MURDER
IN THE MANGROVES
A CLEMENTINE CARTER MYSTERY

ALSO BY JOANNE TRACEY

The Philly Barker series (cosy crime)
Philly Barker Investigates
Philly Barker Is On The Case
Philly Barker and The Muder at Deverell Grange

Clementine Carter Series (cosy crime)
One For Sorrow
Muder in The Mangroves

The Melbourne series (contemporary romance)
Baby, It's You
Big Girls Don't Cry
I Want You Back
Careful What You Wish For
It's In The Stars
Christmas At Mannus Ridge

The Queenstown series
Wish You Were Here
Happy Ever After
The Little Café By The Lake

The Brookford Series
Escape To Curlew Cottage
Christmas at Fountains Hall

MURDER IN THE MANGROVES

A CLEMENTINE CARTER MYSTERY

JOANNE TRACEY

First published in Australia in 2025

by Joanne Tracey

https://joannetracey.com

Print ISBN 978-1-7637768-4-5

Epub ISBN 978-1-7637768-3-8

Cover design by Louisa West

Formatting by coeurdelion.com.au

A catalogue record for this book is available from the National Library of Australia

For Grant and Sarah...
with all my love x

A NOTE FROM JO ...

I'm Australian, writing a book set in Australia. For this reason, I use Australian English. This means some words may have different spellings than you're used to, particularly for American readers. As an example, words like colour, harbour and glamour are spelt with an 'u', and we use an 's' when you might use a 'z'. Mum is with a 'u' instead of an 'o'. Commas may also be missing in places where you'd normally have them. If this causes you any confusion, I apologise in advance.

There might also be some words that are unfamiliar to you, words whose meanings you might not know. Aussie slang can take some getting used to. The general rule is that we like to shorten words: board shorts become boardies. Some of these words – and their meanings – are in the glossary below. If you already know these, feel free to skip ahead.

GLOSSARY

Biscuits or cookies – they tend to be almost interchangeable in Australia, although a general rule of thumb is if it's homemade, it's a cookie; if it's bought and comes in a commercial package, it's a biscuit.

Buggered off – left as in gone, usually in good riddance.

Budgie smugglers – tight-fitting men's swimwear. Also referred to as Speedos, a popular brand of swimwear.

Freddo frogs – an individually wrapped chocolate frog.

Goss – the gossip.

Hide, as in "she's got a hide" – refers to someone with a thick skin and is being cheeky or bold.

Iffy – not sure whether it's good or bad, but tending more to the bad end of the scale. E.g. The milk smells a bit iffy.

Jocks – men's underwear, also referred to as "undies".

No flies on you – means you're too quick for flies to settle. It's usually used to refer to someone quick to figure something out.

No shit, Sherlock – to state the obvious.

Okanui – a popular brand of board shorts (or boardies) sporting a hibiscus pattern.

Op shop – a charity or thrift store usually staffed by volunteers and selling donated (mostly second-hand) items.

Rain on your parade – to cast a cloud over an idea, event or undertaking.

Relos – relatives

Swimmers – as in swimming costume. Also referred to as bathers or togs.

Thongs are the ones you wear on your feet. They are also known as flip-flops or jandals (in New Zealand).

The tip – as in landfill or dump. To take something to the tip is to take it to the place where rubbish is taken for landfill.

Tinny – small aluminium boat primarily used for fishing

Stubby – a bottle of beer – normally holding 375 millilitres

Okay, housekeeping over, let's go and join Clem and the rest of the crew in Whale Bay.

CHAPTER ONE

The sun streaked through the slats in the old venetian blinds, casting a golden, almost hazy, film across the bed and the man in it. Outside, a magpie carolled to welcome the day, its mate joining in the chorus. Life didn't get much better than this. It was *this* close to perfect. As Rose would've said, 'There was just a bee dick in it; it was that close.' Not that I'd ever say as much – there was no one word more likely to wreak disaster than 'perfect'.

Rolling over, I faced Finn, his rhythmic breathing wafting softly against my cheek, his tanned face relaxed in sleep, his salt and pepper curls tousled. I contemplated reaching out a hand to wake him gently. If there's anything better than lazy early-morning lovemaking, I'd like to know what it is. Maybe going back to sleep after lazy early-morning lovemaking, knowing that your partner in lazy early-morning lovemaking doesn't have to get up and open his coffee shop – Beach Brewz – because it's the weekend and someone else will do it for him. Now, *that* would make this morning perfect.

Stretching languorously, I savoured the moment. It wouldn't be long before Finn's labradors, Cosmo and Beans, came tearing through, sticking wet noses where wet noses shouldn't be stuck in their enthusiasm to wish us good morning. Their arrival would break the moment – and any hopes of lazy early-morning lovemaking. Finn would get up and let them out; I'd get up and change into my bathers, ready to head across the road for my regular morning ocean swim. Finn would walk the dogs on the beach and wait for me to finish, and together, we'd go to Bron's bakery for one of her amazing sausage rolls before grabbing a coffee at Beach Brewz. (The whole of Whale Bay knew better than to buy their coffee where they bought their pastries).

When I decided to stay in Whale Bay indefinitely, I moved from my childhood bedroom into Rose's old room. If Finn and I were going to be a 'thing', the single bed in my old bedroom at the back of the house wouldn't be big enough for us – it had barely been big enough for me. Pushing away the familiar pang of loss at the memory of my aunt's death, I'd set to work clearing out her cupboards and drawers.

Then I began to make the room my own. While the mint door and window trims received a fresh coat of white, I revitalised the jacaranda blue that Rose and I had so joyfully applied to the walls the year I turned fifteen. She had stuck with the colour throughout all the years I'd been away from Whale Bay, so who was I to change that? I kept the macramé dream catcher that hung behind the wrought iron bed, gave the frame a fresh coat of white enamel, and sent Rose's lumpy old mattress to the tip, swapping it for something considerably more comfortable. I bought new sheets and discovered a patchwork quilt made from squares of tartans, tweeds, and paisleys with a blue and white striped ticking backing when I dropped Rose's clothes off at the op shop. Although I could still smell Rose's presence – a mix of incense and patchouli – when I closed my eyes, the room was now mine.

Finn groaned and reached out to pull me towards him. Snuggling into his side, my head resting on his chest, I inhaled the rich aroma of coffee mixed with a faint salty scent that was unmistakably Finn. His eyes fluttered open, and he smiled lazily, drawing me closer. 'Mmmm. Is there a better way to start the day?'

'If there is, I don't know what it is,' I murmured, kissing first his chest and then reaching up to brush my lips across his.

'In fact,' he said throatily, 'it's per—' I kissed him again so he couldn't finish the word. 'Perfect,' he murmured.

'You shouldn't have said that,' I moaned. 'Now things will change.'

His body shook beneath me as he chuckled. 'My silly darling'—he kissed the top of my head—'nothing will go wrong.' Lifting my head from his chest, I tilted it to one side. 'What?' he asked.

'I'm just listening for the distant rumbles of thunder … or for the ground to begin shaking. Storm clouds are probably gathering as we speak.'

With another chuckle, he gently pushed my head back to its original position, his finger sliding up my arm, leaving a trail of delightful goosebumps in its wake. 'It's perfect. Waking up with you, knowing you won't be returning to Melbourne anytime soon … all of it is perfect.'

He'd no sooner said the words than two labradors thundered along the hall to the bedroom and launched themselves from the open door to land on top of us.

'Ugh,' I grunted as Cosmo's nose snuffled into my armpit and Beans attempted to manoeuvre himself between us.

Finn released me and stretched his arms overhead before throwing the covers back and sliding out of bed, both dogs rushing to be the first to do the same. With his back to me, he pulled on his jocks and a pair of striped board shorts. He turned and grinned wolfishly. 'Like what you see?' he asked, shaking out a T-shirt before pulling it over his head.

'You know it,' I teased.

'I can always come back to bed after letting them out.'

There was a single knock on the back door, and before either of us could answer, we heard the screen door swing open, hitting the side of the kitchen cupboard, followed by the flip and flop of rubber thongs on the timber floor.

Both dogs, barking loudly, flew in that direction.

'Hello, fellas,' the voice said. A break in the barking revealed this was a friend, not a foe, and the friend was now ruffling ears.

More footsteps, the scrabble of dog toenails on floorboards, and a tousled blond head popped around the door.

'Morning Harry,' Finn said cheerfully.

'Morning,' Harry replied. Upon noting I was still in bed, he added. 'You're still in bed?'

Pulling the sheet and bedspread up to my chin, I retorted, 'So it would seem.'

His eyes squinted with his cheeky smile. 'Are you naked under there?'

Reaching one arm out from under the covers, I pointed for the door. 'Go! I'll be out in a minute.'

'You don't need to be embarrassed, Clem.' Harry said. 'I've seen you in swimmers, and you're pretty hot for …'

'If you were about to say "for a woman of my age", Harry Glover, I swear I'll throw something at you!'

'Is she always in this sort of mood in the morning?' Harry asked Finn as they left the room.

'When uninvited guests barge into my bedroom without knocking, I am,' I yelled after them, unable to stop my smile from spreading across my face. Even with the interruption, the morning *had* been close to perfect.

I slid out of bed and stepped onto something wet with

hard edges that squeaked. 'Bloody hell, Cosmo!' Hopping around on one foot, the other still smarting, I landed on a bra strap, the little hook digging into the pad of my foot. 'Ouch!'

'Are you alright in there?' called Finn.

As the door creaked open again, I yelled, 'Out!'

Flopping back onto the bed, I rubbed one foot and then the other. Finally dressed in the boxer shorts and singlet I usually slept in (when alone), I pulled on a long-sleeved T-shirt and pushed my arms through Rose's batik dressing gown, the one that had always hung behind her door. While I'd swallowed my grief and bundled up most of her clothes for the charity shop, I'd kept this, a few of her cashmere wraps, and some beach dresses that had served as modest cover-ups for her and were more like voluminous mini dresses on me. Sliding my feet into Ugg boots, I was at last ready to face the day – and the men in my kitchen.

Harry let out a low whistle as I entered the room. 'Looking good, Clem,' he said with a chuckle, waggling his eyebrows wickedly.

Patting his cheek lightly, I returned his grin. 'Unlucky for you, I'm taken.' Twenty-something Harry, with his just-got-out-of-the-surf sun-kissed good looks, was a natural-born flirt – and highly sought after by most of the single women (and if the rumour was to be believed, some not-so-single as well) in town. Harry had gotten into some trouble during his teenage years, but that changed when Rose hired him to mow her lawns and do some general handyman work around the house. With Rose's encouragement, Harry grabbed the opportunity with both hands and completed the required courses to attain his building licence.

He'd worked hard to change his bad-boy past, and while some people in town had long memories, he was now in as much demand for his skills as he was for his looks – even though he was known to put work aside if the surf was good. No matter how busy he was, he'd always dropped everything to help Rose – and, by extension, now me.

'So'—I accepted the coffee Finn had made me from the capsule machine that was a recent addition and at least two decades younger than every other appliance in the kitchen—'what brings you by at this hour on a Saturday?'

Harry shrugged. 'Early? Half the day is already done! Besides, you're normally up and swimming by now.'

'Let me guess, no waves?' I sipped at my coffee.

Harry's grin was sheepish. 'Yeah … nah, desperates only this morning, so I thought I'd get a start on measuring up for the deck.'

Although I'd planned a break from my job as a family lawyer at a top Melbourne firm, I quit after only a few weeks and moved into Rose's fibro beach shack in Whale Bay. However, Rose had neglected both it and New Moon – the new-age shop that was also part of my inheritance – over the years, leaving me with plenty to do to bring the shop and this old fibro shack kicking and screaming into the twenty-first century. The first of those tasks was to build a deck at the back.

'Fair enough, but—'

The slamming open of the backdoor silenced anything more I was about to say as two more people burst in, the dogs rushing to greet the newcomers. The first was my childhood friend and the town's solicitor, Maggie King, and the second was her daughter, Siouxsie, whose normally blue-streaked black hair was today striped with green.

'Bloody Ray Cosgrove!' Maggie exclaimed, her blue eyes blazing, her petite form quivering with exasperation.

Finn grinned, immediately took two more cups from the cupboard, and popped another capsule into the coffee machine.

'Hi Maggie,' I said. 'It's a lovely morning, isn't it? A little cooler, but I'm not about to complain about that.'

'Sorry, Clem.' She grimaced at my gentle chiding, smiling her thanks as Finn handed her a coffee. 'Hi Finn, hi Harry.'

'Mum,' Siouxsie said impatiently. 'We don't have time for small talk … hi guys … and Harry.' Her cheeks flamed bright pink as she quickly flicked her kohl-lined eyes towards the latter. Harry had won yet another heart.

'Okay,' I began slowly. 'What's our erstwhile mayor been up to now that's got you so riled up?'

'He's only gone and ordered feasibility studies on the mangrove swamp,' Maggie said. 'You know, that strip of land across the river from the wharf.'

'We take the tinny in there to fish a bit – Mangrove Jacks mostly … and some bream and trevally … the occasional barra …' Harry scratched his head and grinned as he recalled successful catches in his aluminium boat. 'If the weather holds, I'll try and get in there tomorrow.'

Frowning, I ran through potential scenarios in my head. 'Mangroves are protected under the Fisheries Act – the Cosgroves know they can't touch them. Even Martin complained about being unable to build a marina there.' Martin Cosgrove, the mayor's son, ran the family development company.

'What does Ray have planned?' Finn raised his eyebrows as he handed a coffee to Siouxsie.

'It was listed as a late agenda item under "any other business" right at the end of last night's council meeting.' Maggie grinned as I rolled my eyes. 'Exactly – always a sign of trouble with that lot. Justin said there'd been so much discussion about policing the bike path on the boardwalk – you know, that part of the track where cyclists are supposed to dismount and no one pays any attention?'

I nodded. Several times, I'd been walking along in my own world only to quickly get out of the way of a family convoy of bikes who'd ignored the Cyclists Dismount signs.

'Anyhoos,' she continued, 'they'd been going on about it for so long that most of the councillors were either asleep, had left or completely tuned out. Justin said he'd grown suspicious when Ray actively continued the conversation about the cyclists when ordinarily he would've moved something like that on. Then, when Martin also had something to say about it, Justin knew something else was up. Martin couldn't give a flying fig for cyclists. The clincher, though'—she paused to draw breath—'was when Bob Lindsay brought up the parking issues at the surf club.'

I was confused. 'What parking issues?'

Maggie widened her eyes in disbelief. 'About how the signs say to park "front to kerb", but everyone reverses in. Surely you've noticed?'

I shrugged dismissively and suppressed a grin. 'What can I say? I've never noticed, but it's good to know that if people are flouting the rules, the council is on top of it. I'm especially happy they're dealing with the cyclist issue.'

Maggie's eyes narrowed in suspicion. 'Yes, well, my point is Bob is one of the worst offenders in that massive Land Cruiser of his, so Justin smelt a rat.'

'Right …' I still wasn't sure where she was going with this.

Harry waved his finger in a circle in a wind-it-up motion; his mouth twisted into a half grimace. 'Maggie, we don't need the labour pains, give us the baby!'

I choked on my coffee; Siouxsie let out a laugh that earnt her a glare from her mother, and Finn chuckled to himself.

'What I'm saying,' she said slowly, her eyes flashing him a warning, 'is that Justin quickly worked out they were delaying all other business so that by the time they reached the matter of the mangroves, everyone would be fed up and agree to whatever they wanted so they could get a beer in before the club closed.'

'Thank goodness for your husband,' I said, tongue in cheek.

'He's glad he did stay alert because the proposal was to get an environmental study done on the land as someone – he didn't say who – has raised a question as to whether all the land should be designated protected mangroves.'

My eyebrows rose, and my mouth dropped open.

Harry was the first to recover from Maggie's bombshell. 'Nah.' He shook his curly blond head. 'They can't do that.'

Finn frowned. 'Did they happen to mention what they had planned?'

Maggie nodded. 'Only because Justin asked. Ray said that an environmental study was to be commissioned to determine the best way for ratepayers to share in the land's beauty while ensuring it's adequately protected, and Bob Lindsay mentioned something about raised boardwalks.'

'Boardwalks wouldn't be a bad thing.' Harry bent to stroke Cosmo's ears. 'At the moment, you can really only access the area by boat or four-wheel-drive. The road is crap and only gets you so far.'

Biting at my bottom lip, I pondered the issue. Damage to the mangroves was unthinkable. 'I agree. Eco-tourism is a natural extension to the whale watching we're famous for here, and anything that encourages people to stay longer and spend more locally has to be a good thing … although I would've thought neither the Cosgroves nor the Lindsays were interested in boardwalks.'

'That's what worries me.' Maggie grimaced at the bitterness as she took her first sip of coffee.

Frowning, I asked, 'Is Justin concerned this is a back door to a development proposal?'

'That's what I think it is,' said Siouxsie. 'But you know what Dad's like – he's prepared to give them the benefit of the doubt. Despite knowing they're dodgy as, he still thinks they have Whale Bay's best interests at heart, yadda yadda yadda.'

A faint smile played on my lips. Even at school, Justin had always found a way to think the best of people. 'But he thought it was important enough to mention to you.' Maggie nodded. 'How did everyone else vote?'

Maggie shrugged, a silent gesture of indifference. 'As expected – of the councillors who were left, it was ayes all round. They just wanted to get out of there. When Justin said he wanted to debate it, Col Hammond basically told him to shut up and let it pass because it was just a feasibility study.'

'Hmmm.' Lost in thought, I absentmindedly pulled at

my chin.

A twinkle came to Siouxsie's eyes. 'You know what Rose would've done if she was here?'

A wide grin spread across Maggie's face, Harry and Finn following suit.

'What?' I asked, even though I feared I already knew the answer.

'She'd gather the troops …' began Finn, opening his arms to encircle us.

'And get to the bottom of exactly what Ray Cosgrove is up to,' added Maggie, clapping her hands in anticipation.

'And if they're up to no good …' said Harry.

'She'd make sure they didn't get away with it,' finished Siouxsie.

After placing my empty coffee mug in the sink, I gripped the edge of the counter and gazed out the kitchen window. Just at the edge of my sight was the swing chair hanging under the old fig tree near where Rose's lifeless body had been found just a couple of months ago. It was Rose's death that had brought me back to Whale Bay after an absence of more than two decades, and it was while looking into its suspicious circumstances that I'd discovered Rose, who I'd always thought to be my aunt, was actually my birth mother. Closing my eyes briefly I tried to conjure up a picture of her, dressed in the soft denim dungarees she'd favoured when I was growing up, a mug of the herbal tea she favoured in her hands, my heart aching when the image slid away.

Turning back to face four expectant faces, each with hopeful expressions, I sighed, the weight of anticipation settling on my shoulders. While I relished the prospect of making life a little more difficult for Ray Cosgrove – and his business partner and fellow councillor, Bob Lindsay – I decided to wait and see how this one played out. 'I don't know … Maybe it really is about boardwalks. Who knows – the study could show more of the area needs to be protected.'

The ringtone of Finn's phone interrupted further conversation, and his frown when he saw the caller's name made my stomach flip. 'Hello …. What? …. When?' He glanced at his watch, screwed up his eyes and rubbed his forehead. 'This isn't a good time … some notice would've been nice.' As if there was no one else in the room, he stalked across the sitting room to face out towards the road. 'Tamzin … You're not listening to me.'

Maggie's green eyes widened. 'That's his wife,' she mouthed.

Feeling as though the wind had been knocked out of me, I somehow managed to stay upright. 'His wife?'

I hadn't thought it possible for Maggie's eyes to grow any bigger, but they almost reached the sweeping fringe of her pixie cut. 'He didn't tell you?'

Our whispers had reached Harry's ears. 'He didn't tell you he was married?' He shook his head in Finn's direction. 'Bad move, dude.'

'No,' I sputtered. 'He told me … I think he told me …' I'd asked him a few weeks ago, and he'd said … What had he said? Surely, he would have told me. Wouldn't he?

'What's this? Is Finn still married?' Siouxsie asked. 'How did you know?'

Maggie sighed. 'He mentioned something about it ages ago – when he first arrived.'

'Is he divorced?' Siouxsie persisted. 'Or is that what next week's appointment is about?'

'Shhh, he's hung up,' said Maggie sternly.

As Finn pushed his phone back into the pocket of his board shorts, Harry shook his head at him in disappointment. 'Dude, you didn't tell her you were married.'

My gaze went to my sheepskin-covered feet, not wanting him to see how much it mattered to me until I could pretend that it didn't.

'Sure I did … Didn't I?' His voice wavered.

I raised my eyes and shook my head slowly. 'You said you'd been married, but not that you still were married. There's a difference.'

'Did I?' His brow furrowed as he attempted to recall the conversation.

I nodded. 'The day I told you about me and Nick Cosgrove.' Grimacing, I cursed my big mouth. The last thing I needed was for news of my teenage affair to get around.

Siouxsie choked on the last of her coffee, and Harry appeared dumbstruck. Maggie glared at them both and waggled her finger. 'That's not common knowledge,' she warned.

'And it was a long time ago.' I inwardly grimaced. Why did I have to say that?

Finn stared at me for a beat, maybe two, the conversations we'd had playing across his features. Finally, he rubbed his hands across his face, bringing them down to frame his cheeks. 'I said it was a story for another day, didn't I?' I nodded. 'God, I'm sorry, Clem.'

Maggie cleared her throat. 'Right, well, you guys have some talking to do, so we'll leave you to it. Siouxsie?' She grabbed her daughter's elbow.

'Did you know about Clem and Nick Cosgrove?' Siouxsie asked her mother as she was dragged from the room.

When Harry didn't move, Maggie grabbed his arm too and pulled him towards the door. 'Come on … and if I hear any gossip about that around town, I'll know where it came from.'

'I'm here to measure up the deck,' he said with a hint of confusion and curiosity in his voice as he struggled to understand the concept of me with a Cosgrove – even one who'd left town before he was born.

'Then get outside and start measuring,' Maggie said through gritted teeth.

Alone at last, Finn offered a hesitant smile, his gaze not quite meeting mine. 'I probably shouldn't have said the "p" word, should I?'

Letting out a rueful snort, I shook my head. 'I warned you.'

CHAPTER TWO

Finn gathered the used cups and placed them in the sink. 'Do you want to swim first and talk later?' he asked me.

'No. We need to discuss this, and if we put it off …' Finn didn't need reminding that weeks had passed since he'd first mentioned his marriage was a 'topic for another day'. I walked across to the open kitchen door. Outside, Harry, with the dogs' help, was measuring up the area for the proposed deck. He stood suspiciously close to the kitchen window, within hearing distance, and made a show of jotting numbers on a creased piece of paper he'd pulled from the pocket of his board shorts.

'Let's walk and talk,' I decided, my head tilting towards Harry. 'Give me a couple of minutes to get changed.'

Quick on the uptake, Finn nodded with a tentative smile. 'Okay.'

Less than five minutes later, I'd swung my crocheted cotton bag and beach towel over my shoulders and rejoined him. Finn stood at the sink where I'd left him, coffee mugs draining in the dish rack, his hands gripping the counter, his jaw firm and mouth tense. A chill ran up my spine. As if sensing my presence, he relaxed his shoulders and turned to smile at me. If I hadn't seen his expression just a few seconds earlier, I could've believed he didn't have a care in the world. 'That was quick,' he said.

With a strained smile, I gave a curt nod. 'Let's go.' I locked the screen door behind me, and Finn whistled for the dogs. 'We're heading to the beach,' I told Harry.

Harry held up a hand, waving two fingers in a casual goodbye. 'Catch you later.'

'Right,' I said as soon as we were out of range from Harry's keen hearing. 'Tell me.'

Finn opened the wrought iron front gate, grimacing as it squealed its protest. 'Are you ever going to get this fixed?'

'Rose always said it was better than a doorbell.' That gate had alerted me to a late-night intruder a few weeks ago and had earnt the right to remain squeaky. 'Don't change the subject.'

We crossed the road to the beach, the dogs bounding ahead as we paused to take off our flip-flops. While I tucked mine away in my bag, Finn dangled his rubber thongs from his fingers. 'I told you I'd been married,' he began, his focus solely on the sand beneath his feet, 'but I didn't tell you that technically, I still am – even though I haven't lived with my wife for years. When I separated from Tamzin, I needed to get out of Brisbane'—he lifted a shoulder—'and I ended up here.'

'Did Rose know?' His slight nod said a thousand words. 'Maggie obviously did too.' The knowledge felt like a betrayal, as if I'd been deliberately excluded.

'It wasn't a secret – but before you ask, Maggie probably assumed I'd formalised it … the separation.' He shrugged again. 'Everyone probably did. It's what you do, isn't it? Separation followed by divorce.'

My toes sank into the cool, soft sand as we approached where the waves gently lapped at the shore. 'But you never did.' He shook his head, grimacing. 'Why was that?'

He paused at the water's edge, the little lines in the corner of his eyes creasing behind his sunglasses as he squinted out to sea. 'Never really had a reason to.'

'Did you have children?' I waded in a little further, the sand shifting under my feet as the receding water sucked the sand back out, not sure I wanted the answer to the question.

'No.' A wave of what could have been relief washed over me, but the bleakness in his tone prompted me to turn and face him. His smile was tight, the corners of his mouth pulled back in a strained expression. 'That was part of the problem – I wanted kids and she didn't. I shouldn't have been surprised – she'd always been upfront about that. I just thought she might've changed her mind.'

'And she didn't.'

With a frustrated sigh, he shook his head. 'There were other things too, of course.'

'How long had you been together?' Suddenly, even as I

grudgingly acknowledged I hadn't been entirely transparent with him, I needed to know all the details of his past, his marriage, all the other things he'd omitted to tell me.

Finn paused for so long that I thought he hadn't heard me. As I was about to repeat the question, a slight shrug of his shoulder stopped me. 'Forever. I guess you'd say we were childhood sweethearts.' He smiled wryly. 'You know how intense teenage love is – you think you'll be together forever.'

An image of Nick Cosgrove, dripping wet and grinning as he emerged from the water, flashed across my eyes. Tanned and lithe, board shorts clinging to his thighs. He stood over where I lay on the sand and shook his curly blond hair over me like a golden retriever. Salty drops landed on my bare stomach, and his Pacific-blue eyes twinkled. Yes, I knew how intense first love could be.

'Anyway,' Finn continued, pulling me back to the present. 'Long story short, we both woke up one morning and realised we wanted different things out of life. She'd been offered a senior role in Sydney, and I couldn't see myself living there. I didn't even want to be in Brisbane anymore.' His mouth twisted bitterly. 'I was burnt out and … well, I wasn't in great shape. As I said, we wanted different things. I used to joke about wanting out of my corporate job, so when I was made redundant, she told me to take the money and buy a coffee shop or something. "Do it with my blessing," she said. "Go find yourself." So I did.' He bent and picked up a piece of driftwood, examined it for a few seconds and threw it up the beach, the dogs racing to retrieve it.

'Do you communicate these days?'

'Not really. She includes me in her Christmas message mailouts, and we text at birthdays, and whenever I'm in Brissie, I drop by to see her father, but other than that …' His mouth was firm, his bottom lip pressing into the top. 'This morning was the first time we'd spoken in months.'

'Why did she call you?' The water lapped around my shins, still warm despite the calendar proclaiming autumn – or what passed for autumn here in South East Queensland – had arrived.

'To let me know she was arriving in town this afternoon—'

The breath hitched in my throat. 'She what … This afternoon?'

Cosmo triumphantly dropped her stick at Finn's feet. He grimaced and bent to pick up the soggy stick before it could be dragged back to sea, both dogs watching expectedly. 'She said she wanted to talk to me about something,' he mumbled, hurling the stick back up the beach.

'She didn't say what?' A rogue wave hit the back of my knees, dampening the hem of my cotton dress. 'It must be serious if she's coming all the way here.'

His grin was sheepish. 'Maybe she wants a divorce. The timing's right – I was going to get the ball rolling next week.'

My heart skipped into my throat. Heat flushed up my neck, hot and prickly. 'What? You were commencing divorce proceedings against a wife you hadn't even told me you had, and you didn't think to mention it?' Full-blown anger rolled in my stomach now. 'We're in a relationship, Finn … well, I thought we were … yet you didn't tell me this?' Unable to say more, I held up my hands and turned away from him, focusing on the container ships dotting the horizon. What else hadn't he told me? Again I swallowed back the guilt of my own omission. After all, everyone seemed to know Finn was married, no one knew about the baby I'd given away. The two situations were very different.

'Clem … I'm …'

'Don't say it, Finn.' I swivelled back towards him. 'In fact, don't say anything. I can't hear it right now.' I inhaled deeply, needing a moment to process. 'The thing is, I wouldn't have cared that you were still married — I don't mind. You've obviously been separated for so long that there's no doubt you're a free agent. No one is hurting anyone.' Our eyes locked. I had his full attention now. 'What bothers me is that you didn't tell me — and don't try to say it slipped your mind either; it was clearly on your mind enough that you made an appointment to speak to Maggie about it.' I pointed my finger, jabbing it at him for emphasis, to make sure he understood. 'You had the chance to talk about it when I told you about my relationship with Nick, and you had the opportunity when I mentioned what Miles had done.' I'd recently discovered that my ex-boyfriend, Miles, a partner at the law firm where I used to work, had been involved in corrupt dealings. 'And you've had plenty of chances to tell me in the weeks since.' He dropped his eyes from mine, his nose wrinkling in discomfort. 'I … I can't talk to you about this now. I need to swim.' My voice trembled, and I wished it didn't. But I'd been burnt too many times to let this oversight slip. I trudged back up the sand and dropped my bag.

'Are you breaking up with me?' He trailed behind, his tone plaintive.

'What? We're not sixteen, Finn.' I yanked my goggles from my bag, stood and turned to face him. 'All I'm saying is I need some space. After Miles, I can't be in a relationship that's not completely transparent.' Squeezing my eyes shut, I focused on slowing my ragged breaths. 'I want to be with you, Finn,' I said in a gentler tone, placing my hand on his arm. 'But you've obviously got some shit you still need to get in order, so do that.' I kissed him hard on the lips. 'Speak to your wife; sort out whatever needs to be sorted out, and come back and talk to me properly.'

Pulling my dress over my head, I dropped it onto my bag, jogged into the water, put my goggles on and dove under the next wave. When I came up for air, I looked back to the beach; Finn was standing where I'd left him, his eyes on me. Taking a deep breath, I pushed off the sandy bottom and swam, hoping the combination of exercise and saltwater would work its magic and ease the hurt in my heart. With every stroke, I pushed aside my guilt at the one big secret I hadn't told Finn about – the secret I hadn't even told Maggie. Given how I now knew he felt about children, how could I tell him about the baby I'd given up? Besides, it was so long ago I could almost convince myself it had never happened.

CHAPTER THREE

Even though Finn and I had only been together for a few weeks, I'd become used to our Saturday routine – mornings in bed followed by a swim (me), walk (him and the dogs), sausage rolls and coffee. I'd spend the rest of the morning at New Moon, and then later, we'd meet up again for a late afternoon swim (me), walk (him and the dogs), and dinner (sometimes out, sometimes in).

Today, though, felt empty, devoid of the usual banter and bustling energy.

In case Finn had gone straight from the beach to Beach Brewz and not quite heartsore enough to make Bron's coffee palatable, I skipped the coffee and pastries after my swim and went straight home to get changed before heading into New Moon.

'Hey, Nina, Bella,' I said breezily as I pushed open the door to the store, the assortment of chimes and bells alerting the shop's manager and sales assistant to my presence. A waft of neroli and ylang-ylang met me, so faint as if it were carried on a breeze. It curled around me, the floral and citrus notes mixing with a honey sweetness and a spicy sensuality. Delicate yet complex and full of promise, it was also the scent of my childhood and afternoons spent doing my homework in the office or cross-legged on the floor in a corner while Rose tended to customers.

'You're early today, Clem. Is everything okay?' Nina asked, looking up from the box of oracle cards she was unpacking. New Moon's manager was dressed in her trademark dungarees, a long-sleeved T-shirt and Doc Martens boots her concession to autumn.

'Absolutely.' I plastered on a wide smile, even though it was the last thing I felt like doing. 'I thought I'd get some extra prep done. How many do we have booked in?' This afternoon, we were running a new moon workshop – the first of what Nina and I hoped would be a monthly occurrence.

Nina narrowed her eyes briefly, just long enough for me to understand my overly bright smile hadn't fooled her. 'We have twelve booked in.' She hadn't needed to consult the register. 'I thought you were ready? In fact,' she added, 'didn't you say as recently as yesterday afternoon that you had the workshop fully planned and there was nothing more you could add?' Her eyes held a mischievous twinkle.

'Alright,' I sighed heavily. 'You've got me. Finn and I have argued ...' I shrugged and tipped my palms upwards.

The phone rang, and Bella's expression hinted at her disappointment in missing out on the news before she picked it up.

Taking the opportunity to escape, I went to the office at the back of the shop, Nina on my heels.

'Do you want to talk about it?' she asked, taking a seat before I'd even had a chance to put my bag away.

'Not really,' I huffed, crouching to put my bag in the filing cabinet's bottom drawer. When I straightened and turned back, she was sitting calmly, one ankle on the opposite knee, her booted foot jiggling.

'I think you do,' she said, her voice as smooth as warm honey.

With a resigned nod, I inhaled, then let it out in a puff. 'You're right. I do. Finn's wife is coming to town.'

'And that's a problem why?' Searching my face, her eyes widened as realisation dawned. 'You didn't know he had a wife.'

I nodded and shook my head almost at the same time. 'Did you?'

'Sure. Rose mentioned it. To be honest, though, I'd forgotten all about it. What's she back for?'

I shrugged, with a barely there smile, my insides feeling tight. 'He doesn't know but suspects she's ready to ask for a divorce.'

Nina let out a rueful chuckle. 'That'll do it every time.' Still watching me closely, she asked, 'Did you swim this morning?'

I nodded.

'And it didn't help?'

I shook my head.

'I see. Do you want me to pull a few cards for you? To help you understand what you need to consider.'

As my shoulders relaxed, a genuine smile finally graced my lips. 'Thanks. I know he cares about me, but after Miles, I don't trust ...' Who was it I didn't trust? Finn, or my own judgement? After all, I'd had no idea what Miles had been up to, and the knowledge of my ignorance had shaken me more than his betrayal had. Not only had Miles cheated on me, but his shady deals had almost dragged my career under – as well as his own.

Seeming to understand me, she nodded and stood. 'Have you eaten?' I shook my head again. 'And I'm guessing you wouldn't have had your morning caffeine fix because that would've meant going into Brewz.' Without waiting for me to respond, she called Bella in.

'Do you need something?' The teenager poked her head around the door. Like Harry and Nina, Bella was another one to whom Rose had thrown a lifeline. Bella had been struggling at school when Rose gave her some casual work. Then, after Bella's father died, leaving her mother and Bella's three siblings without an income, Rose gave Bella more hours, eventually bringing her in full-time when she left school.

Although Bella was initially shy when we first met, I made sure to involve her in all the planning for the shop and workshops Nina and I were conducting and entrusted her with our social media. As a result, Bella's confidence grew and blossomed before our eyes.

'Clem hasn't eaten'—Nina's grin was cheeky—'and that means she hasn't had a proper coffee today either.'

Bella brought her hands to her face in mock horror. 'And she's still upright? Leave it with me!'

Unable to suppress a laugh, I reached for my purse and handed over some notes. 'Grab some lunch for yourself and Nina while you're out.'

Bella had no sooner left than the door tinkled again, Nina smiling at me before leaving the office to attend to customers.

I sat back in my chair, my hands clasped below my breasts and tipped my head back. After the store had been broken into in April, we'd repainted all the walls – and the ceilings – and the shop now resembled a jewel-like Baroque Aladdin's Cave. Yes, the tangerine, turquoise and navy walls, the indoor plants, and the heavy brocade curtains were over the top, but it was over the top in the best way. Rose would've loved it.

I'd first come to live with Rose when I was twelve. An army brat, my father had been posted to Asia. The initial posting was for just twelve months, so it was deemed that it would be best for me to live with Rose, my mother's sister, and continue my schooling in Australia. One year turned into five, and I completed high school here in Whale Bay, leaving only when my heart was broken twice in one day –

first by Nick Cosgrove and then when Rose had to tell me my mother had died.

Back then, Rose had worked in this shop. She read tarot cards and astrology charts – and had taught me everything she knew. If I closed my eyes, I could still see my teenage self on the floor at the cottage, brown gangly legs splayed out, my hair matted, the sheen of salt and sand on my skin, astrology charts scattered around me. Rose would be at the table, a cup of herbal tea in her hand, saying, 'You know what the symbols mean, darling, but close your eyes and tell me what you feel.'

Rose had bought the shop several years ago when the original owner passed away, and when Rose died, it became mine.

I picked up a deck of Celtic tarot cards from the edge of the desk and shuffled them idly. If someone had told me even six weeks ago that I'd have resigned from my high-powered role as a family law lawyer and would own a new-age shop, I would've laughed at them. Yet here I was doing just that – and about to teach the locals some of the astrology Rose taught me all those years ago.

In the last month or so, my life had been turned upside down. I'd broken up with my long-term boyfriend and had discovered that Rose, my aunt, was really my birth mother. I'd left my swanky apartment in Melbourne for a fibro cottage in Whale Bay, a town I hadn't set foot in since leaving twenty-five years ago. I'd rekindled old friendships and made some new ones. I'd even fallen in love again. I let out a little snort of disbelief. Sure, Maggie had asked me to help her out with some of her case load – as the lone solicitor in Whale Bay and surrounds, she had more work than she could handle – but this shop in this town was now my life, and it was difficult to imagine there'd ever been a time when life had been different.

Bella soon returned, the scent of the best sort of coffee preceding her. She placed a cup on my desk. 'Here you go.' Rummaging in her pocket, she pulled out some coins. 'And your change.'

After pushing the cards aside, I lifted the coffee to my lips and closed my eyes briefly to fully appreciate the sensory experience.

Bella giggled. 'Anyone would think you'd been marooned on a deserted island without coffee for months!'

'Well, may you laugh, Bella,' I said, trying – and failing – to maintain a straight face. 'But it's almost that dire.'

Chuckling, she reached into the crocheted tote bag she had over her shoulder and pulled out a brown paper bag. 'Your favourite.'

'You're a lifesaver!'

Bella was still chuckling as she left the office.

Bron's bakery was one of the few places where you could still get an old-fashioned salad roll—the salad rolls of my childhood. A soft white torpedo bun filled with ham, lettuce, grated carrot, cucumber, tomato, processed cheese slices and beetroot wrapped tightly in the clingfilm we were all supposed to use less of. I tore through the top layer of film and pushed the wrapping down enough to maintain the shape and contents of my roll while allowing me to bite into it.

'Better?' asked Nina, sitting opposite me and unwrapping her roll.

'Much.' I pulled a piece of carrot from the roll and chewed it.

Nina reached for the deck of cards I'd been shuffling and pushed them back to me. 'You know the drill,' she said.

Nodding, I rested my half-eaten roll on its paper bag and shuffled the cards again. I cut the deck into three and, with my left hand, joined it back together. Then, with the cards facing down, I fanned the deck out in front of me and randomly selected five, placing them in a row.

Nina set her roll down and turned the cards over. 'Interesting …' she mused, raising her eyebrows.

'Any spread with the Tower card in it can never be just "interesting".' I chuckled.

'True.' She took another bite from her roll, chewing as she contemplated the spread. 'Alright, let's see what you need to be aware of … The King of Pentacles, a man of wealth and power sitting on his throne, Taurean energy …'

'Probably Ray Cosgrove or Bob Lindsay,' I quipped.

She let out a short laugh. 'Probably, especially with the Seven of Swords beside it warning you to be aware of manipulative individuals and to trust your instincts.' Her eyes narrowed. 'In the centre, we have the Tower – you know what that's about.'

I rolled my eyes. 'Unfortunately, yes – especially over the last month or so. Chaos, revelation, upheaval … it's almost become situation normal, although I had hoped it would've settled down by now.'

'Not anytime soon, I'm afraid,' Nina frowned as she surveyed the remaining cards, chewing thoughtfully. 'Let's see what the trouble is about. Can you pull me another card, please?'

I laid the Empress on top of the Tower.

Nina nodded, her expression unreadable. 'Okay … this woman has something to do with it. Although'—she bit at the corner of her lower lip—'it doesn't necessarily feel like a woman – more like what the card represents. The Empress is another Taurean card and is associated with nature. Look at her, blonde and beautiful, sitting amongst it, a forest surrounding her, a stream winding through. It should feel peaceful and nourishing, but with these cards around it, it's anything but.'

As she spoke, my heart skipped a beat, a vivid image of blonde hair caught up in a rushing current sliding into my brain.

Noticing how I'd stopped chewing, Nina looked up from the cards, concerned. 'Have you been dreaming again?'

'Not like before.' The dreams I'd had before coming to Whale Bay had foretold Rose's death – and had helped uncover the answers and circumstances. 'There was just this image …' I shook my head. 'Do you want me to put another card on this?'

'Please.'

I selected another card from the fanned deck and placed it on top of the Empress.

'Queen of Swords. An independent woman, unbiased, used to communicating and commanding a situation. Her sword is held in the air, and she's looking for truth. She's a woman of integrity.' Nina looked up and met my eyes. 'But check out the clouds behind her.'

The clouds appeared to gather and accumulate, piling on each other. 'Cumulus clouds?'

'Yes, but look also at the trees to the left where she sits; a strong wind is blowing through them.'

'The storm clouds are gathering, and the winds of change are blowing,' I quipped, laughing to mask my sudden discomfort. Again, an image of blonde hair floating through a current flashed across my eyes. 'I told Finn not to use the "p" word.'

Nina didn't laugh with me, remaining stone-faced. 'What are you seeing? You *are* seeing something, aren't you?'

I shook my head. 'Nothing really – just images … hair, water … a current'—I closed my eyes, allowing my brain to send whatever image it wanted to the forefront of my attention—'a white dress … and roots … tangled roots.' I flicked my eyes open. 'That's all.' I picked up the Queen and traced her image with my finger. 'Do you think this could be Finn's wife?'

Nina shrugged. 'That depends on what she's here to do and how he reacts to it,' she said cryptically. 'It could also be you.' Tapping the fourth card, the Six of Cups, she said, 'Oh, this is interesting …'

'Interesting good or interesting not so good?'

She tilted her head to the side and pinched her bottom lip. 'Interesting, interesting. The suit of cups, as you know, is associated with water signs, and I've always felt that the six is aligned to Scorpio.' She slid the card closer to me. 'You have a young boy leaning down to pass a cup filled with flowers to a younger girl.'

I picked up the card and examined it. The girl reached for the flowers, love and hope in her upturned face. Five more flower-filled cups fill the courtyard where they're standing. One of these is on a pedestal.

'This one is about childhood memories and can sometimes indicate a reunion, a teenage sweetheart, perhaps.' Nina chuckled. 'Although it can also sometimes indicate a pregnancy … Anything you need to tell me, Clem?'

I laughed, but it was high-pitched and awkward. 'That bird has flown.'

'Although,' she mused, 'sometimes it can also indicate

that your relationship has moved onto a more harmonious or settled ground and a reminder to give each other the benefit of the doubt.'

'You mean I should trust Finn?' I asked, the morning's revelations still fresh in my mind. 'Couldn't it also be a reminder for me to be more childlike, playful and creative? After all, the last month or so has been adulting in the extreme.' I was looking for any explanation other than the idea that Finn's wife was back in town seeking a reunion. I placed the card back in the line.

'Perhaps,' she conceded. 'I don't think so, though. As for trusting Finn, that one is up to you. Pull another card and place it on top.' She gently tapped the Six of Cups.

I selected another card from the fanned-out deck and laid it on top of the six.

'The Lovers.' Nina lifted the card to examine it. 'Curiouser and curiouser.'

'Isn't that usually about choice?' I asked, pulling what was left of my roll from the cling film.

Seemingly oblivious to the dread beginning to form in a pit in my stomach, Nina nodded. 'Yes. It's about making choices, but it's also about how you connect to others and what you will – and won't – stand for and sticking to that even if it leads to difficult decisions.' Setting the card back on the table, she looked across at me, her gaze steady. 'It's also about soulmates and meaningful relationships – spiritual and lasting connections rather than fleeting sexual ones.'

I dropped my eyes from hers, unable to explain why I suddenly felt uncomfortable.

'Also,' she continued. 'The Lovers is the sixth card in the Major Arcana, so we have a repeat of the number six, and sixes usually have something to do with alignment, harmony, balance and the natural order of things.' She shrugged lightly. 'I'm not sure how that fits here'—she tapped at her lower lip as she considered the possibilities, 'Another card please.'

I set the Death card on the table. A ripple of unease ran up my spine, and again, the image of hair, currents, and tree roots played in my mind. 'I know it doesn't necessarily mean death, but rather the end of something, and, as the song goes, every new beginning comes from another beginning's end …'

'That's right,' Nina said a little too quickly, her smile failing to put me at ease.

'But you think it could be actual death?' I held my breath as I waited for her response.

'Pull another card,' she said, her face grim.

I laid down the King of Cups.

'Stormy seas, disturbed emotions … remaining calm and balanced through turbulence … although it could be a man, maybe a Scorpio. Another card, please.' Her focus was on the cards, her words tumbling out as if in bullet point.

'Justice.' I placed the card on top of the King. 'The law?'

Nina bobbed her head. 'Yes. But this card is also about diving into murky waters to seek the truth – and I have a feeling that these two people'—she picked up the Queen of Swords and the King of Cups—'will be at the centre of whatever this is about.'

The image in my head of the figure floating in the water shifted; her head turned, revealing the face of the Empress.

CHAPTER FOUR

Somehow, I'd managed to put the unsettling tarot card reading and my concerns about Finn and his wife aside to facilitate the workshop. If the smiles and chat among the participants as they left New Moon were any indication, it had been a success.

'Thanks for coming along, and please, take some time over the next twenty-four hours to think about where this Taurus energy will be reflected in your life, how you feel about that part of life, how you'd like to feel about it, and set some intentions.' I listed the points on my fingers. 'Finally, a quick reminder that Taurus is a Venus-ruled earth sign, so whatever you do, take pleasure in it, savour it, lean into it.' As everyone shuffled to put their notebooks and pens back in bags, I added, 'And nature – Taurus is all about nature, so get into it!'

'That was great. Thanks, Clem. It really resonated with me when you said that Taurus rules the throat and that sometimes this means what you want to say can get stuck there – and that you need to listen with more than your ears.'

I was surprised to see Lauren Lindsay among the attendees. While Lauren and I had been friends when I first came to Whale Bay, her high school friendship with Kylie Cosgrove (née Lindsay) had meant we'd spent most of those years ignoring each other.

When Rose died, Lauren expected me to sell New Moon and return to my life in Melbourne. My announcement that I intended to stay in Whale Bay and continue Rose's legacy disappointed Lauren. While Lauren had wanted to buy New Moon from me, her intention to turn it into an upmarket spa specialising in expensive alternative beauty therapies had made my blood boil. Instead, her husband, Michael, surprised her by leasing a shop in the prestigious Whale Bay wharf development to make Lauren's dream become a reality.

'You're welcome, and I'm glad you got something out of it. How's work going on your shop?'

'Slowly, but we should be open in a month or so. Kylie said it was important to be open in time for the July school holidays.' She subconsciously flicked her hair back over her shoulders as she mentioned her friend's name.

'Well, I wish you all the best with it,' I said sincerely. Now that she was no longer after New Moon, I could afford to be magnanimous – after all, our markets were very different, and we wouldn't be in direct competition. While we sold crystals, tarot readings and other new-age books and accessories, her shop would sell holistic treatments to wealthy clients, most of whom wouldn't venture into New Moon.

'Thank you, Clem.' With a subtle shift, she lowered her voice. 'It's probably best if Kylie doesn't know I've been here today.'

I pretended to turn a key to lock my lips shut. 'She won't hear it from me.'

Lauren smiled and stepped forward as if preparing to give me an air kiss but thought better of it and held up a dainty hand to wave her farewell instead.

'She's got a hide coming here.' Once the door closed behind Lauren, Nina turned the sign to Closed. 'After what her brother and her mother-in-law did.'

Following the recent arrest of her brother, Chris, in connection with Rose's death, hostilities between Lauren and I had thawed somewhat. I wasn't sure if we'd ever be friends again – Kylie Cosgrove would surely see to that – but I had seen glimpses of the old Lauren.

Although Chris Walker had also been charged over a break-in at New Moon, we suspected Lauren's mother-in-law, Carmen, to have been behind it – a vain effort to 'persuade' me to sell. 'Perhaps, but what Chris did shocked and humbled her. If she wasn't married to Michael, I suspect Kylie would've turned her back on her – and the rest of their posse would've followed suit.' I didn't tell her that Kylie knew how close she herself had come to social ruin over the whole affair. That I was aware of Kylie's affair with Chris Walker was enough.

While we were talking, Bella had been busy folding the chairs and stacking them against a wall. I stopped her as she picked up two and was about to head into the storeroom with them. 'Don't worry about that, Bella. You've done enough this afternoon, so get off home.'

'Are you sure?' Uncertainty etched a frown on her face.

'Yes.' I glanced at my watch. 'It's just past five, and I'd prefer that you're not cycling home in the dark.'

'I'll be fine.' She grinned with all the confidence of an invincible teenager. 'Whale Bay isn't exactly a hotbed of murder and mayhem, you know.'

'That's beside the point.' My attempt at a stern face didn't hold up to her teasing smile. 'Well,' I said, 'I'd still like to know you've got home while there's daylight.'

'Alright, Mum,' she said with a laugh, the joking term making me wince inwardly. 'But I don't mind staying to help.'

'I know you don't.' As she went into the office to get her bag, I pulled my phone from the pocket of my maxi skirt, flipping through to the messages vibrating on my watch during the workshop. Both were from Maggie:

How did it go with Finn?

And then …

Well??????????

From Finn, there was nothing.

While I sensed Nina's eyes on me, I pretended to be absorbed by the phone. 'We've already been tagged in several social media posts.' I lifted my head and smiled Nina's way.

'That's great.' Nina closed the appointment book. 'We had a few bookings made for readings during the next week or so, too. I think we might be onto a winner.'

'It really was interesting.' Bella emerged from the office, slinging her crocheted tote over her shoulder. 'I'll do what you suggested and keep a new moon journal.' She paused, her hand on the doorknob, her face suddenly alight. 'I know … Why don't we design a range of journals for that purpose?' As soon as the words were out, she dropped her eyes as if not wanting to see rejection in mine.

I didn't need to consider the idea. '*New Moon Intentions and Full Moon Reflections*? I love it! Think about a cover design and we can look at it.'

A flush filled her tanned, round cheeks. 'Are you sure?'

'Absolutely. We can put those graphic design skills of yours to good use.'

As she left with a wide grin on her face, my mind was busy with the possibilities of her suggestion.

'What are you going to do about Finn?' Nina's question broke into my contemplation and returned me to the morning's events.

I shrugged. 'I don't know,' I said honestly, picking up two of the stacked chairs. 'I'm sure he didn't deliberately set out to deceive me, but …'

'After what happened with Miles …' Nina guessed

correctly and followed suit with the last of the chairs.

'Yeah.' Laying the chairs against the wall in the storeroom, I dusted my hands against my skirt. 'I told him to sort things through with her, and then we'd talk, so I suppose I'll do nothing about it for now.' And when that moment came, I had secrets of my own I needed to disclose to him. If we were to have a future, he needed to know everything there was to know about my past, as painful as that would be to disclose.

She flashed me a lopsided grin. 'An Aries choosing to do nothing? That's one for the books.'

'I didn't say it would be easy.' I chuckled at her raised eyebrows.

Between us, we soon had the chairs stashed, the till balanced and the cash in the safe.

As I picked up my tote bag to leave, I said to Nina, 'How did someone so young get to be so wise?'

She shrugged. 'I had great parents.'

'I know you arrived in town about a year ago, and Rose gave you a job, but'—I hesitated before finishing my statement—'I don't know much more about you.' As caring as she was about everyone else, Nina rarely spoke about herself.

Nina looked away, and for a few seconds, I thought she wouldn't answer me. 'I lost my parents a few years ago – a freak accident overseas – and … well, I went off the rails a bit afterwards. I wasn't in great shape when I arrived here, but Rose took me in and gave me a chance.' She chewed at her bottom lip and wrinkled her nose – presumably to keep tears at bay.

'I'm so sorry you went through that.' I reached out and tentatively touched her arm. 'But why Whale Bay?'

She lifted a shoulder. 'Why not?'

'I suppose …' I waited, but Nina added nothing further to the story.

Nina's eyes drifted to the clock on the wall. 'Is that the time? I'd better get moving.' Pink flushed her cheeks.

'Do you have a date tonight?'

The pink grew brighter. 'Yes, and I won't have time to shave my legs at this rate.'

My grin was wide. 'It's like that, is it? Well, enjoy. I'll finish up here …'

Maggie rang as I was locking the door behind me. 'Well?' she demanded. 'How did it go?'

I slipped the keys into my tote bag, balancing the phone against my shoulder. 'Good. We had a full house – even Lauren came, although we're not supposed to tell Kylie about that.'

'I wasn't talking about the workshop,' she chided. I chuckled as I imagined her eye-roll. 'How did it go with Finn? Why is Tamzin coming here? When is she coming here?'

I sighed and crossed the road to the beach. 'He doesn't know why she's coming but Finn thinks she might want a divorce. As for the when? She should be here now.'

As I uttered the words, Cosmo and then Beans came tearing out of the dusk and jumped all over me in pleased welcome. 'Hello, you two.' I ruffled their heads, earning the cutest doggie grins. 'Where's your dad?' While Cosmo took off again, Beans sat by my feet, tail swishing the sand. Further along the beach, in the near darkness, was a couple locked in an embrace. From this distance, I couldn't tell the nature of the hold; was it a hug with added comfort or a hug with kissing, or … The couple separated when Cosmo inserted himself between them. The woman's laugh, soft and melodic, drifted on the sea breeze.

'Where's Beans?' A deep, resonant voice, unmistakably Finn's, cut through the silence.

'Clem? Are you there?' Maggie was asking.

'I have to go.' I hung up, already walking towards home, Beans following me. 'Beans, no, you need to stay, fella.' I quickened my pace, the dog loping easily beside me. 'We're not going home, Beans.'

'Clem?' Finn had caught up to me, panting slightly from the effort.

'Is that Tamzin?' I nodded over my shoulder towards the beach, where the woman was still standing. I didn't break my stride.

'Yes.' He reached for my arm, but I shook it away. 'It's not what you think, Clem.' His palms were upturned, his eyes pleading with me to believe him.

We'd both stopped and were standing face to face near the footpath, puffing, trying to catch our breaths.

'Isn't it? How do you know what I'm thinking?' I started walking again, unable to face him, not wanting to continue this conversation.

'Clem!' Grabbing me by the elbow, he forced me to a standstill. 'Just stop. Please,' he added when he saw my mutinous face.

'Alright, so tell me how it isn't what I think it is.' I planted my hands on my hips, my chin jutting out obstinately.

'She hugged me to say goodbye. That's all it was.' The street lights came on, sending a glint into his coffee-brown eyes.

'Goodbye?' I said disbelievingly. 'Isn't she staying tonight?'

'Yes, but she was saying goodbye to our marriage.' A tentative smile touched his lips as if testing my mood. 'She's met someone else and wants to get married, so she asked me for a divorce and was grateful I'd said yes so easily. That's why she's here.' When I remained silent, his smile grew surer. 'I told her about you.'

My shoulders relaxed. 'I see.' Unwilling to let go of my temper too quickly, I said, 'Is that all she came here for? She could've done that over the phone or in an email.' While Cosmo had remained with the figure on the beach, Beans stuck his nose under my hand, reminding me of his presence and making me aware I'd clenched my fist.

'No,' he said. 'She's here to perform an environmental study on the mangroves.'

My hand stilled on Beans' head. 'What?'

He nodded. 'I thought that would grab your interest. The council has approached her company to perform the environmental study Maggie told us about this morning. Because she knew I lived here, she offered to do it – even though she hasn't done one for years … She's too senior to get her hands dirty these days. There's more,' he said, the headlights from a passing car illuminating us. 'They signed off on the job a month or so ago.'

'But Maggie said the council only approved it last night?'

He shrugged. 'I'm not disputing that. They may have only approved the work last night, but Tamzin said they were commissioned long before that.'

Down on the beach, the woman walked towards us. Finn noticed her too. 'I'll need to keep moving. I'll see if I can find out more and let you know.' He reached out his hand for mine, his thumb moving across my knuckles. 'I love you, Clem.' He lifted my hand to his lips and kissed the back of it.

I nodded but was suddenly choked, the words unable to travel past my heart.

Finn whistled for Beans and walked back down to greet his wife. I watched them disappear into the dark before turning and heading for home.

CHAPTER FIVE

'Another wine, Clem?' Without waiting for my answer, Justin topped my glass up.

As I'd walked home after seeing Finn, Maggie had called back and insisted I come for dinner. 'You know you'll dwell on it, so come here and dwell on it with us instead,' she said. 'Justin has fired up the pizza oven, and now the kids will both be out, so it's just us. It seems a waste to go to all that effort for the two of us.'

While I'd reluctantly agreed, now I was glad I had. Maggie had listened as I talked through Finn's and my discussion this morning and our meeting earlier this evening. As she prepared pizza bases, she nodded at the appropriate times and uttered the occasional 'really?' but otherwise, (uncharacteristically) she'd managed to avoid passing judgement. 'What do you think?' I asked once the telling was complete.

'Well,' began Justin, wine bottle still in hand, and doing his best to avoid Maggie's scowl. 'I think you might be'—he grimaced—'overreacting. Maybe just a little.' He held his thumb and forefinger close together to demonstrate.

'Justin!'

'No, Maggie, it's alright.' I waved away her indignation. 'Why do you say that?'

'Okay, well, think about when you met. You had Miles back in Melbourne – and continually reminded Finn of that – and even if you didn't, you were investigating what you thought was the murder of your aunt.'

'Who turned out to be her mother, not her aunt,' Maggie reminded him, scattering grated mozzarella across one of the pizzas.

'Yes. All I'm saying is, with the emotional upheaval and the investigation into Rose's death, everything had been about you. There was never a good time for Finn to tell you he was married.' Justin placed the wine bottle back in the fridge.

'He could've told me that day before I returned to Melbourne,' I said. 'That's when I told him about me and Nick.'

'Agreed, that was when he should've told you, but to play devil's advocate, he didn't know if you were coming back to town.' Justin lifted a shoulder. 'Your job was in Melbourne – he thought you'd stay there so felt there was no need to tell you.'

'I suppose,' I admitted grudgingly, tracing a bead of condensation down the wineglass with my finger.

'And you two have been loved up ever since so …'

He lifted the stubby of beer and took a sip. 'All I'm saying is maybe there hasn't been a right time.'

Maggie shook her head, a piece of prosciutto dangling from her fingers. 'I disagree. Finn should've found the right time to talk to her after she returned. After all, he'd made an appointment with me to start the divorce ball rolling and he didn't tell her that either.' She paused and glared at Justin. 'Don't look at me like that, I'm not giving away any client secrets. Clem's a big girl, she would have understood if he'd told her. I'm with her; not talking about it was always going to make it seem like a bigger deal than it is.' She laid the ham on the pizza base. 'Even I was shocked when I found out he wasn't divorced and I'm not dating him. I said, "Finn, what were you going to do? Wait until you were walking down the aisle and then say *whoops*, I forgot to get divorced?"'

I choked on my wine. 'No one said anything about anyone walking down any aisle.'

Maggie waggled her fingers in a 'whatever' motion. 'Just saying.' She scattered sliced bocconcini on the second pizza and handed it to Justin. 'These are ready to go in. Clem, can you please grab the salad from the fridge? It's a nice night, so we'll eat on the deck.'

We all trundled outside, Justin heading to the pizza oven, Maggie and me settling at the table. 'There's more.' When Maggie's eyebrows darted up, I continued. 'Tamzin isn't just here about the divorce – she's here to do the environmental study in the mangroves.'

Justin turned back from his supervision of the pizza oven. 'That's quick – the council only approved it last night.'

I nodded slowly, bracing for their pending reactions. 'That's the thing, the firm she works for got the go-ahead weeks ago.'

'What the!' Justin finished his beer and set the bottle on the table with a thump. As he stalked across the deck to look over the pool, Maggie and I exchanged concerned glances at the show of anger from her normally mild-mannered husband. 'Bloody Ray Cosgrove,' he muttered, fists clenched at his sides.

'I think you'll find it's more than just Ray,' said Maggie soothingly. 'Martin and Bob would have to be involved in whatever it is they're trying to cover up. You said how they were all complicit in last night's charade.'

Justin returned to the pizza oven and withdrew the paddle, sliding the cooked pizza onto a wooden board. 'I really thought they were finally listening to the public,' he said, disappointment etched on his face.

'About cycles on the boardwalk and people parking rear to kerb? I hardly think so,' Maggie scoffed as she set out plates and cutlery.

'Why not? No one pays attention to those dismount signs, and if the council does nothing about it, someone will get hurt.' He slid the second pizza into the oven, the glow from the coals emphasising the lines of his disgruntled face.

I raised my hand. 'I second that – I nearly got cleaned up by some teenagers tearing down to the rock wall yesterday on electric bikes. I didn't hear them until they were almost on me. If the bikes hadn't cleaned me up, the fishing rods hanging out to the side would have. And, while we're at it, can we have a sign reminding joggers that the path is there to share with walkers? I swear they think they're more important because they move faster and travel in packs.' I stop my rant momentarily to take a breath. 'And we could also do with a sign reminding people to smile and say good morning too. And don't get me started on those who rollerblade through with their dogs strapped to their back – they take up the whole path and the speed they travel at …'

As if appreciating my attempt to lighten the conversation, Justin grinned faintly. 'It's not just joggers, you know … Seriously though, I really thought they were interested in council business rather than Cosgrove-Lindsay business.' He sighed. 'I should've known they'd have an ulterior motive.'

'We don't know that—' I began, more to avoid conflict than genuine belief.

'Oh, come on,' chided Maggie. 'Of course they've got an ulterior motive – we just don't know what it is'—she smiled cheekily—'yet.'

'Meaning?' I asked, afraid I knew what her answer would be.

Maggie lifted a slim shoulder and plastered an angelic look on her face. It was that look that had got us both into trouble as teenagers. Justin saw the look too and covered his face with his hands. 'As Siouxsie said this morning, if Rose were here, she'd get to the bottom of whatever it is and make sure they didn't get away with it.'

'What if it is about boardwalks, though?'

Maggie shook her head sadly. 'Clem, Clem, Clem. Just when I think you've never been away, you come out with something like that. This is not about boardwalks for the community; we all know that … including you.'

Justin nodded sadly. 'I hate to say it, but maybe Maggie's right. The environmental study wouldn't have been ordered without council approval if this were above board. Whatever the reason is for this environmental study, it's not about boardwalks.'

With both of them looking expectantly at me, I ducked my head and sipped at my wine. 'I just think we should wait and see what Tamzin has to say about it before we get carried away with this,' I said. 'Making a noise now when there might be nothing to make a noise about feels a bit like we're looking for trouble rather than reacting to it.'

Justin shrugged noncommittally and reached for the pizza paddle. 'Perhaps you're right.'

Maggie, however, didn't bother trying to hide her disappointment. 'I don't know,' she began. 'What if we leave it and find out they've … I don't know … made some deal with a developer while our backs are turned. I think we should investigate now.' What she meant was she thought *I* should investigate – the way Rose would've done.

Justin stalled, the pizza precariously balanced on the paddle. 'They can't do that. For a start, the land is designated mangroves and protected and secondly …' He wrinkled his nose. 'Actually, I can't think of a secondly except to say the land is protected.' He slid the pizza onto another board. 'Anyway, these are ready, so let's dig in before they get cold.'

The pizzas were perfect – thin bases and the right amount of topping. When I complimented Maggie, she laughed. 'Oh, I don't make the bases – Bron sells these. They're sourdough, apparently, not that it makes much difference to me.'

'Well, whoever made the bases, it all tastes great.'

'That would be the wood-fired oven.' Justin's chest puffed out with pride. 'It was a fortieth birthday present and the best thing Maggie's ever given me.'

'Except my heart,' Maggie said with a perfectly straight face while I pretended to make sick noises.

'Seriously though, thanks for feeding me tonight. I would have otherwise sat at home feeling sorry for myself.'

'What are friends for?' Maggie clinked her glass against mine.

'You do know, though, this is all Finn's fault,' I said with a chuckle.

'How do you figure that?' Justin leant over to pour

more red wine into my glass.

'He said the "p" word this morning.'

Justin frowned in confusion, rubbing his arm when Maggie punched it. 'Perfect,' she said. 'Everyone knows you don't use that word. You're probably lucky it's only his wife who's turned up.'

'I'm not sure how much worse it could be.' I shook my head and sighed. 'The minute he said it, I swear I heard the rumble of thunder.'

Maggie laughed, and Justin rolled his eyes in exasperation. 'You two …'

While I'd had friends in Melbourne, I hadn't realised how much I'd missed Maggie until I was back in Whale Bay. Over our teenage years, we'd shared so much – yet I hadn't shared the biggest secret of all with her.

'Justin …' I began, a random thought popping into my head. 'If you didn't have a boat, how would you access the mangroves?'

Brows knitted, he considered my question. 'You'd need to access it from the Dolphin Point end. An access road takes you into the bushland adjoining it, although it's more of a fire access track than a road. From there, you'd need to walk in.'

'Is that land state forest?' An idea was forming, vague but full of potential.

He tapped the side of his stubby, his head tilted to one side. 'I always assumed it was, but maybe not.'

'I don't suppose there's a way of finding out who owns it?'

'Do you think this is more about that land than the mangroves?' Maggie's lips held the beginning of a speculative smile.

I lifted a shoulder, not quite ready to show my hand. 'Possibly.'

Maggie's smile widened, and that mischievous sparkle appeared in her eyes. 'So we're going to look into it?'

I shrugged again, the familiar fire of battle beginning to stoke in my belly. 'Maybe we can make a few enquiries …'

Maggie punched the air, almost taking out Justin in the process. 'Yes!'

'We can't complete a search on the property without the details, so I'd suggest that's our first challenge,' I said. 'And we'll need to do it on the quiet – we can't let any of them know we're looking into it.'

'That will make it harder,' mused Justin, pinching his bottom lip. 'There'll be a map of all the parcels of land in the region somewhere, but how we get our hands on that without alerting anyone could be difficult.'

'True,' said Maggie. 'As much as I hate to say it, I don't think we should say anything to Finn until we know Tamzin's either not involved or off the scene.' When I hesitated, she added, 'I'm not suggesting you keep it from him for long, just a day or so until we know she's not involved with whatever it is Ray and Bob have planned.'

'Okay,' I said reluctantly. Keeping something like this from Finn felt hypocritical after our argument this morning. 'But only for a day or so.'

She clapped her hands together. 'Excellent! Time to get the murder board back out.'

'Except there hasn't been a murder,' I reminded her.

She waved my clarification away. 'Minor detail. What else can we call it? The investigation board?' She shook her head. 'No, that doesn't have the same ring. The murder board it is.' Her tone was one that, from past experience, Justin and I knew not to challenge.

I shook my head. 'No, Maggie. I'm fine with making a few enquiries, but it's too soon to get the board out. Let's wait and see.' As Maggie pouted her disappointment, I added, 'That pout is wasted on me, Maggie King. I'm only talking about a few days, so there's no need to throw your toys out of the cot.'

A laugh burst from Justin. 'God, I'm glad you came back to Whale Bay, Clem.'

'So am I,' I said, a lump in my throat.

'At this moment, I'm not sure I am,' said Maggie, the smile she couldn't hide giving lie to her words.

CHAPTER SIX

Despite my head telling my heart that I could trust Finn and that Justin was right, and that I was overreacting, I couldn't shake the images that crowded my head as soon as I went to bed and switched the light off. Images of Finn with the shadowy woman mingled with those of Miles and his business trip flings. Across them all floated the tarot cards I'd drawn earlier. What was it about the six of cups that reminded me of Nick Cosgrove? It was something Nina had said, something about young love, a teenage sweetheart. All that love, hope and trust destroyed when I caught Nick with Kylie Lindsay.

It had been over two decades ago, but the picture was as clear as if it had happened yesterday. It had been bad enough that Nick had cheated on me – we were meant to be forever – but for him to have cheated on me with Kylie Lindsay? That was rubbing salt into my wounds.

I'd run from the Cosgrove's house back to Rose, who told me that my mother had passed away unexpectedly in Melbourne that day. I'd packed my bags, and Rose drove me to Brisbane and flew back with me to Melbourne. Since then, I've not spoken to Nick.

When I discovered I was pregnant, I attempted to contact him, but he'd already left town. Rose asked around, but all she could ascertain was that he had gone surfing in Indonesia and that Ray had cut him off financially and appointed Martin as his successor. After that, it was too late to matter, I'd made the heartbreaking decision to give our baby up. These days, so I've been told, he's a marine biologist and living in Cairns.

Kylie was still in town and now married to Martin Cosgrove, to whom she was perfectly suited. While Martin and Nick were non-identical twins, their natures were very different. Martin was a chip off the old block, Nick, by far, the nicer of the two.

I rolled over and punched my pillow. Nick was ancient history, and Finn was very much my present. Squeezing my eyes shut, I forced the pictures from my mind and concentrated on breathing: In, two three four, hold two three four, out, two three four, hold two three four.

Somewhere around three, I must've finally drifted off, so as a result, I slept late and dressed with more reluctance than usual for my morning swim.

Despite my gloomy mood, the weather gods were definitely smiling on Whale Bay. The late autumn warmth and brilliant blue cloudless sky were the kinds that had advertising gurus raving about Queensland's weather being perfect yesterday, today and tomorrow. Even though it wasn't yet nine in the morning, the sun was tickling my bare back. Refusing to wonder where Finn was and what he was doing (or doing it with), I donned my swim cap and goggles and strode into the ocean, diving under the first decent wave and determinedly striking out.

An hour or so later, I emerged, exhausted, having swum for longer than usual, my goggles and cap dangling from one hand, the other attempting to ruffle my hair back into shape. Towelling off, a voice from the sand beside me startled me.

'Excuse me.' The voice belonged to a woman sitting on a towel close to where I'd left mine. Holding out a bottle of sunscreen, she said, 'I know this is cheeky, but I was wondering if you could do my back?' When I hesitated, she added, 'I've injured my shoulder – boxercise'—she rolled her eyes—'so I can't reach, and the sun is surprisingly strong.'

After wrapping my towel around my waist, I took the sunscreen from her and chuckled. 'That's what we get for trying to be fit.'

'I know. Maybe I should take up ocean swimming instead, although I haven't swum laps in decades.' She grinned up at me. 'And I'm scared of sharks.'

I twirled my finger to indicate she should lean forward and squirted some sunscreen into my hand. 'Sorry, my hands will be a bit cold.' She flinched as I touched her and began rubbing the cream into her skin.

'That's okay,' she mumbled into her towel. 'Do you get many sharks here?'

'From time to time. The beach is netted for most of the year, although I'm not sure how much good that does.' I shrugged. 'I take the only precautions I can – don't swim out too far and avoid dawn and dusk.'

'Feeding time?' The woman laughed, sitting back up again.

'Something like that, yes,' I conceded. Straightening, I wiped my hands on my towel. 'That's you done.'

'Thank you.'

'No problem. Enjoy your day.'

As I was about to walk away, she asked, 'Are you a local?' At my puzzled frown, she added, 'I mean, do you live here?'

'I do, why? Are you looking for the best coffee in town? That would be Beach Brewz, just across the road.' I pointed towards Finn's café. 'Don't be tempted by the coffee at the bakery; just stick to the pastries and rolls from there.'

She grinned ruefully and reached behind to tighten her blonde ponytail. It was a runner's ponytail – one of those that would swish back and forth. The action reminded me of something I couldn't quite grasp. 'Too late. I made that mistake when I was here last week. Amazing sausage rolls, but the coffee?' At my raised eyebrows, she pulled a sour face and chuckled. 'You're thinking I don't look the type to eat pastry?'

I wrinkled my nose in embarrassment at being caught in a snap judgement. While the faint laugh lines around her eyes and mouth showed her age – similar to my forty-four – her body was lean, honed by a disciplined gym and running schedule, not by overindulgence in fatty carbohydrates, no matter how good they tasted.

'You'd be right. Normally I wouldn't, but'—she shrugged—'a little of what we love is a good thing, right?'

'My thoughts exactly.' I returned her smile, feeling a sense of connection. 'It's why I swim as much as I do.'

'I was wondering, what's the café at the wharf like? The Haven, I think it's called.' She grinned again. 'Aside from being one of the only businesses in town without a zed in the name. In the main street alone you have Beach Brewz, Split Enz and Sundaze.' She shook her head in mock exasperation.

'Aaah, yes, the random zeds. As for The Haven, it's nice in an upmarket Hamptons-style way. I don't go there on principle, though.'

'Oh, really?' Bending her knees, the woman sat forward and hugged her legs.

'Yes, it's owned by the Cosgroves.' I scrunched up my nose. 'Ray Cosgrove is the mayor, and his son Martin manages their development company.'

'You have a problem with them?'

Suddenly aware I didn't know who I was talking to and that I was being indiscreet, I casually dismissed the comment with a wave of my hand. 'It's a personal thing. Pay no attention to me.'

'Fair enough.' She brushed some sand off her towel. 'I only ask because'—she twisted her mouth as if deciding whether to confide in me—'I've heard rumours.'

'Really?' I kept my expression bland and stance open and inviting. 'Well, Ray has been mayor for decades, and he and Bob Lindsay – he owns a few whale tourism boats and is in partnership with the Cosgroves on the wharf development and a few other ventures around town – have both been on the council for as long as I can remember. I suppose whenever anyone is that successful – especially in a town the size of Whale Bay – there's bound to be rumours.'

She narrowed her eyes. 'Is that all they are?'

Regretting having said anything, I asked the first question that popped into my head. 'Are you a journalist?'

Straightening one leg, she lifted a slim shoulder. 'No. But I do have one last question. The mangroves you can see from the wharf, how do you get over to them? I was sure I read somewhere about a lovely walk I could do there.'

'Really? I didn't know that,' I said. With her designer bikini, she looked more like a 'lunch at The Haven' than a 'walking in the mangroves' type. Recalling the previous night's conversation about this very topic, I shared what I knew. 'That's all protected land – state forest, I think. There are fire trails for access, but most people go in by boat.' I tightened the tuck on my towel and pushed an errant, salt-crusted piece of hair behind my ear.

'It's a pity it's protected. It would make a lovely marina and luxury resort.'

'If our mayor and his cronies had their way, I suspect that's what would happen to it, but that would be a great loss.' I turned away from her to gaze out over the ocean, giving myself time to gather my thoughts. Although she'd denied being a journalist, there had been something in the set of her mouth and the tilt of her head that made me think these were no idle questions.

'You don't think it should be available for everyone to enjoy?'

Biting back a retort, I twisted back to face her. 'I'm sorry, I need to get on with my day.' I smiled tightly. 'Enjoy your sunbathing.'

'It was nice to meet you,' she said, fitting a big, floppy sunhat on her head.

'You too,' I said through a fake smile as I slung my tote over my shoulder and lifted a hand in farewell. After taking a few steps along the sand, I looked back. She was still watching me from under the brim of her hat, her expression unreadable. Turning, I quickened my pace.

Despite the fear (or was it hope?) of running into Finn, I crossed the road to Beach Brewz.

'Hey Clem.' Lainey greeted me with a smile when I reached the front of the queue. 'No Finn this morning?' Even though Finn left Beach Brewz to Lainey and her sister

Georgina to run most weekends, we still usually called in for coffee.

'Not today.' Lainey and Georgia exchanged a glance, a flicker of shared comprehension in their eyes.

My gaze swept around the bustling café, the gurgle of the coffee machine and chatter from the tables, the usual soundtrack to my Sunday mornings.

Lainey passed me the coffee Georgia, the barista, had already made for me. 'I heard he had a visitor this weekend.'

Were there no secrets from anyone in this town? 'He does. Anyway'—I forced a smile—'I'd better keep moving; I'll see you tomorrow.' I held up my cup. 'Thanks for this.'

I was almost out of the café when Harry sauntered in. 'I've just been up to your place,' he said. 'No Finn?' I shook my head. 'You'll be looking for a distraction then …'

I raised my eyebrows. 'How does that follow?'

He waved my question away. 'I said to myself, Harry, I said, why don't you take Clem out in the tinny with you next time you go out?' Before I could say I could think of quite a few other things I'd prefer to be doing than going out with Harry in his (probably leaky) boat, he held his hand up. 'Now, I'm sure you're probably thinking you can think of a million other ways to spend a Sunday afternoon than going out fishing with me – and you'd be right. What I haven't said is that I was thinking of going into the mangroves and we were only talking about that yesterday.' His smile was bright on his tanned face. Overly so.

'Have you been talking to Maggie?'

'Mags? No, but'—he grimaced and opened his palms—'I might've seen Sioxsie out and about last night, and she might've mentioned how if Rose—'

'Let me guess. She might've said that if Rose were here, she'd be investigating why Ray, Bob and Martin are so interested in the mangroves,' I said wryly.

Harry's triumphant grin told me I was right. 'And I said to myself, Harry, I said, Clem can't understand how important the mangroves are until she sees them, and the best way to do that is by boat. And then I thought, I know, why don't I take Clem out there? It's a twofer.'

'A twofer?'

'A two for one,' he said with a doesn't-she-know-anything look on his face. 'I get to go fishing, and you get to see the mangroves.' That grin was still plastered wide across his face. 'A twofer.'

'And if I decide after I see it that it's worth investigating, that would make it a threefer?' I couldn't help returning his beatific grin.

'Now you're getting it.' His eyes danced with excitement. 'So I'll pick you up at about two?'

Knowing when I was beaten, I nodded. 'This tinny of yours, it doesn't leak, does it?'

'Yeah, nah … she's sound. Besides, you're a good swimmer.'

And with that, he grinned again and approached the

counter. 'Lainey Lane! Now, aren't you a sight for my poor, hungover eyes …?'

I shook my head. He was incorrigible.

CHAPTER SEVEN

Harry's tinny was exactly as it sounded – an old aluminium-framed boat with a single outboard motor and no canopy. 'Sometimes I think I should update it, but it's all I've got left of my dad,' he told me in a rare exchange of confidences.

'How long ago did he pass?' I asked, gripping the side of the boat as we bumped across the wake left by one of the Lindsay's tour boats.

'I don't know if he has.' Harry deftly manoeuvred the vessel using a tiller attached to the single outboard motor. 'He buggered off the year I turned thirteen.'

'Is that why you got into trouble?' Harry's chequered past was public knowledge. His misdemeanours were relatively minor, but sufficient to bring him to the notice of the police and to earn a reputation in town. Maggie had told me that if Rose hadn't stepped in he probably would have completely gone off the rails.

He shrugged. 'Probably. He wasn't a great role model even when he was around, so who's to say I wouldn't have gone down the same path even if he was here.' Despite his sunglasses, he squinted into the sun. 'Rose was the only one who ever gave me a chance. She said, "Harry, the way I see it, you've got two choices – you can either go the way of your father or not. It makes no difference to me, but I'd far prefer you choose the latter."' He chuckled. 'She called it the way she saw it, did Rose. It didn't matter to her what people said; she always made up her own mind about a person.' He shook his head sadly. 'I owe her my life.'

A familiar lump rose into my throat, and I blinked back the hot prickle of tears. 'She was one of a kind.' There was a slight break in my voice, one I had no control over.

'You're very much like her, you know,' Harry said, and there was something in the way he said that made me wonder if he'd guessed that Rose was more than my aunt. Although a few people knew, it wasn't something I'd broadcast. 'And I don't mean you look like her – although there is a resemblance, I suppose. No, it's more that you're *like* her, if you know what I mean. Ready to fight the good fight.'

Despite the cool breeze out here on the water, my face blazed. 'Is this your subtle way of trying to persuade me to take on Ray Cosgrove – the way I've heard that Rose would?'

He shook his head, the expression on his face guileless. 'Nah. I just saw the way you didn't rest until you got to the bottom of what happened to Rose. That's all. Although,' he added with a cheeky grin, 'Siouxsie thinks you should confront them over this environmental study …'

'She told you that last night?'

'Yeah, I saw her at the surf club.' The engine slowed as Harry steered us closer to the mangroves. Before I could reply, he pulled right back on the throttle, a frown marring his sunny features. 'What's that?'

At first, I didn't see what had caught Harry's attention, but then a flash of white floating between the mangroves came into view. 'Is it a plastic bag?'

Still frowning, he shook his head. 'I don't think so …' He slowly steered us closer.

I covered my mouth too late to stop the gasp that left me. Half floating, half caught in the roots, was the facedown body of – I assumed from the white dress she wore – a woman. Her blonde hair wafted around her on the current. It was the woman from my vision. My hand flew to my chest, my heart pounding like a drum.

'Is she …?' Harry's voice was strangled voice, words catching in his throat.

'Dead?' I nodded and swallowed back the bile that rose in my throat as a crab scuttled through her hair. 'I think so.'

The boat lurched, rocking as Harry leant over the side and threw up. Straightening, he wiped his mouth with the back of his hand. 'What should we do? Go back into town and call the police?'

'I'll call Ted, but I don't think we should move from here,' I said, unable to take my eyes off the body. 'We should stay and mark the spot. What's the tide doing?'

'High tide is in a couple of hours.' Harry looked up and down the shoreline. 'At the moment, she looks to be caught in the roots, but the tide could lift her free and if it does …'

'That's what I was afraid of.' Pulling my phone from my shorts pocket, I searched the number for Whale Bay Police Station and selected it, my fingers tapping anxiously against the side of the boat as I waited for the call to be answered.

'Whale Bay Police Station, this is Constable King speaking. How can I help you?'

'Tyson, thank goodness. I was beginning to think no one would pick up.'

'Who is this?'

'Sorry. It's Clem – Clem Carter. Is Ted around?'

'Hi, Clem, Senior Sergeant Winters isn't rostered on today. Is there anything I can help with?'

Taking a deep breath in a vain attempt to steady my nerves, I said, 'I'm out with Harry in his tinny—'

He chuckled. 'You're braver than me. What's up?'

'We've found a body.'

There was silence on the other end of the phone. When Tyson spoke again, his tone was businesslike. 'Where are you?'

'Just off the mangroves near Dolphin Point.'

'And you're sure it's a body?'

'As sure as we can be without touching it.' I gripped the side of the boat as it rode a wash of wake, the body rising and falling, the hair splayed out in a curtain around the woman's head.

'Stay where you are, Clem. I'll get someone out to you as quickly as possible.'

'Tell him to hurry,' Harry said.

'What did Harry say?' asked Tyson.

'He said to hurry. The tide's coming in, and we're worried it will lift her.'

'Understood, Clem. Hold on, we'll have the Coast Guard boat there soon.'

When he rang off, I turned back to Harry. 'He needs us to stay where we are.' I looked around the base of the boat. 'Does this thing have an anchor?'

He smiled weakly. 'Are you implying this fine vessel could be lacking in some way?'

Recognising his attempt at levity, I returned his smile. 'Absolutely not. Your tinny is, indeed, the finest of vessels.'

We'd drifted away from the body, so Harry restarted the engine, brought us in as close as he could, and tipped the anchor over the side. The boat jerked as it reached the bottom.

For a few minutes, we were quiet, neither of us wanting to look directly at the body bobbing in the current but also unwilling to turn our backs on it.

'So.' Harry broke the silence. 'What's this about you and Nick Cosgrove? When did that happen?'

I should've known he and Siouxsie would have wanted

to know more about that. 'Were you and Siouxsie talking about that last night too?'

'It came up,' he said with a grin. 'Don't worry though, no one else heard us.'

'You and Siouxsie – is this a thing?' While I knew Siouxsie had a crush on Harry, he didn't seem to be the dating sort.

'Don't try and change the subject,' he chided. 'Go on, we've got nothing else to talk about – except that poor woman'—he inclined his head—'so you might as well tell me.'

'Well …' I began. 'This had better not get around town.'

He turned an imaginary key to lock his mouth shut. 'No one will hear it from me.'

'In that case … we dated in my last year of high school and for a few months after.'

'Was it serious?'

I nodded. 'Very. Well, as serious as these things can be.' I pursed my lips and tilted my head back, seeing again Nick striding from the ocean, tanned and lithe in his sky blue and white Okanui board shorts, his blond, curly hair glinting in the sun. 'We fancied ourselves as star-crossed lovers, Whale Bay's Romeo and Juliet. His parents would never have allowed it if they knew.' Harry didn't need to know that Nick had proposed and I'd accepted.

'Romeo and Juliet …' mused Harry. 'I know I didn't listen much at school, but that one didn't end well, did it?'

I shook my head. 'No, Harry, it didn't. And nor did we.'

He nodded solemnly. 'Is that why you stayed away for so long?'

'Sort of, but not really. I knew he'd left town not long after I did. It was more that I knuckled down to do my degree and then work and then …' I shrugged. 'Time got away.'

'What's Nick like? I can't imagine you with someone like Martin.'

I snorted a laugh. 'No, I can't imagine myself with someone like Martin either. They might have looked alike – although not identical – but that's where the similarities end. Nick was different. For a start, he was kinder than Martin. He knew he was the heir apparent to the business – but wanted nothing to do with it. Even though he was brighter than Martin, Martin would always be more suited to the business than he was.' The memory of Nick's warm smile and easy-going nature brought a smile to my face. 'He was a conservationist, and you can imagine how his father felt about that!'

Harry chuckled.

'I was going to do environmental law, and together we were going to change the world.' We'd had such big, naïve dreams. 'It's why I feel a bit sorry for Mike.'

'Mike?'

'Mike … Michael Lindsay. He and Nick were best mates. Mike never had any time for Martin back then. To be honest, I'm not sure he does today, either. Mike didn't want to take over from his father either, but he didn't have a brother who could take it on, so he never had a choice. Kylie would've been better placed to succeed Bob Lindsay, but …' I shrugged.

'She and Martin seem well-suited,' mused Harry.

'You could say that.' I grimaced.

'Although there were rumours about her and Chris Walker.' He grinned. 'I don't suppose you know anything about that?'

I arched an eyebrow. 'Now, that would be telling,' I said.

'If it were true, she wouldn't want it to get around that she was sleeping with the guy who'd been convicted of Rose's manslaughter,' he said disingenuously. 'I was surprised she didn't immediately dump Lauren as a friend, but if she had something else she wanted to hide …'

'Perhaps, but that's just conjecture.' His knowing smile told me he knew he was on the right track but understood I didn't intend to gossip about it.

'I saw them together once,' he said laconically. His grin widened. 'And Kylie knows I saw them.'

'I see.' I chuckled at the mischief on his features. 'She wouldn't be happy about that.'

He lifted a shoulder. 'I might usually be below her notice, but she knows that I know.'

I shook my head and chortled in amazement. 'You're a dark horse, Harry Glover.'

'I'm not sure I'd like to be married to Martin Cosgrove.' Harry's face turned serious. 'I've heard he can be nasty if things don't go his way.'

'Well, it's fortunate you're not married to him then,' I teased. 'I have no doubt Kylie knows how to manage him, and any problems between them would damage the family businesses so …'

'So the Crown Prince and Princess of Whale Bay can continue to reign over us,' he finished.

'Something like that.'

'You know,' he began, his eyes on the woman's body. 'I got the impression there was another reason you and Kylie didn't get on. Was that to do with Nick?'

A disbelieving laugh escaped me. 'There really are no flies on you, are there?'

'I see things,' he said.

'You certainly do, and yes, it had to do with Nick. And before you ask for details, I'm sure you can fill the gaps.'

He opened his mouth to say more, but before he could, the Coast Guard vessel pulled up beside us, Ted Winters and Tyson standing at the stern.

'Alright, you two,' Ted called. 'Where's this body you say you've found? The one that's ruined my Sunday afternoon watching the footy. The Lions were up against the Swans.'

CHAPTER EIGHT

The last rays of sun dipped below the horizon just as Harry guided the tinny back into the boat ramp. We were both stiff and sore from spending the last few hours seated in the boat, unable to stand up and walk around. Although Harry had been wearing a long-sleeved fishing shirt, my exposed arms prickled with sunburn. My throat was dry and while I knew I should be hungry, I had no appetite.

I waited with the boat while Harry got his ute and reversed the trailer down the ramp. Once he'd attached the boat to the trailer, I stood to get out, but instead of sliding gracefully over the side, I lost my footing and ended up on my knees in the water. After the experience we'd had, neither of us found it amusing.

He drove in silence, keeping the engine running in the drive when we pulled up outside my house. 'Did you want a coffee? A beer? Something stronger?' I asked.

He shook his head and gave me a weak smile. 'No thanks, Clem.'

'I won't ask if you're okay,' I said, aware I'd done

precisely that.

Another weak smile. 'I'll be sweet. A few beers and an early night is all I need.' He hesitated and added, 'If the weather holds, I'll head out for a surf tomorrow before I start work on the deck. Good way to clear my head.'

'Great idea. I'll see you later.' I patted the side of the vehicle, and with a single finger wave, Harry was gone.

With a sigh, I opened the squeaky front gate, trudged up the path to the front door, opened the screen door with its incongruous wrought iron reindeer and unlocked the wooden front door.

As I stepped inside, I was almost bowled over as a body hurled itself into me, a scrabble of paws on the wooden floor giving me sufficient notice to prepare for the second onslaught. 'Beans! Cosmo! What are you two doing here?'

The kitchen light flicked on, casting a shadow as Finn stepped into the hall. 'Sorry about the welcoming committee.' He grabbed the dogs by their collars and pulled them back before telling them to sit. 'I just thought you might need …' He lifted a shoulder. 'Even though I'm probably the last person you want to see right now.'

Overwhelmed by a torrent of emotions, I shook my head, and a tear spilled down my face, and then another, dripping off my chin. 'You're exactly the person I want to see right now.'

It didn't matter whether he or I took the first step; all that mattered was his arms around me, holding me tightly against his warmth. 'How did you know?'

'It's a small town.' He kissed the top of my head. 'Word is you and Harry found a body? Is that right?'

I nodded into his chest, sniffing as more tears fell. 'In the mangroves near Dolphin Point.'

After a brief silence, he said, 'What were you doing out there?' His voice sounded high-pitched as if he was trying to be casual but failing.

I pulled back, my eyes searching his in the dim light. 'Harry was trying to convince me that the mangroves needed saving.'

'I thought you were going to wait and see what happened.' He stepped away from me and walked back down the hall to the kitchen. I followed, surprised at his accusatory tone.

'I was … I am … But with you otherwise occupied this weekend, I didn't see any harm in going out for a look.' I leant back against the doorframe as he opened the fridge and took out a stubby of beer and a bottle of white wine. When he held up the latter, I nodded. 'What's wrong, Finn? You sound angry and, given the afternoon I've had, that's not cool.'

His back towards me, he paused as he reached for a glass from the cupboard, his head giving a little shake as if he was giving himself a talking to. 'I'm sorry,' he finally said, his voice thick with regret. He poured wine into the glass and handed it to me. 'The thought of you … The idea that you …' He covered his face briefly with his hands. 'I'm sorry … it just shook me. Knowing you were bobbing about out there in Harry's rust bucket—'

'It's quite seaworthy, you know.' I attempted to lighten the mood. When he didn't laugh I put the wineglass on the counter and wrapped my arms around his waist. 'Hey,' I said gently, nuzzling under his chin. 'It's okay … well, it's not okay, but I am. And so is Harry. We're certainly much more okay than the poor woman we found.'

'Was it a woman?'

I extricated myself and picked up my glass, leaning back on the counter. 'It seems to be so. We didn't get close enough to have a good look, though. All I saw was …' I squeezed my eyes shut, but the image I saw was the one from my vision, not the view Harry and I had from the boat. 'She was wearing a white dress,' I said and took a large gulp of wine, breathing in deeply as the cool alcohol made its way down my throat. 'We had to give a brief statement to Ted – what we were doing out there, when we arrived, when we saw it, did we touch her … that sort of thing.'

'Do they think it was an accident?' Finn stood opposite me, hip against the edge of the other counter.

'What else could it be?' I scratched the back of my head. 'Harry said it was probably someone mucking about in a kayak without the right gear – although we didn't see another craft out there.'

'It could have drifted away.' Finn took a long swallow

from his beer.

'Yes, it could have,' I said slowly, working through that possibility.

'You don't sound convinced.' His chuckle sounded forced. 'Or are you keen to get the murder board out again?'

'Hardly,' I scoffed. 'There's no reason for me to assume it wasn't an accident, it's just … well, what was she doing out there?'

He shrugged. 'As you say, it was probably someone up from the city mucking around in the kayak without the proper gear. Her friends will miss her soon, and a story will come out about how she took a kayak out on Saturday night after a few drinks and it didn't end well.' He drained his beer and tossed the bottle into the recycle bin.

'You're right, I suppose.' I searched for something else to talk about. We'd never struggled with conversation before, but now it felt awkward, as though we barely knew each other, the words we'd exchanged yesterday a shadow between us. 'I'm surprised you're here. Doesn't Tamzin mind?'

Finn's brow furrowed in quick surprise. 'What? No. She left this morning to head back to Brisbane. She lives there now. Her father was put into a care home, and she wanted to be closer to him so got a new job.' Sadness shadowed his eyes. 'Her mother passed away not long before we split, but her father has gone downhill in the last few years. Alzheimers.' He shook his head. 'Such a cruel disease – he was an academic, you know. A scientist.' He sucked in a big sigh. 'He'd been so proud of her, and she said he barely recognises her these days.'

'I can't imagine how awful that would be for her.' I said, my heart going out to Tamzin.

His faint smile acknowledged my sympathy. 'She'll be back in a few days to begin the study.' He crossed to the fridge and opened it. 'What do you feel like eating? I can make something …'

Suddenly aware of both the night chill and the fact that I was still wearing the same clothes I'd had on out in the boat – and the shorts were still damp – I said, 'I'm cold and feel'—I rubbed my arms—'filthy so I'm going to have a shower. Let's just order a pizza or something.' I kissed his lips. 'I missed you last night.'

'I missed you too.' His eyes met mine, heat pooling deep in my belly.

This time, when he kissed me, I pressed hard against him. Even though I'd told him I didn't want to see him until he'd sorted things through, tonight I needed his closeness and his heat. I needed to block out the images of the afternoon. Mostly, though, I needed to feel alive.

Although Finn rarely stayed over during the week, tonight he offered and I almost accepted.

'It's okay,' I said. 'I don't think I'll sleep well, so there's no point in both of us starting the week exhausted.'

'Are you sure?' he asked, already moving away from me.

'I'm sure.' Although I'd needed him earlier this evening,

the memory of yesterday's argument had resurfaced and now I wanted to be alone.

While thoughts of Finn and a shadowy Tamzin had kept me tossing and turning last night, images of an entirely different nature kept me awake tonight. Every time I closed my eyes, I pictured it again: this time, though, the body was lying in the mud, the once-blonde hair tangled and matted, a crab scurrying across the woman's head, its claws tangled in her hair. Whoever she was, she didn't deserve to end up where she did.

CHAPTER NINE

By five, I'd given up attempting to sleep, changed into my bathers and a tracksuit and headed across to the beach, walking the length before I decided the sun was high enough for me to swim. While others might talk about the wonder of dark ocean swimming, I wasn't interested in being mistaken for a seal by a passing shark.

While the exercise exhausted my body, it did little for my brain, the vision of blonde hair waving in the current, refusing to be dislodged.

As I always do, I stopped at Beach Brewz for a post-swim coffee, although Finn's warm hug almost brought me back to tears.

I was changing out of my bathers in the bedroom when the front gate heralded my visitors. I slid my arms into a rugby jumper and pulled up my track pants just as the knock came on the door.

'I'll be right with you,' I called, rubbing at my still-wet hair with a towel.

Even if they hadn't presented their warrant cards

through the screen door, I would still have known they were police officers. I'd seen enough of them in court. The older one was dressed in black suit trousers, scuffed black leather shoes, a navy shirt (that either hadn't travelled well or hadn't seen an iron since it was last washed) that struggled to remain closed around an expanded girth, and a narrow charcoal tie with a thin silver stripe. In contrast, the younger one was more snappily dressed, his well-ironed, slim-fitting lilac shirt and black pants clinging to a body that saw the inside of a gym regularly.

The more poorly dressed of the pair introduced himself first. 'Detective Sergeant Osborne and this is Detective Constable Hall.' The younger man nodded. 'We'd like to talk to'—he made a show of consulting his notebook—'a Ms Clementine Carter.'

'That's me.' I held the screen door open. 'How can I help you?' Even as I asked, I knew there was only one reason they'd be here.

'We'd like to talk to you about the body you found yesterday.' Sergeant Osborne watched closely for my reaction.

Nodding sombrely, I said, 'You'd better come in,' and stood aside, allowing them to walk into the hall. 'I was about to make myself a coffee, so if you want one …' Squeezing past them in the narrow walkway, I led them to the kitchen.

Opening the overhead cupboard, I pulled down a mug. 'Was that a yes to the coffee?' When they nodded, I reached for another two and turned to face them. 'What is it you wanted to know about yesterday?'

Detective Sergeant Osborne looked around the kitchen, presumably for a chair, and finding none, leant against the kitchen counter. 'We'd just like to go through the statement you provided yesterday.' Despite his casual pose, his eyes were steely. Two detectives – they'd only call in detectives if the woman's death hadn't been an accident.

Even though I had nothing to hide, my heart jumped into my throat. 'Of course. How do you take your coffee?'

'White and two for me, thank you,' said the constable who had walked across to the back door to look outside. I popped a pod in the machine, slid a mug under the dispenser and pressed the button. As the kitchen filled with the sound of the machine doing its job, my mind stepped through the statement I'd given yesterday. 'And you, Sergeant?'

'White and one,' he said grudgingly, scowling at his constable when the younger man raised his eyebrows.

Chuckling, I spooned sugar into Constable Hall's mug and poured a generous splash of milk. 'Am I guessing Sergeant Osborne is supposed to be watching his sugar intake?' I flashed the constable a conspiratorial smile.

'He's not supposed to be having sugar at all,' the younger man said with a wary sideways glance at his superior.

'Aaaah.' I nodded, popping another capsule into the machine. 'Diabetes?'

'That's enough, Constable,' Sergeant Osborne said

sternly. 'Are you quite finished, Ms Carter?'

'Just a minute, Sergeant.' Still facing the coffee machine, I suppressed a smile. The detective was too experienced not to see the coffee-making for what it really was – an opportunity for me to gather my thoughts. 'Here you go.' I handed him a mug and popped a pod in the machine for my cup. As the machine whirred, both detectives were silent, although I felt the sergeant's eyes on my back. 'Now, you were saying?'

He took a sip of coffee, his eyes holding mine. 'The statement you gave yesterday was a bit light on detail.'

I hadn't left anything out, had I? 'Would you like to take these through to the lounge room?' Without waiting for their response, I walked through the arch into the dining and lounge room and sat on the sofa, setting my mug on a coaster on the side table.

The two men did the same, and the sergeant grunted a little as he sat down. 'Are you right now?' he asked.

Allowing myself a wry smile, I nodded. 'I'm sorry, Sergeant, but I told Senior Sergeant Winters everything I knew.'

'How about you go through it again for us?'

I picked up my coffee. 'Sure. We – Harry Glover and I – were out in Harry's tinny yesterday afternoon and saw what appeared to us to be a woman's body. That would've been around three-fifteen. I called the police station, and then Harry and I sat there until the Coast Guard turned up with

Senior Sergeant Winters and Constable King. They asked us to wait until they'd completed whatever it was they needed to do, took our statements and told us we were free to go.'

'How did you know it was a woman? Did you recognise her?' DS Osborne asked, inclining his head towards his constable who obligingly opened his notebook.

'We assumed it was a woman because of the hair and dress, but as for recognising her?' I shook my head. 'She was face down, and we didn't want to disturb her. Do you know who she is?'

He ignored my question and leant forward on the lounge. 'You'd never seen her before?'

Beginning to feel exasperated, I counted to five in my head. 'As I said, she was face down, and we didn't get close enough to recognise her; as such, I wouldn't know if I'd seen her before.' DC Hall wrote in his notebook. 'Given that you're both detectives and not from here, can I assume her death wasn't an accident?'

The two men exchanged glances. 'It's an unexplained death. We're simply gathering evidence for the coroner,' said DS Osborne. 'What were you and Mr Glover doing out there?'

'It was a lovely afternoon for messing about in boats,' I said, misquoting Ratty from *The Wind In The Willows*.

DS Osborne didn't return my smile and continued with a straight face. 'Our understanding is that you're in a relationship with Finn Marella'—my eyebrows rose—'so,

I'll ask you again: what were you and Mr Glover doing out there?' His mouth twisted unpleasantly.

'Not what you're implying, that's for sure! Have you ever tried doing anything like that in a small boat?' I scoffed at the ridiculous idea he was insinuating. 'If you must know, we were out there because I wanted to see the mangroves.'

'And why would that be?' The sergeant set his empty mug on a coaster.

'Because the council has rushed through an environmental study that I suspect is for different reasons than what was stated.'

DS Osborne raised his eyebrows, a sceptical expression on his face. 'Why do you think that?'

Beginning to feel like a suspect rather than a witness, I pushed my anger back where it belonged and forced levity into my tone. 'You don't know our mayor, do you?' When I received blank faces and shakes of their heads, I looked at my watch. 'Now'—I stood—'if that's all, I need to get to work.'

'What is your employment?' While DC Hall had made to stand, the sergeant had remained seated. What was this guy playing at?

'I own New Moon – the new-age shop in town.' I picked up my coffee cup and strode into the kitchen, leaving the detectives little choice but to follow me. 'I'm also a lawyer.' I met DC Hall's eyes as he placed their cups on the sink.

A little smile played around the corner of the sergeant's mouth. 'We'll bear that in mind. We need to find Mr Glover, but he wasn't at his address.'

'He wouldn't be – the surf was up this morning. But I am expecting him here—' I rolled my eyes at the innuendo in the glance the two men shared. 'He's doing some work for me … and here he is now.'

Harry let himself in through the back door, stalling when he saw the two detectives.

'Harry,' I said. 'This is Detective Sergeant Osborne and Detective Constable Hall. They haven't said as much, but I suspect the body we found yesterday didn't fall from a kayak.' Suppressing a grin at DS Osborne's glare, I continued. 'So they need us to go back over our statement.'

'Sure,' Harry said easily. 'Clem and I were out in the tinny, and we found a body. Clem phoned the police and Tyson—'

'That's Constable King,' I cut in.

Harry nodded at my clarification. 'Constable King told us to stay put until Ted – Senior Sergeant Winters – could get there. So we did. End of.'

'And what were you and Ms Carter doing out there? Was it a romantic assignation?' Sergeant Osborne asked with a sly sideways glance at me. I rolled my eyes. Was he serious?

Harry threw his head back and laughed. 'Clem's hot but taken – and I'd be batting above my average with her.' DC Hall allowed himself a small grin. 'Besides, have you ever tried hooking up in a boat that size? No, if I was lucky enough to be in that situation with Clem, I'd be taking her somewhere more romantic than my tinny.'

'I'll ask again, Mr Glover, what were the two of you doing out there?' DS Osborne narrowed his gaze on Harry, his clipped voice telling me he was losing patience with us.

Harry sighed, looked at me, then sighed again. 'Well, Sergeant … We were out there because I was trying to convince Clem that the mangroves were worth saving. The council's approved this environmental study, you see, and even though they say it's about boardwalks, anyone who knows what Ray Cosgrove is like – and Bob Lindsay, for that matter – would know that the last thing they'd be interested in would be boardwalks. No'—he shook his head, unruly blond curls falling about his face—'this is about—'

DS Osborne held up his hand. 'Enough! I've heard enough.' Exhaling loudly, he said, 'If either of you think of anything you haven't told us …' He nodded at DS Hall who handed across his business card.

'Absolutely.' I led them back down the hall to the front door and held it open.

The older man lingered in the doorway, a frown creasing his brow. 'I heard there was a mysterious death on these premises not long ago,' he said.

'Yes. My aunt.' I glared at him, eyes burning with anger. 'And before you start asking for my alibi for that, you'd also know that Chris Walker has been arrested, has pleaded guilty to manslaughter and is currently awaiting conviction.'

He smiled that unpleasant smile of his. 'Yes, of course. Apologies, Ms Carter, I didn't mean to upset you.'

'Your apology is accepted, Sergeant.' My words were as insincere as his. 'If you need to ask any more questions, here are my details.' I handed him a card from the basket on the hallstand.

As soon as the detectives were no longer in sight, Harry's sunny demeanour faded. 'Was she murdered?'

I shrugged. 'I can't see why they'd send up two homicide detectives otherwise.'

'They're from homicide?'

'They didn't say, but I suspect so.'

'Wow.' Harry's teeth caught his top lip. 'In the mangroves too … You don't think …?'

'It has something to do with the study?' An unwelcome thought pushed itself into my brain. Was there a link between Finn's wife and the dead woman? Surely not. Harry was watching me expectantly. 'I hope not,' I said.

'But it could be?' he persisted.

I met his eyes. 'If there is, we must leave it to the police,' I said sternly.

'To those clowns?' Harry scoffed, his eyes skyward.

'I'm sure they're not that bad,' I said, my words lacking conviction. 'Anyway, how are you? Did you get any sleep last night?'

Shuffling his feet, he said, 'Some. I know there was

nothing we could've done for her, but I kept seeing her, you know?'

'Yeah, I know,' I admitted. 'I wish I could tell you how to make it disappear, but I can't. Did the surf help?'

'A bit,' he said after a short, awkward silence. 'About as much as your swim probably did. The way I figure it, if we hadn't been there yesterday, who knows when she would've been found.'

'Good point.' After glancing at my watch again, I said, 'I'd better get changed and head into the shop. Are you right to lock up here when you're done?'

'No probs. I'll get on with digging the holes for the supports. Catch you later.'

His head was down, and his feet dragged as he left through the back door.

CHAPTER TEN

News had spread, and it seemed as though every time the bell rang on the shop door, it was someone wanting to know the goss about the previous day's events.

By early afternoon, Nina had had enough. 'Why don't you leave? Everything is under control here.' She smiled and added gently, 'I know you like to be here, but …'

'I know, you're the manager, and you've been managing perfectly well.' My sigh was exaggerated so she'd know I was joking. 'You're telling me I probably should take Maggie up on her offer.' Maggie had recently asked me to join her practice. Aside from having more work than she could handle, there were, she said, no decent family lawyers in the region. I'd promised her I'd think about it.

Nina nodded. 'All I'm saying is I think you'd feel you had more … more of a purpose. After all'—she grinned cheekily—'an Aries without a purpose or, God forbid, a fire to fight is dangerous.' A short laugh and, 'Seriously though, Clem, you had a truly awful experience yesterday, don't think you can pretend it wasn't. And while you can't control that, the best way for you to get through it is to—'

Nina really was wise beyond her years. A lump rose in my throat, making my voice catch. 'To find something I can influence and fight that battle. That's what Rose used to say to me.' My smile held a hint of sadness. 'I'd come home from school upset about something – probably something Kylie Lindsay had said or done'—I chuckled—'it would've been Kylie. She was the ultimate mean girl – still is. Anyway, Rose used to say to me, "Don't stand here complaining about it; either stand up for yourself or let it go – it's your choice." She was right.'

'You miss her.' Nina's eyes became suspiciously moist.

'I do.' I pulled her in for a quick hug. 'You know, the first time I saw you, I thought I was looking at Rose. You reminded me so much of her.'

'It must be the dungarees and the Docs.' She did a quick ball change in her Doc Martens.

'Yep, that's it.' Sobering, I said, 'You're right though. I'm of more use helping Maggie with her umpteen million cases than cluttering up the space here.'

'I don't want you to think—'

'That I'm not wanted?' I laid my hand on her arm. 'I don't.' Impulsively, I kissed her cheek. 'But I will get out of your hair.'

Maggie greeted me with a comforting hug. 'Sweetie! How horrible was it?'

'You know she's talking about Harry's boat, don't you?'

drawled Siouxsie, her frown showing her concern.

'Do they know who it was?' Maggie asked, glaring at her daughter.

I shook my head and stepped out of her embrace. 'No. But a couple of detectives turned up this morning, so I don't think it was an accident.'

'Seriously?' Siouxsie stood behind the reception desk. 'Do you think she was murdered?'

'I have no idea. We didn't get close enough to get a good look.'

In my pocket, my phone vibrated; I ignored it.

'Harry wondered whether it might have been someone out in a kayak or something, but there was no kayak anywhere around.'

'It might have drifted off,' Maggie said without conviction.

'Maybe. We didn't see any other boats out there, and she wasn't exactly dressed for kayaking.' An image of her white dress and blonde hair floating in the current flashed across my eyes. That was when the two detectives walked in.

'Can I help you?' Siouxsie asked as they would've walked straight past reception into Maggie's office.

While both men paused, DC Hall's ears tinged pink.

'Actually,' said DS Osborne when I walked into reception, 'we were looking for you. That woman in the overalls at your shop told us we might find you here.'

'That woman in the overalls is the shop manager.' I

planted my hands on my hips. 'Why were you looking for me? I don't remember any more than what I told you this morning.'

The two men glanced at each other. 'The victim has been identified as Tamzin Griffiths,' said the constable. 'It's Finn Marella's wife – she goes by her maiden name.'

My hand shot to my chest to slow the frantic beating of my heart. 'Finn's wife? But he hasn't said … Oh God, I need to call him.'

As I reached for my phone, DS Osborne's raised hand stopped me. 'Mr Marella is currently helping us with our enquiries. When did you last see him?'

'Ummm.' I rubbed my forehead, feeling the dull throb of a headache starting behind my eyes. 'Yesterday … yesterday evening.'

DS Osborne raised his eyebrows. 'My understanding is you two are …' He pinched at his chin as if searching for an appropriate word, even though we both knew what he meant.

'In a relationship? Yes, we are. I told you that this morning.'

'We've also heard you had a disagreement on Saturday morning.' The older man's eyes narrowed. 'Was that to do with his wife coming to town?'

I hesitated briefly before answering. 'If that's what you've heard, it must be right.'

'And?'

My mouth curled into a half smile at the sergeant's question. 'And nothing. We argued. Couples do.'

Again, he consulted his notebook, even though I was in no doubt he'd memorised the contents. 'We've been told the argument was because you were unaware Mr Marella was married.'

Had Finn told them that? Where was this going? 'That's right,' I conceded. 'I told Finn to deal with what he needed to deal with, and we'd talk afterwards.'

'Yet you saw him on Saturday evening.' Sergeant Osborne tapped at his lower lip with the pen.

I shrugged. 'Not by design. It's a small town. I saw them – Finn and his wife – at the beach when I came out of New Moon.'

'Aaah, yes, your new-age shop.' The wrinkle of his nose told me what he thought of that. 'I don't suppose you predicted the death of Ms Griffiths.' He chuckled and looked to his constable to join the amusement. The constable's face held a strained smile. DC Osborne continued after clearing his throat. 'Yes, well. I thought you said you didn't recognise the victim, yet you've just said you saw Mr Marella and his wife on Saturday evening.'

'That's right. I spoke to Finn and assumed the woman he was with was Tamzin.' I lifted a shoulder. 'She was on the beach, and it was dark, so I wouldn't have recognised her again.' I forced a tight smile. 'So you see, Detective Sergeant, my statement stands – I didn't recognise the victim. But I am sorry to hear it was Finn's wife.'

'And yesterday evening?' He flipped the page of his notebook, seemingly to check the details.

'Sorry?'

'You said you saw Mr Marella yesterday evening. Why was that? Had you forgiven him? In my experience, women don't forgive that quickly.' DS Osborne wore a disbelieving smile.

'I suppose that depends on how many times the man in question has needed to be forgiven, I suppose – and how sincere he is. In my experience, some men are slow learners and are sorry only when they're caught. I'm glad to say Finn is not one of those men.' As I raised my eyebrows pointedly, the smile slipped from the sergeant's face. 'But yes, as a matter of fact, I had forgiven him. Finding a dead body tends to put things into perspective.'

'Is that why you called Mr Marella? To tell him you'd forgiven him?'

Was the man being deliberately obtuse? 'I didn't call Finn. He was at my house when I got home, and I was glad he was,' I said bluntly. 'You may be used to finding dead bodies; I am not.'

He inclined his head to imply understanding. 'Did you talk about the body you found?'

'Of course I did.' Was he going somewhere with this line of questioning? Something he'd said earlier came back to me. 'Hold on – you said Finn was helping you with your enquiries. Does that mean you suspect him of being involved in her accident?'

Again, the two police officers exchanged glances. 'Ms Griffiths' death was not an accident,' said DC Hall, his colleague watching my face closely for a reaction.

My heart sprang into my throat as I put what he'd said together. 'And you think Finn has something to do with it? No. No!' My voice rose in disbelief. 'Finn was not involved in whatever happened to his wife.' I shook my head firmly, throwing a glance to Maggie for backup.

'When you say "helping you", does that imply you're questioning him?' Although her expression was neutral, Maggie sounded as incredulous as I felt.

'He has identified the victim and has provided a preliminary statement.' Constable Hall was careful with his words.

'Where is Finn now?' I demanded. I dug my fingernails into my palm to stop the panic I felt from showing.

'We have more questions for him, so he's at the station,' conceded DS Osborne, snapping his notepad shut.

Thoughts whirled through my brain, and anything I wanted to say stuck in my throat. My eyes flew wildly to Maggie.

Touching my arm lightly, she took over. 'You seriously think he …' She shook her head, managing to convey disbelief and disappointment at the incompetence of the detectives standing before us in the motion. 'Has he been offered a solicitor?'

'Of course he has!' DS Osborne's face was thunderous at her implication that he hadn't followed procedure. 'He said he's done nothing wrong, so he sees no need for a solicitor.'

Maggie rolled her eyes. Typical Finn.

'Right,' Maggie said in her best legal voice. 'Unless you intend arresting Clem as well, I think you've asked all the questions you will be asking today. It's obvious you're fishing'—I suppressed a grimace at her tasteless-in-the-circumstances pun—'so if that's all, I'd like you to please leave.'

Finding my voice, I added, my tone firm yet measured, 'And I need to talk some sense into my client.'

'Your client?' asked DS Osborne, eyebrows shooting up.

'Yes. I'm a lawyer, and Finn Marella is my client.' As neither man seemed capable of speech, I added, 'And as you're going back to the station, you can give me a lift.' When neither man moved, she asked, 'Well? Are you coming?'

'Do you think it's wise you represent him? After all'—Maggie paused for half a beat—'you do have a conflict of interest.'

'I know I do, but that makes me the best person for him right now.' My eyes pleaded with her to understand. 'You know what Finn is like – he knows he's innocent and it won't have occurred to him that there are people who won't believe that. I need to get him out of there. But there is something I need you to do for me.'

'Anything,' Maggie said.

I picked up the tote bag I'd left behind the reception counter, fished inside for my keys and handed them to her. 'There's a spare key to Finn's place on this keyring. Can one of you please get Finn's dogs? I hate to think what they must be thinking.' I glared at Sergeant Osborne's back. 'You can take them to my place … and Maggie?'

'Yes …'

'I'm not sure what time I'll be back and …' How could I say this in a way she'd understand? 'You know how I'm having the meeting at my place tonight? The usual crew …'

'Yeeees …?' She frowned her confusion.

'Well, could you remind the others and get out the board for me?' Squeezing my eyes shut, I willed her to understand. 'It's the one that doesn't fit in the kitchen cupboard, so I've kept it in the spare room ever since we had Rose's do – you can't miss it.'

Siouxsie picked up on my meaning. 'You know, Mum … the board …'

'The board! Of course! Leave it with me!' Maggie pulled me into a goodbye hug before I followed the detectives outside.

CHAPTER ELEVEN

The drive to the police station was a short one, but I spent it running through the tasks in my head. Finn's dogs would be taken care of, and Maggie would let Justin and Siouxsie know we were meeting at my place that night. With Finn's freedom at stake, it was time to bring the murder board back out.

When we pulled up outside, I unclipped my seatbelt and tried the door handle. 'Can you unlock the door, please?'

'What's the gathering you're having tonight?' Sergeant Osborne asked, twisting around in his seat.

'Is that really any of your business?' I plastered on the same look I used to reserve for recalcitrant spouses in my family law days. Sighing heavily, I shook my head in exasperation. 'If you must know, it's book club at mine.'

'And you asked Maggie to get a cheese board together if you're running late?' The comment earnt Constable Hall a glower from his superior.

'Exactly. Now, can I please see my client?'

Walking alongside the two detectives into Whale Bay Police Station, I wasn't sure what I expected to see, but

Finn sitting in Senior Sergeant Ted Winters' office, the remains of one of Bron's sausage rolls and a coffee from Beach Brewz on the table, certainly wasn't it. While Finn appeared relaxed as he spoke with Ted, the dark shadows under his eyes told a different story.

As I flew through the door, Finn rose from his chair to meet me. Wrapping my arms around him, I held him as closely as I could. 'Are you okay?'

If it were at all possible, he pulled me in tighter. 'I am now.'

'I'm so sorry, Finn, I only just found out. Maggie will see to the dogs.'

'Thank you, Clem. I was just explaining to Te … Senior Sergeant Winters … that I was worried about them.'

Pulling back, I held his hand. 'You get good service in this station,' I said, inclining my head towards the coffee cup.

'We didn't provide him with that,' said Ted. 'The coffee and pastries just arrived.'

'But how?' began Constable Hall before nodding his understanding. 'It's a small town.'

Sergeant Osborne thrust his phone back into his pocket and stood in the office doorway, face red, legs astride, hands on hips. 'What's going on here?' he demanded.

'I was about to ask you the same thing, Detective Sergeant,' Ted said easily, his tone warning against any further rebuke. 'This man was left in the interview room and told to wait.' He narrowed his eyes on the visiting sergeant. 'My understanding is you brought Finn in to help with your enquiries, following which you decided he needed some "alone time" to rethink his answers. He was denied a phone call—'

'He wasn't denied a phone call; he didn't ask for one,' blustered Sergeant Osborne.

'It's difficult to ask for something when there's no one here to ask. But,' Ted continued, 'I see his solicitor is here now, and I suspect she's going to tell you that unless you have more questions for him or wish to charge him, she'd like him released.' As Sergeant Osborne seemed about to argue, Ted added, 'Do you have any different questions you'd like to ask him?'

The detective scowled and shook his head. 'Mr Marella doesn't have an alibi for the time we believe Ms Griffiths was killed,' he said.

'Do you have a time of death yet?' When DS Osborne lowered his eyes, I said, 'Obviously not. Finn, where were you on Sunday morning after Tamzin left and before, say, two in the afternoon?'

His pause was so minute as to be almost imperceptible. Almost. 'At home, feeling sorry for myself. Tamzin had left for Brisbane early on Sunday morning, or'—he let out a humourless laugh that sounded awkward to my ears, so must also have to the police officers—'so I thought, and after our argument the day before I didn't feel comfortable ringing you.' He shrugged. 'So, it was just the dogs and me. I took the opportunity to update my accounts and order some supplies we were running low on.'

'Timestamps on your banking app and email should be able to prove you were where you said you were.' I grabbed at the information as if it were a life buoy.

'Anyone could've been using his computer at that time,' argued Sergeant Osborne. 'It doesn't prove anything.'

'Agreed, but you have no firm evidence to hold him,' I held his gaze, holding Finn's hand tightly.

'She's right,' said Ted, steepling his fingers under his chin.

Finn shook his head. 'It's okay. I just want to understand what happened to Tamzin.'

Even though I knew his feelings were understandable – after all, he'd once loved Tamzin – his naivety was getting in the way of me protecting him as his lawyer.

DC Hall's phone rang, and he left the office to take the call. His eyes widened, and then, through the half-open venetian blinds, his eyes briefly met mine before skitting away. My heart skipped and the back of my neck prickled. He rang off, walked back into the office, and tapped the sergeant on the arm. 'Excuse me, sir, can I have a word?'

The pair walked out, and as DC Hall explained the call to his superior, a smug smile that made my heart skip again and my neck prickle some more spread over the sergeant's face.

'Ms Carter,' he said, coming back into the office. 'I thought you said you'd never met the victim.'

'That's right.'

'Then why have we found your fingerprints on a bottle of sunscreen in her bag?'

'My fingerprints are on record?' I shook my head as I realised. 'You took them from the card I gave you this morning?'

Finn let go of my hand and stepped away, the look in his eyes a combination of confusion, puzzlement and something else. Accusation? 'Clem? You didn't tell me you'd met Tam?'

His voice sounded distant. Sergeant Osborne asked more questions, but his voice, too, was muted. Vaguely, I registered Ted holding his hand up so they would all be quiet. 'Let her think,' he said.

Sunscreen. Images rushed into my brain, and puzzle pieces fitted together. I turned to Ted. 'It was the sunscreen lady. I saw her yesterday morning after my swim. I swam later yesterday – and for longer'—I cast a rueful glance at Finn whose fault it was I'd overslept—'so it must've been around ten when I got out of the water. And she was sitting on the beach near my things.' I tilted my head back as I walked back through our conversation. 'She said something about the weather like "it's a nice day" or "it's going to be warm for this time of year", something like that.'

'Which was it?' demanded the sergeant.

'Does it matter? It was a comment about the weather,' I bit back, momentarily losing my train of thought. 'Actually, no, it wasn't. She led with asking me to put sunscreen on her back, and then she said it was surprisingly warm. Where was I? She said she had a shoulder injury and couldn't reach around.'

'I didn't know that,' said Finn, frowning.

'To be fair, you said you haven't seen her in a while,' I said.

'Go on,' urged Ted. 'Did she say anything else?'

'Yes, I told her Beach Brewz was the best coffee in town.' Constable Hall wrote in his notebook, and I guessed they'd bought coffee from Bron this morning. 'Then she asked me about the café at the wharf.'

Ted picked up a pen and clicked the nib up and down. *Click. Click. Click.* 'It sounds like she knew who you were and was attempting to confirm that. Did you get a sense of that?'

I twisted my mouth and shook my head. 'Not at the time, but in hindsight … you could be right. She also said something about the mangroves and how she'd seen them from the café at the wharf. She wondered how to get over there and if there was a walk she could take. I said they were protected, but you could access the area by boat.' Heat rose to my face, and I lowered my head – and tone. 'I might have also said that if our dodgy mayor and his cronies had their way, they'd probably rezone it away from mangroves and stick up some posh development that would ruin the environment.'

When I raised my head again, Ted's mouth was slightly twisted as if he were suppressing a grin. 'Did she say anything to that?'

'She said she'd heard rumours and asked if they were true, but I regretted having said anything by then. Besides, it wouldn't have mattered to her – at least I didn't think it would matter to her – to know that the council had commissioned work on the environmental study of the mangroves before obtaining approval … so I made my excuses and left.'

'And that was the last time you saw her?' Ted asked, holding his hand up when Sergeant Osborne would have interrupted.

'Yes. Until …' Again, the image of the mud-splattered body came into view. 'Maybe I should've recognised her, but'—I shrugged—'she was lying face down so I didn't.'

'Do you know how …' Finn grimaced, unable to finish his sentence. 'Was it an accident?'

DS Osborne paused, perhaps deciding how much to disclose. 'It wasn't an accident. Preliminary results have shown some blunt force trauma, and there are marks on her throat, but the final report hasn't been issued.'

A choke escaped me, and Finn staggered backwards, the desk stopping him from falling. 'She really was … murdered?' His voice broke on the final word, his pain stabbing at my heart.

'It appears so.' DS Osborne's gaze narrowed on Finn, watching every emotion play across his face. Horror, disbelief, sadness … regret. 'Do you know who might have had a reason to want your wife dead?'

Finn gave a jerky shake of his head. 'I barely spoke to her these days.'

'And she gave no indication—'

When Finn shook his head, the detective turned his attention back to me. 'We're going to need a statement, Ms Carter.' DS Osborne had been mostly silent as Ted had questioned me but was now reasserting his authority.

I nodded. 'I understand.'

'After all, you may have been the last person to see her alive.'

'With the exception of her killer,' I reminded the sergeant. 'Do I need a solicitor?'

'That's up to you,' the sergeant said gruffly. 'But I can't see why you'd need one if you have nothing to hide.'

Despite his impassive face, a knot of distrust tightened in my gut. 'You know what? I think I'll be safe and call one anyway.'

Pulling my phone from the pocket of my track pants, I rang a number. 'Maggie? Can you come down to the station?'

'Sure, but why?'

'I might need a solicitor – and you're it.'

'I'll be there in five.'

As I rang off, I swear I heard Ted choke back a chuckle.

CHAPTER TWELVE

Once Maggie arrived, my statement was quickly dealt with and Maggie was able to leave. Finn's situation, however, was more problematic.

'Mr Marella, can you please explain why your vehicle was seen on the Bruce Highway heading south at around midday yesterday?'

My head jerked up, startled by this line of questioning. 'Finn?'

He let out a heavy sigh and lowered his head to the table with a thump.

'Mr Marella, why was your car on the highway at the same time you told us you were home'—DC Osborne leant over and consulted DC Hall's notebook—'working?'

Finn lifted his head, his eyes darting from me to the detectives. I held my breath as I waited for him to answer, silence hanging heavy in the air.

The sergeant pursed his lips and nodded once. 'Now, I've never been great with maps, but I know the turn-off to Dolphin Point is about here'—he pointed at the map open on his phone—'and you were last picked up on cameras about here.' He steepled his fingers under his chin. 'I don't need to remind you that the access road to the mangroves is only a few clicks down this road. So tell me, Mr Marella, were you in the mangroves yesterday afternoon? Perhaps you went down there with your wife and'—DS Osborne sent me a sly look I pretended not to notice—'argued, and one thing led to another. Perhaps it was an accident and you panicked.' When Finn didn't react, the detective shrugged. 'It happens.'

It was all I could do to remain silent and expressionless in the face of the relentless questioning.

'Is that how it happened, Mr Marella?' The sergeant repeated his question.

Finn shook his head, strands of his curls falling around his face. He pulled at the leather braid around his wrist, the fear in his eyes telling me he was finally realising how serious his predicament was.

'For the tape, please, Mr Marella?' The sergeant pointed to the recording device in the room's corner.

'Finn,' I pleaded, my hand on his arm. 'Please tell them where you were.'

DC Osborne glared at me, his eyes narrowed and filled with barely suppressed fury, and I glared back at him, my own anger simmering.

'I went walking,' Finn mumbled. 'In the national park.'

DS Osborne relaxed back in his chair, clasping his

hands together. 'That's alright then. Why didn't you tell us that in the first place?'

'Because I didn't think you'd believe me,' Finn said, avoiding eye contact with everyone in the room.

'Can you show us on the map where you went walking?' The sergeant pushed forward the map app on his phone.

'Ummm … about here.' Finn pointed to an area to the right of the highway.

'There, see,' I said, also shuffling forward in my seat and looking over at the screen. 'Nowhere near the mangroves.'

DS Osborne held up his hand. 'Are you here as Mr Marella's solicitor or … something else?'

I reluctantly nodded my understanding, knowing I needed to tread carefully and not cross the line. The last thing I want is to cause more issues for Finn.

'Can anyone corroborate your story?' asked DC Hall, scratching something into his notepad with his pen.

'You mean, did anyone see me?' Finn narrowed his eyes at the detectives as he most likely thought through his actions. 'I wasn't the only person on the track, but would they remember me? And how would I find them?'

DS Osborne lifted a shoulder like he didn't have a care in the world. Dickhead.

'When was the last time you saw your wife?' Again, the sergeant sent a sly glance towards me that I pretended not to notice.

'Yesterday morning,' Finn said. 'She packed up and—'

'She'd stayed at your house?' DS Osborne widened his eyes. 'Even though you were separated?'

'Well, yes.' Finn sounded like he didn't understand the problem. 'Things were amicable between us, and I have a spare room. Anyway, as I said, she packed up on Sunday morning.'

'Did she say where she was going?'

Finn glanced across at me, but his eyes skated away before mine could hold them. 'Yes, she said she was going to Brisbane to see her father – he's in a care home down there. Has anyone told him?'

DS Osborne waved Finn's concerns away. 'We can deal with that.'

'It would be best coming from me. Even though we were separated, he always liked me.'

'I said we'd deal with it,' the sergeant repeated. 'Did she say when she'd be back?'

Finn nodded. 'Yes. She said she'd be back today or tomorrow – to begin the study the council had commissioned her to do.'

'The one on the mangroves?' When Finn bobbed his head with confirmation, DS Osborne continued. 'Yet instead of driving to Brisbane, she first met up with your girlfriend on the beach and then went to the mangroves where somehow she ended up dead.' After a loaded pause, he added, 'Is that right?'

'Well, yes, I suppose so. I didn't see her after she left my house.'

'Hmm.' DS Osborne tapped at his lower lip with the end of his pen. 'Yet how did she get to the mangroves?'

'I suppose she drove.' Finn shrugged.

'That's what we thought, but we haven't found her car. I don't suppose you know where it is?'

'Of course I don't,' Finn snapped. I laid my hand on his, a gentle reminder to remain calm.

'Or maybe'—DS Osborne turned to his colleague—'Mr Marella drove his wife out to the mangroves?'

'That could've happened, sir,' acknowledged DC Hall, referring again to his notes.

'In which case we'll find traces of her DNA in Mr Marella's car,' the sergeant mused.

'Are we going to talk in possibilities, or do you have questions you wish to ask my client?' This detective was really getting on my nerves now.

Another of those unpleasant smiles and, 'You'd better settle in, Ms Carter; we're only just getting started.'

It was early evening before I let myself into the cottage, the dogs jumping around me in pleased welcome. Ducking into the bedroom, I pulled a woollen poncho over my T-shirt and slid my feet into Ugg boots.

'No Finn?' Maggie and Siouxsie were sitting in the lounge room waiting for me. Justin appeared from the kitchen and handed me a glass of red wine.

'Thank you,' I said weakly, blinking back sudden tears.

'Oh Clem!' Maggie was out of her chair and across the room in a flash. Justin took the glass back out of my hand as Maggie embraced me. 'Was it terrible?'

I pressed my lips together and nodded. 'It was.'

'And Finn?' Siouxsie asked, shuffling forwards on the lounge but not getting up.

'He's still'—my voice broke—'there.'

Maggie stepped back, her hand clapped over her mouth.

'They're holding him?' A frown creased Justin's face.

Nodding, I took my glass back and drained it before handing it back to Justin. 'They applied to a magistrate and can hold him overnight and question him again in the morning.'

Maggie took my hand and led me to the throw-covered armchair. 'Tell us about it,' she urged.

'Well …' I took another sip and began to speak, filling them in on the questions the detectives had asked Finn.

'Then they started questioning him about his relationship with Tamzin; how did he feel when she told him she was seeing someone else and asked for a divorce … that sort of thing.' I rubbed my forehead and picked up my wineglass. 'When Finn said he was happy for Tamzin, the sergeant said he'd been told they'd had an almighty row about it, that Finn had flown into a jealous rage!'

'Finn? I don't believe it,' said Justin, shaking his head. 'I've never heard Finn raise his voice.'

'Me neither,' Maggie said firmly. 'He wanted a divorce. He'd made an appointment with me to draw up the paperwork – she just beat him to it. I'd say they made that up to try and get a rise out of him.'

'Did they say who reported this so-called almighty row to the police?' asked Siouxsie.

I swallowed a mouthful of wine before answering. 'Her new boyfriend. He said she called him on Saturday night and told him she was frightened.'

'Of Finn? No way,' said Siouxsie. Siouxsie swung her legs around and sat up.

'Well, if he's to be believed, she must have been frightened of something,' mused Justin. 'Do we know who he is?'

I shook my head. 'They wouldn't tell me. All they said was that he was working overseas, but heard the news so phoned them straight away.' I wrinkled my nose. There was something that didn't ring true about the story. 'Apparently he was scheduled to be back at the end of next week, but is happy to come home earlier if they need him to.'

'That's good of him,' said Maggie sardonically. 'Do you believe Finn?' Maggie gave me a wary look.

'Of course I do!' I snapped. 'Absolutely!' I hesitated for a second and then blurted out what had been worrying me. 'Why didn't he tell me yesterday he'd been hiking? I asked him what he'd been doing, and he said "this and that". Also, he never did tell me how he knew we'd found that body.'

'He'd have his reasons,' said Justin, although his frown had become deeper.

'I know.' I couldn't shake the feeling that Finn knew more than he was saying. 'I just wish he'd trust me with them.'

'As for how he knew, well'—Siouxsie shrugged—'it's a small town.'

'What happens now?' asked Maggie.

'They're holding him overnight while they check his car and search the house. Then, I suspect, they'll charge him tomorrow,' I said bleakly.

'Can they do that?' Siouxsie asked.

'Their evidence is circumstantial, and there's bound to be traces of Tamzin – a hair or fingerprints – in his car, so yes. We'll get him out on bail, but …' I shrugged. 'Osborne and his sidekick haven't looked anywhere other than at Finn for this …'

'Which means'—a gleam appeared in Maggie's eye—'that we have to.'

At Maggie's nod, Siouxsie uncurled herself from the lounge and walked across to the corner of the room where an easel stood, a batik throw hiding the board beneath. With a flourish, she ripped off the throw. 'No pressure, but Finn is depending on us,' she said.

'Thanks, guys.' My eyes filled with tired, grateful tears. 'I should've known when Finn said the "p" word on Saturday that something would go wrong.'

'Well,' said Maggie with a short laugh. 'At least things can't get any worse.'

As if on cue, the front gate squeaked. Maggie frowned. 'Are you expecting anyone else?'

'No. Siouxsie, you'd better cover the board,' I said slowly, the back of my neck prickling with foreboding. Surely there was nothing else this day could throw at me?

When the knock came, Maggie said, 'I'll get it.'

We all heard her gasp of surprise as she opened the door, but when she said, 'Nick Cosgrove! What are you doing here?' my heart stopped.

CHAPTER THIRTEEN

It wasn't until the wine slopped out of my glass that I realised my hands were shaking – and not just my hands. My entire body felt as though the blood in my veins had frozen. I expected my teeth to begin chattering any second.

Justin and Siouxsie both turned to me. While Justin's eyes were concerned, Siouxsie's were wide with curiosity and anticipation. My brain told my legs to walk down the hall to the open door, to greet Nick as if Kylie Lindsay and twenty-five years hadn't happened, as if he were just any visitor calling in to say hi. But my legs weren't listening, and they didn't move.

The chatter in the hall grew louder, and it was only a matter of seconds before Maggie rejoined us, Nick beside her. Yet still I stood, rooted to the floor, my heart pounding so loudly that surely the whole of Whale Bay could hear it. Fancifully, I imagined Martin and Kylie sitting in their glass and concrete McMansion on Nob Hill, turning to each other and saying something like, 'What is that drumming noise?'

'Clem.' Nick's eyes met mine, and in their oceanic

depths, I floundered, my feet scrambling for sand, my breath coming faster, and millions of goosebumps marching across my skin. 'It's been a while.' His eyes ran up and down my body. From anyone else, it would've felt creepy, but with Nick, it was as if he was coolly assessing me.

Self-consciously, I pushed an errant lock of chestnut hair behind my ear and resisted the urge to tug at the hem of the shorts I was still wearing. How must I appear to him? When he last saw me, I was young, lithe and fresh, and now? Now, I was middle aged, and while I hid the grey in my mid-length hair with the help of clever colouring and layering, the fine lines around my hazel eyes and the softness in my jaw proved my age.

I stood my ground and remained expressionless even when his lips quirked as he clocked my ensemble – a granny square poncho (made by Rose during one of her bursts of crocheting) over khaki shorts that left much of my legs bare, with Ugg boots completing my outfit.

'You look good, Clem,' he said with the grin that used to make my knees wobble and my heart melt. 'Although your fashion sense hasn't improved.'

I lifted a shoulder in a show of nonchalance and, with one hand on my hip, adopted a parody of a pose. 'This old thing? You should see me ready for court.'

He tilted his head back and laughed a rumbly laugh that sent my stomach on a rollercoaster ride. 'I'm sure I've seen that wool thing before.' He stepped closer and flicked at the edge of the poncho. 'Wasn't that Rose's?' When I nodded, the smile slipped from his face, and he stepped back. 'I heard about Rose. I'm really sorry, Clem.'

My smile was fleeting. 'Thanks for saying that. She always liked you.'

He'd weathered the years well. Although he and Martin were twins, they weren't identical, and while Martin was shining and golden – all blond hair, gleaming white teeth and obvious charm – Nick's good looks were more … muted. Yet if the two were standing together, it was Nick you couldn't look away from. He had a presence that Martin couldn't replicate. Rose once said it was like adding dark chocolate to chilli. 'You can't taste it, and you can't see it, but it adds a depth you can't replicate any other way,' she'd said. 'Nick Cosgrove is like that. There's something unexpected and complicated about him. Martin pretends, but Nick's the real deal.'

If anything, he'd improved with age, the lines around his eyes – still the same bluey-green as the Pacific – making him more rather than less attractive. His hair had lost some of its lustre, some grey blending into the blond, but again, it suited him. 'I see you're still addicted to Okanuis.' I waved my hand in the direction of his hibiscus-printed board shorts.

'Why mess with a good thing?' he asked lightly. 'Although'—he rubbed at his sweatshirt-covered arms—'it was warmer than this when I left home.'

'I hate to interrupt this touching reunion.' Until

Maggie cut in I'd forgotten there was anyone else in the room. 'What are you doing here, Nick?'

Nick's eyes widened. Had he also forgotten we weren't alone? Recovering quickly, he said, 'Mike told me about the study Dad commissioned on the mangroves, so I hopped in the car, and fifteen hundred kilometres later, here I am.'

'You came back for that?' Maggie made no effort to hide her scepticism. 'You haven't come home when your father's pulled dodgy stunts in the past. Are you sure you're not here because Michael Lindsay told you Clem was back? What?' she asked when Justin scoffed and shook his head at her directness. 'Don't you roll your eyes at me, Justin King. You were thinking it too.'

Flashing me a quick smile, Nick said, 'Okay, yes, that was a factor, but as soon as Mike told me about the mangroves, I put two and two together and came back to help you save it.' He cast his eyes around the room. 'I take it that's what you're all here for? A council of war? Mike told me how you found …' He broke off suddenly, a wide smile on his face. 'That's not …' He turned to me and laughed. 'That's not one of yours and Maggie's murder boards, is it?'

Heat rose to my face, but before I could answer, Siouxsie stepped forward. 'Hi, I'm Siouxsie — Mags' and Justin's daughter.' Justin's brows rose at her use of their Christian names. 'And yes, it is a murder board.' She thrust her hand out for him to shake, her kohl-rimmed eyes narrowing. 'I see the family resemblance.'

Nick's lips quirked. 'In looks only, I hope.'

She crossed her arms, determined. 'That remains to be seen.'

He chuckled. 'I see the family resemblance now, too.' He took a step closer to the board we hadn't yet begun to fill and pulled the cover back off. 'I can't believe you two are still doing these.'

Maggie planted her hands on her narrow hips. 'And why not? These days, though, the stakes are higher than deciding whether or not Kylie is a bitch.' She stared hard at him. 'Not that we'd need a murder board to know that.'

'No,' he smiled tightly. 'You don't need any help to work that one out.'

I resisted the urge to say, 'You didn't used to think that.'

'Is this set up as a council of war for the mangroves?' he asked. He picked up a ball of red wool we'd set out on the table and tossed it idly from hand to hand.

'Not exactly,' I began. Nick Cosgrove. Here. How did I feel about that? How should I be feeling? My head was spinning to fast to make sense of it.

'We're going to solve the murder of Finn's ex-wife,' Siouxsie blurted, defiantly swinging her green-streaked black hair over her shoulder.

A slight furrowing of his brow was the only surprise he showed. 'Mike mentioned something about a body being found. I didn't know it was a murder, though.' He let out a short laugh. 'I don't know, I'm away for two minutes and, all of a sudden, people are getting murdered in Whale Bay. First Rose and now …' When none of us laughed with him, he said, 'Sorry, I didn't mean to sound tasteless. While I was surprised to hear Chris Walker was arrested for that, I'm glad you got justice for Rose.'

I blinked the hot sting of tears away.

Nick frowned as Siouxsie's words must have registered. 'Who is Finn?'

'He owns Beach Brewz,' said Justin.

'He's Clem's boyfriend,' Maggie said simultaneously.

'I see. And why are you solving his ex-wife's murder?'

'Because those morons up from Brisbane think Finn is the prime suspect,' said Siouxsie.

'And … I was the one who found her body. Me and Harry — that's Harry Glover, he's doing some building work for me. Anyway, we found her … in the mangroves.' Raising my eyes, I saw compassion in his, and it was almost too much to bear.

'Oh Clem.' He moved closer and reached out, lightly touching my arm. 'I'm so sorry.'

'Yes, well.' I stepped back, absently rubbing where my skin burnt from his touch. 'I'm more concerned with getting Finn cleared.'

'You're sure he didn't do it?' Nick asked reasonably.

'Of course I'm sure!' I stalked into the kitchen and flung open the fridge door to get more drinks. How dare

Nick imply Finn was guilty of murder? He didn't know Finn, didn't know how gentle he was.

'It's a question that has to be asked.' Nick had followed me in. 'After all, isn't that the most common motive for murder? Love?'

I injected as much disdain as I could into the look I gave him. 'He didn't love her anymore. In fact, he was going to ask her for a divorce – well, he would have if she hadn't got in first – so whatever you're imagining'—I shook my head, my lips pursed—'you can stop imagining it.'

Holding his hands up in surrender, he said, 'Fair enough. I had to ask.'

'Why?'

'Why did I have to ask?' A flicker of confusion crossed Nick's face at my nod; his eyes widened slightly. 'Well, before I become involved in your investigation, I need to know he's innocent.' He shrugged as if he hadn't just announced he was going to help us, as if we hadn't seen each other for over two decades, as if my heart wasn't performing cartwheels.

'Why would you be wanting to help us?'

He leant back against the kitchen counter, his arms crossed, the movement stretching his sweatshirt across his chest. He'd definitely filled out in all the right ways. 'Because I need your help to work out what Dad, Martin and Bob are up to. I know how Rose used to stand up to them, and Mike said he reckons you're the same. Besides, I know you never had any time for Martin.'

I didn't know whether he wanted me to laugh and agree or say something like how Martin really wasn't that bad. As I was deciding on the most appropriate response, the fridge began to beep. I pulled out a couple of beers and held them up. He nodded. 'In that case,' I said, hopefully sounding calmer than I felt, 'you'd better take one of these through to Justin.'

Once he'd left the room, I crossed to the sink and gripped the edge, staring out the window into the darkness of the backyard but seeing nothing other than my reflection. Leaning forward, I peered closer. Nick Cosgrove. Here. Surely the chaos I was feeling should be reflected on my face?

Maggie's face joined mine in the window. 'How are you doing?'

When I shrugged, unable to answer, she gripped my arm. 'I'm not going to say it's all going to be okay with Finn because I have no idea if it will be.'

'Finn didn't do it,' I said feebly.

'I know he didn't, sweetie, but we need evidence to back that up.' Placing her arm around my shoulder, I rested my head against hers, our eyes meeting in the window. 'Nick's looking good though, don't you think?'

'Yeah.' I returned her smile. 'He certainly is.'

'Something must be going on if he's coming running down from Cairns.'

'He said he wants us to help him work out what they're up to.'

Maggie dropped her arm. 'Alright, grab us another bottle of wine and let's hear what he has to say.'

CHAPTER FOURTEEN

Justin and Nick were chatting by the board, stubbies of beer dangling from their fingers in that way men seem able to do. Siouxsie had sprawled on the lounge, her booted feet hanging over the arm, her face lit by her phone screen. Cosmo was curled on the other two-seater while Beans was lying on the mat near the hall. My heart clenched as I realised he was waiting for Finn to come home.

Both men paused as we stepped back into the lounge room. 'You girls right?' asked Justin.

Nodding, I filled our wineglasses and set the bottle back on the dining table, then turned to Nick. 'What have you heard that made you come running back here?'

Nick took a swig of his beer. 'Mike told me that Dad pushed an environmental study on the mangroves through the council. Mike also knows I've always been worried about preserving them. This gave me concern enough to come home.'

'Does Mike know what they have planned?' Justin took a mouthful of his pale ale. 'At the council meeting, they spoke about boardwalks and making the mangroves accessible for more people to enjoy.'

Nick shook his head. 'He hasn't been involved in the discussions, which is interesting as they usually would include him. Martin knows he speaks to me and knows I'd oppose any development in that area, so excluding Mike from their plans sent alarm bells ringing for me.' Still holding his beer, he gestured with the bottle towards Justin. 'When you told me how they delayed the vote with other issues I know they care nothing about, that's when I knew for sure something worth worrying about was going on. Regardless of what was said at that meeting, it has nothing to do with boardwalks and community use. I think Mike is right – a development opportunity is at the heart of this.'

I scoffed. 'Don't they ever get sick of trying to build resorts on every possible piece of land?'

Nick's careless shrug told me he hadn't taken offence. 'You'd think so, but if Mike is right, this is the most ambitious project they've taken on.'

'But aren't those mangroves on state land?' I directed my question to Justin, who was also on the town council and possibly privy to that information.

'I always thought so.' Justin looked to his wife for confirmation.

'Me too,' Maggie agreed. 'And if the state owns it, even your father and Bob Lindsay will have problems getting development approved. Regardless of any study, the mangroves are protected under the Fisheries Act.' She lifted a shoulder. 'I hate to say it, Nick – and you know I'd be the last person to defend anything your father or brother get up to – but maybe you and Mike are worrying about nothing. Maybe the intention truly is to get approval to build a boardwalk on it.'

'And build an access road through to it,' said Siouxsie from the lounge, phone still in front of her face.

'What?' Maggie asked. She pulled a chair out from the dining table and sank into it.

'Think about it, Mags.' Siouxsie swung her feet off the lounge and, after ruffling Cosmo's head, stood and joined us by the board. 'The only way to get in there is by boat or via the fire trail off the main road into Dolphin Point. It's four-wheel-drive only, so your average UFC—'

I choked on my wine. 'UF what?'

'UFC – up from the city,' she said calmly with a don't-you-know-anything lift of her hand. 'As I was saying, they won't want to take their new Merc or Beemer in there. The track is poorly maintained and quite tight in places.'

'How do you know that?' Maggie tilted her head to the side and observed her daughter through narrowed eyes.

'Keep your hair on, Mags,' she said good-naturedly. 'We've been out there a couple of times …'

'Who's "we" and what would you want to be doing …' Her voice trailed off when Justin shook his head. 'I don't want to know, do I?'

'Some details are best not known.' Siouxsie's grin of remembered mischief reminded me too much of the same grin I'd seen on her mother's face when we were teenagers.

What had Siouxsie just said? About access? I reached for a Post-it note, scribbled the word "access" on it and stuck it on the board.

'The only thing I can think of is that they've found some sort of loophole in the land's title,' mused Nick. 'Or the legislation, which is what I'm most worried about. The mangroves are a unique ecosystem and are culturally important to the Traditional Owners. Anything built or developed on that land must be done with full consultation.'

'Even if they can get a new study to prove that the mangroves no longer take up all of the land or …' I shrugged, unsure of the direction my thoughts were heading.

'This is great,' said Siouxsie, her impatience clear in her tone. 'We can speculate about what dodgy deal your relos are up to now, but none of that helps us get Finn off the hook.'

'You're right,' said Justin, giving her a warm fatherly smile.

'Besides,' continued Siouxsie. 'Even if he hasn't lived here for God knows how long, he'—she waggled her finger towards Nick—'is still a Cosgrove. Plus, he's getting his information from Michael Lindsay, who might as well be a Cosgrove. How do we know we can trust him?'

'Mike is one of the good guys,' I said weakly, mentally crossing my fingers and toes that he is indeed one.

'And Nick has always been different from Martin and has never been in his father's pocket. Just the opposite, in fact.' Justin glanced sideways at me. 'We can trust him.'

'I understand your concern, Siouxsie,' said Nick. 'But your father's right. I've never been in Dad's pocket; after all'—he chuckled—'Martin's never left any room in there for me. Besides, I'm a marine biologist, and my remit is to ensure environmental sustainability. I'm not about to look for ways to exploit it.'

Siouxsie scrutinised his face before nodding slowly. 'Alright. I suppose I can give you the benefit of the doubt.'

'Hold on,' I said. 'If you need a four-wheel drive to access the mangroves, Finn couldn't possibly have taken Tamzin in. His car is way too low.'

'What does he drive?' asked Nick, considering the sole Post-it note on the board.

'A small hybrid,' I said. 'For environmental reasons.'

'I don't know,' Nick said slowly. 'My first car was a Corolla, and I recall taking that off-road.'

My cheeks flamed at the look he gave me, memories of a summer long ago pushing to the front of my brain.

'So do I,' laughed Maggie. 'The five of us would pile into that car.'

'The five of you?' asked Siouxsie.

Maggie nodded, a faraway look in her eyes. 'Your dad and me, Nick and Clem and Mike Lindsay.'

'I don't want to know, do I?' Siouxsie asked with a

cheeky grin, echoing the words her mother had said only minutes before.

'Best you don't,' agreed Maggie with a playful smirk tugging at the corners of her mouth.

Justin pinched his chin. 'We might have got away with it with your old car, but these new models?' He shook his head. 'Not a chance. Not with their low clearance and open differential front wheel drive. If one wheel slips, the system sends all the power to the wheel with the least traction, which rarely ends well.'

While Nick nodded his agreement, Maggie and I looked at each other and shrugged, having no idea what any of that meant.

'I don't know about you, Clem,' said Maggie. 'But my eyes just glazed over.'

Nick chuckled. 'You two haven't changed, have you? What he's saying is that most small cars have been built as commuter vehicles. The engine, suspension, steering, wheels and tyres aren't tuned for off-roading.' He took a mouthful of beer. 'In other words, if Finn had been on that road in that car, they'd find plenty of evidence of damage to the undercarriage.'

'Do we know what Tamzin was driving?' asked Justin. 'They'll say he took her out there in that vehicle.'

'I don't know, but the police are resting their evidence on picking up Finn's car on the Bruce before the Dolphin Point turn-off.' Feeling suddenly hopeful, I added, 'They can't have it both ways. They can't say he drove her out there in her car if they've clocked his car on the highway at the same time, and if his car shows no evidence of being there, it stands to reason that he wasn't there.'

'Whatever he wore would also be covered in mud,' Nick pointed out. 'Especially if she was dumped at low tide. No way could you do that and not get dirty.'

'Which we think she must've been.' I tapped my finger on my lips. 'While we can probably prove Finn's car wasn't out at the mangroves yesterday, it would be great if we could prove he was hiking like he said he was.'

'That could be easier said than done.' Justin sighed before emptying his beer. 'Anyone for a top-up?' Nick and Siouxsie nodded, but Maggie and I shook our heads.

While Justin was in the kitchen, Siouxsie, Nick and I stood where we were, the three of us staring at the single Post-it sticker as if it held all the answers until Siouxsie's phone beeped with a message and she transferred her attention to that, a small, secretive smile on her lips.

'Is there any reason Finn's wife—'

'Tamzin,' I interrupted Nick.

'Is there any reason Tamzin would be at the mangroves?' Nick asked. 'After all, if Finn didn't take her out there, it seems quite a random spot for her to be.'

'Well, yes,' I said. 'She was the one who was going to complete the environmental study in there.'

Nick's eyes widened, Siouxsie looked up from her

phone and Maggie's mouth dropped open. Justin, who had rejoined us, tapped his forehead. 'How did we miss that?'

Then Nick said what we were all thinking. 'This can't be a coincidence.'

'No, it can't be.' I picked up the pad of Post-it notes on the dining table and tossed it to Siouxsie. 'That means whatever happened to Tamzin is tied in with plans for the mangroves.' Casting my eyes around the group, I added, 'And that means we need to get to the bottom of what's going on in the mangroves to clear Finn's name.'

After that announcement, we all fell silent; the only sounds were the dogs shuffling at the back door. I quickly let them out, leaving the door open so they could come back in when they'd finished. Nick was the first to break it. 'We need to find out who owns that land.'

'And the adjoining land.' I threw a pen to Siouxsie, and she wrote that on a note.

'Why the adjoining land?' Justin asked.

'It's as Siouxsie said – regardless of what they have planned, they'll need access to the site. Aside from that, even though the mangroves are protected, what if the adjoining land isn't? Think about it. It's worth nothing now if you can't build on it – or access it – but find a tame environmental scientist to sign off that the mangroves have reduced in size or no longer qualify to be protected, and suddenly, you're sitting on a gold mine.'

'By tame scientist, you mean Tamzin?' Maggie latched

onto my train of thought, and a silent understanding passed between us as we exchanged glances.

'Yeah. That's exactly what I'm thinking. I'm not suggesting Tamzin is involved, but …'

'You can't help but wonder,' finished Justin as he took a square note from Siouxsie and stuck it on the board.

'No. And that's made me consider what would happen if it turned out she wasn't so tame after all.'

Nick shook his head, the gesture sharp and decisive. 'No. My father might be dodgy, but he's not a murderer,' he said vehemently.

Unconsciously, I laid a hand on his arm, removing it when his eyes went from my hand to my face. 'I'm not suggesting he is, but if this does involve that land, this is big and much bigger than what Ray and Bob could manage on their own.'

He stared at me, his eyes unwavering, for a few long seconds before nodding slowly. 'You're right. There has to be someone else involved in this, backing them.'

'Okay.' Maggie stepped forward. 'It's getting late, so plan of attack.' As we'd been talking, Siouxsie had been scribbling theories onto yellow stickers, Justin placing them randomly on the board. 'Nick, are you staying with your parents?'

He nodded. 'Yes. Can you imagine Mum if I didn't?'

We all grinned as we imagined Paula Cosgrove on the rampage.

'Right,' said Maggie. 'See what you can find out. Get

Mike to do the same.'

'I have enough supplies here for the dogs so will head to the station first thing in the morning to see what's happening with Finn. Hopefully, without any firm evidence, they'll have no option but to release him. Maggie, I know we don't have the reference numbers we need, but can you do a title search on the mangrove land using the address?'

She grimaced. 'Possibly, but we have nothing we can search against; there's no address as such out there. There are certainly no street numbers or, indeed, streets.'

Justin nodded. 'She's right. We'll need to access the survey maps at the council. I think Len Hartog, the town surveyor, would hold them.'

'Surely someone is paying rates on it,' added Nick with a note of certainty in his voice.

'Not necessarily,' said Justin, stepping forward to place another sticky note on the board. 'If the state owns the land, rates won't be payable.'

Holding my hand up, I said, 'My head is hurting. We have enough to be going on with, so let's see what tomorrow brings.'

'Agreed.' Maggie collected the wineglasses and took them into the kitchen. Siouxsie and Justin followed with the empty bottles, leaving Nick and me behind.

'So the dogs are Finn's?' Nick asked after a brief silence.

'Yeah. Poor Beans is waiting for Finn to come home.' I clapped my hand over my mouth as something occurred to me.

'What's wrong?' Nick asked.

'I can't believe I only just remembered this. When I was talking to Tamzin on the beach—'

'You spoke to her?' Siouxsie asked, her face avid.

'Your mother didn't say? It was just briefly and, at the time, I didn't know it was her,' I explained. 'It wasn't until the detectives questioned me that—'

'They questioned you?' Nick folded his arms and frowned. 'Why?'

'They found my fingerprints on her sunscreen tube. She'd asked me to rub some on her back.' I shrugged it off. 'Anyhoo, as I was saying, she said she'd tried Bron's coffee last week.'

'And?' Nick frowned his confusion.

Maggie ducked back in from the kitchen. 'She told Finn she was arriving on Saturday, so how could she have tried Bron's coffee last week?'

With the beginning of a smile twitching on my lips, I nodded. 'She lied to him. She was already here in Whale Bay, and I'd like to bet she'd already begun that survey.' Turning to Nick, I added, 'We need to find where she was staying—'

'And who she spoke to when she was here,' added Siouxsie.

'She'd spoken to enough people to have heard rumours about Ray.' I turned to Nick. 'Sorry, but that's what she said.'

He lifted a shoulder to show he'd taken no offence. 'What else did she say?'

Squinting, for the second time that day, I recalled our conversation. 'She said it was a pity the mangroves were protected and that it would make a lovely marina and luxury resort. I said something about how if our mayor and his cronies had their way'—I couldn't look at Nick—'that's what would happen to it. And when I said that would be a pity, she asked whether I thought it should be available for everyone to enjoy.'

Nick frowned in thought. 'It sounds more as though she wanted to know what you, as a local, thought about it rather than it being what she believed.'

'That's the impression I got. It felt as though she wanted to know if the rumours she'd heard were true so was trying to get a rise of some sort out of me. By then, though, I was regretting saying anything, so I left her to it. So I was probably the last person to see her alive.'

'Other than the murderer.' Siouxsie pointed out the obvious.

'Yes,' I murmured.

CHAPTER FIFTEEN

The detectives released Finn without charge the following morning.

When I arrived to collect him, he was chatting with Tyson King. Although his face was drawn and his clothes crumpled, he didn't appear any the worse for wear after his night in the cells. When he saw me, his face lit up, and his arms opened for me to run into. 'Are you okay?'

'I'm fine,' he said, his hand warm across the back of my neck.

Stepping out of his embrace, I cast my eyes around the station.

'They're in with Ted,' Tyson said, correctly guessing the direction of my thoughts.

'What did they say?'

Finn's smile was strained. 'I'm not off the hook. They just don't have enough to charge me.' He rubbed his hands over his face. 'They seem to think they'll find evidence in my car.'

Tyson nodded sombrely. 'I tried telling them there was

no way Finn's car would make it along that track without leaving parts of the undercarriage behind, and while DC Hall was prepared to listen, DS Osborne had it in his head to pin this on Finn.' When Finn paled, Tyson grimaced. 'Sorry, mate.'

'Did they search Finn's house?' I asked.

Tyson looked nervously at the closed office door. 'Yes, but I don't think they found anything. Although the DS said they found Tamzin's fingerprints everywhere.'

Finn scoffed. 'Of course they did! She stayed there on Saturday night.' He shook his head. 'It didn't matter how often I explained that, they weren't listening.'

'Finn,' I began. 'Did she—' Before I could ask if Tamzin had mentioned where she was last week, the office door opened.

'Aaaah, Ms Carter.' DS Osborne attempted a smile that didn't quite work.. While today's white shirt appeared to be clean, it hadn't been bothered by an iron. 'Have you remembered anything else?'

Standing straighter, I lifted my chin. 'I've told you everything I know. I'm just here to collect my client.'

'I have no doubt that when we get the results back from your client's car, we'll talk to him again.' DS Osborne was nothing if not persistent.

'Tell me,' I said, the sweetness in my tone laced with a hint of something else. 'Were you able to access the track in your vehicle, Sergeant?'

'We didn't even try,' said DC Hall. 'Senior Sergeant took us out there.'

The crinkles around Ted's eyes told me he knew what I was getting at. 'I told DS Osborne we'd save his vehicle,' he said with barely a twitch of his lips. 'It was best not to risk his – not when I've got a four-wheel drive. I had a quick look at that car of Finn's, and it doesn't look to me as though it's been off-road recently, but'—a conciliatory nod in the detective's direction—'it's best to follow procedure.'

'Has anyone told Tamzin's father yet?' Finn asked, rubbing his face.

'I understand the communication has been made,' said DS Osborne gruffly.

'I'd like to go to Brisbane to be with him,' said Finn. 'Am I allowed to do that?'

DS Osborne folded his arms. 'You'll stay in town until we have the evidence to charge you.'

'Surely you meant to say you need him to stay put until you have the evidence to clear him?' I said through gritted teeth. 'Or have you decided Finn is guilty and you'll find the evidence to fit that theory? Because that sounds awfully like you intend to fit Finn up for this.'

The sergeant dropped his eyes from my defiant stare. 'That's what I meant.'

'So if Finn's car is found to be clear …'

'He may have taken her in her vehicle. I understand her car was a four-wheel drive,' said DS Osborne.

'You can't have it both ways, Sergeant.' I squared my shoulders, ready to fight. 'You have Finn in his vehicle on the highway in what you've led us to believe is the critical window, and now you're saying he might have been taking her out there in another vehicle at the same time? I take it you have found her car on the same cameras?'

DC Hall answered for his sergeant. 'Yes, we have, although we've been unable to locate the vehicle.'

'What time did she drive past that point?' I asked.

DC Hall consulted his notebook. 'She drove through just before midday.'

'And Finn was captured coming through at what time?'

'Around ten minutes later.' The constable seemed oblivious to his superior's glare.

'Right,' I drawled as if struggling to understand. 'In other words, you've assumed that Finn followed her out there in his car, killed her and dumped her body, somehow managed to hide her car where no one has yet been able to find it, came back – presumably on foot—'

'Mr Marella said he'd been hiking.'

Ignoring the sergeant's interruption, I continued. 'He came back on foot to retrieve his car, which he drove back to town with no damage and, I think you'll find, no physical evidence to support either it or Finn being anywhere on that track.'

'He might have killed her elsewhere and taken her body out there.' DS Osborne's tone was a mix of desperation and frustration.

'Absolutely, that could've happened, but if it did, who drove her vehicle out there? At a similar time to when Finn was driving his?' I shook my head. 'You have the wrong man, Sergeant, and I think you know it. And while you've been messing about with Finn – and me – the real murderer has probably left town.'

Ted exhaled and rubbed his eyes. 'Sergeant, I suggest you hurry your forensics up, and if there's nothing to link Finn's car with that access road, allow him to go to Brisbane to be of some comfort to his father-in-law.' He turned to Finn. 'Finn, DS Osborne will be in touch regarding clearance to travel. I'm sorry, but your vehicle has been taken to Brisbane, so you'll need to borrow another car in the meantime.'

'That's okay.' I took Finn's arm when he seemed unable to speak. 'He can use mine.'

As we made to leave, Ted said, 'I hear young Cosgrove is back in town – Nick, that is.'

Finn's eyes flicked to mine but dropped away before I could read their expression.

'Yes, he is.' I shoved my hands into the pockets of my patchwork maxi skirt.

'Have you seen him?' Ted asked.

'Yes, he dropped by last night,' I muttered, my eyes on my boots.

'I don't suppose you know why he's come home now?'

Shrugging, I hoped my short laugh sounded casual. 'Does he need a reason to visit his family?' I risked a glance at Ted; his narrowed eyes and the tilt of his half smile revealed my forced nonchalance hadn't fooled him. 'If that's all, we'll be on our way.'

Once outside the station, we started down the footpath. 'I thought you might like the walk. We'll go via your place, though; after being in that cell, you'd be wanting a shower and a decent coffee, and—'

'Clem!' He stopped walking. 'You're rambling.'

'Sorry, it's just that—'

'I was inside for a night. It was hardly a life sentence. What's this about Nick Cosgrove being back?'

Shrugging like I had when Ted had asked me, I said, 'He's back. No big deal.'

'Except it has to be … a big deal. And he dropped by to see you?' Even though we'd started walking again, I felt his eyes boring into the side of my head. 'Why was that?' When I hesitated, Finn said, 'What's going on, Clem?'

'I don't want to bother you, not with—'

'Clem …' he warned.

'Okay, okay. Nick's back because he heard about what's happening in the mangroves … with the environmental study. He's worried his father is up to something and has returned to help defend the mangroves if needed.' Finn frowned sceptically. 'He knows what his family is like.'

'He didn't come back when they were trying to turn

the wharf into a high-rise resort, and he didn't come back when they wanted to buy Rose's cottage and the others at that end of Beach Road to build Finz. I don't understand what's different this time.'

'Rose isn't here,' I said simply. 'Apparently, Michael Lindsay has been keeping Nick updated over the years and knew Rose was involved in organising the protest efforts, but now Rose is gone …' I turned my palms up. 'Also, this one is important to him.'

'And that's the only reason he's high-tailed it down from Far North Queensland? It wasn't anything to do with you being here?'

Anger bubbled in my stomach. 'Really, Finn? What's with the jealousy? That's not like you! He probably has come back also to see me, but so what? It's been twenty-five years! I'm hardly likely to run into his arms, am I?'

'I don't know, are you?'

His jaw was firm and … Oh my God! He was pouting! Actually pouting. While I was tempted to walk away from him without another word, I reminded myself his wife had just been murdered, and he'd spent the night in jail suspected of that crime. He was, perhaps, bound to be more sensitive than usual. 'Finn,' I said, grabbing his hand. 'Nick and I are ancient history.'

'Are you sure about that?'

Again, I counted under my breath at his snippy tone. 'Absolutely. And the others – Mags, Justin and Siouxsie –

were at the house, so we weren't alone.'

'Will you be seeing any more of him?'

Sighing, I said firmly, 'Yes, I will be. He's going to help us get to the bottom of whatever Ray and Bob have planned for the mangroves.' As Finn would've pouted some more, I added, 'This is too big for them to be acting alone.'

'I thought you weren't going to involve yourself in it.' There was a challenge in his voice, a hint of defiance, which was better than his pouting. 'He comes home, though, and you're ready to get the murder board out.'

We paused in his driveway. 'For your information, we already had the murder board out … for you.' I turned and gave him my full attention. 'Hasn't it occurred to you that Tamzin being murdered in the place where she was supposed to be conducting an environmental study can't possibly be a coincidence?' When he looked blankly at me, I shook my head. 'Finn, her murder and whatever's planned for the mangroves are connected. And I don't trust DS Osborne and his sidekick to get to the bottom of that. So, I'm sorry, but I don't have the time or the inclination to deal with your jealousy.' Finn didn't answer, his eyes focused over my shoulder. 'Finn? Are you listening to me?'

'Clem.' His voice cracked with urgency before turning and hurrying up the driveway. 'My front door is open.'

'What?' I followed him up to the ajar door. 'Wait, Finn!' He paused, hand hovering by the door handle. 'Be careful. What if someone's inside?'

He gave a brief nod and a quick, almost imperceptible flick of his wrist, indicating for me to drop in behind him.

I held my breath as we edged around the open door into the hall and entered his sitting room. Clapping my hand over my mouth, I wasn't quick enough to stifle the gasp that escaped me.

The lounge had been upended, the cushion covers unzipped, and the plush inserts flung around the room. The books, once neatly stacked, had been emptied from their bookcases and strewn about. Finn's precious vinyl records lay scattered, their covers discarded, a chaotic mess of scratched plastic and torn sleeves.

Still silent, we picked our way through the kitchen – where a similar scene of devastation greeted us – and into the hall.

Finn held a finger to his lips, although I couldn't have spoken even if I'd wanted to. With my heart hammering against my ribs, we inched our way along the wall, following the bangs and rustles coming from the second bedroom.

Carefully pulling my phone from my pocket, I silently cursed that I didn't have the number for either DS Osborne or the police station stored, so I texted Maggie:

Call the police – Finn's house has been ransacked & they're still here

A thumbs up came through in response, followed by:

Be careful – wait for backup

Finn raised his eyebrows at me in a "are you alright?"

gesture. Nodding my assent, I inhaled deeply and crossed to the other side of the door.

Inside the bedroom, two black-clad figures had pulled the mattress from the bed. One cursed and said, 'There's nothing here,' while the second said, 'It has to be here somewhere. We can't go back empty-handed.' The first pulled the drawers from the bedside table and said, 'The little bitch had to put it somewhere.'

Another quick nod from Finn and we burst through the door. 'What do you think you're doing?' demanded Finn.

'The police are on their way!' I yelled, standing in the doorway to block their escape.

One flew at me, pushing me hard against the wall, my head banging into the doorframe. The second raised his arm and hit Finn with something. There was a thud and Finn crumpled to the floor. The two men dashed out of the open doorway, their footsteps hard on the wood floor, just as the high-pitched wail of sirens pierced the air. The screen front door crashed against the side of the house.

'Finn!' Scrambling onto my knees, I crawled across to where he lay motionless, blood pouring from a wound on the back of his head. I rolled him onto his side and pressed my hands against the gash, the sticky warmth of blood coating my palm as my eyes darted around the room, desperately searching for something to stem the bleeding.

CHAPTER SIXTEEN

Constable Selina Gupta appeared in the doorway, took in Finn's situation and radioed for an ambulance.

'Are you okay?' Selina crouched beside me, her face etched with worry, her brow furrowed. 'You're bleeding too.'

'I'm fine,' I said, suddenly aware of the trickle of warmth on my cheek. When I touched it, my hand came away red, almost sobbing when I couldn't tell if it was my blood or Finn's. 'The men … Finn …'

'Tyson's gone after them.' She stood and disappeared into the kitchen, reappearing with a clean, folded tea towel. 'Here, press this onto the wound.' I did as she said. 'You stay with him, and I'll see where Tyson is.'

Tyson burst into the room, his hands on his hips, panting. 'I lost them.' Inclining his head back towards the sitting room, he asked, 'Were they responsible for that?'

'If they weren't, DS Osborne's team has some explaining to do,' I said wryly. Finn stirred, letting out a groan of discomfort. 'Shhh,' I soothed, holding him down, my other hand on his shoulder. 'Stay still.'

Another siren grew closer, the door swinging open again and more booted feet pounding along the hall.

Tyson went out to meet them. 'In here, one head injury – looks like blunt force trauma,' I heard him say.

Three figures appeared in the doorway. 'Clem,' said Tyson, 'the paramedics are here. Aaron and Chelsea will take it from here.' He held a hand out to help me up. I staggered, a wave of dizziness washing over me. 'We'll get you looked over, too.'

'I'm fine. Will Finn be alright?' I held my blood-covered hands out, staring at them in disbelief. Was that blood on the floor too? Absently I wiped them on my skirt.

Tyson looked across at Aaron. 'Head wounds bleed a lot,' he said, avoiding a direct answer. 'We'll get him to hospital and checked over.' The paramedics had Finn on a trolley and were preparing to take him out. 'Maybe you should go in too.'

I shook my head emphatically and held Finn's hand. 'No. Finn's dogs are at my place.'

With that, Chelsea approached, resting her hand on my shoulder. 'Is it okay if I check you over?'

When I nodded and reluctantly let go of Finn's hand, she ran her fingers over the cut on my cheek and shone a torch into my eyes. 'Were you knocked out?'

'No. He pushed me into the wall.' I pointed out where I'd fallen.

'Hmmm,' she said. 'You'll be fine and shouldn't need

stitches, but come with me, and I'll clean it and dress it before we leave.'

Obediently, I followed her out of the house and waited while they got Finn settled into the ambulance. It only took a couple of minutes for my cheek to be cleaned and a plaster put over the cut. 'Can I come to the hospital with Finn?'

Selina pulled me away gently and led me back into the house. 'He'll be fine, but we need you here to give a statement.'

Maggie pulled up as the ambulance left, DS Osborne and DC Hall pulling in behind her.

'Oh my God, Clem! What happened to you?' Maggie rushed into the hall and reached for my hands.

Shaking my head, I said, 'No, they're covered in blood – not mine … it's Finn's.' Then I promptly burst into tears.

Avoiding my hands, she pulled me into a hug. 'Finn will be okay, I'm sure of it. But let's get you cleaned up before you answer any questions.' She turned to Tyson. 'Is it okay if we wash her hands?'

'That'll be fine, Mum,' said Tyson, cheeks colouring when DS Osborne, who had just walked in, smirked.

'Mum? She's your mother?' He turned to DC Hall. 'This really is a small town.'

Maggie glared at him. 'Did you lot cause this mess?' She swept her hand around the sitting room.

DC Hall raised his eyebrows. 'We didn't leave it like this.'

'We surprised them in the bedroom,' I said.

'They must have been looking for something,' observed the sergeant.

'No shit, Sherlock,' Maggie said sardonically. 'Come on, Clem, let's get your hands washed.'

When we rejoined them, Tyson was dusting the front door for prints while Selina was doing the same with the guest bedroom door.

DS Osborne was waiting for us in the kitchen. Pulling out a stool from the counter, he motioned me to sit. 'Ms Carter, I think we might have got off to a bad start—'

'You think?' cut in Maggie, who pulled up a stool opposite me.

Ignoring her, he said, 'Can you tell me what happened? Please?' He added the last after another glare from Maggie.

Nodding, I tilted my head back as I recalled our steps through the house. 'We came here directly from the station.'

'Where did you park?'

'We didn't. I thought Finn might need to stretch his legs so didn't bring my car this morning. Anyway, as we got close, Finn noticed the front door was open – we could see it through the screen. I wondered whether you might have forgotten to lock up properly, but when we walked in, we found the … well, we found that.' Grimacing, I turned away from the upturned canister of flour. 'We heard some noises coming from the second bedroom, so that's when I called Maggie.'

'Why didn't you phone us?' asked the sergeant.

I scoffed. 'Even if I'd had your name stored, we haven't exactly got off to a great start, and I knew Maggie would read a text and jump into action. If I called you, I would've had to explain myself and then they might have overheard us.'

DS Osborne nodded, expression unreadable. 'Fair call. What were they doing in there?' He pointed over his shoulder to the bedroom.

'Much the same as what they did out here. They'd taken the pillows from the bed, had tipped the mattress up'—I screwed my nose up as I tried to remember what I'd overheard—'then the one who was closest to the wardrobe – he was the one who hit Finn – said to the other one something like "we can't go back empty-handed", and the other one said something like "the little bitch had to have put it somewhere." Then they saw us, and the one closest to us charged at me.'

'And the other one hit Mr Marella?' DC Hall looked up from his notebook.

'That's right.' I stood and returned to the bedroom. 'With this.' I toed at a wooden lamp. 'He pulled it off the bedside table and held it just there'—I pointed out where I'd seen the attacker's hands—'and swung it at Finn like a baseball bat.' Suddenly feeling ill, I covered my mouth with my hand. 'I'm sorry,' I said, rushing to the bathroom.

When I returned, Tyson was dusting the lamp before

placing it in a large plastic bag.

'Do you know what they were looking for?' DS Osborne asked, pushing a drawer shut.

I shook my head. 'Not a clue, but whatever it was, it must have belonged to Tamzin. Have you found her car yet?'

The detectives exchanged glances, and DS Osborne sighed. 'You'll probably hear some other way anyway'—he looked hard at Tyson whose ears had tinged pink—'but yes. A local found it near the boat ramp. The keys were in the ignition, and the doors were open. Her suitcase was inside, but we didn't find her phone.'

'What about her laptop?' I asked.

'Did she have one?' asked the constable.

'I'd say so. There was a charger on the kitchen counter.'

'Could it have been Mr Marella's?' DC Hall asked.

I shook my head. 'No, Finn's strictly an Apple man - iPhone, MacBook Air. That charger is for a Windows laptop.'

DS Osborne nodded at Selina to dust the charger and place it in a plastic bag. He flipped another page over in his notebook. 'Would you be able to describe them – the perpetrators?'

I closed my eyes, gasping when I saw again the raised arm and lamp coming down on Finn's head. 'They both wore black hoodies, but yes, I think so.' My face fell as I saw the look on DS Osborne's face. 'You need me to come back to the station, don't you?'

'I'm sorry, Ms Carter, but yes.'

'You know what, DS Osborne? If we're going to be spending so much time together, you'd better call me Clem.'

For the first time, he offered a halfway pleasant smile. 'And you can call me DS Osborne.'

Perhaps it was a reaction to all that had occurred that morning, but I tipped my head back and laughed.

CHAPTER SEVENTEEN

While I gave another statement at the police station, Maggie and Siouxsie closed the office (Justin felt the wisest move was for him to do the same), corralled Harry and Nick into helping and together, they all set about putting Finn's house to rights.

The news travelled quickly, and my interview was interrupted when a coffee from Beach Brewz and a salad roll from Bron were delivered to the station for me. The detectives from Brisbane were beginning to understand how Whale Bay operated and barely raised eyebrows in surprise.

I went straight from the station to the hospital. When I arrived, Finn was sitting up in bed, his eyes closed, and the covers pulled up to his chest. Upon feeling my hand on his, though, his eyes snapped open, his smile faint.

'How are you feeling?' I rested my hands on the bed to balance as I leant over to kiss his lips.

'I have one hell of a headache,' he said ruefully. 'They tell me it could've been a lot worse, so I suppose I should feel lucky.'

'I suppose,' I agreed. 'Sorry it's taken me so long to get here. I had to give another statement.'

'I figured as much,' he said with another faint smile. 'I wouldn't have been much help. My memory is blank after seeing the mess in the lounge. Were you able to give them a description?'

Closing my eyes, I saw again the man's arm raised to strike Finn. Just as his arm came down, his hoodie slipped, and for a split second, I saw his face. 'The one that struck you, yes. I won't forget the colour of his eyes – almost amber – and he had a scar just here.' I ran my finger in a line from my dimple down to the side of my mouth. 'It was his hair that was the giveaway, though – it was orange. I'd recognise him again in a heartbeat.'

'Is that how you got that cut on your cheek?' I nodded. 'What about the one who pushed you?'

I shook my head. 'He was a blur. He had his back to us until he pushed me. I had a flash of his face, but it was fleeting. All I recall seeing was the tattoo on his hand.' I wrinkled my nose as I pictured it. 'It was ivy or a vine of some sort.' I shrugged. 'That was all I had.' I shook my head at my failure to identify the pattern. 'Anyway, you're more important. When can you come home?'

'They want me to spend the night here – just to be on the safe side. But even when they clear me as a suspect, I can't drive until Thursday, so I will need to wait until then to go to Brisbane.' His face fell. 'The sooner I can see Tam's father, the better. He won't have understood anything they told him.' He winced and pressed his forehead.

'Your head hurts?' Even though the wound was to the back of his head, I figured he'd still have one hell of a headache.

'Yeah,' he shrugged.

'Any idea when they're releasing her body?'

He shrugged, then winced and pressed his forehead. 'Not yet. They still haven't told me how she died.'

As he said it, the two detectives sauntered into the hospital room. 'Good, you're both here.' DS Osborne cast his eyes around the ward and pulled over a chair from beside another bed. 'How are you feeling, Mr Marella?'

'Like I've gone ten rounds with a front-row forward,' Finn said with a weak smile.

'The doctor said you're very lucky. A couple of inches in the other direction and we'd be investigating two murders,' DS Osborne said solemnly. 'We do have some news for you, though. The forensic team have completed their investigation of your vehicle, and there's no evidence it's been in the vicinity of where your wife's body was found. Your alibi has also confirmed you were where you said you were.' He gave me a quick sideways glance. 'There was a delay as we had to wait for them to phone us back, so we drove out there ourselves.'

Colour rose to Finn's cheeks, and he also shot me a quick look, his eyes sliding past mine. 'So I'm in the clear.'

DS Osborne nodded. 'Yes. I'm sorry you spent last night in a cell, but'—he cleared his throat—'I hope you understand we had to examine all possibilities.'

Still confused about the existence of an alibi for Finn, I snapped, 'Yes, although it seemed that the only possibility you were considering was that Finn did it or, failing him, me.' DC Hall pretended to read from his notebook, and DS Osborne crossed his legs. 'Do you know yet how she died?'

'Yes, she drowned.' The sergeant said bluntly, watching Finn closely for a reaction.

'So it was an accident, after all?' Finn asked hopefully, wriggling to sit straighter against the pillows.

'I'm afraid not. As I said yesterday, she wasn't alone. It appears as though she suffered blunt trauma to the head and'—he swallowed hard and scratched the bridge of his nose—'there's evidence she was held under the water.'

My fingers involuntarily went to the back of my neck. An image of Tamzin came into view. Tamzin, as I saw her on Sunday morning with her runner's ponytail, tanned and healthy, was in the prime of her life. The picture was replaced by the memory of the body floating in the mangroves on Sunday afternoon, the blonde hair muddied, the white dress billowing around her. Hands splayed out on the back of her neck, forcing her head down, hands with a vine winding around his hand and tangling around Tamzin's neck. I shivered and shook my head to dislodge the image.

The others must have also been imagining something

similar as we were all silent for a few seconds. Finn broke the silence. 'When can I get my car back?'

'We'll need to get it transported back here,' said the sergeant. 'So at least another few days to a week.'

'What if I caught the train to Brisbane? Would I be able to collect it then?' Finn said, urgency in his voice.

'I don't see why not, but will you be fit enough?'

'The doctor said I can't drive for twenty-four to forty-eight hours; he didn't say anything about catching a train down.' With a resolute set jaw, Finn lifted his chin.

'But—' I began.

'Clem, I need to see Tam's father and her siblings.' His voice caught, and he swallowed hard before continuing. 'I also need to sort out the funeral arrangements for when the body is released.'

His eyes held mine, willing me to understand that he needed to do these last things for the woman he once loved – and probably still did. I nodded.

The detectives left soon after, so I asked him the question I'd wanted to ask him since last night. 'Finn …'

'What?' He asked wearily.

'When I was talking to Tamzin the other day – on the beach – she mentioned she'd tried Bron's coffee …'

'So what? Most people make that mistake at least once.'

'I know, but she said she'd tried it *last* week.' When he still looked confused, I added, 'She was only supposed to have arrived in town on Saturday.'

'She did,' he said. 'She rang me from Brisbane and drove up here on Saturday. She would have come to see me if she'd been here last week.'

'Would she?' I asked quietly. 'What if she was here starting on the study and needed to keep quiet about it until the approval came through from the council?'

'No,' he snapped. 'You're looking for something that isn't there. Whatever she said or didn't say on Sunday, you've misheard her.'

'I don't think I did—'

'Enough, Clem!' He closed his eyes briefly, his hand going to his bandaged head.

'The detectives told me they'd found her vehicle but not her phone or laptop.' When he lifted a shoulder, I added, 'She'd left a charger plugged in at your place.' I let out a short chuckle. 'I told them it had to have been hers because you were a Mac user.' Another half shrug. 'Do you know what those men were searching for?'

Frowning, he shook his head. 'Of course I don't.'

'Tamzin didn't give you anything to hold for her?'

'No, she didn't. Is that all?' His voice was clipped as if he were trying not to show anger, but what did he have to be angry with me about?

'There's just one more thing … The alibi.' I watched him closely for a reaction but saw none. 'You said you were hiking on Sunday and didn't have anyone to corroborate that.'

He sniffed and turned away. 'Yes, well, I remembered someone who might have seen me.'

Hadn't DS Osborne said they confirmed he was where he'd said he was … 'Why didn't you tell me? If I'd known, I would've been able to push for your release last night.'

'I only remembered after you left last night,' he said. 'I'm feeling quite tired, Clem. Do you mind if I get some sleep?'

He wanted me to leave? 'Sure. I'll come back later tonight.'

'No,' he barked, and then more gently, 'no need to come back. I'll see you in the morning. Do you mind having the dogs for a few more days until I come home?'

'You're really going to Brisbane tomorrow?'

'Yes. I need to get this done, and there's no point in delaying. Can you pass me my phone, please? I'll call Lainey and check she's okay to open without me.'

'Sure.' I passed him the phone and waited for him to make the call, but he didn't. 'I'll see you tomorrow.'

My dismissal felt like a cold wave washing over me, leaving me numb.

I kissed his cheek and left the room, pausing at the door, waiting for him to call me back or say something else – perhaps tell me he loved me – but he smiled tightly and remained silent.

I turned and left, my mind whirling. Why had he got so defensive? Had Tamzin confided in him and sworn him to secrecy? If that was the case, surely he knew he could trust me. Plus, he'd lied to me. He'd had someone who could corroborate where he was, so why hadn't he divulged it? Why wait until I wasn't around to tell the detectives? Why spend a night in the cells when he didn't have to? If he'd lied about that, what else had he lied to me about?

CHAPTER EIGHTEEN

I said as much to Maggie later that afternoon. 'The way that sergeant looked at me when he mentioned it made me think his alibi was someone Finn didn't want me to know about.' I slumped in a chair in her office. 'I know he had nothing to do with Tamzin's death, but it's made me wonder whether he's involved in something else. And you should've seen his expression when Ted mentioned Nick's name. It was so unlike Finn, Mags.' I shook my head at the memory. 'And then, when I mentioned how I thought Tamzin had been here last week, he almost snapped my head off. I thought I knew him, but maybe I don't.'

Maggie rested her elbows on the desk, cradling her cheeks between the back of her hands. 'He's been through a lot in the last few days, Clem. Maybe you should give him some slack.'

'I get that, but I don't do jealousy, and when he started on about Nick, I felt like handcuffs were being clapped on me.' Sighing dramatically, I lowered my head to the desk. When I raised it again, Maggie was grinning.

'Is this because Finn was questioning you about Nick and that makes you feel trapped, or because Nick is back and looking at you the way he used to look at you and a teensy part of you – the part that has never got over him – wishes you were single?'

I wrinkled my nose. 'Don't be ridiculous. Nick is ancient history.' I waved my hand in the air to demonstrate just how ancient history he was.

'What about your'—she waggled her finger in a downward circle—'ladybits? Have they got the ancient history message?'

A laugh burst from me. 'My ladybits? Seriously Mags? What are we – teenagers?'

Unabashed, she said with a 'told you' wobble of her head, 'You didn't answer the question.'

'No, and I don't intend to. I was still a kid when Nick and I were together.'

'And now you're a woman of the world?'

'Exactly.' I picked up a magnetic egg timer that sat on the end of her desk and tipped it up, watching the iron filings fall into the shape of an anemone.

'If that's the case, you won't mind coming along to a community lecture at the surf club tonight that he's bound to be at.'

'Why would I want to do that?'

'Because the subject is the importance of mangroves in coastal ecosystems.' She leant back in her chair and stretched her arms overhead.

'And because I've googled the guy who's giving the talk, and he looks seriously hot,' yelled Siouxsie from the reception desk.

I tapped my bottom lip. 'The timing seems coincidental.'

'Doesn't it just?'

'Why do you think Nick will be there?'

'Didn't I mention? He's good friends with the scientist who's giving the talk.' She wore a self-satisfied smile.

'Do you think maybe you should've led with that little factoid?'

'Nah,' she said flippantly. 'My way was more fun.'

'Finally, mangrove forests act as breeding nurseries for species vital to our commercial and leisure fishing industry.' The speaker, who Nick had introduced to the audience as Angus Jones, an environmental scientist, crossed one jean-clad knee over the other and swivelled slightly in his chair at the front of the function room. 'If we don't protect this land, we risk losing pristine coastal habitats and upsetting critical biodiversity. And'—he smiled at the audience and readjusted his headset microphone—'let's be frank, in Whale Bay, your biggest asset is the environment, and once it's gone'—he shrugged—'you can't replace it. Nor can you replace traditions that have survived for thousands of years.' He stood and opened his palms before clasping them together. 'I'll leave you with that thought. Thank you for listening, and I'll be around if anyone has any questions.' As the audience applauded him, he placed his palms together in a prayer position at his heart. 'Thank you.'

'Well,' said Maggie, fanning herself. 'I could watch him talk all night.'

'Don't you mean listen?' I quipped.

'No,' said Siouxsie. 'She meant what she said. Those eyes …' She sighed dramatically. 'What would you call them? Grey? Silver? Icy blue?'

I shook my head and chuckled at her dreamy expression and soft smile. 'Poor Harry.'

'Harry who?' she asked innocently.

'I wonder what Martin Cosgrove thought of that.' I tilted my head to where he and his entourage were sitting on the edge of the crowd.

'I didn't expect to see him here.' Siouxsie followed my gaze.

'Me neither, but what better way to show the community you have the environment's best interests at heart than to be seen attending an event like this.' I bent down and picked up my bag. 'If you'll excuse me, I need a drink.'

'And Martin just happens to be standing at the bar,' said Maggie wryly.

'So he is.'

Pushing through the scrum surrounding Angus and Nick, I made my way to the bar where Martin was talking to Michael Lindsay.

'Clem,' Martin said brightly as I asserted myself into their chat. 'It's good to see you.' Gripping my arm, he kissed my cheek.

Beside him, Mike raised his eyebrows, a questioning look on his face. 'Release the woman, Martin, so that I can say hello too.'

If Martin was annoyed, it didn't show on his face as he stepped back, allowing Mike to kiss me hello. 'All okay, Clem?'

'All good.' I offered a small, reassuring smile as he nodded his understanding.

'How's your boyfriend?' Martin asked, lifting his chin. 'I hear they've let him out.' He laughed unpleasantly, and it grated on my nerves – but I had to keep my cool. Before I answered, he rambled on. 'So tell us, Clem, did he really knock his wife off? You're not having a lot of luck with men lately, are you?' He slyly grinned as he referred to my ex, Miles.

'Oh, I don't know about that.' My tone was light and airy, carefree even. 'It could be worse.' I caught the bartender's eye and ordered a glass of white wine.

As I went to hand over money, Martin called out, 'Stick it on my tab, Todd.' As I would've protested, he shook his head. 'No, this one's on me.'

'Thank you,' I accepted graciously.

'So Clem, what did you think of the talk tonight?' Mike asked as I took my wine from the counter and savoured the fruity flavour.

'Really interesting; I'm glad Mags talked me into coming along. I have to say, though, that in light of the boardwalk you guys are looking to put in, it was a masterstroke to bring this guy in to remind the community why the mangroves are so important.'

At first, I thought Martin was going to deny all knowledge of it, but he puffed his chest up instead. 'Thanks, Clem. I can't take all the credit, though; the guy just happens to be Nick's mate, and when Nick mentioned he was in town, it seemed like too good an opportunity to pass on.' He narrowed his eyes and said blandly, 'Have you managed to catch up with Nick yet? You two were … friends … back in the day, weren't you?'

Kylie had obviously told him what she knew of our history. 'We were.' I matched his blandness. 'I suspect we'll catch up at some stage.'

'Have you decided when you're going back to Melbourne?' he asked. 'You're on leave from your job, aren't you?'

'Haven't you heard?' I feigned surprise. 'I've resigned, so Whale Bay is now home. Maggie has asked me to help in her practice – apparently, there's nowhere to get a decent divorce in this town, so how could I say no? So if you know anyone who needs a good family lawyer, you know where I am.' Flashing him another insincere smile, I said, 'If you'll excuse me, gentlemen, I'll go say hello to your brother, and

I haven't seen Kylie yet tonight – oh, there she is.' Martin frowned as he saw his wife draped around Nick, dressed to the nines as always. 'They're quite close, aren't they?' My job done, I ignored Mike's muffled choke. 'Thank you for the drink, Martin.'

As I approached, Kylie flicked her long blonde hair back and leant even closer to Nick. Nick extricated himself from Kylie and hugged me. 'It's good to see you, Clem,' he said. 'I hoped you'd come tonight.'

When he released me, Kylie gave me a tight smile and an air kiss. 'This is a surprise, Clem,' she said. 'I thought you'd be at your boyfriend's bedside.' She turned her eyes on Nick to see if the barb had landed.

When Nick said, with concern on his face, 'How is Finn?' she couldn't hide her disappointment.

'He'll be okay,' I said. 'But after yesterday, he needed some sleep, so I left him to it. He's off to Brisbane tomorrow – he wants to be with Tamzin's family.' I shrugged to show I didn't mind. 'They might have been separated, but they're still family.'

'Understandable. Hey, if you don't have to run straight off, I'd like to introduce you to Angus. Have you got a few minutes?'

'Absolutely,' I said. 'I'll see you later, Kylie.'

As he led me away, I couldn't hide my grin. 'Now, now,' he chided softly, a laugh in his tone too. 'But thanks for the rescue.'

'Did you need rescuing?' I asked archly.

He rolled his eyes. 'What did Martin have to say?'

'He was saying how fortunate it was that your friend could be here tonight – that the timing was perfect. You'd think he planned it himself.'

Nick chuckled. 'Of course he did.'

Angus looked up from his circle of admirers – all women, few of which I'd bet were interested in his environmental sensibilities – as we approached, a wide, dimpled smile welcoming us.

'Angus, I'd like you to meet my friend Clementine. Clem, Angus and I worked together in Cairns, but he's not long back from a stint in Scotland.'

Angus held out his hand for me to shake. 'It's nice to meet you, Clem.'

'Likewise. Scotland, hey? I'd hazard a guess there's not too much in the way of mangroves or remnant rainforest that needs protecting there.'

'Especially not in Shetland. There are, however, marine birds at risk, and that's what I was studying there – and, of course, helping with the conservation effort.'

'It's a bit of a change, though, isn't it? Far North Queensland to Scotland? What prompted that?'

Angus sighed and hunched his shoulders like he was carrying the weight of the environmental world. 'The usual: a bad break-up about five years ago. The timing was perfect – the fellowship came up, I applied, and thankfully was accepted.'

'And now you're back in Queensland.'

'Yes'—he exchanged a quick glance with Nick—'although I'm not sure for how long. It depends on a few factors.'

'Well, it was great you could spare us the time tonight.'

Angus smiled at Nick. 'Nick has told me what's going on with the mangroves here, so if I can help, I'd like to.'

Across the room, I saw a frown float across Martin's face. The three of us must have looked as though we were conspiring.

'Thank you. We need all the help we can get,' I said, unable to suppress a yawn. 'I'm so sorry! My only excuse is I've had a few days from hell.'

As if she knew I'd hit the proverbial wall, Maggie joined us. After introducing herself, she turned to me. 'We're heading home and thought you might like a lift.' Siouxsie was already saying her goodbyes to a group near the bar.

'That would be great, thank you.' I turned my attention back to the men. 'Goodnight. It's been nice meeting you, Angus; maybe I'll see you around town before you leave?'

'I hope so,' he replied with a kind smile.

Nick took my arm and kissed my cheek. 'I'll see you.'

'Yes,' was all I could manage.

CHAPTER NINETEEN

'I should've known you still kept up the habit.' Nick pulled his goggles off and shook his head, drops of salty water flying from his hair. Matching me stride for stride, he walked alongside me back onto the beach. Aware of the brevity of his 'budgie smugglers', I kept my eyes firmly ahead. 'The morning beach swims,' he clarified with a cheeky grin.

'Yes, well'—I removed my goggles and poked the straps into the leg of my swimmers—'it's something I've taken up again since returning to Whale Bay. Even though I swam regularly in Melbourne – you knew I lived in Melbourne, right?'

He nodded. 'Mike said you were a lawyer.'

'I *am* a lawyer,' I corrected him. 'I'm just not working for anyone at the moment.' My goggles bounced against the side of my thighs, the cool of the morning giving my wet skin goosebumps. 'Before I came back, I could count on one hand – and still have fingers left over – the number of times I'd been in the ocean in the last ten years. I'd forgotten how much I missed it.' My voice trailed wistfully.

'You, though, I'm surprised you could keep up your morning swims. I've only been to Cairns once, and it struck me how hard it must be not to be able to swim in those beautiful beaches for half the year. When's stinger season? November to May? Or is it the other way around?'

'Your first guess was right. It's November to May. There are stinger nets on the beaches, and you can wear stinger suits, but they're not a hundred percent …' He shrugged. 'I'm in the water all year round anyway – diving, snorkelling off the reef.'

We'd reached where I'd left my towel, and while I pulled a heavy towelling poncho over my head, he wandered a short distance away to where he'd left his gear. 'So you visited Cairns, did you?'

I averted my eyes as he pulled on boardshorts over his wet swimmers and slipped a rugby jumper on. Was he thinking the same thing I was? How close we'd come to running into each other. I kept my answer light. 'It was a conference for work. We stayed up at Port Douglas.'

'In one of those swanky resorts? Did you get out onto the reef?'

I nodded. 'Yes, to both questions. The resort might've been swanky, but the reef was stunning.'

Recalling that day brought a smile to my face. 'The colours … and snorkelling amongst it all.' I shook my head, unable to find the words to describe how it had made me feel. 'It really is one of those places you have to experience, isn't it?'

'It sure is.' He hesitated and then said, 'I still remember my first time out there … it reminded me of you.'

I swung around to face him, more goosebumps prickling my skin despite the warmth of the coverall. 'Me?'

A slight blush crept onto his cheeks as he nodded. 'It felt like being immersed in the mural you and Rose painted on your bedroom wall – all the blues and greens of the ocean, seaweed dancing in the current, brightly coloured fish. All it needed was a mermaid with emerald hair.'

'Oh.' It was my turn to blush, and a wave of warmth spread across my face.

'Did it remind you of that, too? That first time?' I knew he was talking about the first time on the reef, but something in his eyes made me wonder whether he was thinking about another first time – our first time. The first time we made love. Involuntarily, my gaze wandered to the far end of the beach, past Rose's cottage, near where the rock wall led to the lighthouse.

When my eyes came back to his, the look in them made me shiver – and not from the cool breeze. 'Yes,' I whispered, the word catching in my throat. I swallowed hard. He'd called me his mermaid that night. We'd swum, and when we finished swimming, we'd made love under the full moon's light. With a little shake of my head, I dislodged the unsettling image. 'I'd better be getting home.'

'How's Finn?' Nick wandered closer to where I was

standing.

His change of subject threw me for a second. 'Ummm, good, I think. I'll go pick him up shortly. He's going to Brisbane today.' I picked up my bag, shoved the wet towel into it and swung it over my shoulder.

Nick frowned. 'Should he be driving so soon after a head injury?'

'He's catching the train. The doctors yesterday said he'd be fine to drive tomorrow, so he'll visit Tamzin's father and pick the car up from wherever it is the police have it stored.'

'How long will he be away for?' He rubbed his hair with a towel.

I shrugged and bent to put my goggles in my bag. 'However long it takes, I suppose. He's got to arrange the funeral and so forth. She has a couple of siblings, so they'll want to be involved.'

'Who inherits her estate? Is it Finn?'

My head snapped up at the tone in his voice. 'I have no idea, but I doubt it. Why do you ask?'

'No reason. After all, you said they weren't divorced, so if she died without a will, Finn would be her beneficiary.' He lifted a shoulder like it was an everyday conversation to be having. 'I was just wondering.'

'Whether Finn had anything to do with Tamzin's death? Are you suggesting he killed her so he could get his hands on her money? The police have already ruled him out.' I ended my statement with a so-there tilt of my chin.

'Has he told you yet where he was, though?' Nick's jaw was tight, determined. He was like a dog with a bone.

My chin tilted higher, gaze unwavering. 'No, but I'm sure he will. One place I know he wasn't and that's in the mangroves killing Tamzin.'

Nick held his hands up, his palms facing me. 'No need to get upset; I'm not implying anything. You know him better than I do.' He let out a short laugh that did nothing to ease my annoyance. 'Hell, I don't know him at all. Forget I said anything.'

'I will,' I said firmly, knowing I wouldn't.

'Good.' He slung his towel over his shoulder. 'But while you're not thinking about that, can we think about this issue with the mangroves?'

I jammed my hands on my hips. 'Sure. What do you suggest?'

He pushed his top lip over the lower lip and looked towards the ocean. 'You mightn't like it …'

Sighing heavily, I said, 'Go on …'

'Well.' He turned his gaze back to me. 'We need to find the land references for both the mangroves and any adjacent land …'

'Yeeees. Maggie said she has nothing she can search against.' Where was he going with this?

'That's right. The only place we'll find it would be on a surveyor's map—'

'We can't very well march in and ask to see that,' I

pointed out. 'That would immediately alert Ray that we might be onto what they're up to.'

'Exactly. Which is why we need to'—he broke off and seemingly searched the cloudless sky for the words he wanted—'go about it another way.' He grimaced. 'A way that's not strictly legal.'

'You're not suggesting what I think you're suggesting, are you?'

'What do you think I'm suggesting?'

I rolled my eyes. 'That we break into the surveyor's office.'

'Absolutely not!' He appeared affronted. 'As if I'd suggest something like that; if you got caught, you could be disbarred.'

'I'm glad you realise that,' I said with a relieved sigh.

'What I'm suggesting is that Justin lets us in so we can have a poke around.' He shrugged as if it were no big deal.

'And how is he going to do that?' Scepticism dripped from every word. Surely, he can't be serious about this plan.

'Easy. The surveyor's office is in the same block as Justin's, and Len gave Justin a spare set of keys just in case. Len has Justin's spare keys.' Another shrug. It all made perfect sense – not.

'So you're saying we could poke around in the office while Len wasn't there?' I turned the plan over in my head. Nick nodded. 'There's no difference in doing that as there is to breaking in! Either way, we're there without permission.'

For a smart man, he was being very stupid.

'Only if we get caught.' Nick's lips had curled into a cheeky grin, those oceanic eyes of his twinkling. 'The way I see it, there's no risk. Len leaves early on Wednesdays – he plays golf with my father, Bob and Martin – so Justin can let us in and leave us with the keys. We find what we need; we let ourselves back out. Too easy.'

'But if we're caught …'

'We won't be,' Nick said persuasively. 'Do you have a better way of finding out about the land?'

'We could always go through the formal channels and ask.' I set off towards Beach Road and Brewz, Nick falling into place beside me.

He shook his head. 'We've been through that. Dad – or Bob – would only need to get a whiff of that and they'd know we were onto them. The only way we can find out what they're really up to – and stop it – is if they don't know we're investigating. While they think everyone believes their story about wanting to put in boardwalks'—he rolled his eyes at the possibility anyone could believe that—'we'll be fine.'

He had a point, and the risk did seem to be low, and it might be the only way we could get the information we needed. Even so… 'No.' I shook my head. 'I know the risk is low, but if we do get caught, I'll never practice again. If you want to do this, you'll need to do it on your own. I can't have anything to do with it.'

We'd arrived at the pavement outside Beach Brewz.

Nick nodded slowly. 'I understand. And you're absolutely right. Forget I suggested it.' He held the café door open. 'Coffee?'

'Of course.' I searched his face but saw nothing there to indicate disappointment, just an acceptance which, perversely, immediately made me want to change my mind.

Finn had fitted Brewz out to look as if you'd just wandered in off the beach, which I supposed we had. It looked like a beach shack that just happened to be open for coffee. On one wall was a wave mural with swirls of turquoise and blue, and propped up against another timber-clad wall were brightly painted surfboards.

'Hi, Lainey,' I said when we reached the front of the queue.

'Hey, Clem. The usual?' With a narrowed gaze, she eyed Nick suspiciously.

'Thanks. And whatever Nick wants.'

'Nick Cosgrove?' Lainey asked, her eyes wide with curiosity. 'I heard you were in town. Are you even allowed to buy your coffee here?'

Nick laughed loudly, heads turning to observe us. 'Life is too short for mediocre coffee,' he said. 'Besides, what Martin doesn't know won't hurt him.' He tapped at the side of his nose and grinned.

When Lainey blushed and flicked her hair back across her shoulder, I almost groaned out loud.

'How's Finn?' Lainey asked after a minor tussle between Nick and me over who would get to pay for coffee and which Nick won. 'He's off to Brissie today, isn't he?'

'He is. As soon as I get changed, I'll go pick him up.' Lowering my tone so the rest of the café couldn't hear, I added, 'If you need me while he's away, just yell.'

'Thanks, Clem.'

We'd moved to the side to wait for our coffees when, 'Nick! You're up and about early … and Clem – it is Clem, isn't it?'

Nick greeted Angus with an affectionate clap on the back. 'Early morning swim – you can't top it.'

Angus included me in his smile. 'You too? Clem?'

Nick laughed. 'I've always been convinced Clem is part-mermaid, and at some point, her legs will become a tail, and we'll never see her again.'

As my face grew warm at the second reminder this morning of our first night together, Angus ran his eyes lightly down my body. 'That would be a great pity,' he said. 'I've spent some time in the Scottish islands over the last few years, and there's a legend about the selkies who walk out of the sea, shed their skins and live among humans. Naturally, any human who meets them falls in love with them. Then, when they're done, they pull their skins back on and walk into the ocean, and you never see them again.'

'Maybe,' Nick said thoughtfully, 'I've been mistaken all these years, and Clem is really one of them and not a mermaid. That would explain why she left Whale Bay so suddenly twenty-five years ago.'

Although he wore a smile, the expression in Nick's eyes was anything but light. As an unsettling heat rose, though, I tried to read his expression. Was that … anger? If so, what right did he have to be angry? If anyone had a right to be angry, it was me. Yet, of all the confusing emotions swirling through my brain, anger wasn't one of them. I didn't want to attempt to name the rest.

I forced a light laugh. 'What a cool story, Angus. I'd love to hear more about what you were doing in Scotland.'

Nick raised a quizzical eyebrow, a slight half smile on his lips.

'Any time,' Angus said. 'Leave me your number, and we'll catch up for coffee while I'm here.'

'I'll look forward to that.' Ignoring the thunder now clouding Nick's face, I gratefully took my coffee from Lainey. 'Thanks, Lainey.' To Nick and Angus, I said, 'I'll leave you to it.'

Angus held up a hand in farewell, but Nick said, with a completely innocent expression, 'Let me know if you change your mind about later.'

While I shook my head in exasperation, his grin told me he'd seen Lainey – and several other patrons – raise her eyebrows. The news that I'd been swimming with Nick Cosgrove and was meeting Angus Jones for coffee would probably be all around town before I even reached home.

CHAPTER TWENTY

'I hear you went swimming and had coffee with Nick Cosgrove this morning.' Finn was all sulky when I arrived at the hospital to collect him before lunch. 'That didn't take long.'

Putting his uncharacteristic jealousy down to what he'd been through over the past few days, I pushed down my annoyance. 'What didn't take long?'

'You getting back with him.' Finn had dressed and was folding the T-shirt and football shorts I'd brought him to sleep in.

While I managed to scoff, the words I wanted to say were stuck in my throat.

'I also heard you arranged to have coffee with that environmentalist that's floating around.'

My hand came down on the bed with a slap. 'Finn,' I stared, my words measured, 'I'm trying very hard to put this … rubbish … that you're spouting down to a sore head and knowledge of what you have to do when you get to Brisbane.' His eyes met mine before skating quickly away.

'Yes, Nick and I ran into each other this morning. As for Angus …'

'Who?' Finn shoved the clothes into the overnight bag with more force than was necessary.

'The environmentalist,' I reminded him. 'I'm interested in what he's been working on. Now, it's up to you whether you believe it or not and, quite frankly, at this moment, I don't care whether you do or not, but I care about *you*, Finn. Nick is ancient history.'

'Is he? So you won't be seeing him later this afternoon?'

Lainey must have heard Nick's parting comment. Taking a deep breath I bit the inside of my lip. 'Even though I don't need to explain myself to you, I will. Nick is trying to get to the bottom of whatever dodgy deal his father is doing regarding the mangroves and asked me to help him. That's all.'

Finn closed his eyes and put his hand to his forehead. 'I'm sorry, Clem. I'm not normally the jealous type; I don't know what's got into me.'

I walked around the bed and wrapped my arms around his waist, snuggling into his chest. 'I know you're not, and you have no reason to be. You've been through a lot in the last few days …'

'And I'm dreading the next few,' he said, his voice heavy with apprehension.

'I'm sure you are.' I kissed his lips and laid my cheek against his. 'It will be over soon.'

'You think?' He laughed shortly and stepped out of my hold. 'Thanks for having the dogs while I'm gone.'

'It's fine.' My head tilted to the side as I tried unsuccessfully to read his face. 'Finn …'

'What?' The snap in his voice made me recoil.

'I was wondering …' I shook my head and grimaced. Should I ask him?

'What?' He zipped the backpack closed.

'I was just wondering who benefits from Tamzin's will?' I blurted out the question before I could change my mind.

A flush washed up his neck, hands hovering over the bag. 'What are you suggesting?'

'I'm not suggesting anything or implying anything. I was simply wondering who will inherit.'

'Assuming she has anything to inherit,' he said, still watching me through narrowed eyes.

I lifted a shoulder. 'There'd be at least her superannuation. All I'm saying is that if you two weren't divorced and she didn't have a valid will, you'll be the one who inherits.'

He was silent for a few seconds and then said flatly, 'The police know I wasn't involved.' A little shake of the head and, 'I can't believe you think I was.'

Torn between wanting to shake some sense into him and hating that I'd questioned him about this, I counted to ten and sighed heavily. 'I know you weren't.'

'Did Nick Cosgrove put you up to this? To asking me?'

'No.' I shook my head and then shrugged. 'Maybe. Yes, he did wonder aloud.' Damn Nick for putting the idea into my head. Finn had nothing to do with this.

Finn pursed his lips and looked out the window overlooking the car park. 'Maybe you should be asking him where he was when Tamzin died. After all, he calls himself a great environmentalist, and he did appear back in town straight after she died.' He lifted a shoulder. 'That can't be a coincidence. And that mate of his, too. You can't tell me that's not a coincidence, him turning up at the same time as Nick.'

My eyes widened. 'You can't think … you don't think … Nick wouldn't have anything to do with it – he couldn't.'

'Who says he couldn't? You only have his word for it, and by the sounds of it these days, you believe him rather than me.'

'Don't be ridiculous,' I spat. 'I know you had nothing to do with Tamzin's death. You were nowhere near the mangroves at the time.'

'That's right, I was nowhere near the area. But the police told you that. Would you be so convinced of my innocence if the police hadn't told you?'

I turned away from the accusation in his eyes. There was something else there too – disappointment.

'Even though you still won't tell me where you were at the time, I've always known you weren't involved in Tamzin's death,' I said quietly. 'Why won't you tell me?'

'I was hiking,' he said bluntly.

Whirling back to face him, it was my turn for the disappointment to show. 'We both know you weren't, Finn, so don't lie to me. We don't do that – the lying thing.'

'Don't we? After all, there's only been a "we" for a few weeks, so who knows what we do.'

His eyes bored into mine, their coffee depths muted. His tone was flat and defeated. Was he saying what I thought he was saying? Was he ending us?

Finn placed his hands over his face. When I noticed his shoulders shaking, I moved closer and gripped his wrists, dragging them down his face. 'Oh, Finn,' I murmured, leaning forward to kiss him, his tears salty on my lips. 'I'm so sorry.'

He shook his head. 'I'm the one who should be sorry. I just'—a thin, strained smile stretched his lips—'can't seem to think straight. Everything seems to be going wrong. First, Tamzin arrives, then she's murdered, I'm arrested, my house is broken into, and I end up here. On top of all that, Nick Cosgrove shows up, and you're seeing him. I know I'm overreacting, but I can't seem to help it.' He recoiled, his hand rubbing over his mouth and chin. 'I should've known things were going too well.'

'It was the "p" word,' I said with a forced laugh. 'You should never have said the "p" word.' When he chuckled, I said, 'I'm sorry too. I should never have asked you about her will, and my question had no ulterior meaning. I can't stop being a lawyer.' I opened my palms and shrugged. 'Seriously though, I was just wondering if there is something to inherit and whether someone thought they would be getting it. That could be a sufficient motive for murder.' I warmed to my theme. 'Maybe it's this mysterious new man – the one the police said told them you and Tamzin had argued. Maybe that's who we should be trying to find. If we find them, we might find her phone and laptop too.'

Finn gripped my shoulders, a contrast to his usually gentle touch. 'Clem, enough! Leave it alone.' When I blanched at his vehemence he relaxed his grip and looked deeply into my eyes. 'Leave this to the police. Please.'

'But—'

'No buts. Someone broke into my house, they almost killed me, and you were lucky not to be hurt too. I couldn't bear it if something happened to you.' He kissed me hard on the lips. 'Please stay out of it.' When I didn't immediately answer, he repeated his plea. 'Please, Clem.'

I nodded reluctantly. 'Okay, but I'm not giving up on looking into the plans for the mangroves.'

'No,' he said sadly, 'I don't suppose you will. Just promise me you'll be careful.'

'I will be,' I said.

'I mean'—he looked to the door, a pulse beating in his jaw—'be careful of Nick.'

A short, humourless laugh escaped my lips. 'He can't hurt me anymore.'

'Okay, if you say so. I just don't want you getting involved with him.' He glanced at his watch. 'They'll be wanting their bed back, and I still have to pack and have a train to catch.'

'You're right. We'd better get moving.'

It was only as I drove away after dropping him at the railway station that I realised Finn still hadn't told me where he was or who he was with when Tamzin was murdered.

CHAPTER TWENTY-ONE

'I'm still not sure about this,' I said to Nick as we strolled down Beach Road into town. 'What if we get caught?'

'We won't. I'm glad you changed your mind,' he said.

'I'm already regretting it,' I mumbled. After dropping Finn off, I spent the next hour or so replaying our conversation and his instruction – because that's what it had felt like – not to get involved with Nick. Before I knew it, I'd messaged Nick. I just hoped it didn't end up costing me my career.

He glanced sideways, a slow grin spreading across his face as he looked at me. 'What's with the get-up? All that black?'

'Isn't that what people wear when they don't want to be noticed?' I'd donned a pair of full-length black leggings, a black long-sleeved tee, and black sneakers and had caught my hair up under a black cap. He, however, was in his usual Okanuis (today's were pink), a washed-out blue T-shirt that lightened his eyes and made them stand out in his tanned face, and a pair of scuffed canvas trainers.

'If you're a cat burglar and running over the tops of roofs in the French Riviera, perhaps.' He was referring to wintry Sunday afternoons spent watching Rose's favourite movie – the old Cary Grant and Grace Kelly's *To Catch a Thief*. 'Or if you're breaking into somewhere and intent on causing damage.'

'There's very little difference between that and what we're doing,' I said.

'Except we have a key—'

'Which the owner hasn't given us permission to use. Do you realise if we get caught, Justin will be in trouble too?' Aside from my rebellion against Finn's possessiveness, it had been this realisation that had contributed to my agreeing with his madcap scheme. If Justin was risking his career for this, I couldn't allow him to do that alone.

'Then we'd better not get caught.' He finished that statement with a wink. Damn him!

He seemed so breezy that I wondered how often he'd done something like this: broken into an office to find information.

'And before you ask,' he said. 'This isn't something I make a habit of.'

'You mean you don't often break into offices?'

'No, I rarely avail myself of nonviolent means of getting into a place I need to get into.'

If I looked at him now, he'd be wearing a sardonic grin, so I didn't look at him. 'You say tomato, I say *tomayto*.

Anyway,' I added. 'At least I'll blend in.'

'To what? This is Whale Bay, and sure, the sun is down, but it's not like it's completely dark yet. Besides, anyone used to seeing you in the boho getup you usually get around in is going to wonder why you're suddenly all in basic black and think to themselves "Maybe Clementine Carter is going to break into Len Hartog's office tonight?"'

'Oh, ha-ha,' I retorted. 'They're more likely to say "What's Clementine Carter doing out with Nick Cosgrove? I wonder if Finn knows. I wonder if Kylie Lindsay knows …"' I flashed him a quick look and a so-there waggle of my head. 'And then, before you know it, word will be all around town.' Frowning, I focused on the grass growing up through the cracks in the footpath. 'At least Finn is in Brisbane and won't hear this time.'

'Clem?'

I looked across to find him frowning. 'By the time I got to the hospital this morning, Finn had heard we'd been swimming together.'

He grimaced. 'I'm sorry, Clem. I should've remembered what this town is like.'

'It's nothing.' I waved his concern away and continued to walk. 'Finn was fine about it.' To say anything else would be to let him into our relationship, and I wasn't prepared to do that.

Although I felt his eyes boring into me, I held my ground and didn't look his way. 'That's alright then,' he said.

'Well, here we are.'

The double-storey red brick building was home to the professional services in town. A collective of allied health specialists occupied the suites on the ground floor, but Maggie's and Justin's offices and the surveyor's office were on the first floor.

Ignoring the lift, we climbed the stairs to Justin's office, where Maggie was also waiting. Siouxsie had knocked off early to go home and prepare for a date. Although she hadn't said who she was meeting I had my suspicions.

'What *are* you wearing, Clem?' asked Maggie, eyes wide.

'It's her cat burglar outfit.' Nick smirked.

'I've dressed for discretion and warmth,' I said, with a tilt of my chin. 'It's getting cold in the evenings now.'

'How long do you think we're going to be here?' drawled Nick. 'An hour max.'

'Are you sure about this?' Justin directed his question to me.

'No,' I said honestly, 'but I don't see any other way to get the information without alerting people that we're looking into this.'

'Okay.' Justin handed me the keys. 'Be careful. The cleaners have been in, so you should be fine. The main door downstairs is locked from six, but one of the keys on here will open it.'

'Oh, for God's sake, Justin,' said Maggie with trademark exasperation. 'What could possibly go wrong?'

Justin and I exchanged glances, and I chuckled mirthlessly. 'You're asking that this week? A week when everything that could possibly go wrong has gone wrong?' Why had I agreed to do this?

Maggie gave a little wave to show it wasn't important. 'All that means, Clem, is that there's nothing left to go wrong, so you'll be fine. Let us know if you need a pizza delivery or anything,' she added helpfully.

'Thanks, Mags,' said Nick. 'But as I said, we intend to be in and out quickly.'

'Alright, well,' said Justin, hovering in the doorway. 'We'll leave you to it. Good luck.'

'It's not like they're going on an Antarctic expedition.' Maggie picked up her bag from Justin's desk.

'What about CCTV cameras?' I asked in a sudden panic, pointing to the camera outside Justin's door. 'Does Len have one?'

Justin shook his head. 'No, this is Whale Bay, and the main door downstairs is locked overnight. Mine is there for show only.'

'Nothing will go wrong.' Maggie kissed my cheek. 'Have fun kids, behave yourselves and we'll see you at your place in an hour or so.' With a little wave they left, Maggie nudging Justin when he cast an anxious look back towards us.

After a quick check that the coast was clear, I removed silicon gloves from the pocket of my leggings and wiped the keys against my T-shirt.

'What. Are. You. Doing?' Nick asked. 'And what are those?' He pointed towards my gloves.

'Removing fingerprints, of course,' I said defensively. 'And the beetroot gloves are to make sure we don't leave any prints on the keys or the door.'

'Beetroot gloves?' He laughed at me.

'That's what Rose always called them,' I said mock-defensively. 'Remember how she always had pickled beetroot in the fridge in summer? She used to say these gloves were the only thing that stopped her hands from being permanently stained pink.' A memory came to mind. 'There was even one time when she experimented with tie-dyeing using beetroot. The colour didn't last, though.' I tilted my head to the side. 'Why do you think that was? And let me tell you, if you drop even the tiniest drop of beetroot onto something white, you might as well throw it out because that drop will be there forever.'

Nick shook his head, half in amusement and half in exasperation. 'Are you trying to delay the inevitable? Here, give me the keys.' Without waiting for a response, he whipped them out of my hand, inserted one into the door of Len's office and turned the handle. 'After you.'

I glared at him. 'I'll have to wipe the keys down again now … and the door handle.' Pulling my sleeve over my hand, I dealt with the handle. 'There, that's better.'

We'd come into a foyer with two chairs and a low round table holding an assortment of locally produced magazines – the sort made by community businesses to showcase the region and were typically filled with local openings and closures, features of businessmen and women, and advertorials promoting real estate agents and beauticians. Nick picked one up, flicked through it, scoffed, and set it back down. I rubbed my forehead. Great, now he'd left prints all over them, too.

Selecting another key, he unlocked the door to the office itself. A relatively small footprint, there were two white desks in the main office space, behind which was an open door and a small meeting room with a round table and four chairs. A small kitchenette, single toilet and storeroom were off to the side.

'Here.' Nick tossed me the keys. 'Wipe away to your heart's content.'

'Thanks, I will.' After wiping the keys, I left them on the low table while I wiped at the magazine Nick had picked up. No wonder he'd scoffed; beaming from the cover were Ray and Martin Cosgrove, and Bob and Michael Lindsay. The headline read: 'Progress is a Family Affair'. Oh, please.

'Hey, Clem,' called Nick.

Placing the magazine back on the table, I followed the direction of Nick's voice, finding him at the door to the storeroom. 'Where do you think we should start?'

'Maybe the filing cabinets along that back wall.'

As I pointed towards the cabinets, I heard a key in the outside door with muffled voices.

Nick held his finger to his lips, grabbed my hand and steered me towards the storeroom. With a soft click, he shut the door behind us. Not much larger than a cupboard, the room was dark, with the only light chinking through from under the door.

The voices grew louder, closer now, their tones chatty and carefree.

'That's funny,' Len said. 'The door was open. Bloody cleaners! And they've left their keys behind.'

My heart lodged in my throat, and my stomach teetered. Nick instantly realised what had rattled me and mouthed, 'Shit, the keys.'

Afraid that even a slight movement would be heard, I nodded. Pulling my phone from the pocket of my leggings, I checked it was still on silent, almost gasping aloud when I missed the pocket and caught the phone before it dropped to the floor. Nick's eyes widened in a silent warning, but he also checked his phone.

'I tell you, you can't get good help these days.' The voices were drawing nearer. 'At least it looks as though they've cleaned today, although they didn't empty the bins. And leaving the door open like that'—I imagined him tutt-tutting in annoyance—'is just not good enough.'

'I hear you, Len.'

At the sound of Ray Cosgrove's voice, I looked at Nick in horror. He grimaced and ran his hand over the back of his neck.

'Did you receive the results of the survey before that girl got herself killed?' Ray asked.

'No. She emailed me on Friday to say she'd completed the draft report but wanted to talk to a few people before she sent it through.'

'Do you know who?' Ray asked.

'She didn't say.'

'Probably that husband of hers and Rose's meddling niece. I thought Chris Walker had done us all a favour when he finished Rose off – accident or otherwise – but the niece is just as bad, if not worse.' There was a brief silence. 'Actually, she's a lawyer, so that makes her worse.'

'Your son doesn't seem to think she's worse.' Len's voice held a smirk. 'I heard he's been seen with her.'

'Hmmm. I thought I'd fixed that situation twenty-five years ago. He'll be gone again soon, so it won't be a problem.'

Nick flashed an indecipherable glance at me.

'What's he in town for? It's been a while since he visited, isn't it?'

'He said he's here to see his mother and because that environmentalist friend of his – Angus Jones – is here. He'd heard about the mangrove study – God knows how – and I told him the same as we told the council: that we're investigating putting a boardwalk in so the community can access the area's natural beauty.' He chuckled at his own cleverness. 'It's alright, he believed me.'

A stony expression settled over Nick's features, his

eyes cold and unreadable.

'Back to that woman scientist.' Ray was still speaking. 'I bought that sergeant from Brisbane a beer last night, and he told me they hadn't recovered her laptop and phone. That means there's nothing linking her to us. Officially, she wasn't beginning the study until next week and was here over the weekend to see her husband.' There was another brief silence. 'I'm not telling you to delete her emails and phone messages, but …'

'Understood. But she told me she'd spoken to you last week …'

'Did she? I don't recall.'

Both men laughed.

'What about her boss?'

'He's on board,' Ray said confidently. 'We'll get the result we need this time.'

'This time?' Len sounded confused.

'Let's just say it's sad for her family that someone did her in, but maybe they did us a favour.'

Nick moved closer and placed his hand over my mouth before I could make a sound. In the cramped space, his scent surrounded me. Where Finn was a blend of coffee and salt, Nick was fresh air and the ocean, with uplifting notes of citrus, the depth of amber and the earthiness of driftwood. He was elemental, and despite the clamouring of my heart and the fear of discovery – or maybe because of that – my body was responding to him as it used to.

'You didn't have anything to do with it, did you, Ray?' Len's voice was hesitant, unsure.

'Maaaate, of course I didn't. There was a Plan B lined up if her report didn't stack up.'

Nick removed his hand from my mouth but remained so close I could've swayed into him. It wouldn't have taken much for me to lift my chin and for him to lower his and our lips would've met. Cursing my hormones, I took a step back, staggering as I would've tripped against a box of photocopier paper. Nick's muscular arm pulled me towards him before I could fall.

'What was that?'

For a moment, I thought Len had heard us but realised he was asking about Ray's backup plan.

'Need to know, Len, need to know.' Knowing Ray, he would've tapped his nose conspiratorially. 'There are always ways to get women to change their mind.'

'You mean …?'

'Promise them marriage, and they'll do anything.'

Both men laughed knowingly.

My heart beat fast against Nick's chest, and as our eyes met in the near-darkness of the storeroom, it skipped a beat and then another. When he gave a little shake of his head and stepped back, putting a few extra centimetres between us, I didn't know whether to be relieved or disappointed.

'What about Justin King?' Len asked. 'He asked me

about the access road into the mangroves.'

'What about it?' A guarded note had come into Ray's voice.

'About who owns it.'

'I see.' A short silence and, 'What did you tell him?'

'That my understanding was it was state-owned.'

'Good man. That would be that wife of his. Justin is no trouble, but his wife is friendly with Clementine Carter. Have there been any requests out of the ordinary?'

'No. I think everyone from council is on board. They all bought the story. What are you going to do about the parking at the surf club and the cycles on the pathway?'

Ray scoffed. 'Nothing. You think I give a damn about any of that? Now, about these revised plans for the proposed marina, you said you've had comments from the team at RHD.'

'Yes, an email came through just before I left this afternoon. I'll need to fire up the computer.'

For a few seconds, the only sound was the gentle rustling of papers and our breathing.

'Jesus, Len, what sort of idiot uses his kid's name as his password?' Ray asked with a laugh.

'It's more complex than that,' said Len. 'If anyone was to hack in, they'd also need to know where he comes in the birth order. Here we go. It's from their architect, and he says BG is happy with the marina but wants to know how much the council will contribute towards improving that stretch of road off the Bruce Highway.'

'I thought they might go there. With the federal elections coming up next year, I'm sure there'll be an announcement about improving the Bruce, and I think I can wangle some extra funding out of the state government as well. I'll talk to BG about that when he arrives.'

'Will he be here for the vote?' asked Len.

'Yes. He can wine and dine anyone who's on the fence – or find another way to persuade them to vote with us.'

While I wasn't brave enough to risk taking my phone out of my pocket and making notes, Nick nodded to let me know he was taking it all in, too.

'I'll just print this off for you,' said Len. There was a beep and a whirr. 'Bugger, the printer is out of paper; I'll need to get some.'

Nick's eyes widened, and again, he pulled me close against him, manoeuvring us into the cramped space behind the door.

As the door opened, the room flooded with light as Len flicked the switch on. I held my breath and buried my head into Nick's chest; the two of us jammed tightly together.

'Don't worry about it, mate. Just forward it to me.'

'You sure?' Len asked.

'Yeah, besides, I'm into beer time, and I promised Paula I'd be home by seven. She was muttering something about a family dinner at the club.' I lifted my head to see

Nick grimace and squeeze his eyes shut.

The light went off and the door closed, plunging us back into near-darkness, yet Nick made no move to release me. Even if I could have done so quietly, I was incapable of moving, my leg muscles frozen, the fear of discovery leaving me rooted to the spot.

Nick's eyes strayed to my mouth, his breath coming quicker and mingling with mine, his body stirring against mine. When I swallowed hard and moistened my lips, he shuddered against me. When I shifted my hips, he groaned and rested his forehead against mine, his arms gripping me against him. 'We can't,' I whispered, still making no attempt to move.

'I know,' he murmured against my hair.

Outside the closed door there was a beep as Len's computer powered down and the jangle of keys as the two men prepared to leave.

'I'll need you to present those plans to BG,' said Ray.

'What about the plans for the boardwalk?' asked Len.

Ray laughed. 'Have them ready for the next council meeting. We have to at least look as though that was our Plan A, and this opportunity came out of the mangrove reclassification.'

'Your son won't cause any trouble?' asked Len. 'He seemed to be quite thick with that environmentalist.'

'Leave Nick to me,' said Ray, the voices growing softer and more distant. 'At the end of the day, he's a Cosgrove.'

Nick's body stiffened, his arms dropping to his sides as he stepped away from me, leaving a wave of coolness between us.

CHAPTER TWENTY-TWO

We waited in the dark until we heard the front door click, then another few minutes to be sure. Nick opened the door carefully and stepped into the darkened office – the only glow coming from the lights in the common space near the lift. 'It's clear,' he said.

'Nick,' I began, 'that noise as they were leaving … I think it was the click of a lock turning.'

His eyes met mine briefly, relieved and still alert. 'I wouldn't worry,' he said. 'We'll be able to unlock it from this end; we just won't be able to relock it.' He turned the latch on the door into the foyer to prove his point, smiling back at me when it opened as he'd suggested. But when he tried the front door, the handle refused to budge.

'We're stuck in here, aren't we?' Panic began to sweep across me; my breath hitched in my throat. I can't be locked in a room with Nick, not after what had just nearly happened in the storeroom.

He chewed at his bottom lip and then slowly shook his head, his eyes dropping from mine. 'Yes,' he finally said. 'It looks as though we're here for the night.'

When Nick reached for the light switch, I almost screamed at him. 'Wait! It's going to look suspicious if there's a light on in here.' Casting my eyes wildly around the room, I said, 'The only window to the outside is in the meeting room, so if we pull the blinds shut and shut the door, we can turn the light on in here. At this time of night, there shouldn't be anyone walking around the front of the office, so we should be safe.'

'Good idea,' he said with a sheepish smile. 'I told you I don't make a habit of this sort of thing.'

There was enough light in the meeting room from the streetlight outside to see what I was doing, and Nick waited until I had the blinds shut before switching on the main lights.

I sank into a chair in the kitchenette and buried my face in my hands. 'No, no, no, no. This can't be happening. There's no way we can get out now without being caught.' Dropping my hands, I spat out, 'I should never have let you talk me into this!'

'I'm not the one who left the keys lying around for them to find,' he fired back, eyes flashing. 'Now Justin will be implicated too.'

'I wouldn't have needed to leave the keys anywhere if you hadn't refused to put on gloves! If you remember rightly, I only put the keys down to wipe away your fingerprints.'

'Yes, your honour, of course, your honour,' he sneered,

the words dripping with sarcasm.

All the fight suddenly went out of me, and I flopped back in the chair. 'Regardless of how we got into this situation, we need to find a way out of it.'

'You're right,' he admitted, shoulders slumping.

'Once more for the tape,' I quipped. When he continued to stare blankly at me, I added, 'You telling me I'm right.'

'Was that you apologising?' The twinkle returned to his eyes, and I had to look away from them before my heart skipped again.

'I have nothing to apologise for,' I said, my voice light and airy, a casual dismissal of his accusation.

'I remember Rose telling me once that because you're an Aries, the closest I'd ever get to an apology from you was something like "I'm sorry if you've misunderstood me and are upset by that."' He pulled out a seat opposite me at the table and sat down. 'She used to tell me you'd eventually realise I wasn't following and would stop and wait for me to catch up.'

'And she told me that as a Scorpio, you'd dig your heels in and that I couldn't expect you to bend to my will. She said I had to wait until you'd come around to my way of thinking, find a way of persuading you or admit I couldn't always win.'

'And you were never good at losing – or waiting.' He grinned.

'No, I wasn't,' I conceded. 'I'm still not, although the

law certainly taught me that there are some outcomes I can't control, let alone the pace at which they happen.'

He chuckled, the sound warm, comforting. 'You were, however, always an ideas girl … able to find a way through or around a roadblock.' His elbow was on the table, and he rested his cheek in his hand and smiled at me, his eyes as bluey-green as the Pacific, the spark in them reminding me of those days when the sea looked as though diamonds had been scattered over it. *Seriously, Clem? Get a grip!* 'So,' he drawled. 'I admit this was my idea, and it might not have been the best idea I've ever had—'

'You didn't exactly force me into it, and, on balance, the risk was low.' Why couldn't I look away from him? That moment in the storeroom had brought all the feelings I'd tried so hard to forget for twenty-five years screaming back. The highs, the lows, the pleasure, the pain. All of it. Even if I'd managed to convince my brain that I felt nothing for him, my body remembered him, and it remembered how I'd never *felt* as much as I'd felt with Nick. And, if his reaction in the storeroom was anything to go by, his body remembered me only too well.

'Agreed, but it was unfair of me to talk you into it. You have more to lose than I do if we're caught.'

'I think that's more like *when* we're caught,' I said dolefully, already drafting my response to the Law Council. Pushing my chair back, I stood and opened the fridge. 'Hopefully, this isn't one of those offices where the fridge has to be emptied every week.' Pulling out a milk bottle, I checked the use-by date, unscrewed the cap and sniffed suspiciously. Brightening when I saw a coffee pod machine sitting on the counter, I searched for capsules. 'Winning! I can do us a coffee. We have a long night ahead of us.'

Nick sat in silence as I made the coffees, seeming to understand I needed that space to contemplate our next move. 'Make yourself useful,' I said. 'See if you can find some biscuits or chocolates. Len's a diabetic, so he's bound to have chocolates in his drawer.'

Nick scoffed. 'Surely that means he wouldn't have them?'

'You don't know Len's wife,' I shot back. 'She has him on such a strict diet, yet wonders why his blood sugars never seem to come down.'

'How do you know that?'

'She told Maggie, and Maggie told me,' I said with a shrug.

Shaking his head, he walked into the office, returning a few minutes later with a half-empty box of fundraising chocolate frogs. 'Freddos for the win?'

'Perfect!'

I set coffees on the table and unwrapped a chocolate frog, nibbling at the feet first. 'Why do you think they put them in upside down?' I asked. 'Surely when you open it, the head should be where the head is in the packet, yet this one was head down, feet up.'

He laughed, opened a packet and raised his eyebrows when the froggy head appeared. 'I reckon you got an anomaly.'

'Maybe. I'll have to open another one to be sure. Maybe it's a Six Sigma thing – you know, that whole quality assessment theory.'

'I always remember your questions. Things like "Where do snails go when it isn't raining?" or "Where does all the snot go when you don't have a cold?" Clementine Russell, always asking the big questions in life.'

'It's Carter now,' I said idly. 'My surname is Carter.'

'Yeah, I know,' he admitted. 'So you married?'

'Briefly. Someone I met at university; it didn't last long.' I shrugged to show it was long ago, and I no longer cared. 'You?'

'Am I married, or have I been married?'

'Either? Both, I suppose.'

His lips quirked into a rueful smile. 'Like you, I got married, but it didn't last. She's married again and very happy, apparently.'

'Children?'

'No, thank goodness. That would've made it all too messy.'

My heart clenched when he dismissed the question of children. 'True.' I sipped at my coffee. In the ensuing silence to take my mind off Nick and the moment we'd shared in the storeroom, I racked my brain for a solution to our problem. Maybe …

Watching the beginnings of a smile on my lips, he said, 'You've got it, don't you?'

'Maybe …' I pulled my phone out of my pants pocket and scrolled through to Maggie's number.

She answered on the first ring. 'Hey there, how's it going? Have you found anything?'

'We have a bit of a problem.' I grimaced. 'Is Justin there?'

'Yes, we're at your house waiting for you. What's wrong?'

I flicked my phone onto speaker. 'I have you on speaker. Nick's here with me—'

'Yeeees, but where are you?'

'Can you put me on speaker so Justin can hear? There's no one else around, is there?'

'No, just us. Siouxsie's out on her date and won't say who.'

'I think it's Harry,' I said.

'What?' thundered Justin. 'I like Harry, but not as a boyfriend for my daughter!'

'I'm sure it will be fine,' soothed Maggie.

'You know what he's like with women.' Justin sounded like he was in no mood to be appeased.

'Guys! We can talk about Siouxsie and Harry later; right now, Nick and I have a bit of a problem.'

'Go on,' urged Justin. 'Don't tell me you've been caught.'

'Not exactly.' I looked at Nick for support.

'We almost were,' Nick jumped in. 'Len came back with Dad. Clem and I hid in the storeroom.' Again, his eyes went to my lips, and I felt heat rise to my cheeks and a warmth deep in my core. 'On the upside, they didn't find us, and they were talking freely, so we have plenty we need to catch you up on.'

'And the downside?' Justin asked.

'We'd left the keys in the foyer, they found them, and now we're locked in until Len comes in tomorrow, at which time we'll be caught.'

'Christ!' the normally mild-mannered Justin exploded. I cringed. 'I have no way of getting you out of there tonight! What did Len say when he found the keys?'

'He blamed the cleaners.' Before Justin could say more, I said, 'Before you go off again, and yes, I totally get that it was irresponsible to leave the keys where they could be found. It was just that I was busy wiping fingerprints off the magazines and …'

I heard something that sounded suspiciously like Maggie giggling in the background and imagined Justin glaring at her.

'I don't think he needs to know that, Clem,' Nick said. 'How about you tell him your idea.'

'Your idea? It needs to be better than the last one, which has turned out to be—'

'I know, Justin. Perhaps it wasn't the best idea Nick's

ever had'—I ignored his scowl—'but it looks as though the cleaners haven't been through to empty the bins and I'm wondering whether there's a possibility they do that in the mornings.'

A slow smile spread across Nick's face as he caught his bottom lip between his teeth.

'Yes, they do the rubbish removal in the morning,' Justin said slowly, not quite caught up with me.

'Good. What I was thinking is that you get in before they do, and when you see them, call them into your office to talk to them about, I don't know, something or other. We'll use that opportunity to get away.'

'That could work,' Justin said. 'I'm often in early so they won't think anything of that. What about the keys? As soon as Len confronts the cleaners, he will realise they were my spare set.'

'I've thought of that too,' I said. 'When he asks you for them, make a show of going to the drawer you keep them in and pretend you've just discovered they've gone. Say something like you left the office open when you ducked next door to Maggie's, and when you came back, some of the filing cabinet drawers were open, and it felt like someone had been in, but nothing was missing. Tell him you're going to call Tyson and make a report. Len's involved with Ray's plans for the mangroves – it's a long story, and I hope we'll be able to fill in some of the gaps tonight – but I'm not sure that he'll want the police trawling through his office. Ray certainly won't. Besides'—another sideways look at Nick—'we're using beetroot gloves so won't leave any fingerprints. If he thinks someone's been through his documents, he won't want to advertise the fact by making a formal report.'

There was silence on the other end for a few seconds before Justin said, 'That could work.'

'You'll need to be able to bluff it out, though, Justin, and I know how honest you are.'

'He can do it,' said Maggie. 'If he can't, I can. We need an alibi for tonight, though, and so do you.'

'I've thought about that, too. I'll phone Pizza Boyz now and order enough for the four of us, making sure I let them know you're there too. When they deliver, they'll see you, and you can yell out for me or something.' As my voice trailed off, I shrugged. It was lame, but it could work. 'If anyone asks Pizza Boyz, they'll say I ordered for four and was heard to be asking you, and that we were all at the house when the pizzas were delivered.'

'Got it,' Maggie said.

'One last question, Mags,' I said. 'What's Len's son's name?'

'Jayden, why?'

'And what number is he in the pecking order?' Nick looked away and chuckled as he understood my question.

'Number three. Why?'

'Thanks, Maggie, you just got us access to Len's computer as well.' Over her laughter, I had one more thing to take care of. 'Also, can you look after the dogs for me?'

'No problem, Clem,' she said. 'I'll spend the night here.'

When I hung up, Nick was shaking his head. 'You're still an ideas girl.'

'We haven't got away with it yet,' I said.

'No, but now at least there's hope, and we have all night to find what we're looking for.' His face fell. 'There's just one thing ... From what we heard, Mum is expecting me for a family dinner. I'll tell her that I'm catching up with old friends, but when I don't come home tonight, I think we know what conclusions will be drawn.'

'That you spent the night with me,' I said bluntly.

'Yes. And that will get around town—'

'And Finn will find out.' Thinking it through, I tapped at my lips until I noticed Nick watching the action with too much interest. 'I'll have to deal with that when it comes to it and say you spent the night on the couch. If Maggie stays, she can support that. As an alternative to being arrested for break and enter, I'll take the risk to my reputation. After all, who would believe that you and I could ever be together?'

'True.' Nick's expression was indecipherable. 'It's a ridiculous idea. I'd better ring my mother, and then we need to find those documents.'

While Nick made the call, I settled back to enjoy my coffee and Freddo.

'Mum, hi ... where am I? I'm actually at Clem Carter's

with Justin and Maggie King. What? … You didn't mention that earlier. I'm sorry, but I won't make it home for dinner; we've just ordered a heap of pizzas … I'm sorry about that, but I arranged to catch up with Justin and … no, I'm not going to just leave them to it. We've got a lot of catching up to do. You should've said something if you were planning a family dinner … Tomorrow night? Sure, that would work … What about Clem? I know Martin and Kylie don't like her … okay and Carmen doesn't either …' He sent me an apologetic smile. 'I don't have a problem with her. I haven't seen her since school days, and she's Maggie King's best friend. Besides, she's improved with age.' He dramatically rubbed at his arm from where I thumped him. 'Hang on—' He half covered the receiver and said, 'Yeah mate, be right with you. Gotta go, Mum; I'll probably be late, so see you in the morning.'

'I've improved with age, have I?' I said with a laugh when he set his phone back on the table.

'To be honest, Clem, you've barely changed. You might've cut your hair and changed the colour, but you'll always be my green-haired mermaid.' Before I could respond, he smiled sadly and picked up the coffee mugs. 'I'll wash these up, but I don't suppose you've got another pair of those gloves I can use.'

'Sure.' I pulled the spare pair from my leggings pocket. 'Here you go.'

As he put the coffee cups back in the cupboard, I said,

'I have changed, you know. I had to grow up.'

'Didn't we all?' A cheerless, familiar half smile played on his lips.

I quickly looked away before he saw the moisture welling in my eyes.

CHAPTER TWENTY-THREE

Having successfully entered the password, we began our reconnaissance on Len's computer.

'Len and your father referred to someone as BG.' I looked over Nick's shoulder at the screen.

'And Dad mentioned something about an email from the team at RHD. Let's see if we can find that and go from there.'

Nick opened Len's emails and began scrolling. 'This doesn't feel right,' I said. 'Going through his emails like this.'

Nick wrinkled his nose. 'I know, but …' He shrugged. 'I'm trying to think of something that will justify what we're doing. I didn't like the sound of the word marina in that conversation we overheard, and if that's what they have in mind, it needs to be stopped. Besides, this must be a big deal if Tamzin was killed because of it.'

'We don't know that,' I reminded him.

With a slight lift of his shoulder, he dismissed the comment. 'You heard the same conversation I did. Tamzin was supposed to return a favourable study—'

'Presumably one that allowed the building of a marina in or near the mangroves,' I finished. 'You're right, Nick. We do have to stop it.'

'Okay, there's an email here from an architect at Ridley Hawke Developments. This must be the RHD they were talking about. Presumably, the BG who is due to visit is someone high up there.' He looked up at me from the computer. 'I'll print this out. Can you put some paper in the printer?'

My face bloomed as I replayed the scene in the storeroom. The speed with which he refocused on the screen implied he also remembered.

Nick searched for all emails from Ridley Hawke, and we soon had a pile of printed paper – and a fair idea about what they had planned for the land.

'It looks like the marina was part of a high-end residential development to be constructed on the land immediately adjacent to the mangroves.' I flicked through the plans we'd found. 'I'm not an environmental lawyer, but I'd assume there are rules regarding how close to protected mangroves you can build.'

'So Tamzin's job was to produce a report that showed the mangroves had shrunk, therefore allowing development of more of the available land,' Nick added, leaning back in his chair.

'But who owns the land they're talking about?' I wondered aloud.

'We have the reference now; Mags can complete a search. The most helpful thing right now would be to find the maps.'

'Did you find anything to or from Tamzin in there?' I stood and reached my arms overhead, feeling the stretch in my muscles.

Nick scratched his head. 'No, I'll check the deleted folder.' Another few clicks and, 'Here we are. A couple from her verifying the coordinates and access of the land to be surveyed, and another saying she's completed the initial study and would email a draft through in a couple of days.' He read on. 'According to her email signature, she worked for a company called Hawksbill Solutions. We'll need to find out more about them, too. Dad indicated she was sleeping with someone who could influence her findings – a boss, maybe?'

'Finn said she'd asked him for a divorce because she'd met someone and wanted to remarry.'

'That fits.' He clicked the mouse a couple of times, opening and closing emails. 'Maybe she was killed because she wouldn't alter the results.'

I processed that option and nodded. 'And probably by the same hired muscle who broke into Finn's house and assaulted us.'

Nick frowned. 'You two were lucky; you could've been hurt more.'

'I know. Maybe, though, we were unlucky from a

timing perspective. After all, if Sergeant Osborne had his way, Finn would've still been locked up.'

Nick's frown grew deeper. 'You're not suggesting the police—'

Was I suggesting that? The sergeant hadn't seemed to want to look at anyone other than Finn as a suspect and had spoken out of turn to Ray Cosgrove. No, that was laziness more than malice … surely …

Nick watched the thoughts flicking across my face with a wry twist to his lips. 'No,' I said emphatically. 'Of course not.'

'If you say so,' he said. 'I'll print these up too, and then we need to see if we can't find the maps.' He grinned at me, and despite our predicament, I had to admit I was enjoying myself. 'Maybe I should do Len a favour and drag these emails he deleted back out of the trash?'

'That's very public-spirited of you, Nick.'

'I thought so too.'

Sometime close to midnight, as I stifled a yawn, Nick excitedly said, 'Bingo!'

'You've found it?' I rushed into the kitchenette where Nick had unrolled another survey map.

He looked to me with a tired but triumphant smile. 'I have. Here are the mangroves – that area is cleared and marked as state forest. Our interest is in these pieces of land here.' He tapped at the map. 'This parcel that's adjacent to the state forest has a narrow water frontage'—he traced the path with his finger—'and this lot here backs onto it and would be the only viable access to Dolphin Point Road.' He lifted his gaze upward, his eyes searching mine. 'We need to know the owners of these two properties and whether they've been approached to sell.'

I took photos of the maps on my phone and stood aside as he rolled them into the tubes they'd come from and replaced them. Other than the box of Freddos – which was seriously depleted – you wouldn't know we'd been here.

As I wiped every surface we'd touched on Len's desk, computer and the filing cabinets, Nick disappeared into the meeting room and emerged with a bottle of red wine. 'What do you think?' he asked, holding it up.

'Well,' I mused. 'If we drink it, technically, that's theft.'

'Add it to the Freddos and the technical break and enter,' Nick countered. 'I don't know about you, but I need a drink. In fact, we deserve a drink.'

'As you say, we're already in trouble; we might as well make it worthwhile.' I pulled out two coffee mugs and held them out for Nick to fill.

We clinked our mugs together. 'What shall we toast to?' I asked.

'A successful expedition,' he suggested.

'That hasn't been without its trials and tribulations,' I added.

'Yet still, we got what we came for,' he finished.

We each took a long and satisfying drink. 'Thanks, Len.' I held my mug up to toast its absent owner. 'Not a bad drop.'

'Mind you …' Nick swirled the wine in his mug and sniffed it. 'Anything would taste good tonight.'

'True.' I lifted the bottle and squinted to read the label. 'Look at this. Apparently, it's the perfect vintage to pair with chocolate Freddos.'

Nick tipped his head back and laughed as if it was the funniest thing he'd heard in years. 'Did we get to the bottom of the Freddo quality control?' he asked.

'What's the tally?' We were keeping track of head-first versus feet-first on a scrap of photocopy paper.

'Yours was the only feet-first in the box.'

'So far,' I clarified cheekily, reaching for another chocolate. 'Yes! Feet-first!'

'God, I've missed you, Clem,' Nick said, still chuckling.

Heat rose to my face, and I took another gulp of wine. Without another word, Nick topped up our mugs.

'Why did you run?' Nick had waited until we were both settled in the kitchenette chairs before he asked.

'You know why.' I refused to meet his eyes. 'My mother died.'

'Okay, but why didn't you come back after the funeral? I'd asked you to marry me, and then you ghosted me.'

An image of that awful afternoon flashed through my brain – Kylie Lindsay and Nick in his bedroom. She straddled him, her blonde hair falling over his face like a curtain.

'I saw you, Nick – with Kylie Lindsay,' I said glumly, tracing the whale tail design on the coffee mug.

'I don't understand.'

Anger ran through me. 'I saw you – that afternoon. She was in your bedroom, and she was all over you,' I snapped. 'I'd just argued with Mum – she wanted me to go home to Melbourne, and I told her I was in love with you. I went to tell you, but you were with her, so I ran back to Rose, and she told me my mother had died.'

'Christ, Clem …'

'You know, for years, I blamed myself … that she died believing I'd chosen you over her, and that brought on the aneurism.' A tear slid down my cheek.

'Clem …' He reached out his hand to touch mine, but I pulled it away.

'And you were with her.' I swallowed more wine. 'I got it, you know. Your family would never have accepted me. Kylie was always supposed to be the one that united the two royal families of Whale Bay.' I stood, mug in hand and stalked around the small room. 'Kylie saw me and smiled – her cat-got-the-cream smile. We might have thought no one other than Maggie, Justin and Mike knew about us, but the look she gave me told me she knew how I felt about you and she wanted me to know she'd won.'

'I didn't see you—' he began feebly, his eyes wide with a mixture of remorse and guilt.

'No, you were otherwise occupied.' I leant against the

sink. Nick pushed his finger into his forehead, his frown deep.

'Nothing happened.' He held up his hand when I would have interrupted. 'I remember the incident, and I can only imagine what it looked like, but nothing happened. I was never interested in Kylie. Why did you never say?'

I shrugged. 'I was upset. You'd broken my heart, and my mother had died on the same day.'

'I tried to get in touch. Did Rose tell you?'

I nodded. 'She did. But I wasn't ready and then when I wanted to speak to you, you'd gone too. Indonesia, Rose said.'

Nick stood and leant against the sink beside me, his focus straight ahead. 'My father said he paid you to stay away.'

'Mike told me. Until I came back, I'd never properly met your parents, and I wouldn't have taken his money anyway.'

Turning to face me, he reached out, his finger catching a tear as it dripped off my chin. 'I shouldn't have doubted you, but ...'

'I'd gone away.' He nodded. 'And nothing happened between you and Kylie?'

He shook his head, his gaze unflinching. 'No. Nothing happened. She'd let herself into the house – you know how we never locked the doors.' I nodded. 'She came into my room and began telling me how she knew we were destined to be together. She was giggling and doing that hair flicking thing she does. Next thing I know she's pushed me back on the bed and was on top of me. I pushed her off and told her I wasn't interested. She finally left when I told her I was in love with you, Clem.' My chin trembled and my eyes filled. 'I know what it looked like, but I promise you, nothing happened. You should've said something.'

As tears spilled down my cheeks for all the misunderstandings and missed opportunities, Nick gently cupped my cheeks between his hands and lowered his lips to mine, kissing my top lip and then its partner. He tasted of wine and chocolate and … no. No. All the reasons we shouldn't be doing this crowded in my brain. There was Finn, our history, but mostly, there was the baby we had – the one I'd given away.

I shoved at his chest, the wine in the coffee mug I still held spilling on his T-shirt. 'I'm sorry, Nick, we can't.' I brushed at his shirt. 'I want you too, but we can't.' I forced a laugh. 'And certainly not here.'

Raising the back of his palm to his lips, he backed away. 'No, Clem, I'm sorry. I shouldn't have. It was just'—he shook his head—'that moment in the storeroom and now and'—he held his palms up—'you're with someone and I understand that.'

'It's all of those things but also …' Should I tell him? Could I tell him about our baby?

'What is it, Clem?'

'Rose was really my mother,' I blurted. 'She wasn't my aunt; she was my mother.'

'What?' He scratched the back of his head, frowning his puzzlement. 'What do you mean Rose was your mother?'

'I only found out a couple of weeks ago – after she died.'

'Who was your father?'

'I have no idea; I don't suppose I'll ever know. Rose went to England and came home pregnant. My parents had been unable to have children, so they adopted me.'

'How do you feel about it?' His eyes were full of concern.

'It explains a lot,' I said.

'Yeah, I imagine it does.' He sat back down and poured us more wine before glancing at his watch. 'I figure we have another few hours before we can get out of here, so if you want to try and sleep, I can stay awake.'

I shook my head. 'No, let's talk. We've got twenty-five years of catching up to do.'

At some point, I'd fallen asleep, my head cradled in my arms on the table. It was just after six when a knock at the front door woke me. Nick was sitting, his eyes closed, his head tilted back, his mouth open. He started awake at the second knock and, with his finger to his lips, stood and poked his head around the corner. 'It's okay,' he called. 'It's Justin.'

I stood and stretched, rounding and arching my back in a standing cow and cat yoga pose. I was vaguely aware of Nick speaking to Justin through the door.

'Justin said the cleaners should be here in the next ten minutes or so,' he said. 'We need to get this place cleaned up. He's opened Maggie's office door and left some clothes in there you can change into.' When I raised my eyebrows in a silent question, he said, 'Mags said you'd better get changed – no one would be used to seeing you in all black at this time of the morning.' Good old Mags.

I washed the cups and put them away. Nick wiped the empty wine bottle with a tea towel and placed it in the bin along with the empty Freddo wrappers. 'Why wipe it?' I asked.

'In case they don't empty the bin properly and it's evidence.'

'Fair enough. What about the empty box of Freddos?'

Nick grinned. 'Let's put it back where we found it.'

In the end, we escaped quickly and easily. No sooner did we hear a key in the lock than Justin called for the cleaner to come into his office. 'I'm glad I caught you,' he said. 'I've been meaning to get you to quote me to clean these carpets. Do you have a few minutes now for me to show you what I'm talking about?'

Nick grabbed the paperwork, and we snuck out the door and into Maggie's office. I changed clothes, and we were back downstairs within minutes, the printed emails and plans in my tote. While he returned to my house – where he'd left his car – via the beach, I ducked into Beach Brewz for a coffee.

Lainey eyed me with concern. 'You don't look great,' she said. 'No swim this morning?'

I shook my head ruefully. 'No. The spirit was willing'—I patted my tote—'but the flesh was weak this morning.'

'A heavy night?' There was an edge to her voice.

'Yes. Maggie, Justin and Nick Cosgrove came over – we were all friends back in the old days. Pizzas were ordered, and way too much red wine was consumed. When I snuck out this morning, Maggie was still snoring in bed beside me, and Nick was curled up on the lounge. I have no idea what time Justin left this morning, although him leaving was probably what woke me.' I laughed awkwardly, the way you do when you're hungover, and it hurts to laugh, and she relaxed and laughed with me. 'You'd better get me coffees to take back for them too. You know Maggie's order and Nick … actually, I have no idea how Nick has his coffee,' I said, my fingers crossed behind my back.

'That's okay, he ordered a long black yesterday, so I'll make him that. Have you heard from Finn?' she asked.

'He called yesterday afternoon to say he'd arrived safely and seen Tamzin's father.' My face fell as I recalled the pain in Finn's voice. 'It's going to be a rough time for him.'

'It will.' No one was in the queue, so Lainey could talk to me while the new barista, Savannah, made the coffee. 'If you're speaking to him today, can you pass on a message for me?'

'Sure.'

'Ailsa Jacks called – she's from Whale Bay Coffee Plantation – saying she tried his mobile but it must be a digit out as someone else answered it. This is her number.'

'No problem.' I took the slip of paper. 'I'll let him know. And thanks for the coffee.'

Picking up the cardboard tray, I began the short walk home. Whale Bay Coffee Plantation. Why did that ring a bell? As the front gate squeaked, it hit me – I'd seen the sign on the Bruce Highway. If memory served me correctly, the turn-off was very close to where Finn's car had been captured on Sunday. Was that where Finn was when Tamzin was murdered? And if so, why hadn't he told me?

CHAPTER TWENTY-FOUR

Cosmo and Beans greeted me ecstatically when I let myself in; Maggie took the coffee tray from me so I could bend down and give the dogs the welcome they craved. The poor things were completely out of routine and must be missing Finn.

Following a meaty smell, the dogs at my heels, I sauntered into the kitchen to see that Nick had made himself at home and was frying bacon.

'He said he does a good bacon sammie, and who was I to argue?' Maggie said in answer to my raised eyebrows.

'Sorry for taking over your kitchen.' Nick did not look at all sorry. 'Mags said you wouldn't mind and that you're the same as Rose and everyone helps themselves. Thanks for the coffee, by the way.' He pulled the paper cup from the tray and took a mouthful, sighing.

'Yes, thanks for the coffee.' Maggie grabbed one too, and left the tray on the cupboard. 'You guys must be starved.'

'You're welcome. I told Lainey that we'd all had a big night, and when I left, Justin had already gone to work, but you were still asleep in my bed, and Nick was on the couch. Pretty sure she bought it.' I wasn't ready to tell them about the message Lainey had given me for Finn. I told myself it was because it could be nothing, but the truth was I was concerned that wasn't the case. 'As for being hungry, I'm ravenous – although we didn't entirely starve.'

Nick chuckled and buttered bread. 'Brown sauce?'

'Absolutely!' Maggie grabbed plates from the cupboard and set them on the bench. 'What did you find to eat?'

'Freddo frogs. Len had a fundraising box in his bottom drawer. We also snaffled a bottle of red from the meeting room,' I said.

'There were others in the cupboard, so it will be a while before he misses it,' added Nick, laying bacon onto the buttered bread. 'And we put the empty Freddo box back where we found it.'

'For a man with type 2 diabetes, he had quite the stash of chocolates in there,' I said, bending to give Beans another head ruffle.

'When you think about it'—Nick turned and held out a plate—'we did his health a favour by eating them. Mags, here's your sandwich. Yours is coming up, Clem.'

'So now we just have to hope Justin keeps his nerve. That man is honest to a fault, and I know if Ted Winters were to ask him outright, he'd confess to everything,' Maggie said with an affectionate roll of her eyes.

'You can't talk.' I accepted the plate Nick offered me.

'Remember when we were brought in over that nail polish we nicked from the chemist?'

'How can I forget? We would've got away with it if Rose hadn't seen it and marched you down to confess.'

'And Ted only had to look at you, and you caved.' I laughed at the memory.

'How old were you?' asked Nick.

Maggie chewed her sandwich as she thought. 'I don't know … thirteen? Maybe fourteen?'

'We were certainly old enough to know better,' I said. 'And when Ted told us it might have been cheap nail polish, but to the owners, it might have been the day's profits … that really stuck with me.'

'And he said that if someone had been saving for it, they'd be disappointed to find it gone.' Maggie wiped her mouth with the back of her hand. 'It taught us about consequences and working for what we wanted.'

'It was certainly a lesson I've never forgotten,' I said. 'And'—I glared at Nick's back—'the last time I broke the law.'

'Well,' he said, running the pan under hot water, 'let's hope Ted doesn't ask you about last night.'

'Speaking of—' Maggie swallowed her mouthful. 'What did you guys find out?'

Nick leant back against the counter and took a bite of his sandwich, gesturing to me to speak. 'It's as we suspected. The boardwalk story is just a front.' Putting my plate down, I took a long swallow of coffee. 'We'll run you through everything later, but I've got the land references we need to get a search done on the ownership.'

Maggie shook her head. 'I know Justin really hoped they were on the level.'

'Doesn't he always?' I asked wryly. 'He's always quick to believe the best.'

'Even as he's fearing the worst.' She flashed a quick glance at Nick who held his free hand up.

'Hey, don't worry about me,' he said. 'I know what they're like.'

Still chewing on his sandwich, he put the plate in the dishwasher. 'Right, well, I'd better be off. It's walk of shame time.' His grin was cheeky. 'Oh, I've got dinner with the family tonight, so can we reconvene tomorrow?'

I nodded. 'Sure. After last night, I need to catch up on my sleep.' The look he gave reminded me of the moments we'd shared the previous evening. Heat rose to my cheeks. When Maggie looked between the pair of us and smiled knowingly, I ignored her. 'In the meantime, I have jobs for you and Siouxsie, Mags.'

'I'll do the property searches, but what do you need Siouxsie to do?'

'We need to know as much about Tamzin as we can – who she worked for at Hawksbill Solutions, what her position was, who will take over from her, what she does outside of work. Mostly, though, we need to find out who she was in a relationship with.'

'What has Finn said?' When Maggie asked the question, her eyes flicked to Nick again.

'He didn't know much about her at all,' I said. 'They'd barely communicated over the past few years.'

'Okay.' Maggie put our plates into the dishwasher. 'I'll get Siouxsie onto that. Right' —she bent and scratched Cosmo's head—'I'd better get out of here. Do you fancy giving me a lift home?' She directed the question to Nick. 'It'll certainly push home the story of our late night.'

'Good idea. If you're ready …' Opening the fridge, he took out a slice of cold pizza and took a bite. To me, he said, 'Let me know if there's anything I can do.'

I nodded.

Maggie kissed my cheek lightly and said, her eyes straying again to Nick, 'I'll call you later.'

As they left through the back door, Harry walked in, his eyes wide. 'It's true then?'

'What?' I said, busying myself with wiping down the bench Nick had already wiped.

'Lainey said you tied on a big night and Mags, Justin and Nick stayed over.' Over my shoulder, he took in the lounge with its pillow still on it.

'That's right. We ordered too much pizza; there's some in the fridge if you want.'

He examined me through narrowed eyes. 'You heard from Finn?'

Chuckling, I shook my head and patted his arm. 'Harry, it's touching that you're concerned about Finn and me, but there's nothing between Nick and me, okay? Finn is perfectly safe. Anyway, if I were you, I'd lay low – Justin knows you're seeing Siouxsie.'

'Justin has always liked me,' he said breezily, opening the fridge door and pulling out a slice of pizza.

'It's a different matter when his little girl's heart is at risk, and you've got to admit you have a reputation, Harry.'

His smile vanished, replaced by a grim, tight-lipped expression. 'It's different with Siouxsie.'

'Hmmm, she is still young and impressionable.' I grimaced as I said it – I didn't know anyone more able to look after themselves than Siouxsie. Judging by the expression on Harry's face, the heart that was at risk was his. Shaking my head, I said, 'Help yourself to more pizza; I'm going to take the dogs for a walk and call Finn.'

Clouds were forming on the horizon when I clipped the dogs' leads on and left the house. Popping my earbuds in, instead of crossing the road to the beach, we turned right and headed for the park and the path that would take us to the rock wall with the lighthouse at the end. Waving at Gordon Johnston, my neighbour and an old friend (and lover) of Rose's, I tapped on Finn's number.

He took a while to answer. 'Hey, you.'

'Hey yourself. You sound tired.'

'So do you. Are you out walking?'

'Yeah, I thought I'd take the dogs down to the lighthouse, although'—I grimaced at the awkwardness of the conversation—'the weather's a bit iffy; I think we might get some rain. It's actually a little cool when the clouds cover the sun.'

'Well, it is May.'

There was a brief silence. 'How's your father-in-law?'

Finn sighed. 'I'm not sure whether it's a blessing or a curse that his memory is so far gone. He keeps asking where she is; he doesn't remember we've separated'—he drew his breath in sharply—'and to be honest, Clem, I don't know if I'm helping or hindering. Her brothers seem grateful I've visited, although their wives are a bit … I don't know … like Kylie Cosgrove. I have no idea how Tamzin got on with them. They've already been through her house.'

'Her house? She really had settled in Brissie.' I paused as Beans sniffed and then cocked his leg against a tree.

'She bought a nice place down near the water. When I mentioned I wanted to look around, one of the wives got her nose out of joint. I had to remind her that technically, Tamzin and I were still married.' He hesitated and added, 'It doesn't look like she had a will.'

'I see. That could get nasty.'

'With her brothers? Yes, it could. Are you able to help me with it?'

'I don't know, Finn.' With deliberate slowness, I said.

'I'm not a probate lawyer, but as a family lawyer, if she died intestate, as next of kin, you inherit. I can get Maggie to get onto it for you if you like.'

'Thanks, Clem.' His voice, though weary, held a note of relief. 'I'm heading over to her place this morning to go through the paperwork, so I'll let you know if I find anything.'

'Okay. Have the great detectives been in touch?'

'Uh-huh. Just to tell me there's been no progress on Tamzin's death, but they managed to retrieve some fingerprints from the house break-in – a couple of characters they say are known to police in Brisbane. The theory they're working on is they were responsible for Tamzin's murder and that they're probably back in Brisbane already. They're also wondering whether the call they received to say Tamzin had been afraid of me was a fake. The number he left them to contact him on has been disconnected.'

'But who would do that?' I wondered aloud.

'Her murderer, perhaps. They concentrated on me for long enough as a result of that.' He paused, 'I suspect that was the intention – deflect suspicion onto me to buy them time to get away.'

'Do they know what they were looking for in your house?' While the theory made sense, there were still parts that didn't fit. 'And why kill Tamzin?'

'DS Osborne said it's likely Tamzin interrupted a drug deal – or something like that – and was killed to keep her quiet.'

'Right, but what was she doing out there anyway? Hadn't she said she was driving back to Brisbane? And I still don't understand why they turned your place upside down.'

'I don't know, Clem!' His voice rose, the words hitting me like blows. 'I'm telling you what they think, but I don't know! We might never know.' A sigh and then, in a more Finn-like tone, 'I'm sorry, Clem, but the questions … I can't deal with it at the moment. Just leave it, okay? The police know what they're doing.'

'Okay, I get that, and I understand you're going through a lot, but you don't have to do it alone, and you don't have to take it out on me.' I couldn't hide the hurt in my voice.

'I know.' I imagined him rubbing the back of his dark, curly hair the way he did when something confused or exasperated him. 'And I appreciate it. I miss you, Clem – you and the dogs.'

He'd only been gone a day, but it felt like longer. 'I miss you too, and so do the dogs, I think. Speaking of which, hang on a sec; it's plastic bag time.' I waited while Beans finished what he was doing and cleaned up after him. 'I'm back. Before I forget, Lainey asked me to let you know that Ailsa Jacks from Whale Bay Coffee Plantation called. She said she needs to talk to you, but the number you gave her doesn't work – someone else answered.' I waited for him to speak, but he didn't. 'Do you need her number?'

'No,' he finally said. 'I've got it and will give her a call. Thanks, Clem.' As I was about to ask whether he'd been at the plantation on Sunday, he said, 'I'm sorry, Clem, I've got to keep moving. I'll call you tomorrow, eh?'

'Sure, Finn. I'll talk to you then.' But he'd already hung up.

Sitting on the concrete plinth around the lighthouse, a dog on either side of me, I gazed out to sea. Whatever Finn was hiding from me concerned Ailsa Jacks – I was sure of it.

CHAPTER TWENTY-FIVE

Even though I was exhausted and should be trying to get some sleep, my brain was too full to rest. I'd filled the murder board with sticky notes and was staring at it, hoping to see connections, when Maggie phoned to say they'd heard nothing from Len yet about the keys, and didn't expect they would until Len confronted the cleaners this afternoon.

'Did anything happen between you two last night?' she asked.

'As a matter of fact, yes,' I said innocently. 'We got locked in an office and had to survive on red wine and Freddos.'

'You know that's not what I meant,' she said impatiently. 'I was sure I intercepted some looks this morning.'

'Oh, what sort of looks?' Two can play at this game.

'Don't play dumb with me, Clementine Russell Carter, whatever you call yourself now. *Loaded* looks. The sort of look that said there'd been a moment where more than loaded looks were exchanged.'

'Alright,' I conceded after a brief silence. 'There might

have been a moment, but we both realised it's ancient history, and I'm with Finn.'

'Who isn't here.'

'You and I both know that doesn't matter,' I chided softly. 'Anyway, we're friends now.'

'Clem,' Maggie began, her voice barely above a whisper. 'What really happened when you left?'

'What did he say?' I held my breath, waiting for her to answer.

'Nothing. He said nothing. At first, we all thought it was because of your mother, but then he suddenly upped and left, too.'

'It's a long story,' I finally said. 'And not one for over the phone during a workday. Anyway,' I said, 'I have biscuits to bake, so I'll talk to you later.'

'Biscuits? Why? Do you even know how to bake?'

'Well, may you laugh, Mags. I'll have you know I found Rose's old cookbook, and I'm going to bake Anzac biscuits for Ted and the team.'

Her chuckles gained steam. 'You're baking biscuits to take to the police station for what reason?'

'To say thank you, of course. They must constantly feel unappreciated.'

'Thank you, my arse,' she chortled. 'You're trying to bribe information from them.'

'Do you think it will work?'

'If my son is involved, probably. I wouldn't lead with

the thank you, though – Ted can smell a rat a mile off. It's best to be more straightforward with him. Tyson said the Brisbane detectives have left and word is they didn't endear themselves to anyone.'

'Thanks for that … I'll see you tomorrow?'

'Sure will. In the meantime, Siouxsie and I will get onto our jobs.'

'One more thing, Mags …'

'Yes?'

'Can you please do a search on a company called Ridley Hawke Developments? We need to know who the directors are. You might as well do one on Hawksbill Solutions too – the company Tamzin worked for. I'd be interested to see if the owners are the same.'

'Sure. Is this part of what you found out last night?'

'It is. I promise you I'll tell you everything when I see you.'

'Okay. Take care, Clem.'

'I will.'

On another Post-it note, I wrote *Ridley Hawke Developments. Who are they?*

Standing back, I examined the murder board. While it was now covered in yellow stickers and questions, there was no red wool, so no evidence connecting anyone to Tamzin's murder. Despite the documents we'd found last night, there were still many more questions than there were answers.

•

Tyson greeted me at the reception counter. 'I thought I'd drop these by.' I placed a tin full of Anzac biscuits on the counter. 'To say thank you.'

Tyson lifted the lid and sniffed appreciatively. Selina approached and stuck her head into the tin too. 'Yum, but what are you thanking us for?'

'Coming to the house so quickly the other day. It could've been much worse than it was.'

'Well, it's our job,' said Tyson brightly, reaching in for a biscuit, 'but we'll gladly accept the cookies. Rose's recipe?'

I nodded and casually crossed my arms.

Selina, however, was made of tougher stuff. 'What do you really want, Clem?'

'Well,' I drawled. 'I was just wondering if there's anything new in the investigation.'

'Which one?' Ted came out of his office, took a cookie from the tin and smiled knowingly.

'Are you telling me Tamzin's death and the break-in at Finn's aren't connected?'

'No, I didn't say that.' Sighing heavily, he lifted the end of the counter to create a walkway. 'You might as well come in.' Grabbing another two cookies, he said, 'Constable King, could you please get a coffee for Clem and me?'

'Right,' said Ted after I sat down and he was comfy behind his desk. 'What have you heard?'

'I've heard Osborne and Hall have gone back to Brisbane. I've also heard that the prints you found at Finn's place were owned by some men "known to police" and that they believe Tamzin was an accidental killing as a result of coming across a drug deal.'

Ted relaxed back in his chair, his hands resting on his comfortable stomach. 'You don't believe it.'

'No, I don't.'

Another sigh and then the beginning of a smile. 'And why would that be?'

I started listing the reasons on my fingers. 'Number one: what was she doing out at the mangroves that day? She'd told … From what I heard'—I quickly corrected myself—'she'd completed her survey of the area.'

'She'd completed her survey? The council only approved the survey on Friday night. Are you saying she was in town prior to this?'

'It's what I've heard.'

When Ted tilted his head to the side and trained his eyes on me, I felt the same as I had that day in the station when Maggie and I nicked the nail polish. 'We'll talk about that later,' he said. 'So you're questioning why she was there?'

'Yes. That's number one. Number two: there's no sign of her laptop or phone, and I think they're missing because it would tell you who she was meeting there and why. The laptop is important because it would show any correspondence she had with … um … anyone she was corresponding with about the survey.'

Ted ran two fingers across his mouth in thought. 'Are you suggesting she might have been engaged in correspondence with people such as'—he opened his hand outwards—'our mayor or, perhaps, our town surveyor?'

'I wouldn't like to suggest anything like that, Senior Sergeant, but if she was corresponding with anyone in this town, I'd hazard a guess that either – or both of them – would be likely candidates.'

Tyson knocked once on the door and entered, placing two mugs of instant coffee on the desk.

'Thanks, Constable King.' I gave him an appreciative smile, even though the I guessed the coffee would be barely drinkable.

'You're welcome. I heard you, my parents and Nick Cosgrove tied a big one on last night.' He chuckled. 'You'd probably be needing all the caffeine you can get today.'

Even though he made no reply, I could tell Ted noticed my blush by the slight narrowing of his eyes. 'Thank you, Constable.' He bobbed his head. 'That will be all.'

'So,' I continued breezily. 'Number two was the absence of the laptop and phone. Number three is: if this was just a random and completely accidental killing over a drug deal, why turn Finn's house upside down? Those two were looking for something, and if they had access to her vehicle, which we have to assume they did – after all, who else would've moved it – they'd have her laptop and phone. Number four – which is really quite similar to number three, now I think about it – how did they even know where Finn lived and that she'd been staying with him? Number five'—I tapped my pinkie finger with the opposite index finger—'actually, there is no number five.' I took a mouthful of coffee and cringed at the bitter taste.

Ted steepled his fingers under his chin. 'What does Finn say about it? I assume you have talked it through with him.'

Dropping my eyes, I mumbled, 'He told me to stay out of it.'

'But you can't.'

I shook my head. 'Did the pathologist find anyone else's DNA on her body?'

Ted hesitated briefly, then sighed resignedly. 'Yes, there were traces under her fingernails we hope to match against the men who assaulted you.'

'Fingers crossed. Is their DNA on file?'

He nodded. 'Yes.'

I raised my eyebrows. 'They really *are* known to police?'

'Let's just say they're not upstanding citizens and you and Finn were lucky. It could've been a lot worse.'

I opened my palms, seeing again the blood that had been on them. Waving that away, I had to stay on course with my questioning. 'Was Tamzin associated with any drug dealers?'

'Not that I've been made aware of. I will say, though, the questions you've raised are the same ones that have been concerning me, although I wasn't aware she'd commenced the survey.' Meeting my eyes and holding them, I knew the question that was coming. 'How did you know that?'

Hesitating briefly, I focused on my coffee mug, twiddling with the handle. 'It was something I'd forgotten Tamzin had said that day I saw her on the beach. We were talking about coffee, and I warned her not to get her coffee from Bron. She laughed and said she'd found that out last week.' When Ted didn't react, I clarified. 'She told Finn she'd only arrived in town that day, yet she implied to me she'd been here last week.'

'And the survey?'

'That might've been something I overheard,' I admitted.

'Or that Nick Cosgrove overheard.'

I looked up to see a small smile playing around his mouth. 'Maybe.'

'You've seen a bit of him, then?' Even though his expression was innocent, his tone was anything but.

'You mean last night? What Tyson just said?' He nodded. 'That was old friends catching up and too much red wine.'

'Except that as far as Whale Bay is concerned, you two weren't friends back in the day.' Was that pity in his eyes?

'You knew,' I said quietly.

'I have eyes.' He tapped the side of his head. 'The boy was upset when you left like that, and then next thing we know, he's gone too, and his father's not talking about why.' He lifted a shoulder. 'Two and two. Did Ray offer you money to stay away?'

Anger burnt at the back of my throat. 'What do you think?' I snapped.

Another of his enigmatic smiles. 'No need to throw your toys out of the cot, Clem. What do I think? The Clementine Russell I knew would've told Ray Cosgrove what he could do with his money. No, I think there was some other reason you stayed away and why Rose stayed away for that period, too. But I think Ray told young Nick he'd offered you money.' My silence led him to the right conclusion. 'Does Nick know?' he asked.

I didn't pretend to misunderstand him and shook my head emphatically. 'No one does. Anyway, he'll be gone soon.'

'I wouldn't bank on that,' he said.

'Jesus, Ted, do you know everything?' I couldn't help but laugh.

He lifted a shoulder. 'It's my business to know as much as possible.'

'Yes, well, if you know so much, how about you tell me what Finn was doing out at Ailsa Jacks' place on Sunday.'

'You know about that, do you? How'd you come by that information?'

I shrugged. 'Two and two.'

This time, when he laughed, it rumbled all the way up from his stomach. 'Touche. I shouldn't tell you this, but'— he picked up his second cookie and bit into it—'Rose's

Anzacs are a good incentive.' He chewed thoughtfully, seeming oblivious to the oaty crumbs that fell on his desk. 'He told DS Osborne that he was seeing Ailsa, and it wasn't something he wanted you to know about.'

Frowning, I considered this and then shook my head. 'The implication being he was having an affair with her? No, I don't believe it.'

Ted's expression was impassive. 'I didn't think you would, but DS Osborne did. There's no doubt he was out there, but the why is a question you need to ask him.'

'I have,' I said bluntly. 'And he won't tell me.'

'I'm sure he has his reasons.'

This time, I narrowed my eyes. 'Do you know?'

He shook his head. 'No, I don't, but nor do I think he was out there for romantic reasons. He makes coffee, she has a coffee plantation – maybe they were doing business?'

I shook my head again. 'No. If they were, there'd be no reason for him to keep that quiet.'

'Well'—another shrug—'that's a mystery for you to sort out.'

'You don't think it's connected to Tamzin's death?'

'I don't … and if you think it is, it follows you think Finn is involved, and it's already been proven that he can't have been in two places at one time.'

Was Ted telling me something without actually telling me? What did he want me to know or, rather, what did he want me to find out?

CHAPTER TWENTY-SIX

As I walked home, the thoughts in my brain jostled for position, but one thing I knew for sure was that Finn wasn't cheating on me. Pushing aside how close I came last night to doing exactly that to him, it followed that if he wasn't cheating on me and he and Ailsa didn't have a business arrangement, just two options remained. He was either protecting someone else – Tamzin, perhaps – or he was involved in something crooked with Ailsa. Given I refused to believe it was the latter, that just left the former. Was Tamzin somehow involved with Ailsa and the coffee plantation? If so, why wouldn't Finn discuss it? There was only one way to find out. I pulled my phone out of my pocket and dialled a number.

'Hey, Nick … feel like coming for a drive with me tomorrow morning?'

'Sure. Where?'

In the background, I heard chatter. 'Whale Bay Coffee Plantation – I'll explain in the morning. Where are you?'

'Grabbing a coffee with Mike and Angus. Where are

you?'

'I'm walking back from the police station. I needed to talk to Ted about something. Tyson made me a coffee at the station, but …' I made choking sounds. 'I think it's designed to get people to confess.'

'That bad, eh?'

'Worse. I'm calling in at Beach Brewz now to get something to replace the taste, so …' As I walked into the café, Nick stood, his phone to his ear. 'And you're here too.'

Laughing, I shoved my phone back in my pocket; I dropped by the counter, placed my order with Savannah, and made my way across to where the three men sat.

'Clem …' Michael Lindsay stood and greeted me with a kiss on my cheek. 'All good?'

I nodded. 'Absolutely. You?'

'Never better.'

'I didn't realise you knew Angus too.'

Before he could answer, Angus said, 'Yes, I met Mike in Brisbane once when he was down, and Nick was also in town.'

'Aaah, I see.' I turned back to the counter where Savannah was waving to get my attention. 'My coffee's ready, so I'll leave you three to it.'

'Why don't you stay and drink it here?' Angus gestured to the spare chair beside him.

Doing my best not to look at Nick, I smiled apologetically. 'I'm sorry, not this afternoon. But how are you placed tomorrow afternoon?'

'I have a few things to take care of in the morning, but I'm free in the afternoon,' he said with a wide smile. 'I'll get your number from Nick and message you when I know what I'm doing.'

'Sounds good. I'll see you guys later.' Ignoring Nick's frown, I gave them a little wave and left.

I was still greeting the dogs in the passageway when my phone rang. Somehow, while managing to get the coffee down on the sideboard without spilling it on myself or the dogs, I pulled my phone out and answered it. 'Ted, is there something you forgot to tell me?'

'Clem, someone broke into Tamzin's house in Brisbane today. It was torn apart in the same way Finn's had been, and the same fingerprints were found at the scene.'

'Is Finn okay?' My heart rushed to my throat as an image of him beaten and bruised from the last attack flashed through my mind.

'He is. He wasn't there at the time.'

I let out the breath I'd been holding. 'That proves it, Ted. Tamzin was involved in something that likely cost her her life; surely DS Osborne can't ignore that now?'

'Yes,' he said grimly. 'I think you're right and that's a line of investigation I'm sure they'll be pursuing.'

I didn't tell him that I wasn't so certain.

'On the bright side, though, Clem, it tells us that the likely perpetrators are back in Brisbane.'

'There is that. Thanks, Ted.'

What was it they were looking for?

I crossed to the murder board and wrote another question on a Post-it sticker, pinning it below the others I'd pinned earlier.

Where did Tamzin stay last week? Did that have anything to do with what happened to her?

When I phoned Finn he didn't pick up. I tried again a half hour later and again a half hour after that. Finally, at around seven, I messaged him:

Hi, Ted told me Tamzin's house had been broken into. Are you OK? xxx

While I saw the three little dots dancing away, indicating he'd read my message and was typing a reply, they soon disappeared. It was another hour before a response arrived.

I'm fine; the house is a mess. I'll talk to you in the morning. Are the dogs being a problem? x

I sent my reply immediately:

Let me know if you need me to come down and help tidy it up. The dogs are OK but missing you – as am I xxx

I held my breath as I waited for his reply. *Me too. I can't wait to get home. xxx*

Telling myself he was tired and probably feeling confused and overawed by his emotions – after all, what *do* you feel when the woman you haven't quite divorced dies in those circumstances – the dogs and I had an early night.

Friday dawned cool and cloudy as if whoever controls the seasons had decided that maybe it was time to let autumn have her way. With the sun not up until after six these days, my swims had to be later to avoid dawn and prime shark feeding time. I took the dogs for a walk along the beach and left them with Lainey at the café while I went swimming.

As happened on Wednesday, Nick's morning swim coincided with mine, but this time, I welcomed him matching me stroke for stroke, pushing me to swim faster. By the time we emerged back onto the sand, I was panting.

'You've still got it!' He had both hands on his hips as he drew a breath in.

'So do you.' I picked up my towel, quickly rubbing the excess moisture off me before donning my heavy towelling poncho. 'It's colder out than it is in.'

'Nearly wetsuit time?' he asked with a teasing smile.

'Never!' I shot back.

We walked across the road to the café in companionable silence. 'Are you coming in for coffee?' I asked, stepping out of the path of a power-walker.

He shook his head regretfully. 'No, I don't want anyone to talk. We can get away with being seen together occasionally, but not every morning – and not in your boyfriend's café. I'll get it from Bron this morning.'

'Brave man.' I was grateful for his thoughtfulness in protecting me from gossip.

'Not really. I'm craving one of her sausage rolls and

even she can't stuff up a tea bag in hot water.'

'You'd be surprised.' I couldn't help but laugh at his trust in Bron's tea-brewing skills.

'What time do you want to head out this morning?' We stood on the footpath outside Beach Brewz.

'I need to drop in and see Nina – even though she doesn't need me to – so I thought we'd leave about ten?'

'Okay, I'll pick you up from there if you like?'

I nodded. 'Cool. See you then.'

He turned and left. Cool? Seriously, Clem.

Nina greeted me with a hug. Although she was shorter than me – like Rose, she was just a few inches over five feet – she was surprisingly strong. Her embrace felt almost as if she was passing some of that strength to my body. It was enough to have me blinking back grateful tears.

'I'm sorry I haven't been in for a few days,' I said, pulling away. 'Is everything running okay with the business? Do you need me to—'

'Clem!' With a peal of laughter, she held up her hands. 'Stop. The shop is fine. As I said the other day, as much as we love having you around, we don't need you.' She tilted her head to the side. 'And you've got more to be concerned about than our cash flow. Although,' she added, 'while you're here, I do want to run something past you.'

'Go on,' I urged, even though I knew she didn't *really* need my input on what she was about to ask.

'The Whale Festival kicks off each year with a street fair and a blessing of the whaling fleet at the wharf, and I was thinking this year we should nominate to have a stall.'

'Sounds good. When's that? July?' The humpbacks began coming through here on their annual migration in June, with the whale-watching season running from July to mid-October.

'Yes.'

'Okay, go for it. I'll push ahead with the journals we were talking about the other day, and we can sell them as well as other stock.'

'I was thinking'—Nina hesitated—'of offering readings too, both tarot and your astrology.' She watched me closely for a reaction. 'You know you can do it.'

Although Rose had taught me all she knew, I hadn't looked at an astrology chart in the twenty-five years I'd been away from Whale Bay. Yet since I'd been back, I'd been dabbling again, the language almost second nature. It was as if Rose was in the background, talking to me and instructing me as she used to.

'You're right,' I finally said. 'I'm teaching it in our workshops, so yes, I'll do it. In fact, we might start sooner rather than later with a stall at the weekend markets. Let me think about that a bit more though.'

'That's great. Now, how's Finn?'

I sank into the chair behind the counter. 'Oh, I don't know,' I admitted. 'Things are …' I lifted my shoulders and my palms. 'Things are … not the same. It's almost as if a switch has been flicked, and everything has changed. I know he's got a lot he's dealing with, but I would've thought that would bring us closer rather than force us apart.'

'Is that what's happening?' Nina asked in a hushed tone.

'It certainly feels like it.' I sighed. 'Maybe it all happened too quickly between us, maybe it was meant to burn out, but I really thought …' I shook my head, frustrated I couldn't articulate my thoughts and hurting at Finn's rejection. 'It doesn't matter.'

'Who's this Nick Cosgrove I've heard about?' Nina bustled about getting the cash float ready for the day.

'He's Martin's twin. We used to be friends.'

'Rose mentioned him occasionally. The way she spoke of him showed she thought highly of him.'

'She did.' Through the haze of memory, I pictured dinners at Rose's, the three of us – Nick, Rose and myself – talking for hours about astrology, the environment, the sea, our dreams for the future. 'She always thought well of him, even after … well, even after he left town.'

'And now he's back.' Something in her inquisitive tone made me wonder if Rose had told her about our relationship.

'Yes, but not for long. In the meantime, he's helping work out what his father has in mind for the mangroves.'

She nodded her approval and pushed the till drawer closed. 'That's good. Ecosystems like that can't be lost to development. Do you think the murder is linked to that?'

'The police don't …'

'But you do.'

As I nodded, the door opened and Bella stepped in. 'Clem, we've been so worried!' She rushed over to the counter. 'We heard Finn had been arrested, and then someone said you were helping with enquiries and everyone knows that's what they say just before they arrest you, and then the next thing we hear is Finn's house has been broken into and he's in hospital, and then he's gone and—'

'Whoa!' I held up my hand to interrupt Bella's flow. 'Yes, it's been quite the time, but no, I wasn't arrested, and I'm so sorry I haven't checked in with you guys.'

'As I was just telling Clem, we understand, don't we, Bella.' Nina looked hard at the teenager until she nodded.

'Are you investigating?' Bella asked avidly.

'These things are best left to the police.' While Bella seemed disappointed by my answer, Nina wasn't taken in by my evasion and raised her eyebrows.

'What are you up to today?' Nina asked, straightening some bookmarks on display.

'I'm heading down to the coffee plantation – the one just past the Dolphin Point turn-off. Finn was talking to the owner on a business issue the other day, and with him away, I thought I'd …' I looked to the starry ceiling for inspiration.

'Help out?' finished Nina, her green eyes twinkling.

'Yes.' I glanced at my watch. 'We probably should be open.'

Bella trotted back to the door and obediently turned the sign from Closed to Open. As she did, Nick strode through with a confident spring in his step.

'Oh,' I said. 'You're early.'

'Sorry … I can come back,' he offered, eyes darting around the shop.

'No, it's okay. Nina, Bella, this is Nick.'

Bella's eyes were wide, whether because of how Nick looked or because a Cosgrove was holding his hand out for her to shake.

'Bella, it's lovely to meet you. Clem was telling me about your design work and what you've done with the social media.'

Under his scrutiny, the teenager's olive skin took on a pink hue.

'And Nina, I've heard a lot about you too.' As Nick's eyes met Nina's, he took an involuntary step back. 'I'm sorry,' he said. 'For a second, you reminded me so much of a younger Rose.'

'I had the same reaction,' I said. 'Then I decided it must be the dungarees.'

Nick nodded slowly. 'I'm sure you're right. Are you ready to go?'

'I am.' Picking my bag up, I said, 'I'll check in tomorrow some time.'

'Be careful,' Nina said, her expression serious.

'I will.'

I walked through the door and outside, but before it had time to close, I turned back. Nina was still watching us, a thoughtful expression on her face.

CHAPTER TWENTY-SEVEN

'How was dinner?' I asked as we drove down Beach Road and turned left to head out of town.

'Yeah, good, I suppose.' He chuckled shortly, one hand on the steering wheel, the other resting on the window frame. 'If good is listening to my brother big-noting himself and Kylie prattling on about nothing.' He shook his head. 'I used to wonder what Martin saw in her—'

'You mean other than the obvious?' I hated the resentful edge to my tone.

'If you like the obvious.' He shrugged. 'These days, though, I must admit they're perfect for each other.'

'The Crown Prince and Princess of Whale Bay,' I said derisively.

'Pretty much. I know he's my twin, and we have similarities in looks, but sometimes I can't help but wonder how we grew to be so different. As for Dad …' He shook his head once. 'On second thoughts, let's not talk about my father. And, enough about my family. How did you go with the police yesterday?'

I told him what I'd discovered from Ted and also about Tamzin's house being broken into.

He let out a low whistle when I was done. 'The police can't be still thinking Tamzin's murder was random?'

'You'd think not, but they seemed determined to label it as such.'

His fingers tapped against the steering wheel. 'On the upside, those two goons are obviously back in Brisbane.'

'Yes.' Again, an image of Finn's attacker flashed through my brain. His amber eyes had haunted my dreams for the last few nights. 'Yes, that's a relief, although they haven't been able to arrest them yet.'

A short silence followed, both deep in thought. 'What's Nina's story?'

'She arrived here in a combi van with nothing very much to her name, and Rose gave her a job. She's got a good heart but doesn't talk about herself much. I know she lost her parents a few years ago and went off the rails a bit as a result, but other than that, I think she'—I shrugged, struggling to find the right words—'sees things … or knows them.'

'Do you still have those dreams?' Nick sent me a sideways glance.

I turned to look out the side window, not wanting to be under scrutiny. He remembered. Other than Rose and now Nina, he'd been the only person I'd ever told. He hadn't laughed then, and he wasn't laughing now.

'Sometimes,' was all I said, still watching the trees fly

by. 'For years I either didn't have them—'

'Or didn't notice them,' he suggested quietly.

'Or that,' I conceded. 'But when Rose died'—I swallowed hard—'I saw that. And Tamzin—'

'Did you see her too?'

'Not really. Not in a dream. Nina and I pulled some cards on Saturday, and I saw an image – hair and currents and tree roots … that sort of thing.' I should've been embarrassed to admit it, but this was Nick. I swivelled back to face the road. 'It didn't make any sense and then—'

'You found her.' His knuckles had tightened on the wheel.

I nodded.

'Are you saying you think Nina is like that?'

'No … yes … I don't know. I know she's the most insightful tarot reader I've come across. Part of that could be Rose's teaching – you know, the whole "I'm not predicting the future, but let's talk about what you need to be aware of" sort of thing. The way she taught me to read charts – challenges and possibilities with the rest being free will.'

'Did you keep up with that when you left?'

He didn't take his eyes off the road, but the muscles in his forearm were flexed as if talking about the years apart was difficult for him.

'No. I threw myself into my studies and then into my career. I was,' I added without conceit, 'I am good at what I do. In fact, Maggie has asked me to come in with her – apparently, you have to go to the Sunshine Coast or Brisbane if you want a decent divorce.'

He chuckled. 'Is there such a thing?'

'There can be.' I paused and looked at the map on my phone. 'We need to turn here; the farm should be about five hundred metres up to the right ... here.'

We'd driven across a cattle grid and were travelling up a dirt road when the black Hilux came hurtling towards us. When it became clear there wasn't room for both of us on the track, Nick slowed and veered off the road. As they passed us, my eyes met those of the driver. I'd remember those amber eyes anywhere – and that scar. I'd seen them only last night in my nightmare.

'Nick! It's him!' Swivelling in my seat, I caught only the first few letters of the licence plate through the dust they'd left in their wake. 'The one who attacked us!' I pulled my phone out of the console where I left it. 'I'll phone Ted and let him know. Bugger, I only have one bar.'

Nick laid a hand on my arm. 'Clem ...'

'What?'

Nick's jaw was firm, his frown deep. 'That can wait. We need to get to the farm. Those idiots were up here for a reason.'

'Ailsa?'

He nodded soberly and restarted the car.

At the top of the track stood an elevated white timber house with a corrugated roof and a wide verandah wrapping around most of the structure. A little further behind the house was a corrugated shed, and it was from these doors that a woman holding a cricket bat emerged.

'This is private property,' she yelled. Her stance was wide, her work boots planted firmly on the ground, the bat raised high in a threatening gesture.

Nick and I exited the car, our hands held up in front of us. 'Ailsa Jacks?' I called out. 'My name is Clementine Carter. I'm a friend of Finn Marella.'

The bat lowered slightly. 'Finn mentioned you. Do you have any identification?'

With a shaky exhale, I managed a strained, 'Yes, hang on.' Scrolling through the screens on my phone, I found my driver's licence and held it out.

'Put it down there.' The woman pointed to a patch of dirt halfway between us.

Doing as she said, I laid the phone on the ground and stepped back beside Nick. Ailsa – assuming it was Ailsa – picked up the phone, examined the photo on the licence and lowered the bat. Shoulders relaxing, she handed the phone back to me. 'Sorry about that, but …'

'What did those goons want?' I asked, taking in the surrounding area, the farming equipment and sheds.

Ignoring my question, she inclined her head towards Nick. 'Who's this?'

Nick held his hand out. 'Ailsa? I'm Nick Cosgrove.'

Immediately, she raised the bat again and took another

step back, almost disappearing into the shed.

'I thought you said you were friends with Finn,' she cried, flailing the bat around her head.

'I am!'

Nick realised what the problem was before I did. 'Ailsa, please … If you've had any problems with my father or brother, you need to know I'm not involved with the family business.'

'You're not?' While I couldn't see her expression under her wide, felt hat and dark sunglasses, there was scepticism in her tone.

'He's not, Ailsa. I promise.'

'What do you want?' she asked, allowing the bat to dangle by her side but not fully relinquishing it.

'Were those idiots here looking for something Tamzin might have left with you?' I asked. 'Tamzin did stay here last week, didn't she?'

Nick's eyes widened in surprise.

'How did you know?' Ailsa asked.

'I didn't until I saw that pair in the ute.' I turned to look back down the road to where the dust was barely visible. 'I recognised the driver as the one who broke into Finn's house and attacked him.' Turning back to Ailsa, I continued. 'Given that Tamzin's house was broken into yesterday, I assumed they found your address and came here today looking for whatever it was they thought Tamzin might have left with you.'

She licked her lips before nodding.

'You and Tamzin were in a relationship, weren't you?' I added gently. 'That's why Finn was out here on Sunday – because he wanted to meet you.'

Again, she nodded. 'Perhaps you'd better come into the house.'

CHAPTER TWENTY-EIGHT

Nick and I followed her up the timber stairs. Ailsa toed off her dusty boots before stepping onto the polished floors, and Nick and I did the same, automatically turning them upside down the way she did.

Leaving her hat on a row of hooks in the hall, Ailsa retied her ponytail and pushed her sunglasses to the top of her head. Without her hat and sunglasses, Ailsa's appearance was striking. With her strong jaw, chiselled cheekbones in a tanned face, and a stripe of silver hair down the centre of her otherwise dark hair, she had the appearance of a woman who could stand up for herself – something that had been demonstrated when she'd waved that cricket bat at us. She led us into a surprisingly modern kitchen and pulled three coffee mugs from an overhanging cupboard.

'Coffee?'

'Did you grow it?' quipped Nick, hovering by the door.

A faint smile and, 'Yes, I did.'

I gazed around the room as she busied herself with the coffee machine. A massive white marble-topped island dominated the room, with four white-seated bar stools tucked under it. Soft grey shaker-style cabinets sat above a corrugated iron splashback and double-width free-standing stove.

'Take a seat,' Ailsa urged, gesturing to the stools.

'What a great idea to build a bookshelf into the island.' I squatted and ran my fingers along the spines. Cookbooks filled the shelves under the bench's overhang.

'That was Tammy's idea.' Ailsa's voice broke at the mention of her late partner. 'I cooked, but she *loved* to cook.'

'Have you two been together for a while?' I returned to standing and gentled my voice.

'Yes.' Ailsa placed mugs in front of Nick and me and, cradling her own, leant back against the work surface beside the stove where the coffee machine stood. 'We met at work – I'm an agronomist – in Sydney almost five years ago. Growing coffee had always been my dream, so when my father passed away two years ago and left me this farm, I took the plunge. He'd kept cattle, but this area used to be coffee, bananas and sugarcane. The land is perfect for it, but my great-grandfather replaced the coffee in the early 1940s – it wasn't profitable anymore. Anyway, Tammy was all for it. For the first year or so, she travelled up here every few weeks, but then last year, she got a new job in Brisbane, so we saw each other more often. She lived down there during the week and came here each weekend.' Ailsa smiled to herself. It was a sad smile that hinted at the depth of her loss. 'She knew Finn lived in Whale Bay, but our relationship wasn't something she was ready to go public with.'

My heart hurt for both women having to navigate life's obstacles. 'But surely these days … I mean, love is love …'

'Yes, you'd think so, but Tammy worried about her father, and how her brothers would take it, but when this commission came up, she proposed to me. "It's time," she said.' Ailsa's eyes filled with tears and she chewed at her bottom lip. 'So on Saturday, she saw Finn, told him about us and asked for a divorce. She was heading to Brisbane on Sunday to tell her brothers …'

Her voice trailed off, and she took a large mouthful of coffee. Nick reached for my hand and squeezed it briefly, somehow knowing how much their story affected me.

'Finn came here on Sunday.' Alisa smiled again. 'I knew who he was, of course. Tammy had spoken of him, and whenever I was in Whale Bay, I'd drop by and get my coffee from Beach Brewz. It's how I knew who you were too. I saw you there one day and knew you two were dating. Anyway, Finn was so *genuinely* happy for us. He told me about you and how he'd stuffed up by not talking to you about his marriage, and we talked about how we might collaborate in the future.'

'How did you find out she'd been killed?' I quietly enquired.

Tears ran freely down her cheeks. 'When she didn't phone to let me know she'd arrived home okay, I worried but told myself she might have forgotten, or her phone was out of charge or something. But when I didn't hear anything from her on Monday, I rang Finn. He hadn't heard from her either. And then'—she swallowed hard—'he didn't call me back and'—a little sob—'it was on the news on Monday night. When they said a man was helping police with their enquiries, I knew it had to be Finn, and I knew he couldn't have done it.'

'Because he was here with you,' I guessed.

She nodded. 'I rang the police and told them Finn had been with me.'

'They assumed he'd been seeing you on the side, and Finn was protecting Tamzin's memory by not putting them right.'

When her shoulders began to shake, I was out of my chair and took her in my arms, holding her as she sobbed. 'I'm so sorry,' I said into her hair. Nick also stood and walked across to the far wall, his eyes caught by the framed map that hung there.

Sniffing again, Ailsa stepped out of my arms and reached into the pockets of her jeans for a tissue. 'Sorry about that; it comes in waves.'

'Don't apologise,' I said. 'You're holding up so well in the circumstances. Did those men threaten you?'

She nodded, wiping her eyes. 'The one with the scar said they'd found my address at her place and wanted to know if she'd left anything with me. I told them'—her voice broke again—'that I knew her in Sydney, that we were friends but I hadn't seen her in ages. Then I said she'd phoned me and she'd be doing a job up here in the next week or so and we'd made arrangements to catch up, but hadn't managed to do so.'

I gave a slight nod of approval. 'That was quick thinking.'

'Did they hurt you?' Nick's jaw was tight, his lips pursed.

'No. I think they would have, but the one with the scar rang someone and told them what I'd said about not having seen her, and he must have told them not to bother with me. They didn't seem to know we were'—another half sob—'together.'

'Probably just as well,' Nick muttered. He was still looking at the picture on the wall. 'Have you seen them before?'

She shook her head. 'Not those specifically, but some like them.'

'Is this land yours?' He pointed to the map on the wall.

'Yes,' Ailsa said. 'We have the land down the road and a portion on the other side of the highway.'

Frowning, I walked across to where he stood.

'This piece that butts onto the edge of the mangroves?' Nick pointed to an area on the map.

'Yes.'

Suddenly understanding, I nodded. We'd seen the same map the other night in Len's office.

'Has anyone made you an offer to buy this land?' asked Nick. Ailsa nodded. 'Let me guess, the other men who visited began coming after you refused the offer.'

She nodded again. 'Yes.' The set of her jaw told me the visits hadn't been pleasant.

'Who made you the offer?' Nick's face was like stone, hard and unyielding.

'A third party made the original offer,' Ailsa said. 'They said they were acting on behalf of a client with very deep pockets. When I said I didn't intend selling, they seemed to accept it and I heard nothing for a week or so. I'd almost convinced myself it was some scam, and then a man turned up here in a big, flashy car, a Mercedes. He even had a driver.'

'Do you know who he was?' Nick turned to face her.

'He introduced himself as Branden Greene. He said he was an environmentalist—'

The slightest lift of Nick's eyebrow let me know the name was one he recognised.

'He said they were acquiring a patch of land next to the mangroves and needed my plot to run an access road through. The only patch there is this one that used to be owned by my great-grandfather's business partner.' She pointed to the relevant spot on the map. 'Greene said he wanted to buy the land to protect it from development. He said that's what he did, protected land from overdevelopment. He talked a big game, but there was something about him … maybe he smiled too much.' She chuckled to herself. 'I'd been with Tammy long enough to know what was what when it came to that, and it sounded to me like he was green-washing a fancy development that would be anything but environmentally sound. I asked about the mangroves, and he said all of that was taken care of, that the council was on board and they'd be protected too.'

Nick grimaced, mimicking her thoughts.

'This land here—' I pointed to the waterfront section adjacent to the mangroves. 'Do you know who owns it now?'

'No, I'm sorry. But if it helps, this whole portion'—Ailsa traced the lines of the map from the highway around the state forest and down to the water—'used to be owned by my great-grandfather and his business partner. When they decided not to grow coffee any longer, the partnership was split. We were left with this farm and the small strip off the Dolphin Point Road that Branden Greene wants to buy from me. I know it's not good for anything, and I probably should sell it to him, but I always thought the government might need it some day as an access road into the mangroves or an extension of the state forest. I certainly didn't want to sell it to someone like Greene who, despite what he said, I don't think, has the best interests of the land in mind.'

'If that's the case,' I said, mentally filing what she'd said, 'what answer did you give him?'

'I told him I'd consider his offer and would let him know.' She hesitated, crossing and uncrossing her arms. 'I think that's who Scarface rang today – Branden Greene.'

'Why do you think that?' I asked.

'Because when he was off the phone, Scarface told me my thinking time was almost over.'

'I see.'

'You reacted when you heard my name earlier. Why was that?' Nick asked. When she hesitated, Nick added, 'It's okay. Nothing you can say will surprise – or upset me.'

Ailsa nodded. 'Branden Greene told me the council was on side, so I took that to mean he'd done a deal with your father or Bob Lindsay – or both. Then, the following day, I was in Whale Bay doing some groceries and saw him talking to your father.'

Nick sighed and lifted a shoulder. 'I can't say I'm surprised. When did you say this was?'

She twisted her lips. 'A week or so ago. A few days before Tammy began the survey. I told her about it, and she went quiet on the phone. Then she said not to worry; she was sure it had nothing to do with the survey she was doing; it was just coincidental.'

'Did you believe her?' asked Nick.

'No, and I don't think she believed it herself. When I asked her later, she again told me not to worry, but on Thursday, she suggested I might want to reconsider selling the land. She mentioned Branden Greene would ensure the land was used for the right reasons, and the price he was offering would set us up well. She said she'd resign, and we'd open the café here that we'd been dreaming of and do our own roasting. That's when she said we'd get married. We were going to discuss it when she returned from Brisbane. I can't do that without her.' Again, her voice faltered, a choked sob replacing the words she couldn't say.

'Ailsa,' I gently rubbed her back. 'I know it's hard, but can you recall if Tamzin said anyone was pressuring her at work?'

Ailsa lifted her head and frowned. 'Do you mean sexually harassing her?'

'No,' I said emphatically. 'I'm talking about someone putting undue pressure on her to arrive at a particular finding.'

Ailsa scratched the back of her head, then swiped at the tears. 'Not that she mentioned to me. We rarely talked about her work.' Pain flickering across her face. 'I thought she might have been seeing someone else, though.'

'Do you know who?' Nick asked.

'No. And it might have just been a feeling, but I thought she was back in touch with her ex.'

'Finn?' I wondered aloud, frowning.

'No. There was someone before me – a man – who took their break-up hard, but she never wanted to discuss him other than to mention he'd sparked her interest in the politics of conservation. I gathered he was a fellow environmental scientist.'

'What else do you know about him?' Nick asked.

'Nothing, she never wanted to speak about him, although I think I saw him once. We were at a conference – even though we were together, we'd attended separately, if you catch my drift.' We nodded. 'Anyway, Tammy was worried he might be there. She said he attended the previous year. I was on high alert – you know how there's always a curiosity about your partner's past—'

'Especially if it's one they don't talk about,' I observed wryly.

'Exactly. So when she saw someone and reacted strangely, I took notice. Later, she told me it was her ex she saw – the one she left for me.'

'Would you be able to describe him?' I asked.

'It was a while ago, but I remember he was very good-looking – if you like that type, of course. He had twin dimples – one in each cheek. Also, even at that distance, I noticed his eyes – they were so grey as to be almost silver.'

Again, Nick's eyebrow lifted. 'Are you sure it was her ex you'd seen?'

She shrugged. 'Tammy didn't point him out, so I can't be sure, but when she gasped, I turned around to look, and he was the only one it could've been.'

'When was this?' Nick moved from one foot to the other.

'We hadn't been together for long, so I'd say it was almost five years ago. It was at the Sofitel in Sydney – super glitzy – but I can't remember now who had sponsored it.'

'What makes you think they were communicating again?' I asked.

Ailsa wrinkled her nose and bit at her lip. 'It was a feeling I had rather than anything she said. Messages she'd ignore when they came through that normally she'd say something like "Oh, it's so-and-so, darling, I'll deal with them later." These she'd read and then turn her phone over so I couldn't see the screen. Also, she changed the password on her phone.'

'Because she thought you might read the messages?' I guessed.

A little, almost imperceptible smile touched her lips. 'Well, obviously, I tried.'

'But she proposed …' I said with a gentle smile.

Ailsa nodded, her own smile watery. 'I know. It was unexpected. I'd been so sure she was going to break up with me – it's so easy to be paranoid when you're in a remote relationship, let alone one where you're being kept secret.'

'Okay, thanks, Ailsa. One last question – did Tamzin leave anything with you for safekeeping?' I was clutching at straws, but it had to be asked.

She shook her head sadly. 'No, I'm sorry. But if I find anything, I'll let you know.'

A ragged breath hitched in her throat. 'I'll also phone the police and tell them about our relationship.'

Squeezing her shoulder, I said, 'I think that would be a good idea.'

CHAPTER TWENTY-NINE

After our goodbyes and back in the car, I called Ted on speaker and told him we'd seen my attacker at Ailsa Jacks' house. 'I still didn't have a good look at the other one, but Ailsa did, and she confirmed the vine, ivy, or whatever it was on the back of his hand. I recognised the one with the scar, the one that hit Finn. They were in a black Hilux,' I said. 'I didn't get the whole rego number, but I got the first three letters.'

'Thanks, Clem, that matches the information we have on him.'

'Ted,' I said, my voice laced with worry, a knot forming in my stomach. 'Tamzin and Ailsa were in a relationship, and if that becomes known, Scarface and his mate will be back. Speaking of which, why can't you tell me his name? I can't keep calling him Scarface.'

'You know why I can't tell you,' he said. 'At this point, neither he nor his partner can be charged, so until such time that they are …'

I glanced across at Nick. 'I know … Is DS Osborne

looking at them for the murder?'

A brief silence filled the cabin. 'I'm sorry, Clem. The DNA under Tamzin's fingernails doesn't match either of them. Plus, they have alibis – two men answering their description were stopped for speeding by highway patrol on the Gold Coast within the window that we believe Tamzin was murdered. They might have broken into Finn's and Tamzin's house and menaced Ailsa Jacks, but they couldn't have murdered Tamzin, and there's no evidence connecting either of them to Tamzin.'

'Other than they're looking for something they believe Tamzin has left behind.' Hearing the frustration in my voice, Nick took one hand from the steering wheel and patted my arm.

After I hung up, I turned to Nick. 'If Scarface and his mate didn't do it, who did? Branden Greene? They're obviously working for him.'

'Yes, but it doesn't follow that he has anything to do with anything other than wanting to buy Ailsa's land and develop the waterfront near the mangroves. Besides, men like that don't get their hands dirty.'

My heart broke for Ailsa. She and Tamzin had been given a glimpse of happiness, only to have it cruelly ripped away. As we turned up Beach Road towards my house, I said to Nick, 'What do you know of Branden Greene? Could he be the BG your father was talking about?'

He nodded. 'He could be, but he's well known in

conservation circles for all the right reasons.' His jaw was set. 'So much so that I can't believe he's involved with this development. I can't believe he's involved in development full stop.'

'People do compromise their beliefs if the price is right,' I pointed out.

'Greene is not one of them. He's loaded. From what I've been told, he made his money in technology, and he's passionate about the environment. If he is involved in this development, maybe it is above board.'

'Maybe,' I mused. 'Have you ever met him?'

He nodded. 'Once, several years ago in Cairns, Angus introduced me to him. Greene was sponsoring the study Angus was working on. He's also promised finance for Angus' next project.'

Dimples. Silvery eyes. Could it be? We'd pulled up outside my house. 'How well do you know Angus?' I asked.

'I thought I knew him very well.' He turned in his seat. 'You recognised Ailsa's description too. I wouldn't place too much stock on that; thousands of men must have grey eyes and twin dimples.'

'Who are also environmental scientists? I'm wondering whether he's the ex who got Tamzin interested in the environment. The description Ailsa gave certainly fits Angus. And he said the reason he went to Scotland was because he'd had a bad break-up. What if the person he'd broken up with was Tamzin?'

My phone beeped with a message. 'Speak of the devil,' I muttered. 'I just got a message from Angus; he's caught up in something and can't meet me this afternoon. Bugger, I was going to ask him outright if he knew Tamzin.'

'It's probably just as well that you're not meeting him then,' Nick's face was grim. 'I'd like to hear what Siouxsie and Mags have discovered before we talk to Angus who, for the record, I trust.'

'Fair enough.' I unclipped my seatbelt and opened the door. 'See you back here tonight?'

He nodded. 'I'll be here.'

Sliding out of my seat, I held the door open. 'By the way, what were you and Michael talking to Angus about when I saw you at Beach Brewz?' When he shook his head and lifted his palms, I said, 'Nick?'

'I'm sorry, Clem. I can't tell you. I will, though, as soon as I'm allowed.'

Anger bubbled up, my body tensed for battle. 'Are you serious? After all we've done over the past couple of days – I even broke the law for you – and you're keeping secrets from me?'

With a sigh, he ran his hands over his face, pushing back his unruly hair. 'I'm sorry, Clem, I've promised Mike. I can't.'

'Whatever!' I slammed the car door and stomped up the path. As I let myself into the house, his car was still outside. I refused to watch it leave and crouched with my arms open to welcome the dogs into them.

At least you knew where you stood with dogs.

While Harry (with the help of Cosmo and Beans) worked outside on the deck's construction, I spent the next couple of hours researching Branden Greene and found nothing contradicting Nick's impression of the man.

A self-made (multi) millionaire, Branden Greene was a true philanthropist and passionate about the environmental and conservation projects he supported financially. He married his childhood sweetheart, with whom he had two daughters who work overseas with environmental organisations. Conservation and sustainability were, for the Greenes, a family affair.

If his online presence was to be believed, the worst he could be accused of was using helicopters to travel distances within Australia – to which he'd responded that, where possible, he flew commercial and hired cars. Nick was right; this man was unlikely to be involved with anything even slightly dodgy. Maybe we'd got it all wrong? Maybe this development was something to be welcomed rather than something to fear. Yet the plans Nick and I had seen in Len Hartog's office showed a marina built too close to the mangroves and whose activity would threaten that ecosystem. Let alone the impact of the access roads and the development itself.

Then I googled Angus and again found nothing to

concern me. His socials were full of images of him and his colleagues working on windswept coastlines in Scotland with the occasional cute puffin. There certainly weren't any photos of him with Tamzin Griffiths.

A little after four, my phone rang.

'Clem, it's Angus … Listen, I know I've stuffed you around today, but any chance of catching up now?'

'Now?' I glanced at my watch. 'There won't be anywhere open for coffee.'

'I know, but I would like to see you … How about the surf club? We can have a quick drink.'

'Well …' The temptation to ask Angus about his relationship with Tamzin was too strong. 'Okay, although it will need to be a quick one, I have something else on tonight.'

'I promise I won't keep you.'

'In that case, I'll see you in twenty minutes.'

CHAPTER THIRTY

When I arrived, Angus had already seated himself at a table on the balcony overlooking the beach. It would be cool once the sun went down, so I'd changed into jeans and thrust my arms into an old, soft denim jacket before leaving home. While sitting outside was pleasant, I was glad of the jacket's warmth.

'I hope you don't mind'—he greeted me with a handshake—'but I got you a glass of white wine; I noticed that's what you were drinking the other night.'

'Thank you for that.'

We talked about how the day had turned out to be quite lovely despite the cool start and how warm the ocean was despite it being late in the season until I said, 'I really enjoyed your talk the other night. It's obviously a subject you're passionate about.'

'Thanks. I meant what I said – once they're gone, we can't get them back.'

'You don't know what you've got till it's gone,' I quipped.

He returned my smile and held up his glass to clink

against mine. 'Cheers to that. Let's face it, environmental concerns fly out the window once developers get their hands on pieces of land like this. Look at what almost happened with the Daintree Rainforest. That was all about opening the area up for development at the cost of losing the oldest tropical rainforest in the world. I wish I'd been around for those protests.'

I settled back in my chair, crossing my legs at the ankles. 'My Aunt Rose was. I remember her telling me about it. How each winter they tried to build the road through to Bloomfield and each summer it was washed away when the rains came. The best part of the story she told was how, when they finally got the road done, the bigwigs opened the road and began travelling up it, but then the rains came early and they got bogged.' I chuckled. 'Karmic, really.'

'Or'—he tilted his head to the side—'the land taking care of itself?'

I lifted a shoulder. 'Perhaps. But out of those protests, the Daintree was heritage listed – even though back then, the Queensland government fought the proposed heritage listing. It's a different story these days, though. No one would stand for development on state land or desecration of a protected mangrove area.'

'Unless you can get a tame environmental scientist to provide data that shows the mangroves have retreated.' He eyed me across the top of his beer. 'Someone like Tamzin Griffiths, perhaps.'

I frowned. 'What do you know about Tamzin?'

Casting his eyes around to ensure no one else was in hearing range, he said, 'Only what my sister has told me.'

Choking on my wine, I straightened in my chair. 'Your sister knew Tamzin?'

'Yes. My sister Callie is the human resources manager of Hawksbill Solutions, the company Tamzin worked for. They'd also become friends and Tamzin had sought her advice over some'—he raised his eyes to the sky as he thought—'undue pressure she was coming under.'

'In relation to the survey?'

Angus nodded. 'She told Callie that she'd been commissioned to complete a study in the town where her husband lived. She was excited and said she intended to ask him for a divorce – something she should have done years ago. She'd met someone she wanted to marry and couldn't wait to begin their lives together. The problem was, she'd been asked to fiddle with the results from the survey.'

'Did she tell Callie who was pressuring her?'

'No. All she said was that this person was in a position to ruin her career and her life. Callie asked if it was her manager, the company CEO, but Tamzin said it wasn't. Cal got the impression it was someone even higher up the food chain.'

I snorted a short laugh. 'There's not many more levels above CEO.'

'No, there's not. Cal pushed her, but Tamzin wouldn't

tell her anything else.'

Absently, I traced the condensation on my glass. 'Did your sister take what she knew to the police?'

He nodded. 'She told the police – a DS Osborne? He took the details, but Cal got the impression he wasn't very interested.'

'I see.'

'There's more.' Angus hesitated, pressing his lips together. 'It's no coincidence I'm here in Whale Bay right now.'

'I figured that; Nick said he called you.'

'He did, but I was going to be here anyway. I was worried about Tamzin, and, as it turns out, I had good reason to be.'

I had no words. All I could do was stare at him, open-mouthed. Was this where he was going to tell me he'd known Tamzin too? Was Angus the ex who had taken the split so badly?

'Cal had told Tamzin what I do for a living, and a couple of weeks ago, Tamzin asked Cal if she'd give her my number; she had something she wanted my advice on. She knew I'd been on projects in Far North Queensland where similar issues had arisen, so I agreed.'

'Was this the first time you met Tamzin?'

He frowned. 'Yes, why?'

'I just wondered whether—' I shook my head. 'It doesn't matter. So you met Tamzin?'

'Yes, just the once – the week before last. She told me about the survey and said her partner owned some land adjacent to where the survey was being conducted and that someone had approached them to sell it. She didn't think it was a coincidence.'

'Did she tell you who wanted to buy the land?'

'No, but when Nick called to tell me he'd heard the council were planning on putting a boardwalk in there—'

'Surely the boardwalk wouldn't be a problem,' I interrupted. 'After all, it would allow more of the community to share the area without impacting it.'

'True, but Nick didn't believe that was what the council intended, nor do I. So even though I'd intended to be here to support Tamzin, I told Nick I'd help him raise community awareness around the importance of biodiversity in mangroves.' He took another mouthful of his beer.

'Angus,' I began. 'Why did you want to meet with me?'

He smiled wryly, a glint in his eye. 'Mike Lindsay told me you'd recently investigated your aunt's death, and with your boyfriend involved in this one'—he shrugged—'I thought you might want to get to the bottom of it.'

'The police have it in hand,' I reassured him.

He scoffed at that. 'You don't believe that any more than I do.'

I lifted a shoulder. 'Perhaps.'

Angus pinched his chin between his thumb and forefinger, his brow furrowed. 'Why did you ask me if I'd met Tamzin before?'

'Because I had reason to believe you'd been involved with Tamzin in the past.' I didn't hold back my words; they were as sharp and direct as a knife.

'Involved as in involved in a romantic capacity?' His eyes were wide, reflecting surprise.

'Yes.' I sat straight, my eyes holding his.

'Why would you think that?' he asked after a brief silence.

'Because her partner told us—'

'Us?'

'Nick and me.'

He raised his eyebrows. 'What did this person say?'

'That Tamzin had been involved with someone else before she began a relationship with her current partner, and this person didn't take the break-up well.'

Angus' expression didn't change. 'I still don't understand why you thought it was me.'

'The man she'd been involved with was interested in environmental concerns, and Tamzin and her current partner saw him at a conference. The description she gave matched yours.'

He frowned. 'I'm baffled. None of that makes sense. You're saying that a man fitting my description was presumed by Tamzin's partner – whose name you're also withholding – to be Tamzin's ex.'

'That's right.' Put like that, it did sound convoluted.

'How did the description match me?'

My face was suddenly burning. 'They said the man was very good-looking, dimples in each cheek and silver or light grey eyes. And he was an environmental scientist who was quite political about conservation.'

He shrugged. 'That certainly sounds like me.' He grinned. 'Especially the very good-looking part. How long ago was this?'

'Almost five years ago. The conference was at the Sofitel, if that helps.'

He pressed a forefinger into his forehead. 'I recall attending a conference there – a couple, in fact – but whatever Tamzin's partner thinks, I've never been involved with her. Had Tamzin pointed me out?'

'No,' I conceded.

'Then why does her partner think it was me?' Angus wore his confusion on his face.

'Apparently, Tamzin saw her ex and reacted in a way that concerned her partner, but by the time she turned around, yours was the face she saw.'

He lifted a shoulder. 'That may be the case, but as I said, I've never met Tamzin before the other week.'

The more we discussed it, the more tenuous the connection seemed. I turned towards the ocean, tapping my bottom lip with my fingernails. As the sun set, a gorgeous pink and lilac light was cast across the water.

Turning back to Angus, I asked, 'Do you know

Branden Greene?'

Again, he frowned. 'Yes, of course. He's funded a few of my projects. He's made his money in tech but is giving back through conservation projects. But what's he got to do with this?'

'Branden Greene was trying to buy her partner's land'—I hesitated briefly before deciding just to say it—'and his company is interested in developing the land next to the mangroves.'

Angus stared at me for a few seconds and then shook his head slowly. 'No. Branden doesn't have a development company. He wouldn't do that.'

'Not even if there were millions to be made?'

He shook his head again, more emphatically this time. 'Not at the cost of the environment. Do you have any evidence to support this?'

I looked away with a slight shake of my head. 'Not yet.'

'That's because there is none.' He stood and pushed his chair back in. 'Look, I know your partner was accused of Tamzin's murder, but Branden had nothing to do with it. And he has nothing to do with what's happening in the mangroves. Yes, he's rich, but he has integrity. I'm sorry, Clem, you seem very nice, and I know Nick and Mike both think highly of you, but you're on the wrong track.'

I had to make him believe me. 'Tamzin's partner identified him as the man who had approached her to sell her land.'

He scoffed. 'Is this the same partner who identified me as Tamzin's ex?'

Ignoring the comment, I continued. 'And today, the same man who broke into Finn's house and assaulted us and the same man who broke into Tamzin's house turned up at Tamzin's partner's house, making veiled threats about how she needed to sell the land. He had to be working for Branden Greene.'

'Are you sure?'

'About Greene wanting to buy the land and about his plans for the mangroves? Yes. I'm absolutely positive.'

He pulled his chair out and sat back down. 'Have you told the police this?'

'No. As I said, I have no evidence; it is just a supposition.'

Angus reached behind his neck and grimaced. 'He couldn't have had anything to do with the murder, though – he was attending a conference in Brisbane last weekend. He was the keynote speaker. I saw him myself.'

'I'm not suggesting that he did,' I said quietly.

'What's the name of the development company he supposedly owns?'

'Ridley Hawke Developments.' I watched his face closely, but his expression didn't change.

'Have you completed a company search of them?'

'My friend Maggie is completing one – she should have the results now. In fact'—I noticed the time on my phone—'I should be going …' My phone rang, the caller ID showing it was Harry. 'If you'd excuse me for a second … Harry? What's up?'

'Clem, you need to get home. I've just caught a couple of dickheads in a black Hilux trying to break into your place.'

My heart jumped into my throat. 'The dogs … are the dogs okay?'

'Yes, they're fine; they were around the back with me. Some guard dogs, though; these guys were in the kitchen when I noticed them from the deck. I'd been using the circular saw so didn't even hear the gate opening. I don't know who was more startled, me or them. That's when the dogs noticed; they didn't hang around after that. I've called Ted, but—'

'I'll be there in ten minutes.' I rang off and placed a hand on my chest as if that could slow my heart and concentrated on calming my breath.

'What's wrong?' Angus placed a hand on my arm.

'The two men who assaulted Finn just broke into my house.' An unpleasant thought occurred to me, and before I could think about it, I blurted out, 'Did you tell anyone you were meeting me this afternoon?'

'What? Of course not! You can't possibly think I lured you down here so a couple of dickheads could break into your house?' He looked so affronted I immediately felt terrible.

'God, I'm sorry.' My hand went to my forehead. 'I no longer know what to think.'

With a grim expression, he urged, 'Come on, I'll drive you back.'

'No.' I waved his help away. 'I can walk.'

'Clem,' he said through gritted teeth. 'I'll take you. That is if you trust me enough to get in the car with me.'

'Don't,' I said, shaking my head. 'I've already apologised for jumping to conclusions.'

His eyes met mine, his darkening to almost pewter. Finally, he nodded. 'Okay, I probably would in the same circumstances. Have you got your bag?' I nodded. 'Let's go.'

CHAPTER THIRTY-ONE

A police car was already in the drive when Angus and I pulled up; Maggie's car pulled in behind us.

'How did you know?' I asked as she got out of the car.

'Tyson called me, of course.'

Nick was the next to arrive. When I glared at Maggie, she shrugged. 'And I called Nick.'

Nick slammed his door and rushed across to me, frowning when he noticed Angus. 'Are you okay?'

'I'm fine; I wasn't at home.'

'She was down at the surf club with me,' said Angus, folding his arms.

'I didn't think you could meet today.' Nick narrowed his eyes, one fist balled.

'My afternoon freed up – it was a last-minute thing.' When Nick looked at me and raised his eyebrows, Angus added, 'She's already asked me if I told anyone we were meeting, and I told her I didn't.'

'Who had kept you busy?' Nick's eyes were almost navy with barely controlled anger.

'What the …?' Angus laughed, but Nick continued to glare at him.

'You said earlier something came up and you couldn't meet and now you're suddenly free?'

'You're serious?'

'Those two dickheads work for Branden Greene, and come to think on it, so do you, so yes, I'm deadly serious.' He ground the words out slowly. 'Are you sure you didn't mention meeting Clem to Branden?'

'Of course I'm sure. I was doing some work at The Haven, so I might have been overheard when I called Clem, but I certainly didn't tell anyone – why should I?' As the two men squared up to each other, Angus' face had reddened, the colour returning to normal as he looked between us. 'You guys really are serious.' I nodded. 'And about Branden?' I nodded again. 'Did they kill Tamzin?'

'The police don't believe so.' Nick's eyes still held Angus'. Maggie watched in wonderment, seemingly captivated by these men and their egos.

'But you believe Branden has them looking for something they think Tamzin left behind?' he guessed. When Nick inclined his head, he added, 'Why break into Clem's place?'

'My guess is they know Clem is in a relationship with Finn and thought he might have left something at her place for safekeeping.' Nick finally relaxed his stance. 'So you two have been at the surf club?'

I laid a hand on Nick's arm and felt his muscles relax under it. 'Angus told me how Tamzin had contacted him a couple of weeks ago.'

Nick's eyebrows flew up.

'And before you ask, that was the first time I'd met her,' Angus said wryly.

I shrugged. 'I had to ask.'

Ted and Tyson came down the front stairs, Harry and the dogs behind them. When the dogs saw me, they ran to my side, and I crouched down to cuddle them both.

'It's all clear in there,' said Ted. 'I don't think they had time to do any damage.'

'Except to my nerves,' laughed Harry uneasily.

'Clem, Nick,' Ted beckoned to us. 'Can I have a word?'

'Sure.' I turned to Angus. 'Look, I really am sorry I thought the worst; it just seemed like one more coincidence in a heap of coincidences.'

He nodded. 'Don't worry about it. As I said, I probably would've thought the same. I'll leave you to it.'

As he turned to leave, Nick called out to him. 'Thanks for bringing her back here.'

'What? No apology from you?' Angus chuckled.

'Nope.' Nick's jaw was firm, and his posture over me was protective.

Feeling awkward and suddenly hemmed in, I stepped away from him. 'Where's Siouxsie?' I asked Maggie in an effort to drag attention away from myself.

'Closing up at work. She'll be over soon.' Maggie grabbed my elbow and steered me away from Ted. 'Len asked Justin about the keys today. I think Len believed Justin – although, frankly, it was a good thing I was around because otherwise, he wouldn't have held his nerve. Also'—she cast her eyes around furtively—'there's been an emergency meeting called for the council this afternoon.'

The back of my neck prickled, and I rubbed my arms against the cool of the evening. 'Do you know what it's about?'

She shook her head. 'No, but Justin will come by when they're finished.'

'Clem!' Ted had his arms folded, one hand tapping the other elbow impatiently.

'Coming,' I called.

'Are you finished with me, Senior Sergeant?' asked Harry.

'Yes, Harry, you can go. Maggie, you can make yourself useful and make coffees while Clem checks to see if anything is missing.'

'Thanks, Harry,' I said. 'For everything.'

He grinned his sunshiny, toothy grin. 'Life's certainly interesting with you around. I'll catch you later.' With a pat for the dogs and a wave, he was off.

Obediently, we all followed Ted back into the house.

'We've got a locksmith on the way to fix that.' Ted pointed to the front door lock. 'They didn't have to work hard to get through it. If you're going to stay around and continually get into trouble, you might want to think about putting in a proper security door.'

'I love this door.' I ran my fingers over the white wrought iron reindeer that, while incongruous for this part of southeast Queensland, had always been part of the charm of Rose's beach cottage. 'But I will get a proper lock put on it.'

'See that you do.'

I wandered through the house, checking that everything was in order. As we entered the living room, I deliberately ignored the throw-covered easel holding the murder board. Ted noticed with a small smile on his lips but didn't comment.

'Nothing seems to be missing,' I finally said. 'It was lucky Harry was here.'

Ted motioned for Nick and me to sit on the lounge. He took a seat opposite us. 'Alright, you two,' he began. 'What was all that about?'

'All what about?' I asked innocently.

'That little show of chest-puffing,' he said sternly, his eyes on Nick.

'It was nothing,' Nick said.

'It didn't look like nothing from where I stood. I thought for a minute I'd need to send young Tyson in to stop a fight.' As he continued to stare at Nick, Nick seemed to shrink. 'As for you, Clem, why would those two want to break into your house in the first place?'

Fighting the temptation to do as Nick had done and regress into a guilty teenager, I sat taller, my chin tilted out. 'What I want to know is how hard is it to find two dickheads in a black Hilux? They're not exactly hiding.'

Tyson turned away, but not before Ted saw his smile. 'Something funny, Constable?'

'Not at all, Senior.'

Maggie came in with a tray of coffee and took her time placing them on the coffee table and finding enough coasters to go around.

Ted shook his head. 'Enough. You're only going to listen in anyway, so you might as well take a seat too.'

Beaming angelically, Maggie complied, making herself comfy next to me.

'Now, I want the full story this time. What did Ailsa Jacks tell you?' Ted leant forward in his chair.

'Have you spoken to her?' I countered.

'We have. She told me she believes the two men who menaced her were working for Branden Greene ...'

'That's our understanding, too,' I said. 'Although we can link Scarface – the one with the scar – to Branden Greene, there is no evidence suggesting Greene ordered the break-ins.'

'But, surely—' began Nick.

I shook my head. 'We have nothing that would stand up in court.'

'I agree,' said Ted sombrely. 'Do you have any idea what it is they're looking for?'

'None at all,' I said, not quite meeting Ted's eyes.

'Are you sure about that?'

Unable to look at Nick, I said, 'All we know is that Tamzin had been hired to complete a survey on a piece of land. She told Angus Jones—'

'The environmentalist Nick was just squaring up to?'

'Yes. Him. Tamzin told him there'd been some influence applied on her – she didn't tell him who by – to doctor the results of the survey, to make it appear as though the mangroves took substantially less land than had originally been estimated.'

'For what purpose?'

'This is where conjecture begins,' I said.

Ted nodded slowly and sat back in his chair, cradling his coffee. 'But presumably, that conjecture has something to do with why our council is contemplating putting a boardwalk through the mangroves and why Ailsa Jacks is being pressured to sell her land.'

'Yes. I suspect – and again, I'm only surmising – that whatever it is Scarface and his mate are looking for would provide us with the evidence we need to link Branden Greene with Tamzin Griffiths.' I picked up my coffee mug and took a sip.

'Why would Branden Greene be involved? He's a multimillionaire and, from all accounts, an environmentalist.'

Tyson spoke up.

'I can't answer that, but why else would he want Ailsa's land?' said Nick. 'And Ailsa saw him in town one day talking to my father.'

Ted chuckled. 'I know you don't have many reasons to think well of your father, son, but while he bends the rules from time to time'—Nick scoffed—'everything he does is strictly legal. Now'—he eyed Nick keenly—'what was going on between you and Angus Jones? My sources tell me he's a friend of yours and Michael Lindsay's.'

Something passed between Ted and Nick, something I didn't understand, something Ted obviously knew that Nick was hoping he'd stay quiet about. Did Ted Winters know *everything* that went on in this town?

'Branden Greene has financed studies for Angus in the past, and I was concerned that Angus might have arranged to have Clem out of the house so Branden's goons could have a look around. It was too much of a coincidence they turned up when they did. Also'—Nick glanced at me—'Ailsa had given us a description of a man who she believed had been involved with Tamzin several years ago, and that description matched Angus.'

'Clem?' prompted Ted.

'I put that to Angus, but he told me he hadn't met Tamzin until she contacted him recently. I believe him. As for why they thought the house was empty? They might have been watching me, and Angus conceded someone could've overheard his call to me. He was at The Haven, so maybe CCTV can help identify who was in there when he was.' Tyson scribbled in his notebook. 'As for why they were here at all, the only thing I can guess is that I'm Finn's girlfriend, so they might think he'd left whatever it is with me.'

'Hmmm.' Ted pondered that. 'Whatever it is they're looking for, they seem desperate to get it. What worries me is they may try to get in here again. When's Finn back?'

'I'm not sure,' I conceded, ducking my head.

'I can stay here,' offered Nick. 'On the lounge, like I did the other night,' he added.

'Of course, the night you all drank too much red wine and ordered pizza from Pizza Boyz,' Ted said lightly but eyeing us keenly. 'Do either of you have anything to add?'

When we shook our heads, he put his coffee mug on the table and stood, groaning a little as he straightened his limbs. 'Before I go, Len Hartog said he thinks someone might have been in his office over the last few days and'— he turned his gaze on Maggie—'Justin thinks someone has been in his office too. Do you two know anything about that?'

'Us?' I looked across at Nick who shrugged. 'Why would we know anything? Was anything taken?'

'From Len's office? It doesn't appear anything of value is missing.' Ted's eyes flicked between us. 'And the only thing taken from Justin's was Len's keys.'

I frowned. 'That's unusual.'

'I thought so.' Ted pursed his lips and scratched his head. 'And there's nothing to steal in Len's office – unless you're interested in plans and maps.' He pulled his cap on.

'It doesn't sound as if there'd be any reason to be in his office, then,' I said.

Ted nodded as if he believed me. 'I expect you're right. I told Len it was likely some kids had broken into Justin's looking for money – him being an accountant and all – and all they found were the keys to Len's office. And in Len's office, they found nothing but chocolate frogs.'

'Chocolate frogs, you say?' said Nick.

'Len's not supposed to be eating chocolate, I thought,' said Maggie.

'Well, if that's the case, whoever took the frogs did his health a favour. Now, stay out of trouble, you two, and'— he gestured towards the covered murder board—'leave the policing to us. Constable?'

As they prepared to leave, the screen door was flung open, and Siouxsie flew in. 'What have I missed?' she asked, her breath coming in quick gasps.

'Nick and Clem will fill you in,' said Ted with a wink in our direction.

'He knows,' said Nick wryly once the police officers had left.

'Is there anything in this town he doesn't know?' I said.

'If there is, it isn't worth knowing,' said Maggie.

'Well,' said Siouxsie, 'he doesn't know what happened

to Tamzin. Speaking of which'—she removed the wrap covering the murder board—'we've got some catching up to do.'

'I'll get the drinks,' I offered.

CHAPTER THIRTY-TWO

'So Tamzin was living just down the road for a year and never let Finn know?' Maggie shook her head in wonder.

'Are we sure Ailsa had nothing to do with her death?' Siouxsie tapped her marker pen against the pad of yellow stickers she held.

'She has no motive.' I sipped at my wine. 'They were just about to get married, and everything they'd waited for was about to happen.'

'So she told you,' said Siouxsie. 'Did you believe her?'

Nick nodded. 'She was devastated. Also, inadvertently, Finn gave her an alibi when she gave him one.'

'I hate to even suggest it,' Siouxsie began, 'but—'

'Don't go there,' I warned. 'Finn had nothing to do with this.'

'All I'm suggesting is, what if Ailsa found out Tamzin was seeing someone else? She might have been angry and jealous – it could've been an accident.' Siouxsie was persistent.

Maggie stepped forward and examined the board with

a thoughtful expression. 'Siouxsie might have a point. The police haven't looked at her for this—'

'Mainly because they didn't know she existed,' said Nick. 'She was calling them, though, so they'll at least have to check out her story now.'

'Exactly,' said Maggie. 'If we look at it logically, all we know is when Tamzin was on the highway. She and Finn were picked up on the same part of the highway minutes apart. How do we know she turned left to go to the mangroves and not right to Ailsa's as Finn did?'

'Because she was found in the mangroves,' I reminded them.

'You're right.' Siouxsie sighed her disappointment.

I walked across to the board and the map we'd pinned there, tracing the route with my finger and contemplating the possibilities. Maybe …

'As much as I hate the idea,' I began slowly. 'Siouxsie could be onto something. What if Tamzin left for Brisbane as she said she would but called into Ailsa's on the way? Ailsa confronts her about being back in touch with her ex—'

'Maybe she's been having an affair with him,' suggested Maggie.

'Maybe.' Something she said was pinging in my brain, but I couldn't quite grasp hold of it. 'Let's say she's having – or at least Ailsa suspects she's having an affair. While they've been together for several years and are planning a future together—'

'Although we only have Ailsa's word for that,' reminded Nick.

'Perhaps, but Tamzin told Finn she was remarrying, and that's why she needed the divorce,' I said. When Nick nodded, I continued. 'Ailsa confronts Tamzin, and they argue. Maybe she falls and whacks her head on something. While we didn't see inside, I'm sure there are heaps of things she could whack her head on in that shed.

'Finn turns up, and everything gets a bit chaotic. Ailsa asks Finn to help her move the body. Ailsa knows the pressure Tamzin's been under regarding the survey and knows if the body is dumped there, it will make it look as though her death had something to do with the survey; Finn's car might not be able to access the area, but Ailsa's certainly could. Then what? Finn helps her dump Tamzin's car, taking her phone and laptop to reinforce the idea that her death is linked to the survey.'

I found myself nodding as I spoke through the scenario, my heart falling as I realised it could have happened like that, that someone like DS Osborne could see it as happening like that. Something was missing, though. Taking another sip of wine, I read through each of the stickers I'd put on the board over the last few days. 'She drowned,' I muttered. 'She drowned,' I said more loudly. 'The official cause of death was drowning, so she must have still been alive when she was in the mangroves.'

'Maybe Ailsa only thought she'd killed her, but Tamzin

was actually still alive when her body was moved,' suggested Maggie.

'If this is how it happened,' Nick said thoughtfully, 'it's not linked to the survey and the development. It could also explain what Scarface and his mate are looking for: Tamzin's laptop and phone.'

'And evidence of undue pressure to alter the survey results,' I said bleakly, walking across to the lounge and sinking into it. Cosmo rested her head on my leg, and as I patted her with one hand and sipped the wine I still held in the other, I couldn't help but picture the scene. It all made sense, but even so, something stopped me from believing that was the way it happened. It wasn't just that (for Finn's sake) I didn't want to believe it, but *something* else. Something more concrete than an unwillingness to believe the guilt of the man I … loved. But did I love him? I cared about him and *thought* I was in love with him. Everything had moved so quickly, and so much had been happening and changing in my life that maybe I'd been caught up in the heightened emotions of it all.

My gaze was drawn to Nick. Nick's return had brought up feelings I'd thought I'd buried in the deepest of black holes, yet somehow, they'd resurfaced and had confused everything I thought I knew for sure. And one of those things I'd known for sure was that Finn could not have been involved in this. And if Finn wasn't involved, Ailsa couldn't have been either.

Determinedly pushing that aside, I ran through other possibilities, barely registering the chatter of the three around the murder board. It still felt as though the murder and the future of the mangroves were linked, but as I reminded myself, feelings wouldn't stand up in court. If not Finn and Ailsa, who? And why? Downing the last of my wine, I prised Cosmo's head off my lap and stood. 'We need to find this ex-boyfriend of Tamzin's,' I said, pouring more wine into my glass and topping up Maggie's. 'I think he's the key to this. Siouxsie, how did you go with Tamzin's socials?'

Siouxsie opened the laptop she'd brought with her. 'Not very well. She was quite a private person, ridiculously so. While she has a Facebook profile, she hasn't posted in several years. She's been tagged in some photos at conferences – the most recent one was just a month ago. I've made a list.' She handed me a sheet of paper.

I pointed at the top of the page. 'This must be where Ailsa said she saw Angus. The timing is right, and the Sofitel is tagged.' I turned to Nick. 'Maybe we can ask Angus who he remembers being there?'

'If he's still talking to us,' Nick said ruefully.

I lifted my shoulder and pinned the list to the bottom of the board.

'I had to go back six years to find anything interesting,' said Siouxsie with the air of someone about to drop a bombshell. 'I went through the socials of people who'd tagged her attendance at conferences, and even though she wasn't tagged in this post, I think this is Tamzin.' She clicked on a photo she'd saved on her laptop.

The photo was taken on a boat, with Sydney Harbour Bridge in the background. Tamzin – it was Tamzin – was laughing, her hand to her face as if preparing to try to tuck the lock of hair that had escaped her ponytail behind her ears. A dark-haired man had encircled her waist with his arms, his face buried into the side of her neck.

'This is him,' I breathed. 'The ex. I don't suppose you can make the image any larger.'

Siouxsie shook her head. 'No, I lose clarity when I do, but the watch he's wearing looks quite distinctive.'

'And expensive.' Nick peered at the screen. 'Way too expensive for an environmental scientist's salary. Trust me on that.' He chuckled.

Something beat at the back of my brain. 'I feel like I've seen this watch before,' I said.

'Do you know where?' Maggie asked.

I shook my head.

'The only other clue I got from this'—Siouxsie wore a cat-got-the-cream expression—'was I matched the dates up to this conference in Sydney.' She pointed to an item on the list. 'Maybe if we can find matches for the attendees …'

Maggie looked doubtful. 'The nature of these things is that the same delegates attend annually.' She glanced at her watch. 'Justin should've been back before now. I've brought a lasagne – should I put it in the oven to heat up?'

I nodded absently. 'This is good, Siouxsie. Really good. I can't put my finger on why, but it still feels as though the two are connected – Tamzin's murder and the development …' That was it! 'Nick, what was it your father said when we were stuck in that storeroom? About mistresses?'

'I want to know what you guys overheard in that store cupboard too.' Maggie was back from the kitchen and wearing a cheeky grin. 'I know how big those store cupboards are, so I want to know more about what happened there.'

While my face flamed, Nick chuckled. 'I'm sure you do. Dad joked that if she didn't provide the results they wanted, whoever she was involved with could persuade her with an offer of marriage – that's what all mistresses really wanted.'

'Charming,' muttered Siouxsie.

'Maggie, did you happen to find out who owns that section of land next to the mangroves – the patch with water frontage?' I asked.

'Yes.' She frowned and bit her bottom lip. 'But it doesn't make sense … According to the records I found, the land is owned by Whale Bay Council.'

'What? The council owns the land?' I asked. 'Ailsa Jacks said that piece of land was part of the farm her great-grandfather worked with his business partner. When was it last transferred?'

'That's the thing, the last transfer was registered in the

sixties. The previous owner was a Randall Beach.'

'Unfortunate name,' muttered Siouxsie.

'I wonder …' I mused. 'Who do you know in the local historical society, Maggie?'

'May Hartog is the current president. Why?'

'Len's wife?' Maggie nodded. 'It's a long shot, but I wonder whether Randall Beach bequeathed the council that piece of land, and if he did, there might just be records of it held by the historical society.'

The gate squeaked, then the front door opened, and the dogs rushed to greet the new arrival. 'Hey guys,' said Justin wearily.

Walking into the living room, he sighed heavily. 'They've only gone and done it,' he said, his face pale. 'Tonight's meeting was to tell us the council has received an offer "out of the blue" to purchase the land adjacent to the mangroves. This buyer wants the land to protect it from future development.' Justin gratefully accepted the beer Maggie offered him. 'They even provided plans to prove it.'

'Were they these plans?' I opened one of the photos we'd taken in Len's office. 'This is the land, and this is the proposed development.'

Justin examined the photo and shook his head sadly. 'You know, I allowed myself to hope that maybe this time the council was going to do a good thing. These are not the plans presented to us tonight – but this is the land.'

'And the mangroves?' I asked.

'Ray said that given it had only been approved last week, the survey was yet to be completed and was a separate issue to this proposal. He said the council still intends to build a raised boardwalk in there. There was no mention of Tamzin's death.' He took a long swig of beer. 'The council is meeting again on Tuesday night to vote on the proposal. That gives us just two business days to either find a loophole or an argument against the sale.'

'What about support from other councillors?' Nick asked. 'Surely there are some who are sympathetic?'

'One or two, perhaps,' Justin conceded. 'But they may be taken in by Ray's talk of conserving the land for the future benefit of citizens. He has the numbers; I know it. I can see it now – the sale will be approved based on the plans we saw today, a survey will be received stating the mangroves are receding and before we know it, development of something like this'—he tapped my phone—'will be approved.' Justin's voice rose as he spoke. 'We have to stop it.'

'Tamzin knew about this. I'm sure of it,' I muttered. More loudly, I said, 'Whoever she was seeing must be involved, and she overheard something she wasn't supposed to overhear. This deal is worth millions'—I smacked the table—'that's why she was killed. If only we could find out what she knew.'

'I still don't understand what Scarface and his mate are looking for. Surely the killer has Tamzin's laptop and phone and can erase any evidence of both the affair and whatever it is Tamzin knew.' I wasn't bothered to hide the frustration in my voice.

'Unless it was Ailsa who killed her and Finn who moved the body, which means they have the phone and laptop and Scarface and his mate still need to find it,' said Siouxsie.

'No,' I said emphatically, feeling Nick's eyes on me. 'Finn's not involved. He can't be.'

We all stood. Craning our necks, staring at the murder board, half expecting a clue to jump out and wave at us.

'You know what,' said Maggie. 'We're going in circles. Let's get something to eat and keep going after dinner.'

Over Maggie's lasagne, Nick and I filled the others in about the conversation we'd overheard in Len's office and what we'd found.

'We think Ted knows we were involved,' I said to Justin.

Justin ran his hand over the back of his neck wearily. 'Probably. I couldn't believe it when he came to the office. I was expecting Tyson or Selina.'

'Don't discount Selina,' I said. 'She's on the ball.'

'Yes, well, when Ted asked me if anything was missing from my office, I would've caved and told him the truth if Maggie hadn't been there.' Justin shook his head at the memory. 'Len seemed to buy it, though. Especially when Ted asked him if anything was missing from his office and he came over all shifty and said no. Ted went over and had a look, though.'

'He obviously told Ted he was missing a box of Freddos because Ted mentioned it to us,' chuckled Maggie.

'Hey, we put the box back,' I said.

'Empty,' added Nick, causing Siouxsie to collapse into giggles.

'And when Ted gave Len that look he gives you and asked him outright if there was anything in there worth taking or anything he wouldn't want anyone else to find, Len went so red Maggie was afraid he was going to have a heart attack on the spot. Then he said it was fine, nothing of value had been taken, and it was probably kids looking for money or drugs, and he didn't want it taken any further.' Justin grimaced at the memory. 'Ted asked me if I wanted to make a formal report, and I said the same thing Len had said – that it was probably kids after money. Ted gave me another of those looks and commented on how maybe we should get CCTV that works, and then he left.'

Once the laughter died down, Nick said, 'Ted just wants us to know that he knows – he'll be waiting to see what we do with whatever we broke into Len's office for.'

I stared at Nick with mock outrage. 'How many times do I need to say it? We didn't break in – we were simply there without him knowing.'

'Of course.'

Nick smiled, and I smiled back; Maggie noticed, and

she looked at Justin and smiled at us smiling at each other, and it wasn't until Siouxsie said, 'Ummm, is anything going on here that I need to know about, or is this all just ancient history?' that I forced my eyes and my smile from his.

'Alright.' Maggie cleared her throat. 'Where to from here?'

'Well,' I began, 'you and I will call on May Hartog and see what we can find out from her—'

Maggie nodded. 'Tomorrow is Saturday, so May will be doing a shift at the op shop.'

'Heaven forbid anyone in town ever changes their routines,' said Nick under his breath.

Turning my attention to him, I said, 'You need to apologise to Angus and see what he knows about conference attendees.' He nodded. 'And other than that, Justin, can you go through the council by-laws? Mags and I can help if you need it, but we're looking for anything that governs the protocols around the sale of council-owned land. I'd love to find a clause stating a minimum notice period or community engagement, but I suspect I'm being optimistic.'

'What about me?' Siouxsie pouted theatrically.

'Don't worry, I haven't forgotten you. I need you to find out everything you can about Branden Greene – personal, social and the companies he's involved in. Also, whatever you can find about the ownership of Ridley Hawke.'

'Sorry, I haven't completed those searches yet,' said Maggie, not appearing very sorry at all.

'Done,' said Siouxsie.

'Also, we need to get as many people as we can to Tuesday's meeting. While only councillors can vote on the proposal, we need to mobilise public support,' I said. 'It's a pity Finn isn't here.' I suddenly realised I'd barely given him a thought all day. 'We could put some flyers up in Beach Brewz.'

'I'll create some.' Siouxsie scribbled a reminder on a yellow Post-it note.

'Great – and work with Nina and Bella at the shop – they'll also help with that.' Even though we were no closer to discovering Tamzin's murderer, for the first time in days, it felt as though we were taking action – there wasn't much I disliked more than treading water.

'Do you think we've got a chance?' Justin had a hopeful look on his face.

'Now we know what their plans are, we can try and do something about it,' I said. 'Do I think we'll stop the sale?' I grimaced. 'I don't know.' I looked towards the ceiling. 'Rose, if you're up there and have any influence with the woman in charge, put in a good word for us, eh?'

'Any influence?' Nick scoffed. 'If I know Rose, she'd be running the joint by now.' As we all laughed, he said as an aside, 'And she'd be so proud of you.'

CHAPTER THIRTY-THREE

Water rushed over my head as my feet scrabbled for the sand. It was like being caught in a dumping wave, not knowing which way was up and which way was down, but this time, something – someone – was holding me down. Opening my eyes, I watched the bubbles slowly dribble from my mouth, heading up; did that mean I was facing the right way? A little push and I'd find sky and air, but still, the hands on my shoulders held me down. My hands reached for them, but their grip on me was too tight. My hand closed down over a chunky watch – the one from the photo with Tamzin. I screamed even though I knew no one could hear me, my mouth filling with water. 'Clem.'

The voice drifted from the distance, overpowered by the swoosh of the current.

'Clem!'

Louder and more insistent, clearer, but closer now.

'Clem!'

The hands that held me under disappeared and my eyes snapped open. I sat bolt upright, my heart banging in my chest, sweat causing my singlet to cling to me, my breath coming faster. There was a man-shape silhouetted in the doorway.

'Are you okay? You were screaming.'

In my just-awake stage, I'd forgotten Nick had stayed over – despite my protests – in my narrow childhood bed, the same bed we'd lain in together all those years ago. It hadn't mattered then that it wasn't big enough for one tall adult, let alone two; we'd fitted perfectly.

I'd offered him my bed. 'It doesn't seem right,' I'd said. 'I'm shorter than you.'

'Not by much.' He waved the protest away. 'I'll be fine.'

I blinked as he flicked the bedroom light on and again when I realised he was dressed only in his undies … fire-engine red.

'God, I'm so sorry.' I dragged my eyes away from his bare chest and … well, everything else, pinning my eyes to his. 'It was a nightmare. I'm fine.'

Nick entered the room and sat on the bed beside me. 'Tell me about it,' he urged.

I waved him off. 'It's nothing. I'm sorry, go back to bed.' His hair was ruffled, and there were little creases on his face from where he must have fallen asleep on his hand. Feeling a sudden compulsion to run my fingers through his hair and trail them down his face, dipping into every crevice, I gripped the covers so I wouldn't give in to the temptation.

'It sounded like a nightmare, a bad one.' He leant across

and tipped my chin so my eyes met his. 'Tell me, Clem.'

I straightened the pillows and pulled the covers up further. 'If you must know, the man with the watch was drowning me, holding me down.'

Rather than patronising me and telling me it was just a dream, Nick immediately understood what sort of dream it was. 'Did you see his face?'

'No, just the watch.'

'And it was you he was drowning, not Tamzin?' His gaze was intent, his expression concerned.

'No,' I said sombrely, 'it was me.'

'We need to find the man with the watch.' His eyes roamed across my face as if committing every feature to memory. 'I won't feel like you're safe until we do.'

'It was just a nightmare.'

'Was it though? Or was it one of *those* dreams?' His eyes fell on my lips, slipped down to my breasts, and returned to my lips.

'It was just a nightmare,' I said again, feebly, warmth pooling in my core.

When his finger lightly traced my collarbone, I sighed as a stream of goosebumps rose to follow it, and when he bent his head and tasted my lips, the soft moan I heard came from me. 'I've missed you,' he said in a low, gravelly voice.

All the reasons why we shouldn't be doing this gathered and waved for my attention. 'I've missed you too,' I said and ignored them all as the years dropped away and the only thing that mattered was this man and the way he was kissing me.

'Is this okay,' Nick asked softly as he pushed me gently back on the bed, his hand cupping my breast through the thin singlet.

'Mmmm.'

Vaguely I registered barking, but when Nick pulled away, I groaned my frustration.

Placing a finger against my lips he whispered, 'Something or someone has upset the dogs.' Both dogs were now whining.

'It sounds like they're at the back door,' I whispered back, the fear I'd felt on waking returning.

Silently he swung off the bed and padded out to the back door and let them out.

Sitting up in bed I pulled the covers up to my chin, relaxing only when I heard the back door close again, Nick softly praising the dogs for being good. That was also when all the reasons we shouldn't sleep together gathered again. I was with Finn; plus, there was the issue of Nick and my baby – the one I still hadn't told him about.

No matter how much I wanted to, it would be a mistake.

He must have anticipated my change of mind as when he finally came back into my room, he was wearing shorts and had pulled on a t-shirt.

'If there was somebody out there, the dogs scared them off,' he said, sitting on the edge of the bed and trailing one finger down my cheek.

'I'm sorry,' I said, my hormones far from convinced I'd made the right decision.

'It's okay.' He didn't pretend to misunderstand me. 'You have things to sort out.'

'I know it's asking a lot,' —-I smiled hesitantly— 'but I don't want to be alone and I don't want … well, I do want, but…'

'It's okay,' he said, his cheeky grin designed to make me feel better. 'I'm not going anywhere. Lie down and go to sleep.'

Despite the nightmare and despite the lingering heat of his earlier kisses, I did just that.

When I woke, the sun streaming in around the curtains, the other side of the bed was empty, and save for the tapping of the dog's paws on the floorboards, the house was quiet. Turning over, I buried my head into the pillow and groaned. Even though we'd done nothing wrong, if it hadn't been for the dogs we would have made love. Rolling onto my back, still clutching the pillow, I allowed myself a smile. But his kisses were so good. My smile slipped. No matter how good his kisses were, it had been a mistake and couldn't happen again.

After pulling on some clothes and shoving my feet into Ugg boots, I walked out to the kitchen. The dogs were pleased to see me finally up and about and bounced around in their enthusiasm. Unplugging my phone from its charger, I noticed a message from Nick:

Good morning. I figured you'd wake and begin to beat yourself up, so I've made myself scarce even though you looked so beautiful. The dogs have been out and done what they need to do. See you later. N x

Holding the phone to my chest, I breathed a sigh of relief. Even after all these years, Nick Cosgrove knew me better than anyone else.

Thank you C x

I'd no sooner sent the text than my phone pinged with a new one – from Maggie.

Coffee before op shopping? See you at Beach Brewz …

I tapped a quick reply:

Just out of bed, give me 20

'Okay, guys,' I said to the dogs. 'I know you haven't had a walk yet'—their ears pricked up at the mention of the word 'walk'—'but shower first, and you can come to coffee with me. How does that sound?'

Their wags indicated it was the best idea ever.

As the dogs and I walked down to the café, I tried phoning Finn, but he didn't pick up, so my call went to voice message. I'd no sooner shoved my phone back into my pocket when Ted called.

'How are you feeling this morning?' he asked. 'Any more unwelcome intruders?'

Glad Ted couldn't see the way my face had flamed, I said, 'Thankfully, no. The dogs were carrying on about something, but I don't think anyone was there.' I let out a short laugh. 'It was probably just a possum.'

He hesitated briefly. 'Clem, there's another reason for my call this morning; Finn and Ailsa have both been called in for more questioning.'

I released a weighty sigh. When was this going to end? 'Let me guess – Osborne's theory is now that Ailsa murdered Tamzin after finding out she'd been having an affair and Finn helped her dump the body and cover it up.'

Ted chuckled lightly. 'I take it that theory appeared on that murder board of yours?'

'I don't know what you're talking about,' I said, feigning innocence. 'Are they being questioned here or in Brisbane?'

'Brisbane.'

'Right. Does Finn need me down there as his lawyer?'

'At this stage, no. Regarding the theory, do you know if Tamzin was seeing someone else?'

'We believe she'd recently begun seeing her ex-boyfriend again, but we don't know any details about him. As I mentioned yesterday, Ailsa described a man matching Angus Jones' description, but he denies being involved with her.' Both dogs obediently sat and waited before I signalled we were okay to cross the road.

'Okay, well, keep me posted if you come up with anything more plausible than the theory that DS Osborne is working.'

'Will do, thanks, Ted.'

When the dogs and I arrived, Maggie was at a table on the deck, sipping her coffee and chatting with Nick and Angus. While I thought I'd hid my discomfort, Maggie raised her eyebrows.

Despite a quick but very loaded look that made my toes (and various other parts of me) curl, Nick didn't display any awkwardness. 'Good morning.' He reached down to pat Cosmo. 'Angus was just telling us about the conferences on our list.'

'I'd understand if you didn't believe I hadn't been involved with her.' Angus shook his head. 'I've been to all the conferences on this list. I left the country around about when you say she began a new relationship, and she's apparently back in touch with this guy at about the same time as I arrive back in Brisbane.' He ticked off the reasons on his fingers.

'When you put it like that,' said Maggie.

Angus flashed her a dimpled smile. When she preened, I almost groaned out loud. I handed the dog's leads to Maggie. 'I'm getting a coffee. Anyone want anything?'

At the counter, Lainey said, 'How's Finn?'

'I haven't spoken to him today.' I avoided a direct answer. 'Hopefully, he'll be home in the next few days.'

I placed my order and stepped aside to wait for my coffee, a prickling of my skin alerting me to Nick's presence before I turned to see he'd joined me.

'Are you okay?' His smile was lazy, but a quirk of his lips showed his uncertainty.

'Nick—' I began, looking around to check no one was close enough to hear us.

'I know,' he said. 'I know.'

'Thank you,' I said softly. 'For understanding and'— warmth rushed to my face—'you know—'

'But it can't happen again,' he said ruefully.

'No,' I said. 'I wish it could, but it can't.'

He waited as I collected my coffee and walked back to the others. 'I'll be off,' he said. 'I'm due to catch up with Mike, so I'll see you all later.'

Angus stayed for about another ten minutes while I finished my coffee. We talked about the proposed land sale and the special meeting the council had called. 'You don't have long and, not wanting to rain on your parade, but the likelihood of success is low. If you can't find a loophole in the council by-laws, your best bet is to try to discredit the purchaser. You won't find anything like that about Branden, so concentrate your efforts on the company. Find some examples of dodgy dealings – developments with no environmental credentials. Also, some councils have a community buy-back clause, which means any council-owned land must be offered to the community at a reasonable rate.' Angus paused as his phone rang. Glancing at the caller ID on his watch, he apologised. 'I'm sorry, I need to take this.'

Pulling his phone out of his pocket, he pressed it to his ear and answered. 'What's wrong? Really?' Standing, he mouthed to us, 'I'll see you both later,' and stepped off the deck onto the pavement. Settling into the call, he pushed the sleeves of his long-sleeved tee up.

Maggie and I looked at each other, eyes wide. 'Did you see—?'

I nodded. 'That watch he's wearing looks a lot like the watch in the photo.'

I messaged Nick:

When you get a chance, ask Angus about his watch …

His response came through immediately:

On it. N x

CHAPTER THIRTY-FOUR

'What happened between you two last night?' Maggie asked as we walked the short distance to the op shop. 'And before you say you don't know what I'm talking about, I saw that look he gave you when you walked in this morning, and your face went the same colour as that time I died my hair fluoro pink.'

'And your mum hit the roof because we stained the bathroom sink.'

'That's the one – but don't think reminiscing is going to get you out of this. Did you two sleep together?'

'No,' I squeaked, my face, I'm sure, again blooming brightly. 'Well yes, but not like you think.'

She did a little fist pump and twirled on the spot. 'Yes! I knew it!'

'Shhhhh,' I said when people began to stare.

'What?' she asked innocently. 'I'm just demonstrating my joy.'

'This is not a good thing.' Although my body reminded me, Nick's kisses had, indeed, been a very good thing.

'It was crap? I would've thought he would have picked up a trick or two over the years.'

'No, I mean, yes. It wasn't like you think.' My words were tripping over themselves. 'We kissed and would have made love if the dogs hadn't started up over a possum or something. Anyway, it can't happen again.'

'Why not?'

'Hello! Let me count the reasons: Finn. Then there's … Finn. And finally, Finn. Finn and I are only just together, and here I've gone and almost cheated on him. I'm a terrible, terrible person, Mags.' My feet dragged, the dogs slowing to keep up with me. 'Plus, it's not even two months since I was with Miles. I'm not normally that person. I've never cheated on anyone before. Ever. And I came *this* close to doing it last night.'

'Alright, I admit that's not ideal,' she said. 'But Nick was your first love, and first loves are like calories on planes and other people's hot chips – they don't count.'

'Nice theory from the woman who married her first love,' I said, pausing at the entrance to the op shop. 'But I'm not buying it. Now, is this a dogs-allowed-in-the-shop kind of place, or should I tie them up outside?'

Maggie opened the door. 'May's a dog lover; they'll be fine.'

Shrugging, I followed her in, pausing in the doorway as the familiar op shop smell – a combination of old books and second-hand fabrics – took me back to my childhood and the weekly shifts on the counter that Rose used to do.

May Hartog, a trim, busy woman in her mid-sixties with tightly cropped grey hair, was behind the counter serving a line of customers. Maggie and I busied ourselves checking out the collectibles on the shelves at the front of the store. Once the queue cleared, May looked over at us. 'Maggie King and Clem Russell—'

'Carter,' I corrected under my breath.

'And Cosmo and Beans. Finn still away, is he, Clem?' She came out from behind the counter to pat the dogs.

'He is, May. Another few days, I'd say.'

'Are you two looking for something special?' She rehung some clothes that had fallen from their hangers onto the floor.

'Actually, May,' said Maggie. 'We want to pick your brain about historical society stuff.'

May beamed. 'Goodo, I'll grab one of the girls in the sorting room to look after the counter for a bit. Follow me.'

Winding a path through the racks of clothes, shelves of books, and assorted furniture holding all measure of bric-a-brac, May led us into the office.

'Are you sure it's okay to have the dogs in here?' I asked.

'Absolutely. Of course, they're prohibited under the lease, but what Ray Cosgrove doesn't know about won't hurt him. He's our landlord, and I think he can't wait for us to move out. You know, he put the rent up again this year?' She shook her head and tutted. 'You don't want to hear about that. Take a seat.' She pointed at two mismatched chairs against the wall. 'Just put whatever is on them on the floor.'

Suppressing a grin, I removed the contents of my chair – a pile of Harry Potter books, an old camera, and a barometer – and found a spare spot on the floor for them. Maggie did the same with the doll, two (presumably fake) Louis Vuitton handbags and a piece of what looked to be vintage glass with holes in it.

Holding the latter up, Mags said, 'What is this?'

'It's a flower frog.' May reached out and took it from her. 'They're for displaying flowers. I had someone in yesterday asking for one, and for the life of me, I couldn't remember where I'd seen it. I'll price it up and give her a call. Now'—she steepled her fingers under her chin—'what did you two want to talk to me about?'

Maggie settled back in her chair. 'Not sure if you know the name, but we figured if anyone would, it would be you … but have you heard of a Randall Beach?'

'Absolutely. Who did you think Beach Road was named after?'

I looked at Maggie and smiled wryly. 'I guess I always thought it was called Beach Road because it runs along the beach.' For a second, I thought Maggie was going to giggle, but instead, she clamped her lips tight.

'Well, yes, but it wasn't always called Beach Road. Randall's father bequeathed the land at the end of your street, Clem – the parkland that the beach path runs through?' I nodded my understanding. 'He left that to the Whale Bay Council on the basis that it remains available to the community. He was worried Whale Bay would go the way of Surfers Paradise and parts of the Gold Coast and wanted to ensure there was at least some beachfront land everyone could enjoy.'

'I understood the Beach family were in partnership with Ailsa Jacks' family,' I said.

'Yes. They had some land in town and a coffee-growing enterprise to the right of the highway heading out of town and also to the left towards Dolphin Point. They grew bananas too, but mostly to shelter the young coffee plants. When Ailsa's great-grandfather passed, the land was split between the two families. By then, of course, the bottom had fallen out of the coffee-growing industry.' May began to warm to her subject. 'For a time at the turn of the last century, Whale Bay coffee was regarded as some of the best in the world.' Her sigh was for past glories.

'What can you tell me about the land on the Dolphin Point side?' Maggie took out her phone to take notes.

May tilted her head to the side. 'Well, if memory serves me correctly, the Jacks family ended up with the parcel on the Dolphin Point Road side and the most arable land on the rise – where Ailsa is growing coffee again. I hope it works for her.'

'And Randall Beach?' I prompted. 'Did he get the waterfront portion?'

'I was coming to that. Impatient, aren't you?' She smiled to take the edge off the light scolding. 'You're very like your aunt, you know. We were in school together.' Her sigh was pensive. 'I remember she stood up for me one day when Carmen Lindsay, as she is now, was teasing me. She continued to stand up for what she believed in her whole life. You can't say that about many people.'

'No,' I said quietly. 'You can't.'

'Even though she had her own shop, Rose volunteered here as well. They've got all the time in the world you don't see any of them doing that, do you?'

By "them" I assumed she meant Cosgroves or Lindsays. 'No, you don't.'

'Now, where was I? The Beach land. Yes, Randall had no heirs, and he was concerned his closest relatives – some cousins, I believe – would sell the land to a developer. You need to remember this was before the mangroves were protected, so the entire land could've been developed with dire consequences for the adjacent habitat. Queensland, in those days, was a very different place from what it is today. The government was approving anything and everything.' Maggie and I nodded our understanding. 'So he left the land to Whale Bay Council with strict covenants on how they could use the land.'

I looked up, my breath quickening. This could be what we'd been looking for. 'What sort of covenants are we talking about?'

'Development was intended solely for community use, in consultation with the Traditional Owners. He was quite ahead of his time. There were also some strict conditions regarding the sale of the property, although I can't recall it all off the top of my head.'

'And this was in Randall Beach's will?' I asked. Maggie looked as hopeful as I suddenly felt.

'Yes.' May's eyes narrowed. 'Why are you interested?'

'Has Len told you what he's working on at the moment?' I spoke with caution, not wanting to put my foot in it.

'No, although he's been quiet and a bit shady of late, which usually means one of three things: he's up to no good, he's up to no good with Ray Cosgrove, or he's cheating on his diet. He has diabetes, you see – type 2. And the doctor wants him to lose weight, quit smoking and cut back on the beers. Do you think he's doing any of those things? No, he's not. So'—she rested her cheek against her hand, her elbow on the desk—'which is it?'

'Ray announced last night they have a purchaser for that land,' I said.

May's mouth opened in a silent O, but no words came out.

'There's a special meeting on Tuesday evening to vote on the proposal,' Maggie added.

'So soon?' May asked. She gripped the table and leant forward, tapping her fingers on the tabletop, her eyes flicking to the ceiling. 'They mustn't know about the will or its covenants,' she said after a short pause.

'Or if they do, they're hoping no one else does. Once the deal is done, it's done.' I couldn't help the sadness from creeping into my voice. 'That's why we need your help to find a copy of that will.'

May gave a short nod. 'There'd be a copy in the historical society for sure, although it could take some finding. I'll have a look for you. You let me know if there's any other way I can help too. Len might be in with that lot, but I have no loyalty to them.'

Impulsively, I reached across the table and grasped her hand. 'Thank you, May.'

'Don't thank me yet,' she said grimly. 'Bloody Ray Cosgrove. He thinks he owns this town and can do what he likes with it.' She chuckled. 'He probably thought Rose dying was a blessing. If anything, I think you might be even more of a thorn in his side.'

I returned her grin. 'I'm trying, May. I'm certainly trying.'

CHAPTER THIRTY-FIVE

When I arrived home to see the front door wide open, I didn't need to go inside to find out what had happened. With a sigh of annoyance, I called Ted.

'What's up, Clem?' he asked, sounding resigned to having his weekend ruined yet again.

'It looks like the goons who were here yesterday have been back for another look around.' I pulled the dogs back to my side and made them sit.

After checking the black Hilux was nowhere in sight, my intrepid guard dogs and I ventured inside. It was as expected. They'd tossed aside the throw covering the murder board and upturned the board itself. The photo of Tamzin and the man with the watch had been removed.

The dogs and I left it as it was and sat on the swing chair under the fig tree in the backyard, watching the magpies until Tyson and Selina pulled up.

'Do you guys ever get any time off?' I asked.

'You're certainly keeping us busy,' Selina said.

I told them when I had left the house and where I'd

been for the last couple of hours, and I made them coffee. Did I know what they were looking for? No. Had I seen the suspect's truck in town this morning? No. Why hadn't they been able to find two idiots – one with a prominent scar and flame-red hair – in a black Hilux? They didn't know.

Once the police, having taken fingerprints and photos, left, I called, left another message for Finn, and cleaned up as best I could. Knowing they'd been in my house, their hands over my things turned my stomach. For the first time since Harry and I found Tamzin, I felt rattled – more than rattled; I had to admit I was scared.

When the duo had broken into Finn's house and attacked us, my focus had been on him. Even when we came across Scarface yesterday at Ailsa's, my concern had been for her. Now, it was for me. Whether it was the after-effects of last night's nightmare or the invasion of my house – or a combination of both – I felt as though someone was watching me, waiting to get me on my own.

Logically, the likelihood of them coming back was slim, but I couldn't shake the … not so much premonition … but the vague feeling I was in danger, that my time was limited. I wished Nick was here, that he could hold me and tell me everything was going to be alright, but after last night, I couldn't allow myself to get used to having Nick around. I didn't want to think about why my mind went immediately to Nick rather than Finn. Even though I told myself it was because Finn had his own problems, but I was lying to myself. My mind went to Nick because that's what my heart told it to do.

Instead, I rang Maggie.

Maggie and I spent the rest of the day at her dining table with council by-laws and procedural documents spread out around us. Justin popped in from time to time to explain specific procedures and to keep us supplied with coffee.

'What about a heritage listing?' I asked. 'Could we apply for a heritage listing on the land?'

'Potentially,' he said thoughtfully. 'But I think you'll be better served by checking the LEP – the Local Environment Plan – to see if the proposal conforms to it.'

Maggie nodded. 'I agree. What we're looking for here is a loophole. We also need to find the appropriate clause that governs the sale of council assets.'

At around half past four, I laid my head on the desk and groaned dramatically. 'This, right here, is why I specialise in family law.' I lifted my head at Maggie's chuckle. 'This'—I swept my hand to encompass the paperwork—'is my worst nightmare. You were always so much better at the detail than I was,' I simpered.

'Tough,' scolded Maggie. 'We're in this together.'

'I know …'

When my phone rang, she muttered, 'Saved by the bell.'

Screwing my nose up at her, I answered. 'Nina, is

everything okay? I thought you would've been closed by now.'

'I'm about to walk out the door; it's been a steady day. Before I forget, Angus Jones called—'

'Really? Why would he have rung the shop? He has my number.' When Nina didn't reply, I said, 'Are you there?'

'Yes, sorry. He said he'd been trying you but hadn't been able to get through, but asked if you could meet him and Nick at the beach at five. He said the northern end.'

I frowned. 'Him and Nick?' Unease prickled across the back of my neck.

'Yes. He definitely said he and Nick, and he also said he wants to tell you something about a watch?'

Nick must have spoken to him about the watch. 'Aaaaah. Okay, that makes more sense. Thanks, Nina.'

As I was about to ring off, Nina said, 'Clem, have you had any more dreams?'

An image of last night's nightmare flashed by my eyes. 'Don't worry about me,' I said. 'I'll be fine.'

'What was that about?' asked Maggie as the call ended.

'Nina had a message from Angus – he's been trying to reach me, who knows?' I shrugged. 'So he called the shop, hoping to get in touch with me. Anyway, he and Nick want to meet me down at the beach at five to talk about the watch.' I glanced at the clock on the wall. 'If I'm going to make it, I'd better get moving. Will the dogs be right here with you for an hour or so?'

'They'll be fine,' said Maggie. 'Take your time – and if the opportunity comes up to talk to Nick, you need to take it.'

'What's that about?' Justin appeared with some cheese and crackers on a wooden board.

'They almost shagged last night,' Maggie said poker-faced.

'Maggie!' I reached over and slapped her upper arm. 'I told you that in confidence.'

She waved my words away. 'But you didn't mean I couldn't tell Justin.'

Justin's eyes met mine, and we both shook our heads in exasperation.

'That sounds like it could get complicated,' Justin said.

'No shit, Sherlock,' said Maggie. 'But Clem is favouring the head-in-the-sand option.'

'Guys, I *am* here, you know.'

'Yeah, but you shouldn't be,' said Maggie, chuckling around a mouthful of food.

As I walked from Maggie's to the beach, the faint sense of unease I'd felt on the phone with Nina grew. Why the beach, and why now? It was almost dark. Maybe Angus wanted to ensure no one overheard him. Maybe I should've brought Maggie or the dogs. But Nina said Nick would be here, too. If he was there, there'd be nothing to worry about.

I pulled out my phone and called Nick, but he didn't

pick up. Rather than leaving a message on his voicemail, I texted him.

Just heading to the beach to meet you and Angus. See you soon.
C x

There were no streetlights at this end of the beach. Further along were the absolute beachfront homes owned by people like Ray and Paula Cosgrove, and Bob and Carmen Lindsay. Behind me rose Whale Bay Heights, or what the locals called Nob Hill, with their large designer homes with amazing ocean views, but no one standing at any of those expansive windows would notice me standing in the dark on this stretch of beach. The thought sent a shiver up my spine.

Rubbing my arms (and regretting not having put on a jacket), I surveyed my surroundings. The beach seemed deserted. Perhaps I'd got the time wrong? As I pulled my phone out to call Angus, someone tackled me from behind. My knees hit the sand with a thud; the breath knocked from my body. My phone, which had flown from my hands, rang. Scrabbling through the sand, I stretched out my arm to reach it, but a firm grip around my ankle pulled me back. The ringing stopped.

When I opened my mouth to scream for help, another hand clamped over it. 'Shut up,' a voice growled in my ear. 'There's no one here to hear you.'

My phone rang for a second time. I tried to commando crawl forward but only got sand in my mouth, a knee on my back holding me in place.

'Now,' said the gruff voice in my ear. 'You're going to go for a nice swim. You like swimming, don't you?' Blindly, I kicked out, my second assailant laughing and grabbing both ankles. Twisting my body, I managed to free my captured arm, prompting my attacker to release my head for long enough for me to scream, 'Help! Some—' The slap, a sharp sting across my cheek, cut off the rest of my sentence.

'I said, shut up, bitch!' The man at my head held my wrists in one large hand, his other hand back over my mouth. I tried to see who it was, but he remained just beyond my vision.

'Can't you shut her up?' the man at my feet demanded.

'How do you want me to do that? I can't carry her and shut her up at the same time.'

'Then let's make this quick.'

Again, he released his hand from over my mouth, then gripped onto both wrists. Between them, they carried me to the water; I screamed the whole way, my throat raw, my body twisting in a desperate effort to free myself.

Once in the water, the hold on my feet relaxed, and I kicked out, a groan indicating my foot had found its target. That was when the water rushed over my head, hands on my shoulders forcing me down, my feet scrabbling for purchase on the sand. Once more, I kicked out, freeing myself for long enough to get to the surface and scream once more before I was again forced under, one hand on my shoulder, an arm around my neck, its pressure crushing my throat. I opened my eyes, but everything was dark, the water cold, my lungs burning. Was this how Tamzin felt when she was drowning? The ocean had always been my friend. It had soothed me, supported me, energised me, inspired me. How ironic that now it was going to take me.

If I died now, Nick would never know he was a father. He'd never know about the perfect little girl we'd had together. I should've told him when I had the chance. There were so many things I should have told him. If, by some miracle, I got out of this alive, I would tell him.

Rose, if you're watching, please help me. Her image floated through my head – Rose and me painting the mural on my bedroom wall, Rose breaking the news to me when Mum died, Rose holding my hand as I pushed my baby out, Rose yelling at the nurses to allow me to hold her and feed her when they would've ripped her away from me. Rose telling me to hold on just a little longer. *I'm not ready for you yet,* she said.

'Clem!' A voice, faint and distant.

My throat tightened, my head grew lighter, and the urge to open my mouth and take a breath became overwhelming. Just when I thought I could no longer keep my mouth closed, they released the grip on my shoulders and dragged me to the surface. Air rushed into my lungs, burning and cold, with a force that made me gasp, and fresh panic replaced the fleeting relief as I thrashed against the arms wound tightly around my chest.

'It's okay. Clem, I've got you, darling. I've got you.' Nick's voice crooned in my ear, and I forced my limbs to relax enough to let him pull me into shore. Nick held me until I could stand and supported me as I staggered out of the surf and collapsed again on my knees, gasping, aware of nothing more than the sand, the air filling my lungs, Nick's hand gentle on my shoulders, repeating over and over, 'You're safe now.'

Soon came the lights, shouting and scuffles, and I struggled to my feet, Nick holding me up. Angus held one man down while Tyson King snapped cuffs on him. Ted Winters had already cuffed the other, his red hair bright in the light from the police car's headlights, the scar running down his cheek pronounced.

A siren announced the ambulance, Aaron and Chelsea snapping straight into action. Chelsea tried to put a blanket around me, but that meant Nick dropping his arm. 'No,' I pushed against her.

'It's okay, it's okay,' he said again, taking the blanket from her, wrapping it around me and leading me to the ambulance. 'I won't leave you.'

Then, the world went dark.

CHAPTER THIRTY-SIX

Opening my eyes, I blinked twice against the bright fluorescent light, the white sheets crisp under my hands. Panicking at the tightness around my body, I kicked out, calming only when Nick's face loomed over me. 'You're safe, Clem.'

When I struggled to sit up, he helped me, propping pillows behind me. With my hand against my sore throat, I looked around the unfamiliar room. 'Am I in hospital?' I rasped, loosening the sheets. I'd never liked being tucked in, but now their pressure made me feel trapped rather than safe.

'You don't remember?' he asked quietly, his face pale with concern.

I closed my eyes, and the memories crashed in, one on top of the other. My heart raced as panic again descended. Snapping my eyes back open, the images receded. I nodded.

Nick passed me a glass of water. 'Your throat will still be sore, so just sip.'

The water slid coolly down. 'Thank you. You saved my

life.'

Pain flickered across his face, and I knew he was picturing again what had happened, what he'd seen taking place in the water. I reached for his hand. 'How did you know?'

'Nina,' he said. 'Angus and I were leaving the surf club when Nina walked past. She told us she'd passed on Angus' message, and when he said he hadn't left you a message, we realised you were in danger. I called Ted – which must have been when you'd tried to call me – and the pair of us ran to find you. Angus pulled one of them off you, and I got the other. As soon as they heard the sirens, they let go and tried to get away.'

'The watch,' I said. 'How did they know about the watch?'

'They'd seen it on the murder board when they broke into your house,' he said.

'But Angus? He was wearing the watch and took that call at Beach Brewz … I thought…' I'd been so sure it was Angus. My hand pressed against my throat.

'Don't talk,' Nick said. 'The watch Angus wears is the same as the one in the photo, but it was given to him as a farewell present before he went to Scotland. He wasn't involved with Tamzin, Clem, and he didn't give the orders to your attackers.'

'But who did?'

'They're not disclosing anything, and the only number

dialled on the phone Scarface was carrying – as well as the number from which they've been receiving calls – is from a burner phone.'

'Who made the call to Nina?' My voice sounded as though I'd spent a week at a music festival.

'We don't know. But she said something felt wrong when she took it.'

'She asked me if I'd been dreaming, so I think she did sense something wasn't right. Who gave Angus the watch?'

'Branden Greene,' Nick said grimly. 'Thanks to Ailsa, we can link him to Scarface, but there's no evidence linking him to what happened to you tonight or the break-ins. Scarface and his mate have rock-solid alibis for when Tamzin was murdered, and Branden was in Brisbane attending a conference.'

My brain struggled to make things fit. 'Was he involved with Tamzin?'

He grinned. 'You really don't have the hang of this not speaking thing, do you?' I shrugged and smiled weakly. 'We don't have her phone, and Ted told me that her carrier has matched some numbers with the same burner that your attackers were calling; there's nothing that links Greene to that.'

'It has to be him,' I said.

'I agree, but we have no evidence.'

'Unless they confess …' I said, my voice breaking.

'Unless they confess,' Nick agreed. 'DS Osborne and

DC Hall are on their way back here to question them, and they'll probably want a statement from you, too.'

'Does that mean they're finished with Finn and Ailsa?'

He lifted his shoulders. 'I don't know, Clem.'

Glancing around the room once more, the same fear I'd felt in the ocean rose through me. Was I safe here? 'I want to go home, Nick.'

He nodded. 'Let me see what I can do about that.'

Once the medical staff were satisfied that I was – other than a sore throat and some bruising – uninjured, Nick was allowed to take me home. He'd already updated Nina, and Maggie (who was keeping the dogs with her for the night) brought me some clothes to wear home.

Someone – probably one of the paramedics – had found my phone on the beach, and it was returned to me, although the clothes I'd been wearing were being held as evidence. Maggie told me she'd called Finn and told him what had happened, assuring him I was okay and my attackers had been apprehended.

'Is he coming home?' I asked, unsure whether I wanted him here.

She looked away. 'I told him you were in safe hands and he didn't need to come rushing back.'

'And he didn't argue with that?'

She shook her head slowly. 'I think he's been through the wringer down there too. He was very worried about you though.'

Just not worried enough to drop everything and come back. I didn't know whether I was disappointed or relieved.

Nick helped settle me for bed, but I stopped him when he went to flick the bedside light off. 'Please don't,' I said. 'I can't bear the dark tonight.' When he nodded, I added, 'Please don't leave me.'

'I won't,' he assured me and climbed into bed beside me, holding me until I slipped into sleep. When I woke in the night, screaming into the darkness, he held me again until my fear subsided.

It was almost midday when I woke up properly. The pillow beside me was empty and cold but still holding the indent where his head had been. Sounds of voices drifted through the closed door.

My body had stiffened during the night, and I groaned as I clambered out of bed and threw on a dressing gown and my Ugg boots.

I followed the smell of bacon into the dining room, where Maggie, Justin, Siouxsie and Angus sat at the table. Nick emerged from the kitchen, holding a frying pan. 'Good morning,' he said, a warm smile crinkling the corners of his eyes. 'Is your throat up to swallowing a bacon sandwich?'

'Thank you.' While my voice sounded rougher than usual, the pain in my throat had eased.

Maggie sprang from her chair to hug me tightly. 'Don't you dare do that to me again,' she hissed. Siouxsie put her arms around us, and Justin came in over the top of that.

Once they'd freed me, Angus stood and, smiling a little awkwardly, pulled me in for a hug, too. 'Thank you,' I said. 'I'm glad you were there.'

'I'm glad we were too.' Angas exchanged a meaningful glance with Nick. 'I'd hate to think what would've happened if we hadn't come across Nina when we did.'

'Let's put it this way'—I attempted a weak smile—'I was out of air.'

Everyone was quiet for a few seconds as they contemplated that possibility.

'Where are the dogs?' I gratefully accepted the coffee Nick handed over.

'We left them at home in case you weren't up to it,' said Justin.

When a knock came on the front door, Maggie yelled, 'Come in, it's open.'

'Good,' Ted said as he walked in, tucking his hat under his armpit. 'You're all here.'

'I'm making Clem a bacon sandwich,' said Nick. 'Do you want one?'

Ted nodded. 'Thanks.'

'What do you have to tell us?' said Maggie.

Ted eased himself into a dining chair and smiled his thanks when Nick placed a coffee in front of him. 'They're not saying anything. Whoever they're working for has paid them well. They're denying making the call to Nina and said they were out walking the beach when they noticed you were in trouble in the surf and immediately ran in like any good citizens would have to rescue you. You panicked, though, and thought they were trying to drown you when all they were doing was attempting to help you.'

'Surely no one believes that?' Nick's jaw was tense as he set a plate down for me. 'How do they explain the phone on the beach and the fact that Clem was fully clothed?'

'They thought you must have had some man trouble and had decided to ...' Ted grimaced, and I imagined the words my attackers had used.

'We've got them for the house break-ins – their fingerprints were all over that – and we'll charge them with your assault, but they lawyered up quickly. And not just any lawyer – one of the most expensive lawyers in Brisbane turned up this morning. I'd like to know who's paying for that.'

Ted took a bite from the sandwich Nick gave him. After swallowing, he continued. 'There's more. May Hartog phoned me this morning – someone broke into the Historical Society yesterday and turned it upside down. I expect we'll find our dynamic duo's prints all over that, too.' He looked keenly at Maggie and me. 'When I asked her what she was doing there on a Sunday morning, she said she was looking for a document for you.'

Maggie nodded while I chewed my sandwich. 'We needed a copy of Randall Beach's will. He bequeathed the waterfront parcel of land near the mangroves – the same land Ridley Hawke Developments wants to buy – to the council, but with some strict covenants regarding its future sale and use. Without a copy of that will, the council can sell the property to whoever they wish.'

'Surely the council holds a copy too,' said Ted.

'Presumably, but they're not going to admit that, are they? It will have been misplaced or accidentally destroyed or something.' Maggie sent an apologetic glance to Nick. 'If May could find the historical society's copy, there'd be proof it existed in the first place.'

'How do you know it's Ridley Hawke who wants to buy it?' asked Ted. When my face flamed and Nick looked away, he added, 'Or don't I want to know?'

'You don't want to know,' said Nick.

'What about Branden Greene?' I asked. 'Is anyone questioning him?'

'DS Osborne has been warned off,' said Ted. 'By another very expensive lawyer. Unless you can find some evidence linking him to any wrongdoing, we can't even talk to him.' He cast his eyes around the table. '*Do* any of you have anything on him?'

'We know he used to be involved with Tamzin.' I placed the sandwich back on the plate and brushed the crumbs from my hands. 'We had a photo on the board'—I blushed at the mention of the board—'but the goons took it. Siouxsie has a copy, though.'

Siouxsie obligingly brought the screenshot up on her phone. 'The Facebook account I screenshot this from has taken down the photo in the last twenty-four hours. I tried to message the owner, but they blocked me.'

'How can you tell this is Greene?' Ted squinted at the screen.

'It is,' said Angus. 'The watch he's wearing is one he gave me.' He pushed his sleeve up to show Ted. 'He told me it was a limited edition. Plus, I've known him for long enough that I recognise his profile.'

'Also,' said Siouxsie. 'I've completed searches on Hawksbill Solutions and Ridley Hawke. They're both owned by what looks like a shelf company – Leatherback Green Holdings – of which the BG Family Trust is the primary shareholder. I think we'll find Branden Greene is the primary beneficiary of that trust.'

Angus chuckled. 'Very clever – hawksbill, leatherback, green and olive ridley are all species of sea turtles.'

'I've made a list of the developments Ridley Hawke has been involved with, and none have fantastic environmental credentials, but Branden Greene himself has never been linked with them.'

'Thanks, Siouxsie,' I said. 'We'll need that for Tuesday's meeting.'

Angus shook his head in disappointment. 'I really looked up to Branden Greene.'

'Maybe he doesn't know what Ridley Hawke is up to,'

suggested Siouxsie.

Angus looked at her pityingly. 'You don't believe that any more than I do.'

She shrugged. 'No. I was just trying to make you feel better.'

'Where do we go from here, Ted?' I asked. It felt as though we'd hit a brick wall.

'As far as I see it, I understand why you believe Branden Greene is behind all of this, but unless you have any evidence ...'

'Hang on ...' A thought popped into my head. 'You said he was at a conference in Brisbane last week, Angus?'

Angus nodded. 'I saw him make the keynote on Saturday morning.'

'Did you see him on Sunday morning?' I pressed as another theory grew.

Angus considered my question. 'No ... but that doesn't mean he wasn't there. I did see him later in the afternoon for the close, though.'

A slow, knowing smile spread across Ted's face. 'When he attends things like this, does he usually hire a car?'

Angus nodded. 'With a driver. He gave me their card once; I needed a ride to the airport at an ungodly hour, and Branden told me to call them. He even put it on his account.'

'If it's the same Mercedes he used to go to Ailsa Jacks' place, those things keep a record of their trips on their GPS,' added Nick.

'I'll get someone onto that.' Ted jotted something in his notebook. 'Let's see if he was anywhere near Whale Bay on Sunday. As for you, Clem, take it easy today.' As I would've opened my mouth to protest, he silenced me with a stern look. 'I'm serious, Clem. You were very lucky Nick and Angus reached you in time last night – the outcome could've been very different.'

I nodded, the weight of the reality settling heavily. 'I understand.'

'Good.' He stood. 'Thanks for the sandwich, Nick. The rest of you had better keep an eye on this one until it's all over.'

'Why do you think they tried to kill Clem?' asked Justin.

'That's easy,' said Ted. 'I'd bet Branden Greene's name is all over that board of yours – and his cronies told him as much when they broke in here for a poke about.' Turning back to me, he said, 'Take care, Clem. Rose would never forgive me if something happened to you on my watch.'

His concern brought tears to my eyes. 'Thanks, Ted.'

With a curt nod, he turned and disappeared down the hall once more. The squeaky gate confirming he'd left.

'Right, you lot,' said Nick, clearing the plates. 'Bugger off; Clem needs to rest.'

'I'll stay with her,' added Maggie when she saw the mutinous expression on Nick's face. 'Just until you can go home and get a change of clothes. It might be a good idea to have a shower, too.' She wrinkled her nose. 'I don't know when those clothes you have on were last washed.'

'I found them in the gym bag in my car,' he said ruefully. 'Mine were soaked.'

'I thought as much,' she said with a teasing grin. 'Don't worry, nothing will happen to her.'

As I gazed around the table, my heart swelled with gratitude. I felt lucky to be alive, but more than that, fortunate to have these people in my life.

CHAPTER THIRTY-SEVEN

While we were waiting for Nick to return, May Hartog phoned Maggie. 'I'm so sorry,' she said.

'It's not your fault, May. In any case, Ted has the suspects at the station. Clem's here too – I've got you on speaker.'

'Is it true what they're saying around town?' May asked avidly. 'That someone tried to drown you last night?'

'It is,' I said. 'But thankfully, they weren't successful.'

'And they were the same people who broke into the historical society office?'

'Ted thinks so,' said Maggie.

May was silent for a few seconds. 'Oh dear, I hope this wasn't my fault.'

'Why would you think it was your fault?' I asked.

'After you two visited me yesterday, I called Len and gave him a piece of my mind. "Shame on you, Len Hartog," I said. "Randall Beach bequeathed that land to the community of Whale Bay with the purest of intentions – not for Ray Cosgrove and his cronies to line their pockets."

Then I mentioned there was a copy of the will at the Historical Society, and I intended to go down first thing in the morning to find it. "Let's see how Ray Bloody Cosgrove likes it when we present that at the meeting on Tuesday," I added.' Maggie rolled her eyes, and I grimaced. 'Then Len said that even if there were a will, it wouldn't be legally enforceable, and I replied that we had two very competent lawyers in town who would ensure it was.' She paused for breath. 'So Len must've told Ray, who must've hired those two dreadful men to break in here and to eliminate you.'

'Ray is a lot of things, May, but he would never do that.' I hoped my assumption was correct. If not …

'I agree,' said Maggie. 'I think it's more likely that Len told Ray, who told the person who wants to buy the land, and *he* ordered the break-in and the assault on Clem.'

'Could that be the man I saw with Ray and Martin Cosgrove yesterday?' May asked. 'They were coming out of Martin's office at the wharf, and he got into a black Mercedes with a driver. When I asked Len about him, he pretended he didn't know who I was talking about. I love my Len, but I always know when he's lying – and let me tell you, he was lying when he said he didn't know who the bigwig in the black Merc was.'

I suppressed a smile even though May couldn't see my face. 'Would you be able to describe him?'

'I could do better than that,' said May. 'I took some photos of him, so I'll message them to you.'

Maggie laughed and we high-fived. 'Oh, May, you're a good woman!'

'Well,' said May. 'When Rose died, we wondered who would keep the likes of Ray Cosgrove honest. We ought to have known that Rose's niece and Maggie King would go a long way towards filling the gap Rose left. Besides, I always remember how you two stood up for my Bethany when Kylie Lindsay was giving her a hard time at school. Kylie is the original mean girl, and her mother was the same. I've always wished Bob Lindsay had ended up with Rose instead of Carmen. He had such a thing for her, you know.'

'I've heard that,' I said. Since discovering Rose was my birth mother, I enjoyed these snippets into her life before me even more than I used to – even though to most of Whale Bay, Rose was my aunt.

'How is Beth?' Maggie asked.

'She's doing well.' There was a smile in May's voice. 'They have three kids – the eldest two are at uni. It's such a pity we don't get to see them as often as we'd like.' Her voice trailed off in disappointment. 'Oh, there's one more thing I wanted to tell you – and I'm certainly not telling Len – but all might not be lost in terms of finding a copy of that will.'

'Really?' I looked across at Maggie, the beginnings of a smile on her lips.

'Yes. About a year ago, I brought home some boxes of documents that I always meant to catalogue and scan, but I never got around to it. They're in the last place Len would ever think to look – my sewing room. I'll go through them this afternoon when Len heads out to golf.'

'Thanks, May,' said Maggie. 'We'll keep our fingers crossed.'

Once May rang off, Maggie said, 'Here's hoping she finds it.'

'And that it has the sorts of covenants in it we hope it does.'

Maggie's phone pinged. 'It's the photos May promised us.' She let out a low whistle. 'Is that Branden Greene?'

The first image showed a tall, lean man shaking hands with Ray Cosgrove. He was dressed in a city-meets-country uniform of designer moleskin jeans, a navy polo and R.M. Williams riding boots, a chunky watch on his wrist. May had zoomed in for the second photo, and he was pictured with his hand on the open car door. His short, dark hair was peppered with grey, his defined cheekbones giving him a look that could grace the cover of a business magazine or an R.M. Williams catalogue.

'Yeah.' A shiver ran up my spine. 'It is. And he looks like the sort of man used to getting what he wants.' I didn't say he also looked like the sort of man prepared to pay to have someone else do his dirty work for him. Had Branden Greene ordered my death? Had he ordered Tamzin's? Even if Scarface and his mate couldn't have killed Tamzin, who's to say he didn't contract someone else to?

Maggie flashed me a sideways glance. 'Well,' she said, 'let's show him that Whale Bay can't be bought.'

Finn phoned on Sunday afternoon to hear how I was after my ordeal. At first, he seemed more upset by the fact that Maggie had called him rather than concerned about what had actually happened. 'I can't believe you didn't tell me yourself, Clem,' he said. 'And what was Nick Cosgrove doing there?'

Anger had bubbled in my stomach, and before I could stop myself, I retorted, 'In case you didn't get the message, I nearly died; Nick and Angus saved my life. Be grateful Maggie thought to inform you because I was certainly in no position to do it. If you want to make it about your feelings, that's up to you, but as far as I'm concerned, this one is all about me.'

After that, he settled down, apologised and listened as I caught him up on what had been happening.

'If you'd done as I asked and stayed out of it, you wouldn't have been attacked,' he said when I finished speaking.

'True,' I conceded, 'and you and Ailsa would probably have been charged with Tamzin's murder.'

That seemed to take the wind out of his sails.

'I'm sorry, Clem. All I seem to be doing lately is stuffing up and apologising for stuffing up.'

'Well, we've both had the week from hell, so neither of

us is at our best. On the upside, though, Cosmo and Beans spent a night at Maggie and Justin's, but they're back with me now. They're perfectly happy.'

'Thanks, Clem. I … we need to …'

'Talk when you get back?' I finished his sentence.

'Yes,'

'I know we do, but let's just get through these few days, hey?'

Nick spent the night again with me but had stayed in my old room. Despite the promise I'd made myself, I hadn't told him about the baby and couldn't have a relationship without telling him that. Somehow, he understood I had things to work through, and neither of us referred to what had almost happened between us the other night. The memory of it was, however, in every glance and every fleeting touch.

I overheard him talking to Justin and knew he was coming under family pressure both for the time he was spending with me and for helping organise the opposition to Ray's plans, but Nick didn't seem to be concerned by that.

Monday was spent finalising our arguments for Tuesday's council meeting. May hadn't yet come up with anything on the will front. Still, we discovered some clauses in the Local Environment Plan that permitted the acquisition and protection of vulnerable areas of land requiring conservation and rehabilitation for both fauna and flora. It wasn't much, but it was potentially sufficient for us to argue that the piece of land should be subject to a heritage listing, although none of us believed we would be successful. Given the current circumstances, the best possible outcome would be a delay in the sale for our arguments to be reviewed – and that was only feasible if we could gather enough people to attend the meeting and protest the sale.

Bella had helped Siouxsie design a flyer, which they had posted around town. Lainey handed one to everyone who bought a coffee, and Bron gave them out at the bakery.

Angus knew someone who knew someone from the local radio station and had been on air talking about the importance of protecting coastal habitats and the dangers associated with approving developments intended only to benefit a small proportion of the community at the cost of the community's biggest asset. He'd also received a call from Branden Greene expressing his disappointment and threatening to pull future funding.

'He said he's surprised I hadn't contacted him before I expressed my opinions publicly,' Angus told us when we convened at my house on Monday night.

'We'd understand if you wanted to back off,' said Nick. 'He has the power to stuff your career.'

'He does,' agreed Angus. 'But if I'm quiet about this, what else will I have to be quiet about in the future? No …' He shook his head. 'He can do his worst.'

Support came from a surprising angle when Michael

Lindsay dropped around on Monday night. While Siouxsie initially treated him as the enemy, Mike stood his ground.

'I totally understand why you don't want me here, but I just want you all to know I'll be sitting with you tomorrow at the meeting and not with Martin.' He looked at me fondly. 'No piece of land is worth killing for, and even though Martin thinks he's the best thing since sliced bread, I don't trust that Branden Greene as far as I could throw him.'

'You've met him then?' I asked.

'Yes. Ray and Paula had us all over for dinner on Saturday night. Martin spent the night sucking up to him, and Kylie didn't stop flirting.'

So Branden Greene was being wined and dined just metres from where his henchmen were attempting to drown me.

'Did he take any phone calls during the evening?' I asked.

Mike narrowed his eyes. 'You don't think he …?' When Nick nodded soberly, Mike scratched his head and pursed his lips. 'Earlier in the evening, Ray said something about roadblocks, and he joked about how one of his personal roadblocks was in the process of being removed, and then later he took a call that seemed to make him angry. He went out onto the balcony to take it. All I heard was him saying, "They know better than to talk but get them the best – money is no object. Argue she was unstable, you know the drill."'

My hand involuntarily went to my throat, trembling slightly as a chill ran down my spine. He'd dismissed me as a roadblock, as something to be sorted. For a land deal? No, there had to be more at stake.

Nick watched me, concern in his eyes. 'I'd like to bet that call was from his lawyer telling him that Scarface and his mate had been arrested.'

'Knowing what I know now, yes,' said Mike. 'I agree with you. Can't Ted question him?'

I shook my head. 'Apparently not. We … the police have no evidence linking him with the two men who attacked me.'

Before he left, Mike, Nick and Angus huddled to one side; something was going on with these three, but I didn't want to push Nick to tell me about it until he was ready. Then Nick patted Mike on the back. 'I'll see you tomorrow.'

Mike gave me a quick but heartfelt hug. 'I'm glad you didn't drown.'

'So am I, although I'm sure your sister would see it as a disappointment.'

'I don't know.' He grinned. 'I think she'd miss sparring with you.'

CHAPTER THIRTY-EIGHT

On Tuesday morning, we were all putting on a brave face, and no one was willing to admit we probably didn't have a hope of blocking the sale of the land. It would be, we figured, enough that Ray would see there was opposition to the sale and to know that the people of Whale Bay wouldn't let him do what he liked with community property without making a noise. That is if anyone other than us showed up.

I spent the morning at New Moon, going through accounts that I already knew were in order and approving Bella's designs for the journals we'd spoken about.

Nina, predictably, felt terrible about her part in Saturday's near tragedy, but I did my best to convince her none of it was her fault.

'You weren't to know,' I said, patting her arm. 'And the message was so believable. If anyone is to blame, it's me for not ringing Angus to check – I did, after all, have his number. My only excuse is my head was full of the ins and outs of Local Environment Plans, legal precedents and the like. I never did like commercial law when I was at uni.'

'Even so, when I took the message, I'd had a feeling about it I didn't listen to,' said Nina. 'I never go home via the surf club and don't know what made me go that way this time.'

'I'm glad you did.'

'I hate to think what would have happened if—'

'Don't.' I held up a hand. 'Please don't. You did go via the surf club and you did see Nick and Angus, and they did get there on time.' I smiled tremulously. 'Okay?'

'Okay.' She nodded slowly.

The bell rang, and a courier stepped into the shop. 'I have a delivery for a Clem Carter.' He held out a yellow envelope. 'I need you to sign for it.'

'Sure,' I said, perplexed.

'Should you open it? What if the envelope is rigged …?' Nina whispered, her eyes straying to Bella.

'Good point. There's a sender's name and address on the back,' I said. 'Let's see if we can find a phone number.' A few quick clicks of a keyboard soon brought up the name and number of a solicitor in Brisbane. I dialled the number.

'Good morning, Morgan and Murphy Solicitors. This is Hayley speaking.'

I raised my eyebrows at Nina. So far, so safe. 'Hi, Hayley. My name is Clem Carter, and I've received an envelope from your firm this morning. I was wondering if I could speak with'—I referred to the address sticker on the rear of the envelope—'whoever sent it to me?'

'Of course,' she said. 'Putting you through to Mr Morgan now.'

'Ms Carter,' said a deep, well-modulated voice. 'Matthew Morgan. How may I help you?'

'I've received an envelope from you this morning, and I wondered—'

'I must apologise for the delay in getting this to you,' he said. 'I've been in Fiji on holiday with my family and arrived back yesterday to find the documents sitting on my desk. Ms Griffiths had obviously posted them a week ago, and then, of course, I read the news of her death, so I arranged for a special courier.'

Ms Griffiths. Tamzin? 'Ummm, what's in the envelope?'

'You haven't opened it yet? I don't know exactly what's in there – other than her last will and testament, which she signed the week before I went on holidays. There was, however, a letter for me stating that in the event of her untimely death within the next thirty days, I was to send the enclosed documents to you and you'd know what to do with them.'

'Oh.'

'Ms Carter?'

'Yes, sorry, thank you for your time.'

Hanging up, I pinched my top lip. Tamzin had posted her solicitor documents to be forwarded to me in the event of her death. She must have known she was in danger, and if she were in danger, those close to her would also be at risk. This must contain the information Scarface had been employed to locate. The information I was certain Branden Greene was desperate to find.

'What is it?' asked Nina.

'I think it might be Tamzin's insurance policy,' I said. 'I'll just—' I waved towards the office. 'If anyone asks, you haven't seen me.'

Gingerly, I opened the envelope, finding inside a smaller envelope addressed to me and another containing various documents, photos of Tamzin and Branden Greene together, a thumb drive and a mobile phone. Putting the rest aside, I opened the smaller envelope and pulled out a handwritten letter. And began to read.

Dear Clementine,

Can I call you Clem? Even though we've never formally met, I feel like I know you. Since I heard you were dating Finn – Ailsa has been keeping tabs on Finn for me – I learnt as much as I could about you, and what I learnt, I liked. I hope I can trust you; I can't trust anyone else, you see. If I send the contents of this envelope to Finn or Ailsa, I know he'll come to them looking for it. Instead, I'm sending it to my solicitor, and if anything happens to me – as I fear it will – he's to send it to you, and I have to trust you to do the right thing with it. Above all, I need to keep Finn and Ailsa safe.

I'm writing this on Saturday evening. Finn is asleep in his room, making those little snuffling noises I always found so endearing. If you're reading this, though, the worst has happened, and Branden Greene is to blame.

You've probably heard about him being an environmentalist, a philanthropist, a millionaire who married his childhood sweetheart and gives back to the community. He's all of those things and none of them.

Once upon a time, I was taken in by him; we were lovers. It was soon after Finn and I had separated, and Branden dazzled me. I knew he was married, but he had all the usual stories, and, to be honest, I didn't care that he had a wife. After a while, I began to see that there were two sides to him: the side that cared about conservation and the environment — the side of him I'd fallen in love with — and a more ruthless side. He was also possessive, controlling and cruel.

Once I overheard him making a deal to buy some remnant rainforest on the New South Wales north coast. He promised the land would be protected, but he ripped it up and built holiday apartments on it. Not that he did that — Ridley Hawke, his development company, did. He paid bribes to councillors to get it through, and he arranged accidents for his opponents. If you've met him, you probably won't believe the last — you'll have thought him as charming as everyone else does — which is why, in this envelope, there are recordings of phone calls where he arranged these accidents.

When I met Ailsa, it was love at first sight, and I tried to leave Branden. To say he didn't take it well was an understatement. I told him there was no one else, that I'd realised

I wanted more — marriage. I didn't, but I thought it would scare him away. He told me he'd leave his wife, but she'd just been diagnosed with breast cancer, so now wasn't the right time. I told him I loved him too much to share him. He finally accepted that but told me he'd come after me if he discovered I was with someone else.

I laid the letter down. This was why Tamzin never went public with Ailsa. It had nothing to do with her family's feelings; it was to protect Ailsa.

After a few years, I relaxed enough to believe that I might be safe to make our relationship public. I began using my maiden name again and applied for a job in Brisbane so Ailsa and I could spend our weekends together. I didn't realise Branden owned the company I was working for. He immediately wanted to rekindle our relationship.

He told me about the land near Dolphin Point, mentioning that the town mayor had uncovered its ownership by the council and was looking to partner with someone to build a world-class resort there. The only issue was its proximity to protected mangroves. He said I had to return the right findings, and if I did, he would marry me as I'd asked all those years ago. He knew Finn lived in Whale Bay and when I didn't immediately agree, accused me of wanting to reconcile with Finn. He said if he, Branden, couldn't have me, no one could. He also said if I tried to leave him again, he'd have me killed — along with whoever I was involved with. I believed him and promised I'd ask Finn for a divorce.

You can find all of these conversations on the thumb drive in this envelope. I recorded them all because it was the only way I could think of to keep those I love safe. Also included here is my will. I leave everything to Ailsa. If you see her, please tell her how much I loved her. I hope she knows, and I hope she forgives me.

There's a phone in here too. On it are messages Branden sent to one of his henchmen — a nasty piece of work with red hair and a scar.

It's been lovely seeing Finn again this weekend. While we weren't right for each other, I'll always love him. Branden has asked me to meet him tomorrow morning and I'm to drive him out to the site. He's supposed to be at a conference but has arranged to get away. He told me he wanted to show me what he has planned for the site, but I think he knows I stole the phone and copied some of the other documents you'll find in this envelope. He also overheard me on the phone to Ailsa and knows I'm in love with someone else, but thinks it's Finn. I've told him it's not, but I don't think he believed me.

If he does kill me, he'll come looking for this — which is why I'm sending it to my solicitor first and then to you. I hope it's enough to have him charged with my murder.

I wish we'd been able to meet. I think we could have been friends.

Kind regards

Tamzin Griffiths

CHAPTER THIRTY-NINE

My heart beat fast as I read the letter. It was almost as though Tamzin's pain was in the letter, and reading it transferred the same pain to me. What to do? I needed to keep it safe.

Opening the scanning app on my phone, I scanned the letter and sent it to Maggie and Nick. The rest I secured in the small key safe in the bottom drawer of my desk. After that, I rang Ted.

'Ted, can you drop by the store, please?'

'What's wrong, Clem?'

Surely Branden Greene wouldn't have my phone bugged? Shaking my head at my fanciful thinking, I said, 'That evidence we're after was just delivered.'

'I'll be there as soon as I can. Stay right where you are.'

I sat back in my chair and contemplated what I'd just read. While I hadn't listened to any of the recordings, what Tamzin had said would surely have to be enough to allow Branden Greene to be brought in for questioning. Unless, that is, he'd also paid off senior members of the police force. After all, DS Osborne had quickly jumped on Finn as being the prime suspect.

The bell on the door rang. I heard Nina say, 'Can I help you?'

'I certainly hope so. I'm looking for Clem Carter.' The man was well-spoken, his voice pleasant.

'I'm sorry,' said Nina. 'We haven't seen Clem for a few days. She had a nasty accident on the weekend and is recuperating.'

'Now,' said the man. 'You and I both know that's not true. Ms Carter is here and it would be in your interests to tell me where she is.'

Something clattered to the floor, and I heard Nina say, 'Get your hands off me. You're hurting me.'

'I'll do more than that if you don't tell me where she is.' A short silence. 'Who's this crouching down behind this shelf?'

Oh God. Bella. Without thinking, I came out from behind the curtain that enclosed my office. 'Leave them alone. You don't need them.'

'Do you know who I am?' he asked.

'Branden Greene, I presume.' I bit the inside of my lip in an effort to maintain a calm facade even though my heart was beating fit to burst from my chest. 'What do you want? If it's about this afternoon's meeting, nothing you can pay me will stop me from standing up this afternoon and telling council exactly what you've got planned.'

He dismissed my words with a little wave. 'I don't care what you have to say about that. Nothing you can say will change the outcome.'

I gave a little shrug of my shoulder. 'Even a copy of the will from the original owner stating that the land must first be offered to the community if the council wishes to sell?'

'You don't have a copy of the will,' he said, straightening slightly, the barest downturn of his mouth showing me he wasn't entirely sure.

'Don't I?' Another shrug. 'You'll need to wait and see, won't you?'

He narrowed his eyes and stared at me; I willed myself to stare back.

'You have something that belongs to me,' he finally said, smirking.

'Really? I can't think what.' I held my ground.

'A short while ago, a courier dropped off an envelope to you. That envelope had been sent from a solicitor in Brisbane, and I believe it contains documents and … other property that belongs to me.'

How did he know? Did he have my phone tapped, or had he been watching the store and paid the courier off?

'What makes you think that? The envelope was addressed to me and contained papers pertinent to a divorce case I'm working on.'

'Prove it.' An unpleasant smile curled around his lips.

'Sorry. Client confidentiality and all that. I could show

you, but then I'd have to kill you.' I tilted my head to one side. 'But then, you'd probably know all about that – or at least where to find someone to do the job for you.'

With that, he lunged at me, his hands latching onto my throat. 'You will give me that envelope,' he growled. 'Why couldn't they do the job properly and finish you off?'

My hands flailed at his face as I fought for air.

Nina pounded on his back with her fists. 'Is this what you did to Tamzin? You have witnesses this time!'

With that, he released me and whirled around to face her. Bella held her phone up in the air. 'Once more for the recording,' she sneered.

As he would have lunged at Bella, Nina put her foot out, and he tripped and fell into a display of candles used for rituals and spell casting. As he attempted to get up, Ted and Tyson burst through the door.

'We'll take it from here.' Ted crouched beside Branden, pulling his arms behind his back. When I rubbed my throat, he said, 'Are you okay?'

I leant against the front counter, gasping. Managing to nod. 'Thanks to these guys, yes.'

'Did you get all of that?' he asked Bella.

She nodded. 'He didn't see me at first, so I could turn on record. When he went for Clem, I videoed it.'

Ted nodded approvingly. 'Well done.' To me, he said, 'You better give me the rest of what you have. We've got the testimony of his driver saying he lent Greene the car and the record from the GPS showing he was here on Sunday morning. The Merc was also picked up on CCTV only a couple of streets away from where Tamzin's car was found. With the DNA from her fingernails, we've got him. Tyson, read him his rights.'

'What are we charging him with, Senior?'

'The murder of Tamzin Griffiths, conspiracy to murder Clem and the attempted murder of Clementine Carter. That'll do for starters.'

Nick and Maggie charged through the door, Nick taking me in his arms and holding me tight. 'It was easier on my stress levels not knowing what you were up to,' he said with a forced laugh.

Ted chuckled. 'If she's anything like her mother, you'll need to get used to that.'

I pulled away from Nick, my mouth open. 'You knew about that?'

With another chuckle and a wave, he and Tyson led Branden Greene away.

'Rose was your mother?' Nina asked, her eyes wide.

I nodded. 'I was adopted at birth but didn't find out until after she died that Rose was my birth mother.'

Before she could ask more questions, Maggie grabbed my arm. 'May Hartog called me – she found the will, and there is a condition that in the event the council decides to sell, the property has to be offered to the community to purchase – here's the best bit – at the estimated value at the time of the transfer plus an annual adjustment for inflation.' She held her hand in the air, and I clapped it. 'We've got them.'

'Somehow, I don't think we'll need the will now,' said Nick, his eyes on the police car pulling away from the kerb.

'How did you come to get here so quickly?' I asked.

'I was at Maggie's running through some documents when your text came through with Tamzin's letter. Then Siouxsie returned from getting coffees and said she'd seen Branden Greene walk into New Moon. She rang Tyson, but he said they were already on the way.' Nick grinned. 'This town, eh?'

'Yes,' I said. 'This town.'

Maggie glanced at her watch. 'We need to get to the council meeting!'

Hugging Bella and then Nina, I said, 'I'm so sorry you were here for that.'

'It's not your fault,' said Nina. 'And thanks to Bella's quick thinking, he won't be able to hurt anyone again.'

'Clem!' said Maggie impatiently.

'I'd better go … again, thank you both.'

'Clem!' Maggie held the door open.

'Alright, alright. I'm coming. God, you're impatient.'

She wound her arm around my waist. 'And you're not?'

CHAPTER FORTY

We shouldn't have worried, Whale Bay came out in force to support us. Angus, Justin, Harry and Siouxsie were already in the bowling club auditorium waiting for us, Justin's anxious glances at his watch turning into a relieved smile at our entrance. I waved at Gordon Johnston who was sitting with Rose's book club friends; and exchanged thumbs-up greetings with Bron. There were so many people in the room there must be tumbleweeds blowing up the middle of Beach Road.

True to his word, Mike sat with us, as did May Hartog. When Ray saw her in the gallery he had a quick word with Len who strode with purpose through the crowd to reach us.

'What are you doing here, love?' he asked in a conciliatory tone.

May stood and planted her hands on her hips. 'Helping save our mangroves.'

When Len cast a nervous look back towards his boss, May added, 'You should be ashamed of yourself, Len Hartog!' After an embarrassed cough, he went scuttling back to his position on the stage with Ray and the other councillors.

Of the Lindsay and Cosgrove women there was no sign. 'Hardly surprising,' said Mike when I commented as such. 'It wouldn't occur to Kylie, Carmen or Paula that Ray's proposal wouldn't get through. And Lauren,' he added sadly, 'will always go where Kylie leads.'

Justin gave Maggie a quick kiss on the cheek and squeezed my arm. 'I'd better be getting up there too. I'd say good luck but you don't need it now.'

In the end the meeting was an anticlimax. Maggie presented the will stating the land had to be offered to the community before any external purchasers could bid for it. When the cheering from the floor died down Nick announced that the prospective purchaser was currently in Ted's lock-up and charged with murder and other offences. Ray Cosgrove was speechless for the first time in anyone's memory.

After the council meeting, we'd gathered at the bar in the bowling club to celebrate our victory, with the barman declaring our first drinks were on the house.

Nick and I drifted outside and sat on stools at one of the high tables overlooking the bowling green.

'I suppose you'll be going back now,' I said.

'I'm not going anywhere.' Nick's eyes met mine, and for the second time in almost as many days, I feared I was drowning. 'I couldn't say anything before, but Mike and I are going into business together.' My mouth dropped open. 'We'll be running eco-tours where the objective is to learn about the animals, the environment and the importance of conservation and sustainability. We've consulted with the Traditional Owners and would like to incorporate culture into our offer. Angus has been helping us too.'

'That's what you three were discussing that day at Beach Brewz,' I guessed.

'Yes, I just couldn't tell you then. If word had got out before we were ready, it could've ruined everything. So …' He tilted his head to the side. 'What do you think?'

'About the business or about you staying around?' Unable to deny the rush of warmth that infused me at the thought of him staying in Whale Bay, I played for time.

'Both.'

'I'm glad you're back, Nick,' I finally said. 'I'd miss you again if you left. What does your family think about it?'

His laugh was short. 'Mum's happy I'll be in town, but you can probably imagine what Martin had to say'—he rolled his eyes—'and Dad ranted and raved about how I was competing with the family business.'

'I imagine he also had something to say about my influence, too,' I said wryly.

'Yeah, your name did come up,' he said with a lopsided grin. 'Dad said something along the lines of how he thought he'd dealt with that problem twenty-five years ago.' He wrinkled his nose. 'The conversation went downhill after that.' He lifted a shoulder. 'Mike's getting it too from all directions, although Bob seems to understand he wants the opportunity to do something he believes in; he'll come around. Carmen though'—he inhaled sharply and raised his eyebrows—'she's a different proposition.'

He drained his beer and wiped his mouth with the back of his hand. 'Clem, I know we haven't had time to talk about it—'

'Things have been a little busy around here,' I quipped.

Under his gaze, I dropped my head, and he continued to speak. 'I know you're with Finn, but I was wondering, is there a chance for us?'

'Oh, Nick …'

'It's okay, I understand; you're in love with Finn, and anything between us was a combination of muscle memory and heat of the moment.'

I looked up and met his eyes, unable to read anything other than sadness in their oceanic depths. 'It's not that, and you're right, there was a moment'—I snorted a half laugh—'or moments. Finn and me'—I shrugged and lifted my palms—'I don't know where we're at. That all happened so fast; Rose died, and I got caught up in finding out what happened, and … he was there. I jumped straight out of a relationship with a senior partner in my law firm into a relationship with Finn. My whole life changed in a matter of weeks.' I snorted a laugh. 'And that was less than two months ago.' This was the moment. But' —my breath caught in my throat— 'there's something you need to know.'

This was the moment. Regardless of what happened with Finn and me, any future relationship with Nick – even if it was just a friendship – had to be built on honesty … the way it had started.

He frowned, his smile forced and weak. 'You're beginning to worry me.'

Taking another deep breath, I said, 'Do you remember how I told you I'd tried to find you?' He nodded. 'Rose did too.'

'I went to Indonesia surfing. I needed to drop off the grid for a while. And before I knew it, a month had turned into six months and then a year. What was so urgent?'

'I … I needed to contact you to tell you'—I looked to the sky, my eyes burning, my throat closing—'I needed to tell you I was pregnant.' As I swallowed the lump away, a tear ran down my cheek. I dashed it away with the back of my hand, but then another came and another.

'You were pregnant?' he whispered, his eyes wide. 'And I didn't know.'

'I tried to find you, to tell you …' Tears flowed freely, and I did nothing to stop them. 'I wrote to you as soon as I knew, but when I didn't get a response, I thought you wanted nothing to do with me or the baby. My father wanted me to … well, I'm sure you can guess, but I couldn't. But nor could I keep her.' Through my tears, I saw Maggie and Justin approach, stop suddenly and make a quick retreat. It was enough for me to realise the inappropriateness of the location for the discussion we were having.

Sliding from my stool, I dashed to the darkness at the end of the green until I was out of sight from the bar.

'Clem, wait up.' Nick was right behind me. 'When did you write to me?'

'As soon as I knew, so a few weeks after I left. Although I knew you were probably with Kylie, I thought'—I leant back against the outside wall of the club—'I thought you should know. I asked her not to, but Rose kept trying. Part of me hoped'—I sighed—'you'd turn up and everything would be okay.'

'Oh Christ, Clem, I'm sorry. I didn't get your letter; I didn't know you'd even tried to contact me until I got back in touch with Mike.' His eyes glittered with the reflections from the streetlights in the carpark and something else. Tears? 'You'd been gone a month before I gave up hope,' he said. 'That was when Dad told me he'd paid you to stay away. He must have got your letter and read it.' He kicked the wall and covered his face with his hands. 'I didn't know.'

I don't know how long we stood there, me slumped back against the wall, him rigid with anger – whether at me or his father, I couldn't tell. 'You said "her",' he finally said. 'You said you couldn't keep her.'

'We had a baby girl,' I choked. 'A beautiful baby girl with your eyes, and I couldn't keep her. Rose offered to help, but my father was adamant, and I knew he was right.'

'You gave her away,' he said bluntly, hurt in every syllable, his fists in balls.

When I nodded, he wiped at his eyes, turned and left. I watched his back until it disappeared into the darkness, then I sank to the ground and sobbed.

Maggie found me there sometime later and pulled me to my feet and into her arms. 'Let's get you home,' she said gently.

Bundling me into the car, she secured my seatbelt and didn't speak again until she'd helped me up the path and into the house.

'Straight to bed?' She directed me towards the room.

When I nodded, she helped me undress and put me to bed. 'Stay here and I'll see to the dogs.'

I was still sitting on the edge of the bed when she got back.

'The dogs have been fed, watered and toileted,' she said,

'Thank you,' I whispered.

'What happened, sweetie?' Maggie sat beside me and placed an arm around my shoulders.

'I told him,' I said.

'About the baby?'

My head turned slowly to face her. 'How did you know?'

'I didn't – not for sure. But when Rose was trying to get in touch with Nick, and when she stayed away as long as she did'—she gave a little shrug—'I put two and two together. How did he take it?'

Unable to get the words out, I sobbed. Maggie held me until I could cry no more. 'He needs time,' she said gently. 'He'll be feeling so many things right now—'

'He hates me,' I said.

'Maybe,' she conceded. 'But there's also guilt, regret and a million other things wrapped into it all.' She brushed my hair off my forehead and kissed me there. 'Give him time.'

CHAPTER FORTY-ONE

A week later …

Harry had finished the deck, and I'd invited everyone—Siouxsie, Harry, Maggie and Justin, Angus, Nina, and even Michael and Lauren—over for a barbeque to help me christen it. Bella said she was going to a friend's house, and I understood she would feel uncomfortable with the adults. Tamzin's funeral had been held yesterday and Finn would finally be home this morning. As for Nick? I didn't know. He hadn't spoken to me since I told him about our baby, and I knew I needed to give him time to process it all.

Pushing concerns about him to the back of my mind, I'd made a pavlova and some salads, and they, plus a butterflied leg of lamb and some sausages, were in the fridge. The dogs and I were sweeping the last of the sawdust from the floor when we heard the front gate squeak. The dogs raced to the gate barking. When their usual *someone's here* warning bark turned into a more excited *someone's* here bark, I put the broom down and followed them.

'Hey.' Finn had dropped to the ground to hug his

ecstatic dogs until first Beans and then Cosmo struggled out of the head-lock he had them in. Scrambling to his feet, Finn brushed the bum of his shorts. He opened his arms, and I walked into them, but while he hugged me tight, and the kiss was hard and lingering, there was none of the urgency I would've expected after his absence; it felt strangely subdued.

'Thanks for looking after them, Clem, and thanks also for what you did to find out what happened to Tamzin. I know Ailsa's grateful too.' He rubbed his hands up and down my arms as he spoke, his words lacking emotion.

'It wasn't just me, you know.' I pulled away, feeling awkward.

'I know, but'—he shrugged—'you're the one who nearly got herself killed as a result. Are you okay?'

I nodded. 'I'm fine.' He didn't need to know that for the first few nights afterwards, when I closed my eyes, the water rushed again over my head, filling my lungs. And he didn't need to know how I no longer felt safe on my morning swims, but I was pushing through. Branden Greene might have tried to take my life, but I was damned if he was going to take my enjoyment of the ocean from me.

'Finn …'

'Clem …'

Our words collided. 'You first,' I said, leading him back towards the deck.

'I'm sorry, Clem. These last couple of weeks have been

'…' He grimaced, unable to continue.

'They certainly have been,' I said ruefully, climbing the three stairs to the deck.

'So much so that the last few weeks have felt like a dream someone else was living.' His deep brown eyes were shadowed, and I knew what he wanted to say without him saying it. I also knew I had to let him say it. 'I thought I was ready for another relationship, but …' He shrugged.

'You're not?'

He shook his head slowly. 'And you're not either, are you?'

'It was too perfect, wasn't it?' I tried to laugh but couldn't.

'Maybe if I hadn't said the "p" word?'

'Maybe.' I stepped back to look him over. He'd lost weight, his long-sleeved T-shirt hanging loosely. 'What happens now?'

'I know it's a cliche, but I hope we can still be friends.' His gaze dropped to his feet and then back up at me, biting his bottom lip.

'Yeah, Finn.' Hot tears welled up in my eyes, blurring my vision. 'We can be the best of friends.'

'What about you and Nick? What's happening there?' He didn't quite meet my eyes; instead, they flicked to the swing in the backyard.

'I don't know,' I conceded. 'There's history, of course, and … I don't know,' I said again, feeling again the stab of pain at the look in Nick's eyes when I told him about our baby. At that moment, he hated me, and I couldn't blame him.

'I heard he's staying in town.' His eyes finally settled on me, heavy with unspoken emotion.

'He is. He and Mike are going into business together.' I chuckled. 'Carmen Lindsay is incandescent, and Kylie has told Lauren she's dead to her.' Finn laughed when I held up my hand, tossed my head and mimicked Kylie.

'Lauren's going to need a friend too, then,' he said.

'Yeah.'

He gazed around the deck. 'Harry's done a good job here. What's next? Are you still going to open up the kitchen?'

I nodded, happy to be back on safe ground. 'Yep. I want to take the kitchen window out and pop a servery window in. Also, we'll open the whole wall and replace the kitchen door with concertina doors so it flows.' I paused. 'I'm christening the deck later this afternoon … You will come, won't you?'

'Will Nick be here?'

'I don't know.' I shrugged. 'We've had … let's just say our history caught up with us. He's gone back to Cairns to pick up some of his things, so I don't know if he'll be here tonight. Please say you'll come.'

He began to shake his head and finished up nodding. 'Yeah, I'll be here. I still haven't met him, and if he's staying,

I'll need to get used to seeing him.' I knew Finn meant he'd need to get used to seeing Nick with me. 'You can all catch me up on how you saved the mangroves. Rose would be proud.'

'I hope so.'

If anyone noticed that Finn and I weren't exactly together, no one commented. It would be, I assumed, something we'd just need to deal with until our apartness was as normal as our sudden togetherness had been. Maggie took me aside to ask if I was alright and I could answer honestly. 'I'm fine, sad, but fine.'

'And Nick? Is he coming?'

My half shrug was the only answer I had to that question. She squeezed my arm and I plastered on a wide smile to greet Lauren Lindsay. 'The shop looks lovely, Lauren; you must be proud.'

'Thanks, Clem, but it won't amount to anything if Kylie snubs it. She's so angry with Michael and Nick.' She looked so crestfallen, and I felt a pang of sympathy. 'I don't think she'll speak to me again – and if she doesn't speak to me, no one else who matters will either.'

'Don't worry about her,' I said, handing her a glass of bubbles. 'Kylie Lindsay needs to understand the world – and Whale Bay – doesn't revolve around her.'

'That's nice of you to say, Clem, but new businesses like mine need influencer support if I'm going to attract the clientele I want, and if Kylie and her friends ignore me, it doesn't matter if I've paid top-dollar to lure the best therapists up from Noosa.'

'What about Marta Cametti? Would she be enough of an influencer for you?' I'd negotiated Marta's divorce for her a couple of months ago – although she ended up reconciling with her husband. She'd reached out during the week to let me know she'd be up this way on holiday and was I interested in doing her postnup. Naturally, I'd had to clear it with my old employers, but they were happy for me to take Marta's account.

'No. Way! Marta Cametti? You know her? She's so much better than an influencer – she's a major celebrity.'

Her excitement made me grin. 'I do know her, and I'm happy to put a word in for you.'

Lauren beamed. 'That will really get up Kylie's nose.'

'Then my work here is done,' I said with a laugh.

When Michael Lindsay found me, I was in the kitchen dressing the pavlova with strawberries.

'Lauren told me what you're doing for her; thank you. I know she hasn't been the nicest to you over the years, so I appreciate this.'

I waved his thanks away. 'I've never had a problem with Lauren,' I said. 'Only her choice of friends. Your sister, as we know, is not one of my favourite people.'

'Nor you, hers,' he said with a sly smile. 'Kylie hates that you're back, but I think she hates it more that you've made a success of your life.'

'As Siouxsie would say, too bad, so sad. I've got better things to do than worry about what your sister thinks of me.' I unwrapped a flaky chocolate bar and sprinkled it over the strawberries.

'Nick told me.' Michael made himself comfy against the kitchen doorjamb.

'You didn't tell—' My heartbeat quickened at the thought that my past – our past – could be front page news around Whale Bay.

'I've told no one,' he reassured me, 'but Nick was so angry he tackled his father about a letter you wrote.'

My over-beating heart sank. 'Do you hate me too?'

'Hate you?' He frowned. 'What for? You did nothing wrong; it was just one of those'—he wrinkled his nose— 'things that happen.'

'Nick hates me.' The pain I'd felt last week returned; a sharp, stabbing pain washed through me in a wave. Through it I vaguely registered the squeaking of the front gate.

'He doesn't hate you,' said Mike. 'He just needs time.'

'I don't hate you.' Nick had let himself in through the front door, joining us in the kitchen. He smiled weakly at Mike, who slapped him on the back, but his eyes stayed on me. 'Can we talk?'

It had only been a week, but he seemed drawn and faded, as if the colour had leached from him.

'Umm, I have to …' I waved my hand towards the

pavlova.

'I'll deal with this.' Mike stepped forward and took the chocolate packet from my hand and shooed me away.

'But—' I protested.

'Go, Clem. I'll rummage about until I find what I need, and if in doubt, I'll ask Mags.'

'You'll ask me what?' Maggie had entered the kitchen, too, her eyes wide with a mix of curiosity and concern when they landed on Nick.

'Where to find plates and spoons and things so these guys can talk,' Mike said.

'Go.' Maggie ushered me in Nick's direction. 'Mike and I will make it happen.'

Nick sent me a weak smile, and we left the house through the front door without a word. I followed when Nick crossed the road to the beach and sat on the dunes above the high water mark, patting the sand beside him. There were no street lights near where we sat; the only light was from the houses across the road.

'I don't hate you,' he repeated, staring out to the ocean. 'I … I'm sorry, I reacted badly and'—he scratched the back of his head—'I didn't know what I should be thinking or feeling, so I reacted poorly.'

'You seemed so angry,' I said, digging my feet into the cool sand.

'I was. So angry.'

Racked with guilt, I lowered my head. 'I understand,' I

mumbled. 'I would've been too.'

'Not just at you, although I was angry with you too – for believing I could've been with Kylie, but if I'd been presented with the same image, I probably would've reacted the same way you did. I was also angry with myself for believing what my father told me; I was angry the letter you wrote me had been destroyed—'

'Destroyed?'

'Yes,' he said grimly, his profile firm. 'Dad admitted that. It was for my own good, he said. He wasn't going to stand there and watch me throw my future away on … well, you can imagine.'

Yes, I could imagine. A burning anger at Ray Cosgrove, hot and prickly, bubbled within. He'd denied Nick and me a future; Ray had denied us our child.

'I did some thinking while I drove to and from Cairns,' he said, 'and behind all the anger, there was also regret for a life I could've had – with you and with our children. Mostly though, what I felt most was guilt – that my stupid pride sent me running away when you needed me. I can blame you as much as I like for not telling me about it, but I can't blame you for making the decision you made.'

'I blame myself,' I whispered, tears running freely down my cheeks. 'There's not a day that's gone by when I haven't thought about her. I go between wishing I'd been strong enough to keep her and raise her on my own and days where logic tells me she had a better chance at a life full of opportunities with parents who were more mature than I was and much less messed up. Because I was messed up, Nick. Really messed up. Mum had died, I was pregnant and'—I swallowed hard—'during the birth, there were complications, and the doctors told me I'd never be able to have more children. I fell apart. It's one of the reasons I stayed away as long as I did – I couldn't bear to come back. I'—I choked on the words—'wasn't sure I wouldn't fall apart again.'

Nick reached for my hand and gripped it. 'I'm so sorry you had to deal with it all on your own. I'm sorry I wasn't there.' He dashed at his eyes, and I let my head fall onto his shoulder.

We sat like that for a while, with him holding my hand and my head on his shoulder and the weak first quarter moon lighting the top of the waves. His warmth and the rhythmic sound of the waves rolling in began to soothe a pain I had lived with for so long that I had ceased to be aware of it.

'Tell me about her,' he said softly. 'Tell me about our little girl.'

'She was perfect, Nick. I wanted so much to keep her, but they didn't want me to hold her or feed her, but I had to. Just once, so I could always remember how it felt. So when they tried to take her off me, Rose screamed at them until they agreed. "Just once," she said. "Let her hold her just once."' Tears clouded my vision, and my throat felt thick with them. I didn't need to see Nick's face to know he was crying too. 'It's only now I realise she must have been reliving her own pain, but at least she got to see me grow up.' I sniffed, and Nick released my hand to put his arm around my shoulder. 'The name on her birth certificate was Nicola Russell—'

'For me.'

I nodded. 'She'd have a different name now, but I hope she had nice parents and they love her how she deserves to be loved. I have a photo of her in my wallet, and Rose has the duplicate in the top drawer of her bedside table.' I lifted my head and looked into his eyes, feeling again the undertow of their Pacific depths. 'Do you want to see it?'

He kissed my forehead. 'I'd like that.' He struggled to his feet and dusted the sand from his jeans before holding out his hand for me. 'We'd better be getting back'—he smiled down at me, his eyes dark pools—'before they eat all the pavlova.'

While he held my hand as we crossed the road, he dropped it at the gate. 'I know we need to take things slowly and get to know each other again, but I'm not going anywhere, Clem.'

'Nor am I.'

BEFORE YOU GO ...

If you enjoyed *Murder in The Mangroves* I'd love it if you left a review in the usual places. If you'd like to stay up to date with what Clem and the crew from Whale Bay get up to next, you can sign up for my newsletter at my website: https://joannetracey.com.

You can also drop by and see me – virtually speaking, of course – here:
My blog: https://andanyways.com
Facebook: https://facebook.com/joannetraceywriter
Instagram: https://instagram.com/joanne_tracey_author/

ACKNOWLEDGEMENTS

Story ideas come from so many different sources, and this one was no exception, with its genesis being from a cruise through the Mooloolaba canals I took with my friends Heather and John. As we sailed through the canals, we also sampled native ingredients and learnt a little about the culture of the Traditional Owners of the area and the importance of the mangroves to the ecosystem. That cruise gave me the title; I just needed to come up with a story.

Even though this is just the second Clementine Carter adventure, writing about Whale Bay feels like coming home. A fictional town somewhere above Queensland's Sunshine Coast, it's a combination of Mooloolaba (where I walk daily) and Urangan in Hervey Bay. The characters, however, (especially the dodgy ones) are figments of my imagination.

It's fair to say that my only knowledge of murder cases and police operations comes second, third and fourth hand, so much of this (if not all) is made up. I make no apology for that. However, I have a soft spot for Senior Sergeant

Ted Winters and would like to think there are country coppers out there just like him.

The usual thanks to the usual people. To my editors – Nicola O'Shea and Jo Speirs – for wrangling my words into shape. I'm so sorry I missed my deadline on this one.

Thanks to Louisa West for another fabulous cover and to Keith Stevenson for turning this manuscript into a real-life book. Thanks also to Bel from Blurbs By Bel for crafting the blurb for this novel. As always, to my early readers and cheer group – my sister-in-law Pieta and the ladies from the Simply Stunning Classic Book Club – thank you for your friendship and unconditional support.

To the regular crew at Writing Friday, thank you for your encouragement and for eating my baking. You know who you are. Speaking of which, thanks to Queensland Writers Centre for the Writing Friday initiative. It's a great way to bring writers of all genres together, so if you're in Queensland and you're a writer, seek out your local group.

A special thank you to my nephew Barry for diligently (and selflessly) eating his way through bags of Freddo frogs to test Clem's theory about how many end up upside down in the packet.

As always, the usual thanks to my family – Grant and Sarah. I couldn't do what I do without you. This was the first book I've written entirely without Kali (Adventure Spaniel) beside me and to say I struggled with the change would be an understatement.

Mostly, though, my thanks go to you, my readers. Thank you.

ABOUT THE AUTHOR

An unapologetic daydreamer, eternal optimist, and confirmed morning person, Jo, who lives on the Sunshine Coast in Queensland, writes contemporary romance, women's fiction and cosy crime. When she isn't writing, Jo loves baking, reading, long walks along the beach, posting way too many photos of sunrises on Instagram and dreaming of the next destination and the next story.

Jo's life goals (apart from being a world-famous author) are to be an extra on *Midsomer Murders* and to cook her way through Nigella's books.